THE ROYAL FIFTH

by

JAMES PEYTON

The Royal Fifth

ISBN: 9798441643306

Printed in the United States of America.

Adventura Real Press

For my beloved wife, Andrea, whose unstinting support and encouragement made this and so many other things that make life worthwhile possible.

EL PASO, PRESENT TIME

Martín Cortés stood on the pedestrian approach to the international bridge that would take him into Mexico. Through the pollution that daily turned the high-desert air of Ciudad Juárez into a toxic haze, he focused on the nearby vehicle traffic. The U.S.-bound lanes were choked with line after line of barely moving cars and trucks. Turning to the southbound lanes, he watched the sparse traffic moving fast and free.

He looked back at the new-old skyline of downtown El Paso and dwelled for a moment on the tragic events of the last few months. He knew what had happened. Why they'd happened still eluded him. The inner voice that brought him to this place told him all would soon be revealed. And then he wondered: *Is that destiny or some karmic trickster?* He shook his head. Only time would tell.

Turning again, he raised his eyes to the smog-shrouded sprawl beyond the border where his trip would begin. He had no idea where it would end. He took a deep breath, fished in his pocket for the bridge toll, and resumed his southbound journey.

MEXICO, 1531 A.D.

Spanish Captain Federico Alvarado pulled his horse to a halt. Directly in his path, the boulder-strewn mountain seemed to rise forever into the robin-egg sky, like a giant's stairway to heaven. He glanced behind him at the eighteen men in peaked iron helmets riding stout horses and the ten mules laden with the captain general's treasure. What exactly they carried, Federico did not know. Only six of their burdens weighed enough to indicate gold or silver. Based on the amount of the one-fifth promised payment—*the royal fifth*—that was normally sent to the king, the others obviously held something of great value. Possibly some of the priceless emeralds he'd heard Cortés had taken from the Aztec king.

Over the last two days they'd lost six men to Indian attacks and were dangerously low on food and water. But he calculated they were no more than a day from their destination, the valley of Huaxyacac.
For a moment Federico reflected that if this mission ended well his star could rise like lightning in reverse. A grand home would replace the mud hovel where he lived with his Mexican wife. They could afford a servant and help her family. But gazing at the seemingly impassable range, he wondered if his commander had understood the conditions on the ground.

Again, Federico looked at the mountain. The trail zigzagged steeply upward through volcanic rock. The horses would never make it, but the more surefooted mules could. He turned in the saddle and yelled,

"Leave the horses. Keep only the mules with the

2

treasure and our food and water!"

He hoped the abandoned animals would satisfy the Indians he knew were not far behind them. As he dismounted, he called out, "Follow me, single file. If all goes well, tonight or tomorrow we'll drink the finest cactus liquor in New Spain!"

Late that afternoon, the weary column of sweat-drenched soldiers crested the top of the highest peak. They'd seen no further evidence of Indians. The broad mountaintop was nearly flat, except for a column of rock in the center with a cave at its base. Federico spoke to the man behind him. "Pass the word that we'll rest here and issue the men a small ration of water."

He walked to the edge of the mesa. In front of him a sheer cliff dropped precipitously to a wide valley checkered with cultivated fields. In the distance he made out a settlement he assumed was their destination. To the left of the cliff, he saw a trail with a more gradual descent. About an hour and a half of daylight remained, enough time to reach the valley. After dark, the lights from the settlement would guide them in.

Without warning, from his right Indians yelling battle cries swarmed over the mesa's crest. Horrified, Federico discovered another war party rushing them from behind. "To that large rock with the cave!" he screamed. At least their backs would be covered.

With the crossbowmen returning fire, the Spaniards retreated quickly but without panic. An arrow sliced the calf of Federico's right leg, but he ignored the pain and continued to the mouth of the cave. He found that while the entry was barely large enough for one man to pass, it opened into a space large enough to

3

hold his remaining troops and the treasure. Haphazardly strewn boulders flanked the entry and provided decent cover from both sides. While ideal to secure the treasure, he hated the idea of putting his men into a place that could become a deadly prison. More calmly, he ordered, "Unload the mules behind the crossbowmen and haul the treasure into the cave. The rest of you form up in front of the entrance."

The first crossbow volley barely slowed the attackers, and two more of his men fell. Federico now had no option but to send the rest inside the cave with the treasure. That accomplished, he ordered their two small cannons primed and loaded with grapeshot and placed at the entry, and then commanded the crossbowmen to ceasefire. The Indians seemed to view the unfamiliar mules as enemy weapons and paused to slaughter them before resuming the charge. When the war party came within thirty paces, Federico yelled, "Cannon number one!" Explosive thunder and the acrid smell of gunpowder permeated the cave. Indians fell in pieces as grapeshot cut a bloody swath through them. Federico ordered the second one to fire. More Indians were blown apart, and the warriors dispersed, fleeing to either side.

Time passed with no further sign of the enemy. Federico examined his wound and concluded it wasn't serious. Before he could attend to it, his second in command, Emilio Saenz, a veteran of many battles, pulled him aside. "They can keep us here as long as they want, and we only have enough water for two more days."

Although parched with thirst, Federico waved away the offer of a drink. "You're right, Emilio. It'll be dark before long, and they can sneak close enough to kill the cannoneers and swarm over us like ants. Or they might decide to wait until we're too weak to resist."

Although the chances of survival were slim, he knew someone must go for help. As the commander, he desperately wanted to remain with his men. But he remembered Cortés's order that only he, Federico, communicate with the captain general's representative. He spoke softly to Emilio. "The moon won't rise for a while, and my wound isn't serious. I'll take one man and try to reach the settlement. Have the men use pikes to lever a boulder partially across the entrance to protect the cannoneers. If you don't hear from us by tomorrow afternoon, assume we're lost."

Night came an hour and a half later, as dark as Federico had predicted. He and a sturdy young soldier from Aragon wet their mouths with water and crept cautiously out of the cave. Besides the sabers and daggers on their belts, they each carried a crossbow. They crawled slowly, snaking between the boulders toward the path down the mountain. The young soldier looked back every few seconds to prevent surprise from the rear.
Federico was nearly at the edge when an Indian leapt at them from the side. The young soldier immediately loosed a bolt from his crossbow into the figure and sprang to his feet. He drew his sword and hacked the warrior to the ground.

Federico crawled two more paces and disappeared over the edge of the mesa onto the trail. He heard a babble of cries and looked back to see dark figures swarm over his companion, who roared with anger and then pain. Against his nature, Federico moved as quickly as he could down the path, away from his countryman. Without reinforcements his men would not survive. Slowly, he felt his way in the darkness. A mistake on the rough terrain would mean the loss of all their lives.

Twenty minutes later, the rising moon showed Federico that he was two-thirds down the mountain, and he increased his speed. Near the bottom, he detected the grate of displaced soil and rocks behind him. He flattened himself beside a boulder, placed his sword on the ground beside him, and brought his crossbow to bear on the trail.

Higher now, the moon illuminated two figures moving toward him. When they came within six feet the lead Indian froze, staring directly at Federico's hiding place. Thinking he'd been spotted Federico fired a bolt into the man. Ignoring the pain in his leg, he grabbed his sword, sprang forward, and thrust it at the second warrior. He struck flesh, but only wounded the man. Something smashed violently into Federico's iron helmet and then crushed the thin armor on his left shoulder. Although pain flooded his body, he managed to withdraw the sword and lunge again. This time he found his mark, and the Indian slumped silently to the ground. Again, he withdrew the sword and stumbled down the trail.

Reaching level ground, he limped along the base of the mountain to the top of a low hill, hoping to see the lights of the settlement. He found only darkness. His head throbbed, and he thought his shoulder was broken, he assumed by an *hacha*, a stone hatchet made of the same volcanic rock as the Indian grinding stones. Although increasingly dizzy, he knew he could not afford to rest. When daylight came, the Indians with their incredible tracking skills would find him, and that would be the end of them all. He hobbled in the direction he believed the settlement lay.

What seemed like hours later, he used the last of his strength to plunge into a field that the moonlight revealed as wheat. His last conscious thought was that he must be on the land of a countryman.
In New Spain, only Spaniards grew wheat.

He awoke on a bed of straw, a clean piece of cloth around his leg and a clay jug of water beside him on the floor. A bearded man looked down and spoke to him in Spanish. "*Capitán*, I'm Rogelio Salazar, commander of this fort. Two days ago a settler and his son found you. Recognizing your uniform, they brought you here."

After groggily identifying himself, Federico said, "Two days! My men were surrounded by *indios* on a mountaintop, and their water will be gone. We must get help to them!"

What you describe could be anywhere, *señor*," said Salazar, sadness in his eyes. "Come see." He motioned to the two soldiers who helped Federico to the doorway.
Federico looked at the now distant mountains ringing the valley and saw the truth of what the man said.

"Then I must see the captain general's emissary, Alfredo Sandoval."

"I am sorry. *Señor* Sandoval was killed last week."

Federico's stomach fell. "I've got no alternative instructions, but beg you to help me find my men, even though they may already be lost. Following that, I must return to the City of Mexico."

"Of course, *Capitán*, tomorrow you shall have my best troops."
Even though his head and shoulder ached and he was weak, Federico insisted on joining the search party. It

was three days before they found the site. The men searched the edges of the mesa while he went to the rocky projection. He found the bones of the mules and four of his men. They had been stripped of their flesh by the fearsome Mexican vultures called *zopilotes*.

He raised his eyes to the cave and realized what had happened. The entrance was almost completely blocked with one of the huge
boulders that had rested near it. No one could have escaped. Obviously, the men tasked with levering the huge stone to defend the entrance to the cave had misjudged the angle and center of gravity. Instead of protecting the entrance, they had sealed it and left themselves stranded outside.

The strong smell of death from the cave's interior confirmed Federico's worst fear. Although he longed to open the entrance and see that his men received a Christian burial, he dared not expose the treasure to anyone not authorized by Cortés. He waved off the search party.

"The entrance is too small for a man to pass through. Only God knows where they've gone." The fact that he had told the literal truth failed to console him.

The next day, Federico left Guajaca, which would soon be renamed Oaxaca, with a company of soldiers assigned to escort him to Mexico City. On the evening he arrived, he reported to the captain general's private office next to his ample quarters at the far end of the stockade. He averted his eyes as he described the disaster and its aftermath. When he finished, Cortés patted him on his good shoulder. "*Capitán* Alvarado, do not punish yourself; you did everything possible under the circumstances. Now describe the location of the cave where your men perished."

Federico did so. Cortés asked many questions and took copious notes. Then rising from his ornate desk, the captain general put his arm around Federico and guided him to the door.

"You must stay in the barracks and speak to no one about this matter. In a few days I'll provide you with a new command to see that our men receive a proper burial."

After being shown to a small room within the fort, Federico lay down to rest, but could not stop thinking of his lost troops. Their faces appeared in every shadow in the tiny space. In the middle of the night, he was awakened by the sound of men entering his room. The ensuing tribunal concluded that Federico had left the fort against orders and was murdered by unknown attackers, undoubtedly Indians.

SANTA FE IN PRESENT TIME

Three months before he approached the international bridge, Martín Cortés drove through the gates of his parents' home in Tesuque, just outside Santa Fe, New Mexico. Invariably that caused something powerful to stir inside him. That particular day, as the rambling adobe came into view, what stirred inside Martín was a witch's brew of emotions. The last time he was summoned to a business meeting by his father had been three years ago. It concerned his decision to pursue a career as an artist rather than take over the family bank. That had ended badly—for everyone.

As he turned into the driveway, Martín slowed. He scanned the wooded, thirty-acre site at the base of the piñon-covered hill and then moved his gaze to the house. His eyes traced the rounded corners of the traditional two-story adobe. Irregular roof lines dipped gradually, almost whimsically, on both sides to meandering one-story additions. The structure was pinkish-tan and looked like it had been fashioned by a sculptor, which in effect it had.

Stubby piñon trees and patches of snow dotted the edge of the gravel drive and parking area. Still cold in early March, smoke curled from one of several chimneys, caressing the bare branches of tall trees flanking the driveway. Although the sky gleamed clear and blue through the clutter of spidery branches, Martín felt like a small plane flying into a thunderhead.

As he neared the hacienda, his heart sank. Rumors about problems with the bank were all over town. He had stayed away from Santa Fe and not returned the calls from financial reporters. He even avoided his fiancée, Laura Hudson.

As the tires crunched to a stop, Martín sat for a moment, dreading the inevitable. Surely his father had heard the rumors. The old man was an icon in the Spanish community, as Mexican-Americans in Santa Fe liked to be called. People had turned out in force to comfort him after his stroke and many continued to do so. Surely, one of them had mentioned the gossip.

For the rest of his life, Martín would wonder if he had been given any hint of the deadly spiral that would begin within the next half hour—what, if anything, he could have done to avert it.

The door opened to reveal his mother, Rosario. "Martín, *hijo mío*," she exclaimed throwing her arms wide for an embrace. Although of Hispanic heritage, nobody in the Cortés family except the elder Martín spoke much Spanish. However, through the generations certain phrases of endearment had joined the family lexicon.

After stooping to give her a generous hug, Martín pulled back, holding her at arm's length. His stomach churned as he noticed the toll his father's illness had taken on her. Once black hair had turned as gray as a foggy morning. She had always been plump but had recently lost weight and had aged ten years during the last two.

"I'm fine," he said. "How about you, *mamá*? You look tired."

"It's not me," she said, brushing wispy hair from her eyes. "It's *Papi*." She shook her head. "He's alive, for which I thank God, but he's not well, particularly not today. These rumors about the bank..."

"Is that what he wants to talk to me about?"

"I think so. He met with Abel earlier and is going to see him again later. He said he wanted to talk to you—alone. Please be careful, I..."

"Don't worry; no amount of money is worth *Papi's* health. Should you call the doctor?"

"I don't know. Tell me when you're finished."

Martín edged past her into the spacious living room. The floor was reddish-brown tile, worn smooth by generations of use. The white plaster ceiling, high above walls of the same material, was supported by immense, carved, wooden *vigas*. Navajo rugs dotted the floor, setting off Spanish colonial furniture of oak and pine.

Martín strode across the room to the tall, double mahogany doors to his father's study. He knocked once, opened one of them, heart pounding as his father motioned him to enter from behind the familiar oak desk.

What he saw alarmed him. While Martín was tall and slender with nearly straight, shoulder-length black hair, his father rose only to medium height, his frame heavyset rather than fat. But like his mother, Martín senior had lost an alarming amount of weight. The skin on his face hung in wrinkled folds, nearly covering the once-bright eyes. His thinning, curly hair had turned a dull white, as had the small, still carefully trimmed mustache. Martín took some cheer from the voice, which remained firm. "Come in, *hijo. ¿Como estas?*"

"Bien, Papi. The real question is: How are *you*?"

The older man shifted awkwardly in his oak chair. Each day he insisted on being transferred to it, refusing to confine himself a wheelchair. Although icicles still clung to the outside drainpipe behind him,

12

the winter sun streamed through the panes of French doors that opened onto the back of the property.

"I've been better. It's not pleasant to hear that your life's work's bein' destroyed. Now have a seat." He gestured toward a straight-back chair in front of the desk.

The old man frowned and began, "First, I'm gonna remind you—actually remind myself—what happened with the bank. You were just twenty-eight when I asked you to take it over, and did so in spite of the fact that Abel had more experience and an MBA. I thought you had the better judgment. It took a while after you said no, but I finally accepted your decision after you agreed to remain on the board. Then I gave both you and your brother twenty percent of the stock."

The old man dabbed his brow with a crumpled handkerchief. "God knows that arrangement wasn't perfect, but it worked, at least for a while. Then Abel started try'n to get into risky ventures. Time after time, I told him we made plenty of money taking care of the depositors and borrowers. I also had to constantly remind him to visit with customers. I don't know how many damn times I told him that you don't build profitable relationships sitting in your office staring at your computer like it can predict the future. But things did work for a while, didn't they?"

"The dividends helped me live while I tried to sell my paintings, but that's about all the good I can think of now."

His father shook his head. "Then I had the stroke and the doctors ordered me to stay away from the bank. I tried to ignore them, but for the first time in her life your mama bucked me, made sure I stayed completely away. A few months later, someone told

13

me you resigned as director. The reasons you gave—everything was going well and you needed to spend more time on your work—didn't make sense. But again, your mama, who had never been real assertive, threw a fit and barred the subject. I think I know what really

happened next, but I want to hear it from you."

Seeing no way out, Martín cleared his throat. "At first, I did everything I could, but without you being involved Abel ignored me. I couldn't stop him from taking risks. I also realized that I had selfishly rejected my responsibility to the family by refusing to take over, which didn't help my attitude. In any case, Abel and I continually quarreled. Other than bring you into it, which would likely have killed you, I saw no way out but to sell my shares to him. I figured that involving you would be a disaster. Of course, if things did eventually go bad that would have the same result. It came down to one being certain, the other a future possibility."

"Probability is more like it," interrupted the old man, "and unfortunately the future's here. But go on."

"Based on the $25,000 a year I got in dividends, I settled with Abel for $300,000 in cash and the Espanola adobe on five acres that he owned."

"And then what happened?"

"Abel replaced me on the board with one of his cronies, a fellow member of the Young President's Club. He also replaced Herb Gonzalez as the bank's lawyer with a friend from an Albuquerque firm."

"That's what I figured. I knew you took your responsibilities seriously, that concern for me kept you away, hoping nothing would go wrong. Do you know what happened?"

"No, nothing other than what's been in the news: vague allegations of unspecified irregularities. *Papi*, you're right about the decision. Obviously, it was the wrong one. But after the stroke you were so...fragile."

"I know." The old man waved his hand in frustration. "That's water over the bridge, and here's what's on the other side. You knew Abel wanted to get into land development. And you probably knew that a bank can't legally do anything except provide construction financing—and except in extenuating circumstances, do that only when there's a permanent take-out loan."

"Yes."

The old man sighed and continued, "Well, here's what happened. You probably also knew that just before I got sick, I authorized a loan to Johnny Carillo."

Martín knew that Carillo owned four hundred acres not far to the north, land that his family had ranched for generations. He also knew that Johnny had recently built an inn and restaurant and that the family bank was involved in the financing.

"Johnny's a nice kid, and his dad was a friend. But he doesn't have any experience outside ranching. He wanted to do something more profitable with the land: build an inn and restaurant. I thought he had something, but told him to get a good management company on board. He tried but couldn't interest anyone in such a small project. I advised him to consider a financial partner. He refused, determined to keep it in the family."

The elder Martín stopped and feebly slapped his forehead. "Your mother, bless her heart, will kill me. I

15

forgot the hot chocolate, and *biscochitos*. She made them specially." He motioned toward a tray with a thermos and bowl of cookies on an ornately carved chest by the empty wheelchair.

Martín poured two mugs of steaming chocolate. He took a cookie and placed the bowl in front of his father. The old man shook his head. "I'm getting forgetful. How's Laura?"

"I'm embarrassed to say I don't know," replied Martín, sheepishly.

"Since day before yesterday, when I first heard the rumors, I've pretty much stayed away from everyone."

"She's attractive and seems nice, but forgive me…. Truth be told, you belong to an old Spanish family and her people are old Anglo. The divide still exists if you scratch deep enough, and this business we're talkin' about's a pretty
deep cut. I just wanted to warn you."

"I understand."

"Now, where was I? Oh yeah. Johnny got pissed when I told him the project needed a permanent loan. I figured if I didn't make the construction loan, we'd not just lose him as a friend, but the entire family. Of course," he smiled, eyes twinkling for the first time, "with the value of the land it was also a pretty good loan for the bank. I also figured that I could get him through any temporary problems, like a glitch in the economy."

The old man sipped his chocolate and then from under bushy gray brows and sagging lids he gave his son a pointed look. "Of course, I also thought you'd take over and that I'd be involved at every step."
The younger Martín's heart sank. "Believe me, *Papi*, if I had it to do over…"

16

"I know," his father grumbled. "You're a good boy, and would've done what was necessary, if you'd realized... As much as I wanted you to come in, I didn't want you to spend your life doing something you disliked."

Martín met his father's eyes. "I appreciate your telling me that.

Now, let's see what happened and what can be done."

"Not a great deal, as you'll soon see. I made the loan. Johnny built the Tesuque Valley Inn, finished it a little over a year ago, ten months after I stopped working. It came on the market just as the economy and tourism tanked. Bottom line, he lacked the cash to pay the note by about $25,000, with no permanent loan in sight. What would you have done?"

Martín didn't have to think before answering. "I would have counseled Johnny to sell a few acres, probably some commercial property on the highway. Once on the market, I would've used that as a basis for extending the loan and waived penalty fees."

The old man sighed and inclined his head. "That's what I would have done too. But that's not what Abel did. He was working with an out-of-town developer looking for acreage for a high-end residential project. They told Abel that if he could find the right land at the right price he could come in as a partner." The old man wiped his brow again.

"Are you okay?" asked Martín, leaning forward in his chair.

"Yes, yes," grumbled his father. "By now you've guessed that Abel foreclosed on Johnny and immediately put all the property on the market. That same day he accepted an offer from the developer at well below the land's market value. He raised his voice and his hand shook. "Allocating less than $1 million to the building that cost nearly $3 million!"

Fear stabbed Martín as he saw the pain on his father's face. "Why didn't Johnny come to you? He must have known you wouldn't stand for that."

"Out of respect for my health, I'm told. That is, once he realized what was happening. Johnny had assumed that Abel was me, that he was just going through some pro-forma hocus-pocus. Well, he's come to his senses and hired Emilio Valdez to represent him in a lawsuit against the bank and the developer. Among other things he's alleging fraud. I understand he's discovered that Abel has a ten percent personal interest in the development."

My God!" exclaimed the younger Martín. "What did Abel say?"

"He said he did nothing any other executive wouldn't have done to...what the hell did he call it?" His voice trembled as it rose in anger. "To maximize shareholder benefits!"

He raised his fist as if to slam it down on the desk and then began to lower it, unclenching his fingers as they began to shake. Martín blanched as he saw the old man begin to twitch all over, jowls quivering over his dark turtleneck.

"*Papi*, where's your medicine?"

His father motioned weakly toward the credenza with the thermos on it. Martín leaped from his chair. He wrenched open a tiny plastic bottle, got a pill out and into his father's mouth, then helped him wash it down with some of the chocolate. As he started for the door, his father waved at him frantically, drops of hot chocolate dribbling down his chin.

"Don't bother her. Not till we're finished."

Martín was halfway out the door. Turning back, he said, "May I say something that will finish it?" His voice was icy as the frost on the drainpipe. "I'll call Herb Gonzalez. Maybe we can stop the sale of Johnny's land. In any case we should take Johnny's side, even if we end up losing. The main thing is I don't want you involved anymore. It'll kill you."

The old man remained motionless, nearly all the color gone from his face. Raising his eyes to his son's, he said, "If Abel won't agree…the way he's got the Board packed. I'll have to call a stockholder's meeting."

"There's only you, *Mamá*, and Abel. No big deal. If you want, you can appoint me to represent your interest. I'll call Herb. Right after *Mamá* calls the doctor. First things first." Then he walked back into the room, reached down, and took both his father's hands in his own.
Finally, the old man said, "Abel's not a bad boy; I know that in my heart." Martín slowly released his grip, then turned and went to find his mother.

When Martín and Rosario returned, Martín Senior was slumped in his chair, still as the air before a storm. Martín rushed to him, pressed his lips onto his father's, and breathed desperately in and out, trying to remember a long ago first aid lesson. After several minutes, he straightened, tears flowing down his cheeks. "Oh, *Mamá*, I think he's gone. Call 911, quick!"

Paying no attention, Rosario flung herself on her husband, weeping uncontrollably. Martín snatched the phone and made the call. Returning to the desk he saw a piece of notepaper with a pen beside it in front of his father. Picking it up, he could barely read the faint, almost childish scrawl. Taking it over to the window he held it to the light. "Martín, take care of your mother—and your brother."

At the time, the request seemed appropriate. Within days Martín would realize the impossibility of fulfilling it.

SANTA FE

For Martín, the rest of the afternoon passed in a blur. EMS confirmed the death and Abel arrived demanding to know what Martín had done to upset their father. Remembering the note, Martín somehow managed to keep his temper. The brothers agreed that over the next few days at least one of them would stay with their mother day and night. At Martín's suggestion, they also scheduled a business meeting for the following morning.

Martín left a message with the news for Laura, his fiancée. Thirty minutes later, at the last glimmer of twilight, her red Porsche nosed into the parking area. Tall and slender, with medium-length, curly blond hair framing her face, flushed from an afternoon's skiing, she entered the living room in light-blue ski pants and a pink cashmere sweater. She embraced Rosario, hugged Martín, and ignored Abel.

Following Martín into the kitchen, she put her arms around him and pulled him close. "I'm so sorry, darling. And on top of whatever's going on at the bank." She paused and looked at him inquiringly. "What *is* happening?"

Martín remembered his father's words. He had known that even a well-to-do, old Spanish family— one that actually had mostly Spanish blood—was considered problematical by the old Anglos, especially when it came to intermarriage. "I don't really know," he replied, carefully. "It seems to revolve around some mistake Abel made."

"I knew it," she exclaimed. "He's a fucking idiot!"

"Laura, this isn't the time. I'm going to meet with him tomorrow, and we'll see what happens after that.

21

In the meantime..."

"I know, sweetie, keep your big mouth shut." She hugged him again. "Don't worry, my lips are sealed. You going to stay all night? Somebody damn well better."

"Yeah, Abel and I agreed on that. I took first watch!"

She reached up and kissed him hard on the lips. "That's why I love you."

SANTA FE

When Martín's eyes opened the next morning, he recognized his old room as the enormity of the previous day's events flooded his consciousness. He cringed in denial. Surely when he went downstairs, he'd find his father reading the paper at the kitchen table, while his mother bustled around prying waffles out of the iron and pouring juice. Finally accepting that would never happen again, he buried his face in the pillow and burst into tears.

A half hour later, showered and composed, he found his mother crying in the kitchen. There was nothing to say, so he held her tight. In his father's study he discovered the scrawled note still on the desk. He slipped it into his shirt pocket, hoping it would give him strength in the coming days.

He called Herb Gonzalez, the family lawyer, and until Abel took over, the bank's lawyer as well. He caught him still at home, and gave him the news.

"Shit, Martín," the man said in his Spanish-accented drawl. "With all the talk, I was afraid something like this would happen. One thing you can be sure of, there'll be no fussing between you and Abel. Anyone who contests the trust gets cut off!"

Martín related the old man's desire to stop Johnny Carillo from being cheated. "I don't know what can be done," said the lawyer after some thought. "Depends on what's already happened. But Rosario's got his stock now. That totals sixty percent, a majority when I was in
law school. Only problem is, can she deal with a fuss, now or ever?"

"Not now for sure." Martín checked his watch. "In about forty-five minutes I'm meeting with Abel to see if that can be avoided."

After hanging up, Martín took out his father's last note and read it again. "Martín, take care of your mother—and your brother."

An hour and fifteen minutes later, Martín sat next to Abel in the study, amazed at how much his brother resembled their father. While Martín was tall and rangy with sharply chiseled features and straight black hair, Abel was just over medium height, his curly hair more brown than black. He had recently gone from chunky to fat, adding jowls to his otherwise handsome face.

By unspoken agreement they left their father's chair vacant, bringing in a second straight-back from the dining room. Martín recounted the old man's description of the problem, without mentioning his brother's reported share in the development company. Abel agreed with the facts, but defended his actions as being entirely proper.

It was when Martín explained his solution, emphasizing that their father had agreed to it, that the trouble started.

"It's too fucking late. The deal's done, and Johnny's out of luck" was Abel's truculent assessment.

Martín shook his head. "Not when he has what some might call an airtight case for fraud against the bank—and against you personally."

"What the hell you talking about?"

"Keep it down! *Mamá* has enough grief without us adding to it."

Then with a hint of steel in his voice, he added, "Remember that, because you may be agitated for quite some time." A sudden vision of himself

24

strangling his brother kept Martín from saying more. Abel merely nodded, flexing his fleshy jaw.

Martín continued, "I forgot to mention that whoever told *Papi* about the problem also told him that Johnny's lawyer discovered that you have an ownership position with the developer. Is that true?"

"How the...? There's no fucking way…!" Again raising his voice, Abel started to rise from his chair.

Martín shot out his hand, quick as a karate chop, pushing him back down. "I guess it's true."

"Damn it all, it was too good a deal to pass up. Supposed to be secret. My percentage could be worth more than the whole bank."

Martín barked a cynical laugh. "That's especially true now, because unless we work together to pull off a miracle the bank's going to be worth nothing." He refrained from adding, *And what will the Young President's Club think of that?*

Abel shook his head like a nervous colt and took a deep breath. "Okay, okay, I see what you mean. If they know about my deal with SpanGlobe, they may have a case, even though I did nothing any other banker wouldn't have done."

Again, Martín relied on his father's note for strength. "That's over and done. It's all over and done. What we have to do now is pull together as a family, for all our sakes, but especially for *Mamá*."

Abel sat still for a moment, then his whole demeanor changed, like a mental patient switching personalities. The truculence evaporated, and like a punctured balloon, he slumped and put his face in his hands. After a minute he looked up and met his brother's eyes. Very slowly he offered his hand to Martín, tears trickling down his cheek.

Barely above a whisper, he said, "I'm so sorry. I've fucked everything up and probably killed *Papi*."

The tears kept flowing as the cadence of his speech picked up. "I know *Papi* wanted you to take over. I was trying to be more successful than either of you thought I could." He waved his hand wildly in the air. "I know it's way too late, but I'm as sorry as anyone can be."

Martín accepted the offered hand, but instead of shaking it, he held it tightly. "I knew that wasn't really you," he said softly. "Like I said, we've got to pull together. You want to talk about it now?"

"There's no time to waste," said Abel, wiping the tears from his cheeks. "What do you think?"

"Well," said Martín, "it all depends on the status of the foreclosure and sale to... Who's the developer?"

"SpanGlobe, out of Colorado. I checked, and everything's final. The foreclosure process is lengthy, but Johnny didn't protest until too late. The sale to SpanGlobe's done."

Martín scratched his chin. "Herb can tell us for sure, but it sounds like only the court can reverse the sale, unless of course SpanGlobe is willing to pull out?"

"I can't see that happening," said Abel. "I've met the president, Colin Glendaring, just once. But I've spent a lot of time with some of his people and they're all pretty...*serious*."

"You make them sound like mafia."

"No...not really. I checked out the company, and they have a long history of profitable projects, with a minimum of legal problems. They just seem completely committed, and once they have something they want, I don't think they'll let go of it."

"Well," said Martín, thinking aloud, "you could tell

26

them the jury will undoubtedly rule for Johnny out of sympathy. Explain that damn near everyone in the area's related to him one way or the other.

That's why *Papi* agreed to work with him in the first place. Tell them that alone will kill the deal and make any development there politically impossible. Say you're going to give up your interest and take Johnny's side. In any case, you better get the documents to Herb right away and then see if we can meet with him this afternoon. Bring in your other lawyer if you want, but please let Herb know we're together on this."

"I'll call Herb, see *Mamá*, and try to get my head clear."

He stared blankly through the window for a moment and then added, "What a fool...maybe I should..."

"Abel, *Jesus Christo hermano*!" exclaimed Martín jumping up, putting an arm around his brother, squeezing his shoulder affectionately.
"This is family; we'll get through it together."

SANTA FE

Martín parked near Herb Gonzalez's office on Agua Fria, a street of adobes and small commercial buildings, thankfully away from the center of town. With the news of his father's death now out, plus the rumors about the bank, it would have taken him the rest of the day just to get across Santa Fe's central plaza. It would also have demanded a level of diplomacy he didn't possess.

Inside, the adobe had been lovingly converted to office use and decorated with Herb's passions: Indian blankets and baskets. Abel impatiently tapped his foot on the waiting room's tile floor. Before Martín could sit, the door to Herb's inner office opened and the lawyer stood in the doorway. A big, shambling man of sixty, his wavy salt and pepper hair, sideburns, and droopy mustache made him look like an old west saloonkeeper. He wore a baggy tweed suit that dropped unevenly over massive, rounded shoulders, as if all his possessions had been stuffed unequally into the side pockets.

"Well, boys, life must go on. Since there ain't much time, forgive me if I dive in." He waved them in and then at a stack of papers on his desk. "I've gone over the documents Abel brought me. He's right, they're pretty much in order—but the foreclosure does have a problem that gives Johnny an appeal." He looked at Martín. "That being said, I understand you've got some thoughts."

"If Johnny can demonstrate Abel was personally involved with the developer, isn't a jury likely to rule in his favor?"

28

"In this county that's as safe a bet as you'll get."

Martín pondered a moment. "Our family has a legacy of goodwill that might give us a chance if we admit we made a mistake and support Johnny against the out-of-town developer. We plead naiveté, repent, and show we have every intention of making things right, no matter the cost."

"You gonna send me a bill for that advice, Martín?"

"Maybe, but it'll be a lot less than one of yours, *amigo*. If we don't, we lose anyway with no credit for good behavior."

Herb nodded. "Martín has identified the only reasonable course of action. Thankfully it's also the right thing to do, so here's what I suggest. Abel, you tell SpanGlobe you've concluded you made a mistake. Say you've decided to withdraw from the venture and also from the bank. Before they start to threaten you, explain the problem in the documentation. I'll give you all the specifics. I know I'm suggestin' a bitter pill, but maybe you can come out of this with some skin."

Abel met his gaze. "My problems are nothing to what I've caused everyone else. I'll do it. Should I call Colin Glendaring now?"

"No," said Herb, "I need to make sure you understand the issue with the foreclosure first."

"You don't need me for that, do you?" broke in Martín. "I have to feed Pancho and get back to *Mamá*."

"Go ahead," said Herb. "Abel can fill you in later."

"Just one thing before I go. Is there any hope of saving the bank?"

"Too soon to tell."

SANTA FE

Martín spent a few minutes patting Pancho, his part St. Bernard part Rottweiler, then jumped back in his Tahoe and headed for his parents' house in Tesuque. Everything seemed out of focus and disconnected. He'd start on a thought and lose it, unable to remember where he'd begun, as if he'd arrived in a strange land wearing someone else's glasses. Overload and shock, he guessed.

Snatches of his family's history popped into his head. Tradition said that the first Martín Cortés descended directly from the Conqueror, Hernan Cortés. The oilskin packet of bark paper drawings in his father's safe made the story plausible. They showed the Conqueror, himself, painted by spies sent by the Aztec king to investigate the arrival of ships near Veracruz. Called codices, they arrived in New Mexico with that first Martín and remained with the family ever since.

That recollection segued into the memory of how he had once used the drawings to his benefit at the University of New Mexico, where he first majored in archeology. In a scheme to improve his grade point average, he got his father's grudging permission to take one of the drawings to the chairman of the Archeology Department. The man's eyes grew large and within minutes a panel of experts convened around the cluttered table in the tiny office. The codices received tentative authentication, subject to further study, which Martín was implored to allow.

Sensing the opportunity he'd hoped for, Martín said he wasn't sure.

He agreed the document needed to be someplace where it could be properly cared for and available for study. He then mentioned that his father was beginning to think along those lines. Just maybe…

He received nothing lower than an A in archeology courses until the middle of his sophomore year when, after realizing that unless one had a burning desire to achieve a doctorate and teach, archeology had few practical applications.

Martín kept his foot on the gas as the memories continued to unfold. After a fair amount of tequila, he'd concluded that his infatuation with archeology came from the artistic impact of the images and designs of the ancient Mexicans, and he changed his major to art. Before graduating, he entered several exhibitions where his paintings sold quickly at prices that convinced him to consider art as a career.

At first his work continued to sell. Then he hit a plateau in both inspiration and sales. Part of it related to his technique, which involved realistic landscapes juxtaposed with surreal but time-consuming renditions of ancient Mexican design elements—a frightening serpent's head in a desert, or a pyramid swarming with jaguars blended into a rainforest. He was unable to produce anywhere near the volume of paintings turned out by his abstract artist friends, who he thought made a living selling the equivalent of inkblot tests.

The turn that would take him to his family's home snapped Martín back to the present, a place he was not certain he wanted to be.

SANTA FE

A dozen relatives and close friends supported Rosario Cortés at dinner in the paneled dining room, where she insisted on saying a tearful grace. After the meal, Martín motioned Abel to follow him to the study.

As the doors closed, Abel told Martín he had reached Colin Glendaring, explained the problem in the foreclosure documents, and said he was going to side with Johnny Carillo.

"I apologized for the inconvenience, said I realized he'd spent a lot of time and money on the project, and asked him if we could work things out without a lawsuit."

After several moments of silence, Martín prompted his brother.

"And?"

"I want to make sure I remember right, because I was surprised. Glendaring said, 'I understand and sympathize with your position and am glad to know that you are a man of integrity.' He actually talks like that, very proper and old-fashioned. He ended up saying he thought we could work out something and suggested we meet tomorrow afternoon."

Martín gave his brother a sharp look. "Does that make sense; I thought you called these people *serious*?"

"Actually, it doesn't. I've heard them discussing similar situations, and I expected big problems."

"Where will you meet?"

"He was in his office in Denver but said he was flying in tomorrow and could meet me at the Hilton around four. He always stays in one of the ground floor *casitas*."

"Is Herb going with you?"

"I suggested that, but he said he wanted the two of us to agree in principal before putting anything on paper."

"Something doesn't smell right," said Martín. "Remember, you characterized your deal with SpanGlobe as secret. If you didn't tell anyone, who else could have?"

"Who knows how stuff gets out? Maybe I misjudged him. After all, his company's record shows no serious legal problems."

"I wasn't thinking about lawsuits," retorted Martín.

"Don't worry. We're meeting in his suite at a public hotel for God's sake."

"Okay, but can I ask you a favor? When all this began, I had six paintings I needed to take to a new gallery in Durango. If you could stay with *Mamá* tomorrow and make sure relatives are here when you're at the meeting, I can do it. I should be back by nine at the latest."

"No problem. Give me a call when you get back, and I'll let you know what happened."

"I hate to wait that long. I'm not sure of the service between here and Durango, but call me on my cell as soon as you finish."

Later that night when Abel returned to his Palace Avenue townhouse, he pulled his black Land Rover into the carport. Getting out, he detected movement to his left. As he turned toward it, viselike hands covered his mouth and something cold and cylindrical pressed into the side of his head. "One sound and your brains will be splattered all over the neighborhood," growled a raspy male voice.

SANTA FE

Just after eight-thirty the next evening, Martín topped a rise on the rough dirt track that led to his home. Lightning exploded ahead, momentarily illuminating the distant Sangre de Christo Mountains. Wind slapped the old Tahoe as he swerved to avoid a gully. Another burst of electricity, this time closer, backlit his small adobe nestled at the top of the next hill.

Although his cell phone showed a constant signal, Abel hadn't called. His own calls reached only his brother's recorded message.

He parked and trotted to the front door, hugging himself for warmth. The door was barely open when the first big raindrops thudded onto the porch like tiny sandbags. As he entered the house, lightning crashed nearby, followed immediately by an artillery blast of thunder. Then all hell broke loose.

Slamming the carved pine door behind him, Martín flicked on the light as rain hammered the tin roof. Then he froze. To his right, on the rough-cut cedar counter separating the kitchen from the living area, the answering machine beeped and blinked mindlessly. That was all. There was no other sound or movement, except the rain pounding on the roof.

That was the problem.

"Pancho," he called.

Nothing.

"Pancho!" he repeated, a little louder, adding the command:

"Come!" Still nothing. Surely the dog had not failed to seek shelter through the hinged panel that Martín had built into the back door. It was just large enough for Pancho but too small for a man or most women. Pancho always met him at the door, a 130-pound frenzy of flailing paws and lapping tongue.

Senses straining, Martín glared at the answering machine—beep/flash, beep/flash, beep/flash. An annoying one-beat metronome.

"Pancho!" he repeated, even louder.

Through the storm noise, a whimper followed by scratching came from his bedroom. Surprised to find the door securely closed, he stood outside listening. "Pancho, you in there?"

He heard what sounded like muffled snuffling. Slowly pushing the door open, Martín found the dog lying on his stomach, eyes rolling upward. What passed for his tail jerked frantically from side to side.

"What the hell you doing in here with the door closed?"
Hands on hips, Martín looked down with mock severity at the huge brown and white dog as he continued to beg for whatever he wanted— forgiveness maybe? "Are you going to tell me how you got into that room and closed the door on yourself? I left you outside."

The dog spun in circles and wagged his stumpy tail.

Although anxious to check his machine, Martín's curiosity about the dog won out. His eyes settled on the unlatched bedroom window he clearly remembered securing before he left. Someone small could have gotten in through Pancho's door, a child maybe, then unlatched the window and left. In spite of his fearsome appearance Pancho was easily seduced. Another careful look revealed no evidence of an intruder. In the top bureau drawer, the hundred dollars he kept for emergencies remained untouched.

Shaking his head, he made for the answering machine.

"Martín, I can't find your cell number—call me immediately. This is serious!" Through the rain pounding on the roof, Herb Gonzalez's voice lacked its characteristic good nature and folksy humor.

Hands beginning to shake, Martín grabbed the phone. The first ring hadn't finished when Herb picked up.

"Martín?" he barked.

"What's going on? And speak up, it's raining like hell!"

His voice now much softer, Herb said, "Martín I don't know how to tell you this. I'm about to give you more bad news than I've ever heard of anyone getting at one time. But I've got no choice. Don't say anything till I finish."

Martín cringed and his heart pounded as he heard the man take a deep breath. "At about two-thirty this afternoon the police got a call from one of Johnny Carillo's cousins who'd come for a visit. She found Johnny, Gloria, and their five-year-old daughter, Jenna, shot to death in the kitchen."

Martín gasped. Without giving him a chance to break in, Herb continued like a freight train putting on steam. "At a little before four o'clock a patrolman stopped to investigate a black Land Rover parked near Rancho de Chimayó. He found Abel's body in the front seat. Preliminary conclusion is he shot himself. They found a gun on the seat next to him."

At Martín's moan, Herb said, "Don't say nothin' yet, man. Oh God, Martín! At a little after six, a fucking sheriff's deputy arrived at your momma's house. Before your uncle could get to him he asked her if she

36

knew where Abel had been all day. Just the question upset her, but she answered, saying she didn't know; he was supposed to have been there by mid-morning and didn't answer his phone. The mother-fucker then just flat out told her that Abel had been found with his brains all over his car, after he murdered the Carillo family! Rosario couldn't take it. She simply dropped dead. No pain, no struggle, not a word. She blacked out and never regained consciousness. Oh, Martín. I am so sorry."

Martín felt like he'd been hit by a tornado. He staggered, put his left hand to his head, and emitted a long, wailing "Nooooo!"

"Martín, I know I should've waited till I was with you before sayin' anything, but you'd have known somethin' was wrong and I didn't want to jerk you around. Now, I'm coming over there. There's more news and a lot we need to discuss, including your own safety."

"What about my safety, and what other news?" snapped Martín.

"Martín, this obviously relates to the SpanGlobe deal, and you're the only principal left alive."

"What do you mean? I sold my stock in the bank and wasn't involved in the deal?"

Herb's voice softened. "Yeah, you sold your stock, but with your daddy, momma, and brother gone, it's all yours now. Your father was awful particular about keepin' things straight. I've got wills and trust agreements stacked up in my safe. I checked this afternoon and you get everything. I'm sorry to say that may not be a blessing. Which leads me directly to what we got to talk about, but I'd rather do it in person."

"Give me a summary," exclaimed Martín, fighting

for control. "I can't wait."

"Okay, but then I'm coming over. A little before lunch today I went into the office and found an urgent message to call Frank Haines. That's the dumb-ass attorney Abel had handlin' the bank stuff. I figured it must be important since it was Saturday and he gave me his home number. I got him, and he told me he'd been tryin' to reach Abel all morning, but couldn't. Said he'd been served with a lawsuit by SpanGlobe claiming damn near everything in the book and demanding enough to break the bank."

"Okay," said Martín, feeling like he'd just stopped absorbing anything at all. "So, what have we got to talk about after that?"

"Martín, I understand how you feel; unfortunately, it ain't just your momma, your brother, and the damn bank."

"What the hell does that mean?" blurted Martín in frustration, nearing his breaking point.

"Look man, I can be there in less than thirty minutes."

"No, tell me now, then we'll see," said Martín, fearing he might black out.

"All right, all right. As soon as I finished talking to Haines, I decided to go through the bank's files to get ahead of the curve. What I came across damn near floored me. You may never have heard this; I know I'd completely forgotten. What happened is that when your grandfather started the bank he came up short on capital and didn't want to go outside the family. He pledged the hacienda in Tesuque, now your parents' home, as part of the bank's assets. When he died and your daddy took over, the bank was prospering and no longer needed the property for the balance sheet. I tried to convince him to remove it, but he refused. He said if he was goin' to ask other people to entrust their most valuable assets to the bank, how would it look if he didn't do the same?"

"You mean," said Martín, stuttering with incredulity, "we could lose the house with everything else?"

"All I'm sayin' is that you and I need to talk and real quick decide how to handle this mess. You didn't do fuck-all to create it, but you're stuck with it, and I'm gonna do my best to help you get out of it. Now I'm on my way..."

"Just a moment," said Martín. "None of that means shit at the moment. Wh...what about *Mamá*. What about..."

"As soon as Eddie—that is, Sheriff Jaramillo—heard what happened he got over to the house real quick, had EMS there on the double. As a favor, they took her to the hospital, and I called Vasquez Funerals to make the arrangements. I knew that's what you'd want. And you should know that Eddie knocked the shit out of his deputy for the way he treated your momma. Ripped his badge off, threw him against the wall, and kneed him in the balls. By that time I was there and held him back. Eddie and your father were great pals."

"Thanks, Herb. I appreciate what you're doing. Now all I want is to get over to the house."

As he said it, from somewhere a thought hit him like a sucker punch. "Herb, what kind of gun killed Abel?"

"I assume a .357 magnum," replied Herb. "Same as killed the Carillo family."

"Hold on a minute." The panic that comes from the sure knowledge that something awful is about to get worse struck Martín. He set the phone down, dashed to the bedroom, and jerked open the drawer below the little table by his bed. Empty!

Back in the kitchen he snatched up the phone. "When I got in a little while ago it seemed like someone had been here. Pancho was closed in the bedroom, and the window I locked this morning was unlatched. I did a quick check and the only thing missing is my Ruger .357 Magnum."

"Martín, before you do one thing else, we've got to call the sheriff's office and get an investigation started. I'll call Eddie personally, but you gotta stay there till they come and don't touch anything!"

SANTA FE

Martín's home lay on five acres at the eastern edge of Española, on the way up to Chimayó, beyond which loomed the Sangre de Christo Mountains. Herb and Sheriff Eddie Jaramillo arrived at the same time. Martín opened the door to find them huddled under the overhang. The rain had stopped and the temperature neared freezing.

The sheriff entered first, his bulky frame filling the doorway. Bronzed copper by the sun, his face had full lips accentuated by a gray mustache, discolored by his trademark Red Man chewing tobacco. He removed his plastic-shrouded Stetson as Martín hustled Pancho out of the room. Wavy salt and pepper hair topped Eddie's large pumpkin-shaped head. He delivered condolences to Martín, profusely apologizing for the behavior of his deputy.

Herb strode to Martín and hugged him. Then he turned to the sheriff and removed his faded baseball cap. "Eddie, did I screw up by callin' you? I forgot this is Rio Arriba County."

"Yeah, but this is part of a case I'm already on. Bernie and I cooperate. He gave me the green light on the way up, as long as I keep him in the loop."

Minutes later, a photographer and crime scene investigator arrived. Martín gave the men the details as accurately as he could. He had delivered his paintings to the gallery in Durango at about 1:30 p.m., gone to lunch with the owner, and then toured two other galleries
with him. He hadn't left until four that afternoon. The policemen silently noted that Durango was a good

four-and-a-half-hour drive.

"I bought the revolver a year ago and another one I keep in the car. I still have the original box and sales slip." Martín went to his closet and handed the deputy the sales slip.

The investigator pulled a small notebook from his pocket. "The serial number matches the one on the revolver that killed Abel Cortés."

"You positive it was suicide?" Herb asked the sheriff.

Eddie spit into a Pepsi can and shook his head.

After the cops left, Herb put an arm around Martín's shoulders. The young man began to sob and didn't stop for several minutes.

"You've had enough," said Herb. "Come back to the house with me. The spare room's ready, and Margo's anxious to see you."

"Thanks, Herb, but I'm going over to the house. It's something I need to do."

"Let me come along. You're done in."

"Thanks, but no."

"Okay," Herb relented. "I was the last one out and made sure the doors were locked. I was gonna leave the lights on, but I just couldn't, remembering how careful your folks were to turn them off. It was almost a religion with them. What I'm sayin' is, check around before you go in; burglars are famous for striking after a death."

"That reminds me," said Martín, "do you think *Papi's* funeral could be delayed so they could all be at the same time?" Again, tears ran down his cheeks.

When Martín calmed down, Herb said, "That makes sense. When you get up tomorrow come by the office. I'll be there by nine. We've got a lot to do, and maybe that's good."

The men hugged each other, neither realizing they would see each other much sooner than they expected.

SANTA FE

The temperature dipped below freezing as Martín followed the winding road down to Española. Turning left onto the highway to Santa Fe, he crept past shuttered paycheck loan and tire repair shops and then increased his speed to fifty until he reached the turnoff to Tesuque. Five minutes later he turned into the hacienda.

The house had never seemed so dark, and tears filled his eyes. As the tires crunched slowly down the icy pathway beneath the bare trees, Martín remembered Herb's admonition about burglars and looked carefully around but saw nothing of concern.

He parked near the gate to the front yard and started to get out, hesitated, and then got back in and reached under the car's seat. He pulled out a .357 Magnum revolver, the twin of the one stolen from his home. *Better safe than sorry.* While Abel had scoffed at Martín's preoccupation with self-defense, his father had encouraged him, sending him through several National Rifle Association programs. At sixteen he'd begun studying karate, and he still worked out. At eighteen, the sheriff had allowed him to take a combat pistol course intended only for sworn officers. Martín kept that aspect of his life under close wraps. In politically correct Santa Fe, where bands of teenagers were known to haze tourists for wearing leather jackets, the knowledge that he was a gun-toting martial artist would have made him a pariah.

He'd started off with one revolver, but often forgot to take it back and forth from his bedroom to his car. Following a spurt in painting sales, he bought a second one. After all, he told himself, he lived on the edge of the area around Chimayó, known as one of the heroin capitals of the nation. He shoved the pistol under his jacket between his belt and hip and unlatched the gate.

After unlocking and opening the massive front door, Martín listened carefully. Not a sound broke the stillness, as if the house itself were quietly mourning. For twenty minutes he ranged through it, turning on every light. He touched familiar objects and looked at a generation of family photographs. "*They can't be gone!*"

He poured a stiff drink of his father's favorite scotch and went to the study. On the wall above the chest, where the cookies and chocolate had been when he'd last seen his father, was a painting of a handsome young man, a nineteenth century portraitist's conception of his ancestor, the original Martín Cortés. Family lore and the historical record indicated he came to Santa Fe in the late 1600s and spent most of his time killing Indians and seducing settlers' wives.

Instead of the usual, steel-helmeted Conquistador, the painting depicted a handsome young man with longish dark hair—not looking at the viewer, but seemingly through him into the far distance. Martín had always admired the eyes; they portrayed an unlikely combination of resolve and wonderment, as if the man's unswerving purpose had, for a moment, been tempered by the discovery of an unexpected pleasure.

He removed the painting and placed it carefully on the desk. Returning to the now empty wall, he pressed firmly on one side of the paneling. With a muted click, a two-foot section of the polished mahogany swung open to reveal the steel door of a safe. Martín's father had made him learn the combination by heart, and he

45

dialed it
from memory. The door remained locked. Guessing his nerves caused the problem and realizing he was at the end of his tether, he stopped to take a pull of scotch and tried again. This time the door opened. He drew out an oilskin packet that held the bark-paper paintings thought to be of Hernan Cortés and placed it on the desk next to the painting.

He returned to the safe, extracted a large envelope, and opened it. It contained miscellaneous family documents: car papers, insurance policies, and his and Abel's high school and college diplomas. He placed it on the desk. Once again, he returned and felt back to a far corner and touched a small cloth bag. He pulled it out and opened the drawstring. Inside he found his mother's jewelry and one other item, something he'd only seen once before, an uncut emerald, slightly bigger than a quail egg, handed down from the original Martín.

He replaced the jewelry and emerald in the bag and added it to the other items on the desk. He was not overly concerned that burglars would find the safe, but his father had once quietly advised him that if something happened to him and his mother, Martín should remove and hide anything valuable. He feared his heirs could be forced to sell the family heirlooms to pay the inheritance tax.

As the panel snicked closed over the re-locked safe, Martín turned to retrieve the painting and froze. Although he had heard and sensed nothing, a man dressed in black pants and parka stood nonchalantly in the study's doorway. About forty, his tan, ruggedly handsome face had a jagged scar running across one cheek. Although he appeared relaxed, there was a

46

tension and athletic balance to his stance that suggested military or martial arts training. The man wore no hat and his platinum blond hair gleamed in the light. Noting that the intruder held no weapon, Martín exclaimed, "Who the fuck are you?"

The man's smile was mocking as he replied, with what Martín judged to be a slight German accent, "This property's part of a lawsuit you're going to lose. It's my job to ensure it remains intact." He glanced pointedly at the three packages on the desk.

Martín reached for the phone next to the packets. Through gritted teeth, he said, "This is private property and you can leave now, or I'll have you arrested for trespassing."

"That's fine," replied the man, his smile now an outright taunt.

"Just so long as those items remain on the premises."

Martín's fatigue, grief, and frustration ignited into a white-hot vapor. In one fluid motion, he whipped out the revolver and assumed a two-handed combat stance, the barrel aimed at the man, rock steady. "You son-of-a-bitch!" he yelled. "I've just lost both my parents and my brother. If you think you're going to pull that shit on me you're fucking crazy!" Struggling to regain his composure, he lowered his voice. "My attorney warned me that thieves often strike where someone just died. I have a right to protect myself and my property. Do what I say or you're going to be one dead fucking burglar. Now get over to that wall, lie down on your stomach, and put your hands behind your neck!"

The man's grin evaporated as he obeyed. Martín guessed the intruder had a gun, but disarming him would be risky. Years of martial arts had taught him what an experienced practitioner could do to someone who got too close. He had also learned to discard emotion at critical moments but knew that it was his rage that made his threats credible.

He considered calling the police. If he did that, the property he was trying to remove, no matter how legitimate his right to it, would become known. Then the solution hit him.

Martín kept the revolver trained on the man and gathered the items on the desk into his left arm. "Get up and keep your hands on your head," he hissed. "And remember how much I want to kill you." He cocked the revolver with a click that echoed in the stillness. After the man rose, Martín continued, "Now you're going to follow me out, very carefully. He backed toward the study's doorway, then through it, his eyes and the revolver in his right hand riveted on his prisoner.

Just outside the door, Martín suddenly realized the man might have someone with him, and he snapped his head from side to side. *No one.* At the entry, he opened the door and punched the button in the inside handle so it would lock automatically, something he knew he should have done when he came in.

The man said nothing, just did what he was told; this time he preceded Martín through the door. Martín didn't like the way the man looked at him, like a lion deciding how best to kill a wildebeest.

"Try one thing," Martín said through gritted teeth, "and I'll blow a hole in you and drag your sorry ass back inside the house to keep the sheriff happy. I assume that's your car," he added, nodding at a white, late-model Ford parked next to his Tahoe. "Let's go."

Stepping gingerly over the ice, they reached the parked cars. Martín instructed his prisoner to sit down in front of the white Ford. This time the man, fair hair gleaming in the moonlight, looked him in the eye briefly before obeying. *He thinks I've calmed down enough to lose my nerve.*

"I didn't say squat down, asshole, I said *sit down*," he almost screamed. When the man complied, he added, "Now, keeping your right hand on your head, untie and remove both shoes and socks with your left."

The man began to unlace one shoe, then stopped, and shook his head. "No," he said, with the trace of a smile returning. "I don't think so."

A fraction of a second later flame and a thunderous boom erupted from the revolver. The man on the ground screamed in agony and clutched his right arm. "Okay," said Martín, "now you don't have to keep your right hand on top of your head. That was meant to get your attention. Next time it'll be an inch to the right and most of your arm'll be gone. Now get those fucking shoes and socks off, with your left hand."

Shooting the man had been instinctive to Martín. It had also stoked his adrenalin. The intruder sensed this and did what he was told. When he had removed his shoes and socks, Martín ordered him to crawl six feet away and lie down on his stomach.

Martín placed his packages carefully on the ground. With his left hand, he picked up the shoes and socks and threw them as far as he could in different directions. Then he picked up his belongings and backed to the Tahoe. He got in, fitted the key into the ignition, and twisted it. The engine rumbled to life and then settled into a rough idle.

He returned to the man on the ground. "I'm going

to call the sheriff and report that a thief surprised me in my house and tried to rob me. When I ran, he chased me. I was able to get the gun in my car and winged him in self-defense. I also…" He paused, aiming the revolver, which once again boomed deafeningly in the frozen night.

"Shot out a tire so he couldn't come after me. I left the scene because I was afraid he might be part of a gang and that others could be on the way."

"I won't give him your license number, but I'll remember it. Changing that tire one-handed should occupy you until they get here."

The man clutched his injured arm and glared at Martín with such hatred that he shivered, even though he held the pistol.

"And just because you're walking away this time," Martín added, "don't count on it in the future. I intend to get justice for what's been done to my family, and I'll be happy to begin with you." With that, he quickly backed to his car, leapt in, and took off as fast as the slick surface would allow. In case the man had a gun, he left the lights off and bent low until he reached the gate at the driveway. His spine tingled the whole way, expecting bullets to smash into the car.

SANTA FE

Since staying at the hacienda was now out of the question, and the last thing he wanted was to involve Laura in whatever was happening, Martín decided to accept Herb's invitation. The threat to call the sheriff had been partly a bluff as he'd inadvertently left his cellphone at his house. He would make that call from Herb's to get his version of what had happened on the record. Setting his revolver on the passenger seat by the other items, he slowly made the right turn from the hacienda's driveway onto the narrow two-lane road to Santa Fe. Nevertheless, his tires slid on the treacherous surface. As he regained control, a pair of lights blazed in his rearview mirror.

He decided the vehicle must have been driving without lights or parked by the side of the road and suddenly switched them on. It appeared to be a pickup truck and was rapidly gaining on him. Although Martín increased his speed on the icy road to the point where he was barely in control, his pursuer drew closer, bright lights illuminating him like a performer in a spotlight.

Maybe I'm being paranoid and it's just some yahoo with a couple of beers trying to get home. He was beginning to ascend a steep grade in a wide, left-hand turn and thought about slowing to the right, hoping whoever it was would pass him. But if he was wrong, he could easily be forced off the road into the increasingly deep canyon. He released the wheel for the few seconds it took to fasten his seatbelt.

Now tailgating him, the truck suddenly lunged forward and rammed the Tahoe, sending its rear end skidding to the left. Through the shock of the collision Martín fought for control. Just as he began to straighten out, the truck slammed him again, and he heard the sound of shattering glass. Out of control, he started to spin to the right in a circle whose arc brought him to the edge of the road—then over it. For a moment there was a sensation of flight, then a bone-jarring crunching of glass and metal as the Tahoe rolled end over end, down the hill.

The sturdy old car lacked airbags, but the seatbelt held, as did Martín's iron grip on the steering wheel. Miraculously, the vehicle ended right side up at the bottom of the ravine, with Martin in essentially the same upright position as before the impact. The windshield and rear window were gone and he was covered with shattered glass. But other than a few cuts and bruises, he felt okay. He guessed the heavy brush had cushioned the descent. Mainly, he worried about the family heirlooms and revolver he'd placed on the passenger seat. Feeling carefully in the darkness to keep from cutting his fingers, he could find them nowhere in the front of the car.

Terrified they had been thrown out through one of the smashed windows, he scrambled over the seat into the back, where he'd folded the seat down to accommodate his paintings. He quickly found the oilskin packet of drawings, the large envelope, and his revolver. The little bag of jewelry was nowhere. Back in the front seat, he tried opening the driver's side door. No luck. *Probably wedged tight.* Fortunately, the passenger door opened. Shifting his things to the driver's seat, he got out as quietly as he could. He heard voices above him.

"What the fuck you think, man?" Martín heard a

high-pitched, almost girlish voice.

"We gotta go check," replied a more normal male voice.

"It's too fucking cold!"

"Tough shit, let's go."

Martín peered upward and made out what appeared to be two figures dressed in white silhouetted against the dark sky. They immediately disappeared, presumably heading downward.

Thankful that the interior light had not come on, he wrenched open the rear door and felt along the floor beneath the folded-down back seat. Nothing. He heard the voices again and saw a light bobbing slowly toward him, followed by the sound of breaking brush and dislodged pebbles. Dashing around the car, he got the driver's side rear door open and reached below the platform to run his nearly frozen hand along the floor. The jewel bag was in the corner. He snatched it, retrieved the other items, and darted sideways, away from the vehicle and into a patch of brush.

The shock of the accident and the frantic search for the family treasures had temporarily submerged Martín's anger. Hearing the voices and seeing the light descend, his rage returned. Enough was enough, and he decided to finish his pursuers then and there. He placed the bag with the emerald in his pocket, dropped the bark drawings at the base of a bush, and drew and cocked his pistol.

The two men took their time descending the steep slope into the canyon, which gave Martín time to think. What if he shot them both and they turned out to have no connection with the blond man, were only a couple of drunks coming to rescue him? He doubted that, but realized he had no proof either way. Killing someone without being able to demonstrate the need for self-defense would only multiply his problems. Also, he could barely see his hand in front of his face and only had four more bullets. Poor odds.

Lowering the revolver's hammer, he shoved it inside his belt
and picked up the codices. Moving as soundlessly as he could through the rocks and brush, he pushed his hands into the warmth of his parka's pockets. As he went, he tried to figure out why the voices seemed so distinctive.

Fifteen minutes later, with no further evidence of pursuit, Martín became less concerned about noise and more so with getting out of the cold. Luís Perez's house should be just up ahead. The two had been neighbors and played together in these hills as they grew up. Before they died, Luís's parents had owned a gas station and mechanic shop in town. On more than one occasion, Martín's father helped them with financial problems. After high school, the boys drifted apart—Martín to college in Albuquerque and Luís to take over the family garage. But they still greeted each other warmly, and Martín had attended Luís's wedding a few years ago.

Five minutes later, the ravine widened into a valley, and there was the one-story adobe, built just high enough above the valley floor to avoid the spring runoff. Shivering, Martín heard a dog bark as he approached the house. Nearing the doorway, he called out. "Luís, it's Martín Cortés. I need help!"

A light came on, and moments later the door opened. Luís wore jeans and an untucked flannel shirt. His tousled black hair, like Martín's, hung nearly to his shoulders. Without waiting for an explanation, he waved Martín inside, offering condolences about the Cortés family tragedies. When he saw Martín in the light, he explained, "What the hell happened to you—been in a fight or something?"

"Might as well have." Martín explained what had happened to his family and how he had nearly been added to the toll. When asked to describe the men, Martín could remember only his impression that they wore white and sounded like—now he had it: hippies.

"Like out of the '60s, man?" Luís grinned at his imitation.

"Yeah, one of them had a high, whiney voice."

"I'll tell Sonia everything's okay, and we'll get you something warm to drink, but first you might want to clean up a bit. You know where the bathroom is."

After combing his hair and cleaning the cuts on his face, Martín called the sheriff's office and reported both the incident at the hacienda and being forced off the road. He told the dispatcher that the sheriff had been with him earlier in the evening and would want to be informed immediately. After providing Luís's address, he called Herb, who said he was on his way. As he finished, Sonia placed a steaming mug of hot chocolate in front of him.

"Perfect," said Martín, beginning to warm up. Then motioning toward the packages he had placed on the table by the phone, he added, "Luís, you got anyplace I can stash this stuff until everyone leaves?"

Luís looked at him suspiciously and Martín quickly added, "No drugs, just some family stuff that could affect the inheritance taxes."

Luís waved at an old cupboard in the corner. "Stick 'em in there behind the sack of beans."

Martín stowed away the oilskin package and jewel bag but left the envelope with miscellaneous items on the table.

Fifteen minutes later Eddie Jaramillo arrived, a slightly disheveled version of his earlier self. "Okay, Martín, what the hell's going on?" he began. Martín searched in vain for the familiar twinkle.

Martín recounted his story, exactly as he'd told the dispatcher.

The sheriff gave him a hard stare. "What was the guy at your house trying to take?"

"I'm not sure. I only had family stuff, like my and Abel's diplomas." He gestured toward the envelope.

Eddie looked at him speculatively. "We got a call from some guy. Anonymous, from a booth outside of town, saying you tried to run *him* off the road. Said your driving seemed drunk. You had anything to drink, Martín?"

"Just one drink at the house, probably about two hours ago."

"Mind takin' a breath test?"

Martín readily agreed, and they finished the test right before Herb arrived.

"He's probably more sober than I am," said Eddie.

In response to Herb's sharp questioning of the need for the test, the sheriff replied, "Herb, I got an itchy feeling that everyone involved in this thing's going to need some cover, and I got to make sure everything's by the book."

Herb's forehead creased in thought. "You're probably right. It's pretty obvious what's goin' on. We better get a line on these people, pronto. Martín, did you get the license number of the truck that hit you?"

"No, they had their brights on me, but I gave Eddie

the license number of the guy's car at the house."

"He's probably gone, but let's take a spin by there," said the sheriff.

Martín called Luís, who had disappeared when the sheriff arrived. He came out from the back, and Martín thanked him for his help and suggested Eddie go ahead. He and Herb would meet him at the hacienda. After he left, Martín retrieved his possessions from the cabinet and grabbed the packet of files from the table.

SANTA FE

The blond man and the white Ford were gone. The sheriff's flashlight revealed only some tire tracks, a few drops of blood, and one dark sock on the ground.

"The Ford belongs to a rental place in Albuquerque," said Eddie. "We'll check it out tomorrow." Although the house was still locked, they searched it thoroughly but found nothing disturbed.

Half an hour later at Herb's home, Martín began to describe the contents of the packages.

Herb stopped him with a raised hand. "I don't want to know. I assume you want me to handle the estate. When it comes to the IRS, I got no obligation to disclose what I don't know. You want a drink?"

Realizing he was wiped out, Martín shook his head.

"I thought so," nodded Herb. "Follow me. By the way, tomorrow's Monday, and the bank's gotta open. Hope you don't mind, but I called Odette, and she'll take care of everything, including gettin' a couple of security guards to keep order. I told her no comment to the press. They're probably stakin' the place out already. I did say she could tell customers there's no problem with the bank, just a heap a bad luck for the family."

Martín smiled his thanks, too tired to do more.

Martín awoke to find sunlight streaming through his window. As he remembered the horrors of the day before, his first reaction was to crawl back under the covers and disappear from the world. Realizing he didn't have that luxury and remembering a plan he had conceived to safeguard the codex paintings just before falling asleep, he inched stiffly out of bed, feeling as if

58

every part of his body had been severely bruised. A glance at his watch told him it was just after nine. He followed the aroma of frying bacon down the narrow hallway and found Herb's wife, Margo, in the kitchen. At sixty, she was tall, willowy, and still beautiful. "I'll bet you're starving," she smiled, motioning toward a pile of bacon
and scrambled eggs on an electric warmer. "After that, the bath next to your room is yours. Herb's gone for a walk."

"Thanks, Margo, but first may I use the phone?"

"Sure, second door to the right in Herb's office."

The house was on Acequia Madre in one of Santa Fe's oldest neighborhoods. It had originally been a small adobe with yard-thick walls. Successive owners had added to it, creating a warren of narrow passages lined with white plaster.

Martín opened the carved door to Herb's home office, ducked under the wooden lintel, and entered the book-lined room that was not much more than a cubby hole. The brick floor was covered with what he guessed were priceless Indian rugs. He called the University of New Mexico and, after confirming that Dr. Geoffrey Lassiter was still chairman of the Archeology Department, asked to be connected to him. The man's abrupt "Hello" became a welcoming purr after Martín identified himself.

"Of course I remember you, and I want to extend my condolences on the loss of your father."

Surprised that he was still remembered after nearly ten years and that the professor apparently had not heard the news of yesterday's
tragic events, he said, "Do you also remember the drawing you tentatively identified as being of Hernan

Cortés?"

"Yes, certainly. In fact, not long ago I mentioned it to a donor who's building a Pre-Hispanic display gallery for us. He's passionate about the subject. When I heard your voice, I thought perhaps he'd contacted you and persuaded you to add it to our collection?"

Martín remained silent, and after a pause the professor continued.

"His name is Colin Glendaring. Like me he used to be an archeologist, then he got into land development. Apparently a good choice because he's loaded! Have you met him? He said he's doing something with your brother."

Martín was stunned as pieces of the puzzle crashed into place, like immense concrete blocks dropping from the sky to land in perfect alignment. The president of SpanGlobe was a former archeologist and aware of his family's treasures!

"Well," Martín finally said, trying to deal with the thoughts flashing through his brain like a sky full of tracer bullets. "I just wanted to see if you still had an interest. You apparently haven't heard that my mother and brother died yesterday, and a customer of the bank was murdered." Then, his rekindled anger getting the best of him, he blurted out, "Probably because of a business deal your donor was involved in."

Before the man could respond, Martín said, "I've got a lot on my plate. I'm trying to find a safe place for the items, and I may get back to you. Now, I'm afraid I've got to run." Martín hung up and ran for the door.

Acequia Madre is well up the mountain, roughly parallel to but a block higher than Canyon Road, where many of the area's best art galleries were located. Turning up Camino Don Miguel, he spied

Herb entering a small neighborhood convenience store. Nearly out of breath, Martín followed him in.

"How you feelin'?" asked Herb as he turned from paying his bill.

"I just had an interesting telephone conversation," said Martín, still breathing hard. "We need to talk."

"Let's walk. It's a fine day."

It was indeed one of those crisp, cloudless, Santa Fe spring days where the sun bakes through the thin air, instilling a feeling of well-being. They walked back down to Acequia Madre and then away from Herb's house. Still sore and limping, Martín found it difficult to keep up with his friend's shambling stride. After hearing Martín's story, Herb wiped his mustache and passed over a plastic package. "Try some of this, beef smoked with chile *pasado*. A little hot, but just what you need to get you goin'."

Martín impatiently declined, and Herb looked at him sharply. "Are you tryin' to say all this was about those drawings?"

"Not entirely, but maybe partly."

"But from what you said, he could only have known about the one you showed the school."

"Abel could have told him about the others. As eldest, I would inherit them, but he sure knew all about them—and didn't think much of them."

"I see what you mean, but that don't make no difference now. Before the end of the day, we need to deal with the bank and that means the FDIC. I talked to Odette earlier and sure enough the place is crawlin' with reporters. But I think she handled everything okay. Probably just as well you stay outta sight today."

Martín was relieved. Odette O'Reilly was a feisty, middle-aged redhead who had worked for the bank for twenty years. He knew that if anything was left after Abel's irresponsibility it would be due to her efforts. She bore the title of vice president, and her high energy level enabled extended hours at the bank, as long as the rest of her time was free to pursue her passion for amateur theater. She and Martín got along well, but he knew she had developed an intense dislike for Abel, whose outspoken disdain of their father's management style had nearly caused her to quit.

"Herb, I can't thank you enough!" exclaimed Martín.

"Wait till you get my bill," he chuckled. "Now we better get you home for a change of clothes, then down to the office. We got a lot to do."

"First, I need to get the things in your house into my safe deposit box and some clean clothes. And my damn car's wrecked."

"I'll take you by the house and you can get your parents' car, and the cops should be releasing Abel's Land Rover before long."

An hour later, after a visit to his own home to pick up his safe deposit box key and Pancho, Martín pulled into the parking lot of his bank in Española. He had opened an account there after selling his stock in the family bank to Abel. He had invested $100,000 from the proceeds of the sale of his bank stock in a certificate of deposit, $150,000 in bonds, and $50,000 in gold coins that he kept in a safe deposit box.

SANTA FE, SIX WEEKS LATER

Exactly six weeks from the day his father died, changing his world forever, Martín sat in his father's office in the bank. He had endured the combined funeral of his mother, father, and brother and then tried to sort out the bank's problems. Herb proved right in that the Feds called the shots. Deposit insurance meant they stood to lose millions if the bank went under.

Some depositors closed accounts, but most did not. That reflected the attitudes of people toward Martín. Some considered him part of a wealthy family that didn't mind ruining the common man in the form of Johnny Carillo for their own gain. Others—which included most of the people who actually knew Martín—considered him the victim of a tragedy caused by his brother.

At first, Laura supported Martín. But soon, likely due to pressure from her family, her ardor waned. Not in big chunks, but steadily, little by little. Phone calls and drop-ins came further apart. She took longer and longer to return messages he left for her. Planning for the future ceased altogether. Martín actually felt relief. Avoiding her social agenda and parents topped the short list of things he could look forward to. How could he have considered her his soul mate? It dawned on him that her family embodied the arrogance and prejudices he'd always disdained, and he wondered why he'd ignored his father's concerns about their relationship.

His relatives followed suit. His father's only sister, who'd died several years earlier, had left no children. But his mother's large family—aunts, uncles, and cousins—after an initial outpouring of sympathy remained conspicuously absent. He had the distinct impression that some of them welcomed his family's fall.

As for his friends, Martín verified what he'd always suspected—that they were merely acquaintances. Most of his high school buddies had either drifted away or, like Luís, entered different worlds. He usually hung out with the art community. That often meant big egos and intolerance of anyone outside their clique. Although many of them were vain and self-centered, more than a few were also perceptive. It didn't take them long to discover the conservative aspects of Martín's nature. Although he kept his gun ownership and self-defense skills closely guarded secrets, they quickly sniffed out his propensity to put reason ahead of emotion. They chided him endlessly, saying that relying on his brain rather than his heart made him boring, and they predicted it would keep his work from achieving greatness. Although coming events would prove them at least partially correct, for whatever reasons, after receiving appropriate condolences he rarely heard from them. That was fine; he had no time to waste.

Martín made it a priority to reverse the Carillo foreclosure. In the process he learned that shortly after Johnny's murder, a lawyer representing an unnamed client had met with each of Johnny's potential heirs. For substantial sums he purchased whatever rights or money they might receive from a future lawsuit against the bank.

Johnny had left no will and had no immediate family. So, who within the family would eventually inherit remained uncertain. Because of that, they accepted the money—a sure thing—as opposed to fighting with each other over something that might never materialize. The lawyer then filed suit against the bank for $50 million, plus treble damages for fraud and more trumped- up grievances than Herb had ever heard of.

Determined to salvage what he could of his brother's reputation, Martín had retained Herb to try and prove that Abel had not killed Johnny and his family. Herb hired a private detective, and three weeks earlier had summoned Martín to receive his report.

In his office, Herb handed Martín a thick envelope. "Here's the full report, but let me hit the high points: The detective discovered that Glendaring, although now president of SpanGlobe, started his working life as a professor of archeology and that his career ended badly. Although the university he worked for hushed it up, Glendaring stole valuable artifacts from a dig he managed in Peru and was fired. After that, he worked as a stockbroker, mortgage broker, and car salesman. All those jobs ended with legal problems that, for reasons unknown, never came to trial. Later the police arrested him for impersonating a Baptist preacher while soliciting funds in Kansas. Those charges were also dropped."

"Shit, I knew it," exclaimed Martín.

"Wait, it gets better. After several years with no clues to his whereabouts, two years ago Glendaring turned up in Colorado working as a project manager for the founder of SpanGlobe. Last year the owner died in a hunting accident, and Glendaring quickly acquired ownership of the company from the man's widow. That explains why Abel's research gave the company a clean bill of health. The inquest indicated that a person or persons unknown shot the former owner accidentally, a conclusion the private detective considered suspect."

"Did you give that to the sheriff?" asked Martín.

"Course I did, but it doesn't prove anything."

Martín left the meeting as frustrated as ever. In a subsequent deposition regarding the foreclosure, Glendaring confirmed the facts of his last conversation with Abel, claiming he intended to honor the decision to reverse the foreclosure on Johnny's land and search for other property for his project. In reality, SpanGlobe seemed to have disappeared from the Santa Fe scene.

The foreclosure was reversed and the attorney who had purchased the interests of Johnny Carillo's family was told that he needed only to keep current with the loan and tax payments. He had done nothing yet. Martín suspected the attorney worked for Glendaring.

Interrupting Martín's review of recent events, Herb walked into the bank's office, waving a thick manila envelope. Here's the examiners' report. "You want the good news or the bad news first?"

"If there's any good news better save it."

"Actually, a lot of it's good, except that the examiners turned up a mess of other stuff that Abel did, including a two hundred-fifty grand unsecured loan to a pal of his in Albuquerque. The guy started some flaky high tech-company. The land deal made the most noise. Bottom line, it looks like the bank ain't gonna fail, at least not technically. The bad news: you need to sell it for nothin' to achieve that outcome. And the Feds have found a buyer."

"Who is it?"

"A bank holding company, *BancFrontier.* They're

new. I'm told they just bought your bank in Española last week. Did you know that?"

Martín shook his head. "Not really. Now that you mention it, day before yesterday when I went in to renew my certificate of deposit, I didn't recognize any of the staff."

"Unfortunately, Martín, I couldn't talk them into allowing you to buy the family home back from the bank at what it's carried for on the books. I even told their lawyer it was a deal-breaker, but they knew better. The FDIC assumes total liability for all present and future suits, and they won't give anythin' up. won't budge an inch. The chief examiner was actually surprised that anyone was willing to buy the bank, especially with a lawsuit pending. Said everyone else turned him down. He thinks these folks are reachin' for market share."

"Herb, that house is on the books at $100,000, the value in the late '40s when my grandfather started the bank. Now, it's probably over $4 million! Whoever bought the bank has a hell of a deal if the lawsuits come to nothing."

"That's the risk, ain't it. Unless you just won the lottery, what can you do about it?"

"We still don't know who that lawyer who bought the Carillo family interests represents. Since it's not the Carillos themselves, there damn sure won't be nearly the favorable sentiment. Something's fishy. Can't you smell it?"

"Martín, don't you think the buyer is counting on not havin' to pay too much to settle the suits? Fishy? Possibly, but it don't matter; there's no choice. The examiners can do any number of things, including preferring criminal charges if they don't get their way.

They want to eliminate any risk they'll have to pony up if the bank goes bust. Thing is, they're bein' reasonable."

"Okay, okay! I thought you high-priced lawyers could work miracles. In that regard, the bank has paid a lot of your fees, but you haven't sent me a bill for the stuff that's personal, like handling the estate and defending Abel at the inquest. I hate to say anything, but I

imagine the cost of that private detective alone is a bunch of money."

The estate was almost settled, and Martín had analyzed his situation. For him the results were devastating. His father's main net worth came from his shares of the bank and the hacienda. He had some emergency cash in a savings account and a few shares of publicly traded companies, but not much else. In better days the stock alone was worth several million dollars, certainly enough for a comfortable retirement. But not with accounts closed and the lawsuits hanging over it. The house belonged to the bank and it charged the family $5,000 per year plus taxes and insurance for rent. His father had believed that was a fair return on the $100,000 place it held in the bank's capital account. Never mind the probable market value of several million.

Martín realized his entire inheritance consisted of the items in his safe deposit box plus whatever he could get for the hacienda's furniture. Considering that he had no moral right to sell the family heirlooms, that meant his entire net worth had not really changed after the deaths of everyone he loved.

He had never cared much about money, so that didn't bother him. He had simply hoped the legal bills would not force him into a job that would interfere with his painting, which he longed to return to. That would now be difficult in high-dollar Santa Fe. He hadn't realized how important the family had been to him. He was now the only direct heir to the line begun in the seventeenth century and would soon have to make some difficult choices.

"Martín," said Herb, "all those fees do add up to a fair amount of money, but I've been saving the statements until after the bank sale's complete, probably within the next couple days. You don't need to
pay it all at once or, for that matter, ever."

"Thanks, Herb. I treasure your friendship! But I want to clear everything out so I know where I stand and can go on with my life."

"I understand. I'll call you when they set the closing."

SANTA FE

A week later, just after 2:00 p.m., Martín walked out of the bank for the last time. He had just signed over his one hundred percent ownership for a hundred dollars and indemnification against future lawsuits.

"Come with me," said Herb, pulling him gently to the left. "We need to celebrate the end of this mess and the beginning of whatever's next for you."

Ten minutes later, they entered the Inn at La Fonda, one of the town's most historic and picturesque establishments, located just off the main plaza. Reaching the lobby, they turned right and entered La Placita, the Inn's restaurant, an atrium-like space set beneath the balconies of the second floor and topped with a high glass ceiling. Stepping down tile steps onto the area's dark, polished flagstone floor, Martín groaned. Of the five occupied tables, two held acquaintances. The buzz of conversation lapsed into awkward silence until Martín summoned all his will and waved cheerily, first to the former mayor of Santa Fe and then to Laura's brother and his wife. The normal noise level resumed, accompanied by curious glances.

"Fuck 'em," whispered Herb out of the side of his mouth, as he steered Martín to a table in a far corner by a whimsically painted banquette.

When they'd ordered drinks, Herb said, "Well, my friend, what you gonna do now?"

Martín had been thinking about nothing else. "I've decided to give the art six months to work. In the meantime, I'll come up with an alternative."

Herb frowned. "You need to wake up from this nightmare. You're so damn close to the trees, you can't see the forest. Take a month or two, go somewhere else, relax a little. One day you'll wake up and the answer will smack you in the face. You either want to be an artist or you don't. If you can imagine an alternative, you probably don't."

"You may be right. Although Laura hasn't said it in so many words, the Spanish boy without the family bank won't cut it. Actually, that's the only relief I feel over the whole damn thing. Now, what about that bill you promised me? Might as well clear that out."

Herb smiled. "You sure? This'll just make a bad day worse?"

Martín nodded. Herb reached down, slid an envelope out of his briefcase, and handed it over.

"I did what I could, but… And like I said, take your time—or forget it."

Martín tried not to gasp as the printed amount, $50,000, swam in front of his eyes. He shoved the statement back in the envelope and tried to smile. "If you don't mind taking some of it in gold coins I'll go to the bank and drop them by later. I may decide to sell a bond or two, so that may take a few days."

"Think on what I said about gettin' away."

SANTA FE

A pleasant lunch and several drinks under his belt, Martín entered his bank in Española. After completing the requisite form, a young woman climbed a short ladder and unlocked his box. She was short, so he slid it out of the top bank of boxes.

Immediately he sensed a problem. Fifty thousand dollars in gold coins weighed around two pounds at the time, and the box felt empty. Rushing to a viewing room, he fumbled the latch open and pulled up the lid. Inside he found some miscellaneous papers, including the deed to his home, insurance policies, and the one bond that had been in his name, with a face value of $10,000.

Nothing else!

He had the largest box available and he stared blankly into the nearly vacant interior. Frantically, he shuffled through the papers again. The missing items included the gold coins, the stack of bearer bonds that represented most of his wealth, the priceless codex paintings, his mother's jewelry, and the huge emerald. Eyes glazed over and heart beating like a snare drum, he ran with the box to the barred entry to the safe deposit area and shouted for the receptionist. "Nearly everything's gone!" he yelled when she arrived. "Get the manager!

She turned on her heel and returned moments later with the attractive brunette who had assisted him in renewing his CD earlier in the week. Opening the gate, she said, "Mr. Cortés, I'm the assistant manager. How may I help you?"

Feeling the blood and alcohol from the late meal rush to his head, he explained what had happened.

When he finished, the woman glanced at his sign-in card and looked him calmly in the eye.

"Mr. Cortés, I don't know what to say. Nobody else has access to your box, and this shows you last went to it on Monday, the day you cashed in your CD."

"When I what?" yelled Martín. "I didn't cash it in, I renewed it, and I only went to the box to add the receipt!"

She shook her head. "I'm sorry, but I helped you myself. I remember being surprised when you requested the proceeds in cash. One hundred thousand dollars took some time to arrange."

"I don't know what you're trying to pull, but you better get the manager—now!" he nearly shrieked, unconsciously stuffing the few papers into his jacket pocket.

"Certainly, sir." She turned on her heel.
Minutes later she returned with a security guard. Crew cut, in his early thirties, he had the fit look of a combat soldier, very unlike the usual flaccid security guard. But the man who came behind him nearly sent Martín into orbit. He'd last seen the blond man in his bare feet outside his parents' home. The man he had wounded but who now seemed completely recovered!

"What the hell's going on here?" yelled Martín. "You're the sonofabitch that tried to rob me. Looks like you found another way!"

The man, looking as tough and dangerous as the security guard, wore a gray suit, white shirt, and regimental tie. He gave the same mocking smile Martín remembered.

"I'm sorry, sir, I've been here just since my company took over this bank, and I don't remember seeing you before." He sounded as unctuous as a waiter in a pretentious restaurant.

Snatching out the remaining bond, Martín turned and threw the steel box as hard as he could at the wall. It hit the surface with a crash and clattered onto the concrete floor. Turning, he saw that the woman had gone, and the security guard had his hand on the handle of the huge holstered revolver. Ignoring him, Martín stared into the blond man's eyes, noticing again the prominent scar on his cheek. "I'm on my way to the police and then the FBI. If it's the last thing I do I'll make sure you don't get away with this. Now get the fuck out of my way."

Never losing his taunting smile, the blond man stepped aside and motioned the security guard to do the same. Martín barged by them and left the bank, clutching his remaining bond to the stares of employees and customers.

SANTA FE

Rio Arriba County Sheriff Bernie Mendoza gazed calmy across his desk at Martín as the young man gave an emotional description of the theft of his property by his bank. "Calm down, Martín," cautioned the sheriff in his slightly accented voice.

Buzz-cut, salt and pepper hair, and a perfectly shaped pencil mustache accented his knife-thin features, making him about as opposite to Santa Fe's bearlike and rumpled Eddie Jaramillo as could be imagined.

Mendoza continued, "Eddie told me what happened with the blond guy at your folks' house, and I saw what you claim was his blood on the ground. But even if we'd taken samples, what's the use? You said he came inside through an unlocked door and demanded you hand over some things and that he was unarmed. Then you said that after he assaulted you, you got the gun from your car and winged him. He'll undoubtedly say he works part-time for the law firm that filed the lawsuit and wanted to protect disputed property, and that you assaulted and then shot him."

Bernie paused, locking eyes with Martín. "I know you're damned good at karate, so for you to say you needed a gun in that situation is a stretch. Anyway, nothing he did qualifies as breaking and entering, attempted robbery, or anything else—except maybe bad manners. I *will* grant you that the fact he didn't report the shooting *is* suspicious."

Martín frowned, regretting that he hadn't fabricated a better story to explain why he shot the man. The sheriff shifted in his wooden swivel chair, becoming even more erect. "Now about this other thing with your bank. I'll start an investigation, but I think it involves the Feds more than me. And I have no idea how you can prove you had those things in your box, or, for that matter, that you ever had them. It'll be your word against theirs."

He raised his hand to restrain Martín, who gave every indication of a man about to vault out of his chair. "Dammit, just settle down! That's my official take, but I'm not gonna leave it at that. I'll question the bank employees and run background checks on them. These are serious charges and, in spite of your recent problems, you're a credible source."

Martín leaned across the desk and locked eyes with the sheriff. "Bernie, I've had my entire family taken from me—basically murdered—by these people. And there's no doubt in my mind that this bank holding company is related to SpanGlobe and probably to whomever bought the interests in Johnny Carillo's estate from his heirs. That's why they could buy our bank, risk-free; they knew all the lawsuits would disappear and they'd end up with valuable assets and a going concern, including the hacienda and the Carillo property."

Martín took a deep breath and continued. "In spite of $50,000 in legal fees, I couldn't prove my brother's innocence. The bank that took two generations to build was taken away just like that!" He snapped his fingers. "And in a few days, I have to turn over the keys to the home my family has lived in for over 120 years. Of course, the sons-of-bitches realized they'd missed a few things, and now I've been personally stripped. I didn't cash that CD and haul $100,000 in cash out of the bank on Monday. I didn't remove

$50,000 in gold coins or $100,000 worth of bearer bonds that legally belong to whomever possesses them."

Still wary of possible tax consequences, Martín did not mention the loss of the emerald or the codices. During the previous month, his subtle inquiries indicated that the emerald alone might be worth several hundred thousand dollars. And the missing codices? To a passionate collector—perhaps a former archeologist like Colin Glendaring—they could be priceless.

Martín leaned closer to the sheriff. "Anybody who thinks I'm going to take this lying down is dreaming. I haven't got much to lose and I plan on getting justice."

Mendoza raised his hand again and his eyes turned hard. "Martín. I understand how you feel but I'm warning you, no more threats. Besides pissing me off, they have a way of coming back to bite you in the ass. I told you, I'll investigate this thing and that includes contacting the FBI just as soon as you leave. Now get the hell out of here, behave yourself, and call me tomorrow afternoon."

Martín shook his head. "Be sure and examine the documentation of the supposed cashing of my CD against my signature. Then check the bank's security cameras for Monday. Under normal circumstances they'll prove I didn't take anything out. I've no doubt you'll discover the system was 'down.'"

Back at his house, Martín took Pancho for a run on the hillside. The air was cool and clear, and a dusting of snow lingered on the distant mountains. He noticed none of it. An all-consuming desire to obtain justice had overwhelmed his customary focus on aesthetics.

Earlier, when he'd stopped at the hacienda to lock

his remaining papers in the safe, he had picked up the phone to tell Herb about the thefts that had wiped out his net worth, at least other than the one

bond and his home. He couldn't do it. Herb would tell him not to worry about paying his bill, which a quick scan showed was mostly fees for the private detective, expert witnesses, travel, and other large but legitimate expenses, with very little going to Herb. Herb would then counsel him not to do what he intended to do. No, he wouldn't call. All along he'd taken advice, played by the rules, and where had it gotten him? His plan was simple. He would find the blond man and do whatever it took to retrieve his belongings. If that didn't work, there was always Colin Glendaring, the man he was sure was behind the whole thing.

SANTA FE

Martín parked Abel's black Land Rover in a strip center across the boulevard from his bank. A detailer had removed the blood from the leather upholstery, but the bullet hole in the front seat, although now covered with duct tape, remained.

Just before 5:00 p.m., a convoy of black clouds had rolled in and the temperature rose with the humidity. Martín's eyes moved back to the bank. The adobe building, framed in a pre-twilight shaft of light from between the storm clouds, was nearly new with a *kiva* ladder leading to a fake second-story balcony.

He had surmised that both the blond man and the woman, and perhaps other bank employees, were brought in to do to him what had been done. To avoid an inquiry, they might disappear. Delay being the principal ally of the guilty, he guessed that the investigation would be met with something like, "He's been transferred," or "She's taken a leave of absence." The bank was his only connection to the blond man, and intuition told him that link would soon disappear. Five o'clock came and went. The bank's door opened periodically to disgorge one employee after another, but not the right ones. Then, just before 6:00 p.m., the door swung open once more, and through it came the blond man and the woman who had so blatantly lied to him.

Martín started the engine.

The wind had picked up and the pair leaned close together, like lovers. Each carried a large rectangular suitcase of the type favored by accountants for transporting important documents. Going directly to a silver Mercedes, they got in and pulled out of the parking lot onto the highway toward Santa Fe. Martín followed. He kept his distance, glad the traffic was light. As he passed the opera grounds on the right, he reached over and touched his revolver on the passenger seat and found its presence reassuring.

The Mercedes went by the first exit and continued straight to Cerrillos Road, where it turned right. Traffic was heavier and Martín closed the gap. Could they be heading for the airport? That would fit his theory. *How would he handle that?*

After about two miles, the Mercedes suddenly swung right into an industrial area of adobe and cinder-block buildings between Cerrillos Road and Agua Fria. As he followed, he saw the car turn left at the second block. Realizing his was the only other car on the road, Martín fell back and then slowly made the left turn.

Ahead at the next cross street, the Mercedes turned right. When he reached that intersection, Martín slowly turned the corner and saw an empty street flanked by warehouses. The Mercedes had not had time to reach the next block, so it must have turned into one of the buildings. He crept past the first and second warehouses. As he approached the third, a one-story block structure surrounded by a chain-link fence with an open gate, a pickup truck without lights burst from the driveway directly at him, then slammed on its brakes. As Martín put his own brakes to the floor, the truck's right front fender clipped the passenger side of the Land Rover just in front of the door, slamming him sideways.

Furious, Martín flung himself out of the car and rounded the hood to confront the other driver who had already gotten out. For a moment Martín gaped.

The other man was tall and thin, with a full blond beard below a bony, crooked nose. He was dressed in the white robe and turban of a Sikh. *Probably from the colony near Española.*

Martín took a step closer, and the tall, white-gowned man said in a high-pitched voice, "Gee, man, I'm really sorry—wasn't looking."

Martín recognized the voice of one of the men who had run his Tahoe off the road, a moment before a blow to the side of his head knocked him unconscious.

TAOS HIGHWAY

When Martín regained consciousness, he lay in the back seat of a moving car. His hands were securely tied behind his back, his ankles were lashed together, and his head felt like someone had used it as a bowling ball. He had no idea how long he'd been out. The hole in the back of the driver's seat and the smell of cleaning chemicals told him he was in Abel's Land Rover. In front of him, smoke with the unmistakable aroma of marijuana swirled around the white turbaned head of the driver.

Martín's involuntary groan caused the man to glance over his shoulder. "Hey man, you okay? Hope so— you're not supposed to be dead yet." The voice rose in a shrill giggle.

"What the fuck's going on?" croaked Martín.

"What's goin' on, baby, is that you're goin' to meet the man in the Rio Grande. And guess what, it's almost time!" He giggled again and blew a cloud of smoke toward the open window.

"Yes, sir," he continued. "It don't matter that you know. We're goin' to fill you fulla tequila (he pronounced it *tek-uh-luh*), then in you and this piece a shit go, victims of lack of spiritual oneness."

Martín tried to ignore the ache in his head. The car made regular, gradual turns, and he guessed they were heading north on the Taos highway, alongside which the Rio Grande flows swiftly. Night had fallen, and bright lights that never stopped reflecting in the rearview mirror told him that someone followed close behind, probably in the pickup that had hit him.

"Yup," said the driver, his voice now lower, "just about another half mile."

A couple of hearty tugs told Martín he had no hope of releasing his hands. It would be less than a minute before they stopped, knocked him out, untied him, and doused him with tequila. The car would then be shoved into the swiftly flowing river.

Martín did the only thing he could think of: in one fluid motion he flipped onto his back, cocked both legs until his knees touched his chin, and, with all the strength and focus of a thousand karate lessons, he kicked the driver in the back of the head with both heels. The man swore in surprise. Martín repeated the action three times in quick succession and the Sikh fell forward over the steering wheel.

The car began to drift to the left and then smashed through a barrier, became airborne, and landed with a crash. The forward momentum continued, and the Land Rover bumped and slid down a hill and into the water with a huge splash. As the force of the current took hold, the vehicle began to spin in a wide circle.

Panicked, Martín threw himself upright and, with his feet on the floor, drove himself headfirst over the seatback into the passenger seat, landing on his side. The driver moaned and tried to grasp the wheel. Shifting onto his back, Martín again kicked, this time striking the man on the side of his face and jaw. He did it twice, with every bit of force he could muster, and the man finally slumped forward, his turban falling off to reveal stringy hair, spider-webbed over a mostly bald head.

Scrambling from behind with his feet, Martín wriggled snakelike over the driver and got his head out of the car's open window. Feet churning on the body of the Sikh, he shoved himself far enough out so that gravity took over, and he splashed into the frothy water.

Down he plunged until his shoulder met the rocky bottom. Martín was an excellent swimmer and drove himself to the surface with a dolphin kick. Breaking the surface, he coughed and choked, desperately trying to keep his head above the icy water. With both hands and feet bound, he could only do so on his back. Even then it required incredible effort, and he was only partially successful. He was able to rest a second with his head upstream, but the powerful current flipped him over and he ended up face down with his head pointing downstream.

With the strength born of panic, he again turned onto his back and found that he could keep his head mostly above water by rocking along with the current, using his body in a sort of upside-down butterfly kick. Even then he constantly swallowed water and rapidly tired. The other problem was that his head pointed downstream and would bear the full impact if he hit a rock. If that wasn't enough, he knew the cold water would soon bring death from hypothermia.

As he tried to turn, Martín was again thrown to the bottom and again resurfaced, sputtering and choking in the darkness. Although in the water probably less than a minute, the extreme cold, lack of oxygen, and breath-stealing panic had taken a serious toll. He knew that the next time he went down could be the end. Just as he was on the verge of giving up, the surface of the water became smooth, almost glassy. He had left the rapids and found he could now keep his head above water most of the time and was gradually able to maneuver toward the shore.

A minute later he reached the riverbank and snagged his shoulder on a protruding rock. Pain knifed through him, but the maneuver allowed him to remain still long enough to get his feet on the bottom and to push his upper body onto dry land. With the last of his strength, he rolled his legs onto the bank.

For several minutes, Martín lay still, retching and gasping for breath as his body shook from the cold. As his breathing returned to normal, he estimated that in the short time he had been in the water the current had carried him less than a quarter mile downstream, not far enough to be safe from whomever had been following the Land Rover. He had no idea what had happened to his brother's car and the man in it.

Staggering to his feet, he saw headlights whisk by on the highway, about fifty yards away. Just in front of him sat a rocky outcropping. Hopping to it, he quickly found a sharp edge and sawed vigorously on the thin rope that held his wrists. The frantic up and down motion of his body created some warmth, and shortly he freed his arms and untied his feet.

After massaging his wrists and ankles, he rose and saw a vehicle stop on the highway shoulder. Shivering, he dropped behind the outcropping and peered over the rocks. The dome light of the vehicle glowed as one of the doors opened, but he could see nothing from this angle.

Without warning, a dazzling light blazed through the darkness and began to traverse along the river's edge and the rough terrain between it and the highway. Chancing another glance over the outcropping, he saw two people behind the light, both dressed entirely in white. Did that mean the man driving Abel's car had escaped? Had they seen him, or was it a coincidence they had stopped at this place to check the river?

He peeked again and saw they had scrambled down

the steep
roadbed and were walking toward his hiding place.
Realizing he had no choice, Martín hunched down,
snatched up the rope that had bound him, trotted to
the edge of the river, and, gritting his teeth, slipped
into it. Pushing off, he took a few strokes, disappeared
below the surface, and swam to the center. He held his
breath as long as he could before surfacing for air,
then again submerged.

The cold was bitter, and Martín felt groggy as he
came around a bend in the river. He was no longer
afraid of being seen but knew he needed to get out of
the icy water. He reached the bank, climbed out, and
began to jog downstream. After ten minutes, he felt
the chills abate and slowed to a fast walk. After
another ten minutes, the highway was a good quarter
mile from the river. He made out a dim light in the
distance. As he drew near, he realized it was a security
light beside an adobe farmhouse.

Martín staggered toward it and, despite the clear
night, blundered straight into a barbed-wire fence. He
managed to climb over it, adding to the cuts and
bruises on his body, but the cold numbed his pain. He
knew that most rural people kept a shotgun or rifle
handy, but was so tired he plunged heedlessly ahead. A
dog began to bark, then another. Approaching the
house, Martín stopped to yell his name and that he
needed help.

Five minutes later, a tall Hispanic man with a full
head of wavy hair leaned his shotgun in a corner by
the front door and led Martín, teeth still clicking
uncontrollably, to a bathroom and switched on the hot
water. Martín had gasped out a summary of what had
happened. In return he'd learned that the man's name

was Stevie Perez, coincidentally a distant cousin of Johnny Carillo. Martín told him he believed that his attackers had killed Johnny. Perez nodded thoughtfully.

Warming up under the stream of hot water, Martín hoped the steam would continue to fog the mirror. Before he had gotten into the shower it revealed considerable damage to his body and face.

Martín was too tired to cope and didn't even know which of the two sheriffs he should call first. He would have to call Herb and regretted not telling him about the theft of his property from the bank. He guessed it was around 9:00 p.m.

Although Stevie Perez was about Martín's height, he outweighed him by at least twenty pounds. The jeans he lent Martín required a large tuck, secured by a huge safety pin. Although slender, Martín had broad shoulders. "Like a cowboy," Laura had always said, and the red flannel shirt fit okay.

Martín reached Herb and explained what had happened and where he was. Herb said, "We'll talk about what you did later. Stay where you are and let me handle things."

An hour later, in the midst of his fourth cup of steaming coffee, a procession of headlights down the long driveway signaled the arrival of both sheriffs and Herb.

Forty minutes later, Martín finished his story. "I fully realize I set out to do something wrong, but the assault and kidnapping stopped me before I had a chance to do anything illegal."

The sheriffs immediately relayed instructions to their offices. Within minutes, a squad was headed upstream to where the Land Rover had gone into the water. The description of the truck that rammed Martín and the people dressed like Sikhs went to law enforcement throughout the region.

Before the law officers left, Eddie Jaramillo placed his huge hand
on Martín's shoulder, causing him to wince from his injuries. Then the hawk-faced Bernie Mendoza said, "I was afraid you'd do something like this, but maybe in a way you got lucky. Sure can't blame you for what those guys did. No law against following someone under the circumstances you described. But no more!"

Martín nodded wearily.

After profuse thanks to Stevie and a promise to return the borrowed clothes, Martín walked stiffly to Herb's car.

"I'm takin' you to the hospital and then to my house. No tellin' what might be waitin' at yours," the lawyer said.

On the way to the hospital, Martín explained why he had not told Herb about the theft of his property.

"I confess," said Herb, "I'm a little out of my depth. I never heard of a bank stealin' from a safe deposit box. I don't know what's involved, but I'm sure as hell gonna find out tomorrow. Now we better start thinkin' about what you're gonna do. What kinda money you got left?"

Through the wave of fatigue, Martín struggled to think. "I've got about $2,500 in my checking account...if they didn't figure out how to steal that too. The gallery in Durango owes me another $2,500, and there was one bond in my name that they left with a face value of $10,000; what it's worth now I'm not sure, probably somewhere around $7,500. Most of my parents' stock went to pay funeral and other expenses, so that and the furniture in the house are everything. Not enough to pay you in full, I'm sorry to say."

"Don't worry about that. If you knew how much money I've been paid by your family over the years and how much I made because of your father's help, you'd be pissed I haven't already written the damn thing off. Anyway, you've got enough to live on for a few months. That's what counts."

SANTA FE

The next morning Martín could barely crawl out of the Herb's guest room bed. Nevertheless, he smiled through the bruises, cuts, and scrapes, thankful that the hospital examination showed no concussion or broken bones. At breakfast, he caught Margo averting her eyes from the bandages on his face as she poured coffee.

Herb said, "I heard from Bernie, and they found the Land Rover washed up on the bank—a total loss. No sign of the guy in the car with you, so he managed to get out. I guess that brings you down to your parents' Buick. There's no word on your attackers or their truck. I also called a friend who specializes in bank law. He'd never heard of a situation like yours. No one expects a bank to steal from a customer." With a chuckle, he added, "at least not from their safe deposit box. And since I seem to be bearing bad news, don't forget that you need to turn over the keys to the house next week."

Two hours later, Martín and Herb stopped at the hacienda to pick up the Buick, Martín's papers, and his remaining bond. After retrieving the documents, they discovered that the Buick's battery was dead and went to Martín's adobe to pick up jumper cables. As he eased himself carefully out of Herb's car, Martín froze for a moment and then said, "What's that?"

Herb got out of the car as quietly as he could and stood still, ears straining. They both heard it, a pitiful whimper coming from the right side of the house.

Following Martín as he limped around the corner, Herb saw his friend fall to the ground beside the back door, screaming obscenities. He found him cradling Pancho's bloody head in his arms. Only the weak moans indicated life.

"Help me get him into the car! We've got to get him to Dr. Benchley. We can call ahead."

When they got to the veterinary hospital, Dr. Benchley, a short, slender man with a well-trimmed gray beard, and his assistant, a young Navajo woman, waited outside with a gurney. After a quick examination, they loaded Pancho onto the contraption and wheeled him inside.

"Obviously a severe blow to the head," the doctor said to Martín. "I'm not joking when I say that the fact that he's still alive is a good sign, but it'll be touch and go. I'll do everything I can and call as soon as I know something."

Back in the car, Herb said, "I called Bernie, and he's gonna meet us at your house. Shit, Martín, it's gettin' so damn near every day we have to decide which sheriff to call."

Martín shook his head like a punch-drunk fighter. "What the hell do they want? They've got the bank, the house, and almost everything else, including the codex drawings."

"I think," said Herb, stroking his mustache with his right hand as he steered the car up the hill toward the mountains with his left, "they want to get rid of a pain in the ass. With you out of the way they got no problems."

A minute later they turned right, heading parallel to the distant mountains. As they neared the turnoff to Martín's house, they spotted a police car pulling up the hill toward the house.

"That's Bernie," said Herb. "I recognize the car."

As he finished the sentence, an explosion thundered, shaking the ground under the vehicle. The police car ahead fishtailed as it accelerated up and over the hill and disappeared from sight in a cloud of dust and black smoke that dimmed the sunlight, like an eclipse.

Herb sped up but kept his car under control. As they topped the hill, Martín uttered a cry, like an animal caught in a trap. Before them two police cars stood at odd angles. Bernie Mendoza sprinted toward where Martín's house had once stood. Nothing remained of the adobe but a portion of the back wall. A few flames danced and crackled among the wreckage; the house had little wood except the doors, cabinets, furniture, and the vigas that supported the roof. Some black smoke continued to curl heavenward.

As Herb slid to a stop beside the patrol cars, Martín already had his hand on the door latch, but Herb's arm shot across his chest.

"Hold on!" he said. Best to stay back a moment till Bernie has a chance to check things out. I have a feelin' he's gonna be pretty upset."

They watched as the sheriff squatted near what used to be the adobe's doorway and then rose, swiveling his gaze over the wreckage. Finally, he turned and walked slowly back to his car, shaking his head. He got in and began to use the radio.

Martín and Herb stood by the car until Bernie walked over to them, his eyes and face red and swollen. "I told Beto not to go in until I got here," he said, his voice raw with anger. He clenched his fists. "He ignored procedures when he thought he was wasting time. Shit!"

Walking up to Martín, the sheriff looked him in the eye. "Martín, I only half believed you before yesterday.

92

After you went into the river, your credibility reached three-quarters. Today when your bank told me the security cameras malfunctioned earlier in the week, I got near a hundred percent. That's why I told Beto not to go into the house until I checked it. Damn it to hell!"

He pounded his right fist into his left hand, tears filling his eyes. "I should have told him the place might be booby-trapped to make him pay attention." He shook his head in frustration. "Anyway, everyone from the medical examiner and fire department to the FBI are on the way. Undoubtedly to be followed by every reporter within a hundred miles. Get ready for a long day."

The dying sun slanted across the distant mountains as the last policeman and journalist left. Crime scene tape ringed the site. The smell of wet smoke seemed to get worse no matter what the fire department dumped on it. An investigator from the Bureau of Alcohol, Tobacco, Firearms and Explosives was the last to leave, proclaiming that he had never seen so much explosive used for such a small job. A deputy sheriff stood at the end of the drive to keep curiosity seekers and looters away. Martín told his story countless times.

Two FBI agents, a clean-cut young Anglo man and an intense Hispanic woman, had listened attentively, especially to the accusations of theft by the bank. Martín had sarcastically suggested that since the blond man who had first claimed to be working for the people launching legal action against his family bank—SpanGlobe—later turned up working for the bank where his property disappeared, that there might just be a connection between the two. Sheriff Mendoza interjected that he had recently discovered that the Española bank group's home base in Denver was in the same building as SpanGlobe's offices.

At an informal press conference, Martín calmly explained to the reporters that he believed the same individuals who had killed Johnny Carillo and faked his brother's suicide had destroyed his house. "I had no involvement with the bank until after the death of my family, and this was nothing less than an attempt by the real perpetrators to cover up their crimes by removing someone with the motivation to bring them to justice. Make no mistake, that blast was meant to kill me, not the brave young deputy who lost his life!" He then told them that both the local authorities and FBI had active investigations underway and asked the media to keep up the pressure.

"Yes," he confirmed to one enterprising young woman who had associated the registration of the Land Rover hauled out of the Rio Grande this morning with himself. "That was the second attempt on my life. The first took place nearly two months ago when my Tahoe was run off the road, and this was the third."

He refused to provide further details, including naming whom he suspected. The sheriff also remained tight-lipped. The reporters treated him well. The obvious damage to his face and arms, as well as the wreckage of his home, convinced even the most cynical among them not to harass someone so obviously abused.

In spite of everything, Martín remembered to call Dr. Benchley to check on Pancho, and he smiled for the second time that day. His furry companion had the canine version of a serious concussion, but would recover. "Thanks, my friend," he told the vet, "for the only good news I've gotten lately, as you will see in the media."

As the sun sank lower in the sky, Herb patted Martín on the shoulder. "I don't know what to say. You're welcome to stay with us until you work out something with your insurance company; they'll probably provide rent money until you rebuild. You do have insurance, don't you?"

"Of course! At least I did. The policy was in the safe deposit box I left on the floor of the bank."

"Don't worry about that. They'll have records." Herb paused and shook his head. "Hell, Martín, the way things have been goin', for a moment I wondered if maybe SpanGlobe has bought the damn insurance company. Talk about paranoid! Anyway, you about ready?"

"Yeah. If you don't mind, I'd like to get the Buick started and say goodbye to the hacienda. The auction company's coming tomorrow for the furniture, and this will be the last..." Tears streamed down his cheeks, soaking into the bandages, as his body heaved in silent sobs.

After they started the Buick and left the engine on to continue charging the battery, Martín said, "Once again I can't thank you enough for what you've done, but please go home. I want to be alone."

"I understand," said Herb, "but after what's just happened, are you out of your fucking mind?"

"I doubt they'll try anything else. Too much heat."

"Shit," said Herb, "and you ain't got no more guns."

"Actually, I do. *Papi's* shotgun's still there. I'll come to your place tomorrow."

SANTA FE

Entering his father's study, Martín first saw the half-empty glass he'd had when the blond man—soon to become the bank manager—surprised him. He took it to the kitchen, dashed the contents into the sink, and gave it a quick rinse. Back in the study, he filled it to the top with scotch, took a long pull, and lowered himself gingerly into his father's chair. So much had happened so quickly that he had no idea what to do. His situation reminded him of a monkey he'd once seen at a rodeo tied onto a sheepdog. On command, the dog began to herd calves with violent, unpredictable movements. Like the monkey, Martín had had no idea where he was going and no choice but to go there.

Money was now his biggest problem. His net worth consisted of a few thousand dollars, the proceeds of the coming estate sale, the land in Española, and whatever the insurance paid for his destroyed house. That meant he needed a job. But what could an art major do? Teach? In Santa Fe where artists were thicker than flies at a picnic, people stood in line for the few available jobs. It seemed hopeless. Maybe, as Herb had suggested, he needed to get away and let the scattered debris of his life sort itself into some sort of order. But where, he wondered. He took another long drink, relishing the smoky flavor on his tongue and the way the warmth of the liquid spread through his body. Then he sat very still, wondering if one of the ghosts he felt must be nearby would communicate with him.

Twenty minutes and another glass of scotch later, his cell having been lost in the river, Martín reached for the landline, afraid it might have been cut off for lack of payment. Relieved to find a dial tone, he called Herb.

When the lawyer answered, Martín said, "I don't know what I was thinking. I suppose the hacienda was mentally gone, so I forgot that I've still got it for a few more days, and I need all the time I can get to recover. I think there's some clothes in my old room that'll fit, so I'll just stay here."

After a long pause Herb said, "Don't forget to turn off the Buick."

Three nights later, Martín awoke in his second-story bedroom. For hours he had tossed and turned in a world of nightmares, and then in one moment he jolted fully awake. Familiar shadows on the wall told him it was around 2:30 a.m. He strained his ears for some hint of what had awakened him, but for several moments he heard nothing. Then he thought he detected a creak on the stairway from the living room. Retrieving the shotgun from the floor by the bed, he listened more intently, but he didn't hear it again. After what seemed a long time, he finally heard something palpable. It began as a soothing whisper, like a breeze on a lazy afternoon playing in the trees. Over a long minute, it gradually rose in pitch and intensity until it resembled the freight train blast of a tornado shaking the house to its core. Martín could hear the rattle of the windows and things falling throughout the building. Slowly, the commotion morphed into a melodious wail that rose once to the top of the scale and then gradually diminished into a repeat of the comforting sigh he had first heard.

What had happened? As far as he knew, Santa Fe had never had an earthquake. Maybe he should turn on the news? Instead, he lay down and went back to sleep, this time peacefully and without dreams.

SANTA FE

Martín awoke next at seven-thirty. A glance out the window revealed another brilliant day, with no evidence of any weather-related event. A quick check of both radio and television uncovered nothing to explain what he remembered. And what fallen books and other objects proved actually happened. What about the supernatural? He'd always treated the subject with ambivalence. If what happened came from that realm, what did it mean? Perhaps something to do with the fact that he unexpectedly felt in control of his life.

Why am I not depressed? The auction house and movers would soon be there to catalog and strip the family possessions. They would be sold to newcomers, many of whom would have more money than sense, certainly no appreciation for what those things meant. *Mean only to me.*

Consideration of the imminent dissolution of household belongings and the turnover of the hacienda, combined with what had happened during the last week or so, led him to the phone.

"No," said the operator at the Santa Fe Hilton, "Mr. Glendaring has not checked in; we don't expect him until later this afternoon. May I leave him a message?"

"No thank you, I'll try later," replied Martín.

As he replaced the receiver, a grim smile traced his lips. A half hour later he had showered and dressed. As he buttoned his shirt, he realized that the aches and pains had receded to the point that his body was once again approaching decent working order. Almost eagerly, he awaited the movers and the remaining events of the day—whatever they might be.

99

Before anyone arrived, he walked the property, revisiting the hiding places of his childhood. Often, he turned to look at the hacienda, studying it from every possible angle, imprinting it on his memory. The smile never left his face. Incredibly, he could not detect even a hint of nostalgia, nothing but detached curiosity.

By early afternoon, all the family possessions were gone. In spite of some lingering soreness, his step had an unmistakable spring as he walked into the post office in Española. Because of the high incidence of petty theft in the area, he kept a box there. In it, he found the gallery's check in payment of $2,500 for his sold painting and a letter with foreign stamps. Closer inspection revealed a Mexico City return address.

"What the...?" Then he remembered. About six months ago—in what seemed like a former life—he had read a magazine article that informed families with roots in Mexico how to go about tracing them. It had concluded with, "If all these methods fail, you may want to try one of the following reputable genealogy services located in Mexico." On a whim, Martín had emailed one of them, saying he wanted to know if he was really descended from the son of Hernan Cortés named Martín, as family legend and previous amateur investigations indicated. He also included all the information he had about his lineage and his credit card number to pay the $250 for a report."

Fully expecting never to hear from them, he had forgotten the whole thing. After stuffing the check into his shirt pocket, he carefully opened the letter. In precise schoolbook English, it   ,
informed him that Dr. Felipe Gallardo had the "utmost confidence" that the conqueror's son, Martín Cortés, was indeed his ancestor. But—no surprise—

Dr. Gallardo ended with, "Remarkably little has been written on the subject of the children of Hernan Cortés, making more research advisable."

Martín considered what he had just learned, and then made what would be the most important decision of his life.

Half an hour later at the veterinary hospital, he found Pancho much improved, and Dr. Benchley said he could take him anytime. Martín told him he didn't have a place to live. In any case, he would be leaving town for a while. The vet said that his daughter had just opened a boarding kennel and assured Martín she would give him a good rate.

Martín thanked him and said, "I'll make arrangements with my attorney to pay the bills."

Martín returned to the hacienda and called Mexico City. Through the researcher's secretary, he authorized him
to proceed at his earliest convenience and to charge the fee to the same credit card. When the secretary asked him if he wanted the results sent to the same address he didn't hesitate. "No, I'll pick them up in person, probably in a week or two."

He reached Herb at his office. "I'm going to take your advice and go away for a while. Could you prepare a power of attorney and whatever else you need to act on my behalf while I'm gone?"

"Where the hell you goin'? You ain't heard about telephones, email, and fax machines?" snapped Herb.

"If it's all right I'll be by to sign it in an hour. Oh, and since I'm out of banks, could you cash a check I just got from the gallery for $2,500?"

An hour later, Herb exchanged an envelope full of cash for the gallery check and waved Martín to a seat, thrusting his shaggy head aggressively toward his young client. "Martín we've been friends a long time and particularly close during these last months. I know somethin's up with you. What is it?"

Martín smiled innocently, as if he had not a concern in the world. "Old friend, reality is what's up. Like the estate tax stuff, it's best you don't know any more than you do." Then relenting, he added, "Don't worry, I may seem a little crazy, but I'm not suicidal."

Martín continued. "As I said, I'll be gone for a while, exactly where and for how long I'm not sure. Now here's what I'd like you to do: except for a couple minor items it can be summed up as use your own judgment. The exceptions are the property in Española, this bond that I've endorsed, a few things left in the house, and Pancho."

He handed over the bond and continued. "I want you to cash it in, collect as much money as you can from the insurance company, and then sell the land. I hope we can settle the claim without actually rebuilding the house. Then I want you to take your fees out and put the rest away for me, except what Dr. Benchley's daughter needs to take care of Pancho. I'll probably need some cash within a month or so. And could you also have the few personal items left in the house stored? That's all I'm going to say, except that I'll never be able to put into words how I feel about what you've done for me."

Apparently sensing that nothing would be served by further questioning, Herb handed Martín the power of attorney. Martín signed it, gave his friend an *abrazo*, and walked out the door.

SANTA FE

That afternoon Martín called the Hilton again.
"Yes, replied the receptionist, "Mr. Glendaring just checked in. I'll ring his room." Martín hung up.

A few minutes later, propelled by an impulse he feared could lead to serious problems but one he could not resist, Martín pulled the Buick into a metered parking slot three blocks from the hotel. He felt the chill of air-conditioning on the unusually warm and humid day as he entered a souvenir store.

"¿*Martín, como estas*?" welcomed the proprietor, Josefina Castro, an old friend of his parents.

Quickly selecting an item from a display stand, Martín said, "Can you wrap this in a box and deliver it to a guest at the Hilton right away?"

"Of course, Martín." She turned toward the back of the store. "¡Pablo, *ven aca*!"

A boy in his late teens hurried over. The expression in his eyes and his odd gait implied a handicap, but the smile on his face warmed the room.

"I'll wait and follow Pablo over if that's okay," said Martín. "I want to surprise someone," he added.

Josefina smiled and nodded.

A few minutes later, Martín walked out the door with Pablo.

"When we get to the hotel, tell the person at the desk that you can't leave it with them," said Martin. "Say that you have to deliver it in person and get a receipt."

The boy nodded.

When they got to the hotel, Martín trailed behind Pablo. Feelings of apprehension banished by a mysterious infusion of self-confidence, Martín followed the boy through the elegant Southwestern-style lobby and lingered at the far side of the room. After a short conversation with the clerk, Pablo walked by Martín with the box, which measured about two feet tall and a foot wide. The boy disappeared through a doorway.

Martín followed him, and when he caught up, he asked, "What's the room number?"

"It's the second *casita*," replied Pablo.

"Just deliver the package and say you don't know who sent it. I want to surprise them."

They went down some stairs and into a patio. Martín moved back to where he could remain hidden, while Pablo made his way to the room. Two minutes later, the boy returned without the package.

"Look, Martín, they gave me a dollar!" he exclaimed, displaying the money.

Martín thanked him and put five dollars into his hand. As the boy left, Martín stepped to the door of the suite.

He knocked confidently, like a recent messenger returning after having forgotten something. The door opened, and he found himself confronted by the blond man he had shot outside his parents' house, the man who later posed as the manager of his bank.

Before the man could react, Martín placed the flat of his hand on his chest and shoved. Attempting to keep his balance, the blond stepped back two paces, giving Martín just enough space to slide into the room and kick the door closed behind him. As he did so he

caught sight of a figure sitting behind a leather-covered antique desk at the far end of the living area of the suite.

By this time, the blond man had recovered and was reaching inside his jacket. Martín held his hands up, showing he had no weapons, and spoke to the man behind the desk.

"Mr. Glendaring, I presume. In case you're wondering, I'm Martín Cortés, and I'm sure you'll be pleased to learn I've just come to say goodbye. However, if your boy-toy pulls a gun on me I assure you it will become a matter for the courts, something you seem to have avoided with great skill."

"Gabel!" snapped Glendaring, turning to the man. "Although Mr. Cortés misunderstands our relationship, let's see if he is as good as his word. There will always be time for sterner measures."

As Gabel eased his hand slowly out from under his jacket, Martín examined Glendaring. He was tall and wide, but seemed to be constituted mostly of skin and bones, like an oversized coat hanger with a huge, frilled buckskin jacket draped around it. His shoulder-length salt and pepper hair hung in obviously styled waves. Around his neck he wore a silver and turquoise bolo tie. At first, Martín could not decide whom he most reminded him of: Buffalo Bill Cody, or the famous criminal lawyer who affected the same look. Then he had it! The man was a ringer for radio personality Don Imus.

"Well, Mr. Cortés, in deference to your recent, tragic losses, Gabel and I are being quite tolerant. I would, however, appreciate it if you would say your piece and take your leave."

Martín realized that Abel had not been exaggerating when he described Glendaring's speech as formal and old-fashioned. He said, "Thank you, you are most kind. In return I'll be short. First, you'll be happy to learn that, although I know you were directly responsible for the deaths of my brother and the Carillo family, and that you attempted to murder me on at least three occasions, I haven't been able to prove it. Nevertheless, the FBI is suspicious and has you in its sights."

Glendaring nodded several times, as if marking off a checklist.

Martín continued, "However, here is something you will not be so pleased to learn. Because, in addition to the above, I consider you responsible for the deaths of my parents, the loss of my net worth and family heritage, not to mention the injuries to my dog, I intend to keep on looking until I either find what I need to put you on death row or come to the conclusion that I'll be unable to do so."

"In which case...?" interrupted Glendaring, placing his elbows on the desk and resting his chin in his hands.

"In which case, the last time you see me will be just before you cease to exist," replied Martín.

Glendaring chuckled and looked at the blond man. "Well, Gabel, I hope you are appropriately apprehensive—and prepared to provide testimony to the authorities."

Martín shot a glance at Glendaring's blond employee. "If you think the likes of that will protect you, you're sadly mistaken. Did he present himself as some sort of special-forces commando? Truth is, he looks more like someone who provides special services at male bath-houses in San Francisco—at least during his younger years."

Like an out-of-control pile-driver, Gabel's fist lashed

out. Having anticipated that reaction, Martín slid back a step and moved his head to avoid the blow. Spinning a half turn, he cocked his right leg and drove the side of his foot into the man's left knee. Yelping, Galbel

bent slightly, switched his weight to his right leg, and plunged his hand under his jacket. Martín slammed another side-kick to the man's other knee, causing him to crumple to the floor. Gabel jerked his hand from his jacket to break the fall.

"See what I mean!" remarked Martín, as if soliciting agreement on some minor point. "Besides being incompetent, he can't follow orders. He'll also be disabled for the foreseeable future."

Glendaring stiffened and his skin flushed purple with anger, but he remained still and silent.

"I wasn't quite finished," said Martín, keeping an eye on the man looking up at him from the floor. "I'll be gone for a while. I'm not sure how long, certainly weeks, probably months, maybe years. But the process will continue. I'll never stop, and you'll never know when a knock on the door will be a policeman with a warrant or something more fatal."

Having noticed Gabel's hand again reaching toward his jacket, Martín cocked his leg, at which the man stopped the movement. Martín feigned a kick, causing the disabled man to cringe in fear.

Martín spun on his heel and left the room, making a point of closing the door softly.

Less than a minute later, he exited the hotel and trotted to his parents' Buick. Ten minutes after that he pulled onto IH 25 with the radio tuned to a country western station, heading toward El Paso and the border with Mexico at Ciudad Juárez.

As he drove, he tried to fathom why he had done what he did. Totally unplanned, it was as if his body had been shanghaied by aliens. He had played his part and spoken his lines as if he had rehearsed them. Maybe a defense mechanism: blow off steam or go crazy? He had no clue.

He doubted Glendaring would call the police. After all, no report had been made when he had winged Gabel's arm. But he was not certain. He kept to the speed limit and took the back way to Albuquerque via Madrid. At Albuquerque he rejoined IH 25, aimed the Buick south, and set the cruise control at just under seventy.

As he left Albuquerque, he wondered what Mexico would hold for him. Was it simply a question of the grass being greener? He shook his head, realizing it was another puzzle for which he lacked an answer. All he knew was that Santa Fe had nothing left to offer him.

Colin Glendaring glared at his employee, still in agony on the floor, his mouth forming the same expression of distaste he would have used if served bad wine.

"Gabel," he said, "I have never seen you up against any sort of capable opponent. I was not impressed."

Consumed by the pain in both knees, the man said nothing.

"Might as well see what he sent us." Moments later he opened a box to reveal a large clay statue of a howling coyote.

Glendaring pursed his lips in reflection and again looked down at Gabel, who continued to focus on his pain.

"Are you aware," he said, "that the Navajos both

fear and hate the coyote because of his uncanny ability to fool them? They refer to him as 'The Trickster.'" After musing for a moment, he muttered, "We shall just have to see." Taking a step toward the ornate desk, he extracted a cellphone from his pocket.

TEHRAN, IRAN

On Esfand, 11 1396, according to Iran's Persian calendar, the same day that Martín began his southward journey, two Iranian brothers sat close together in one of Tehran's traditional bathhouses. Alone in a secluded pool, only Reza and Parwis Tonhamani's heads broke the water. Above them, stone arches rose to a dimly lit ceiling above walls covered with colorful tiles etched in Persian script.

The Tonhamanis were barely a year apart and could be mistaken for twins. Although their black hair was thinning, they sported bushy mustaches that rippled the water as they whispered. Their portly bodies lay beneath the surface, so only their ample jowls would have indicated to an observer that the pair had the sleek—some indelicate foreigner might have asserted oily—look of pampered bureaucrats.

"Have you considered what I said yesterday on our walk?" asked Reza.

"Yes. That our Islamic administration may soon be in serious trouble. And if the worst happens, those associated with it will undoubtedly be removed from their positions—or worse. Everyone knows that. But what can we do about it?"

"I have a solution—for both of us. It will require careful planning and execution to limit the risk. If things go badly, I doubt the rabblerousers screaming for democracy will leave either of us—the second in command of the Foreign Affairs Directorate or the third assistant director of the Central Bank—in place, or maybe even alive. Do you?"

Reza looked carefully about him, then continued without waiting for an answer. "As you know, my foreign travel is virtually unrestricted, with almost no oversight. Nearly anything I do abroad can be made to look like part of my job. You have unlimited access to the Central Bank, which houses the national treasure, most particularly some of the most valuable jewels in the world."

"Allah must have relieved you of your senses, Reza," hissed Parwis, "if you are suggesting what I think you are."

"On the contrary, Parwis, Allah esteems me. That's why he's given me this plan. No, I'm not proposing we touch any of the items on display, or even those in the vault that are nearly as well known. But you once told me there are numerous lesser pieces, some consisting of unset stones of great value, but difficult to catalog—and trace. And for many items, like rubies, sapphires, and emeralds, copies can now be made that are both inexpensive and difficult to detect. All it would take is for you to replace a few of them— perhaps one or two to begin—with reasonable copies and to do so without leaving a trace. I will then see to their disposition somewhere far away and place the proceeds in a confidential offshore account in our names."

Parwis looked carefully about him, straining his ears for any echo of human activity. His brother had finally gotten his attention. "I admit, Reza, that what you say has possibilities. But doing it 'without a trace' will be difficult. Let me think about it. I'll call you."

A week later, the Tonhamani brothers were in a far corner of a nearly deserted sidewalk café in an upscale suburban Tehran neighborhood. After their greetings and ordering—tea for Reza and Arab-style coffee for Parwis—and ensuring they could not be overheard,

111

Parwis winked at his brother. "I've found what we're looking for: two very large emeralds of ordinary cut and excellent purity."

He handed a photo envelope to Reza. "The inventory we have describes them only by their weight and cut, and could pertain to any stones of similar size and quality. Together they should provide a modest nest egg, even if we get nothing else."

Reza extracted a stack of photographs from the envelope and began to flip through them. The first few glossy prints depicted Parwis's family. In the middle he found two oval-cut emeralds, not very sharp but adequate. As the waiter approached with their orders, Reza said, "May I borrow these? My wife will kill me if I don't show them to her."

"Of course," smiled Parwis. "That's what they're for."

When the waiter had gone, Reza said, "You have done well, brother. I will send these to my contact in Thailand. The copies should be ready in two weeks, and I will personally pick them up. Will that timing work for you?"

"Perfect," replied Parwis. "Our most conscientious employee monitors the collection and hasn't taken a vacation in three years. I ordered him to take some time to recharge his batteries. He leaves in exactly two weeks, thrilled that I offered to fill in for him. That will explain the record of my entrances to the vault and access to the files. Later, if the fakes are discovered, when the theft occurred will be a mystery."

"Excellent." Reza rubbed his chubby hands together. He was not referring to his tea, which remained untouched.

Once again, the brothers Tonhamani met at the café. This time Reza and Parwis exchanged identical briefcases. Upon returning home, Parwis found copies of the emeralds in the photographs he had given to Reza, produced after-hours by an otherwise legitimate operation in Bangkok. Parwis examined them carefully, confirming they were adequate. While they would not bear professional scrutiny, no one other than a member of the bank staff had been near the collection in over fifteen years.

A week later, the two men met for dinner at Parwis's home. While their wives cooed over their children, the brothers retired to Parwis's study and poured some highly illegal brandy of questionable provenance into tiny coffee cups. "Well?" said Reza.

Parwis raised his eyebrows. "Do you think I would have invited you here if I didn't have good news?" He pulled a small leather bag from his pocket and handed it to his brother.

Tugging open the drawstring, Reza pushed two sausage-shaped fingers inside and then added his thumb. Extracting one of the stones, he raised it to the shaded bulb of the only lamp in the room. "Magnificent," he exclaimed, as rich green tones danced over his fingers. "You've done it! Allah be praised. And the copies?"

"Snug in their places. Only an expert could tell them apart, especially with the poor quality of the photographs in the files, which I managed to make even worse by rubbing them against the folder."

Standing up, Reza replaced the stone in the bag with its mate, pulled the drawstrings closed, and carefully dropped it into the inside pocket of his suit coat. "I leave day after tomorrow for Europe," he said. "By the end of the week, with any luck we'll have a small fortune linked to us only by secret numbers."

"We can only pray to Allah for luck and thank him when we receive it." Parwis smiled and rose to embrace his brother.

Two weeks later, Reza returned from Europe and the brothers met again, this time in the late afternoon at a park near the center of Tehran. Reza looked forward to announcing the success of their venture, to reporting that he had sold the emeralds for more than anticipated. But the tone in Parwis's voice warned him there was a problem.

"What's wrong, brother?" asked Reza as the two sat on a bench in the nearly empty park.

"What's wrong? I'll tell you! Yesterday I learned that a detailed inventory of state treasures will begin in six weeks. A French firm of gem experts has been retained to assign a value to every item in the collection. That's never happened before. Why now, I don't know, but those fakes won't fool them. Boucheron of Paris curated the original collection in 1960, and this firm may have access to their records, perhaps more detailed information on individual items than I thought existed. We have to return the real stones."

Reza raised his hands in frustration. "Parwis, that's impossible. They've been sold, and the money is in a numbered account in our names."

"No, no," whined Parwis. "Allah must be punishing us. We have to do something. When they discover the real emeralds are gone, there'll be an investigation that will identify anyone who had access to them, including me. Specific queries will be made to the international banking community. Even in Switzerland, account information is now divulged if deposits are thought to be the result of criminal activities. Couldn't we try to buy them back?"

"It's too late," said Reza. "Because of our, ah, special situation, the transaction didn't go through ordinary channels, and can't be reopened."

"Well, we have the money," exclaimed Parwis, as if grasping a lifeline. "We must find two real emeralds that closely resemble the photographs and replace them—the cheaper the better—and we have six weeks to do it. Perhaps your contacts in Thailand can help?"

Reza nodded. "I'll check immediately, but very carefully."

The next afternoon, Parwis again joined Reza in the park.

"Your call came sooner than I expected," began Parwis.

"I can move quickly when necessary," beamed Reza. "I called Thailand and learned that there are two emeralds possibly available in Mexico, in the state of Oaxaca, wherever that is. The description makes them sound perfect for our purposes. I was already going to schedule a trip later in the month to cement an alliance with a new revolutionary leader, also in Oaxaca. Because of the increased scrutiny by the Americans— and our personal needs—I created a new cover for the trip. You and I will travel together, two brothers taking a much-needed vacation together to view the nearby archeological ruins. Indeed, Allah is once again smiling on us."

EL PASO

Martín joined the mass of humanity walking toward the international bridge at Ciudad Juárez. For a moment he turned back toward El Paso, as if to imprint memories of the familiar before heading into the unknown. From the sea of people in the crowd behind him, a face caught his eye. Where had he seen the burly Latino with the bushy mustache and bulldog jowls before? Was it in Santa Fe after the confrontation with Glendaring that had sent him scurrying southward sooner than he'd planned, or earlier that day in El Paso? The man averted his gaze.

Martín ignored the churning in his gut, turned again toward the border, and raised his eyes to the smog-shrouded sprawl of Juárez. He took a deep breath, fished in his pocket for the bridge toll, and resumed his southbound journey.

On the other side of the Río Grande, Martín joined a short line before the Mexican immigration barrier. Each pedestrian was required to push a button attached to a pedestal that caused a light to turn either green or red. When it flashed green, the person was passed through with no inspection. When it turned red a bell clanged, like an alarm designed to wake the dead, and the unfortunate traveler was questioned and searched.

"Like the old *Gong Show*!" chuckled Martín as his light turned green. That reinforced his feeling that his luck was changing for the better. In addition to avoiding the immigration search, the used car dealer in El Paso had given him several hundred dollars more for his parents' Buick than he'd anticipated, and the bank had obligingly converted the dealer's check into travelers' checks. Had he seen the man there? He turned quickly but couldn't find him in the crowd.

Well aware that drug cartel conflicts had made the city one of the world's most dangerous, he clutched his small canvas bag with his right hand, patted his jeans with his left to confirm the presence of the genealogist's letter, and walked into downtown Juárez.

Before him stretched a boulevard flanked by brightly painted storefronts—liquor stores, bars, restaurants, and tawdry tourist shops. After the traffic with its diesel stench and blaring horns, he noticed that the temperature felt several degrees warmer on this side of the border. At the first cross street, a gaggle of touts fought for Martín's attention. "Hey, meester, you wan taxi, you wan see live show? I gotty young girls, cleen reel cheep."

The scene reminded Martín of the only time he'd come here before or anyplace else in Mexico. He and a carload of college friends drove from Santa Fe to carouse in the redlight district, which he thought was somewhere off to his right. Like so many of his Hispanic friends, that brief border town experience became his only exposure to his roots.

In the next block he fought off more touts and learned that the bus station was still some distance ahead. Because Juárez had become the murder capital of the Americas, he was anxious to reduce his exposure, so he signaled a nearby taxi. As he swung into the back seat, he glanced down the street. The large Latino he'd seen at the border gazed raptly at a life-size papier-mâché donkey in a nearby tourist shop. *Not likely.* His stomach tightened, but he needed more certainty before altering his plans.

By the time he got to the bus station and checked in

vain for his

shadow, his watch said 1:00 p.m. Chihuahua City, about 250 miles distant, seemed about as far as he could get that day, so he bought a ticket and boarded a departing bus.

He found a two-seat row to himself halfway back in the old, nearly full vehicle. He leaned back in the rickety window seat and began to relax—until he saw the last two passengers enter and sit behind the driver. One of them was the big man, now certainly following him.

As they left the suburbs and entered the vast Chihuahuan desert, Martín concluded he could do nothing until Chihuahua City and forced himself to focus on the desert landscape flashing by at what seemed a dangerous speed.

Besides trying to put the man in front of him out of his mind, he desperately sought to ignore the events of the last few months. At first, he concentrated on the parade of artistically shaped cactus plants, interspersed between stunted mesquite trees. But knowing that if he had agreed to take over the bank, the entire tragedy could have been prevented, feelings of guilt ate at him like a slow-acting poison.

He exerted every ounce of will he possessed and forced himself to open his guidebook. He had gotten through the history chapter's description of the Mexican Revolution when the bus stopped at a town of old-fashioned storefronts and dirt side streets. A few passengers got off, but more got on, and a man approached the seat next to him. In his late fifties, he was dressed in a dark plaid western shirt and jeans, thin from many washes. His naturally dark face had been burned to an even deeper bronze. He removed

118

his sweat-stained cowboy hat and smiled a greeting, revealing a full head of graying hair and two missing teeth.

Martín nodded obligingly at the seat, figuring the wiry man was a better bet than the obese woman looming impatiently behind him. Shaking hands with Martín, the man said, "*Mucho gusto, me llamo Julio Castro.*"

"*Mucho gusto,*" stammered Martín, realizing that, although his Spanish vocabulary had once been adequate, he had not spoken the language, except for everyday phrases, since high school. "*Me llamo* Martín Cortés."

Julio nodded at Martín's last name. "*El Conquistador,*" he repeated, grinning. Then seeming to conclude that, in spite of his name, Martín's Spanish was not up to serious conversation, he put his hat over his face, leaned back, and went to sleep.

Martín tried to resume the annals of Mexico, but his seat-mate's reference to his illustrious—some maintained notorious—ancestor reminded him why he'd come to Mexico. *El Conquistador*, mused Martín, *supposedly the founder of my family. I'll soon know for sure, and also if I have more family than I thought.* He knew the powerful feeling—now virtually a premonition—was illogical, but nevertheless had been driven to act on it, much the way he had behaved yesterday with Glendaring.

"*Oye,* Martín!" His seatmate patted his shoulder, jerking him from his reverie. The man had awakened and probably decided that imperfect communication beat none at all. "Where you go?" He pointed at the bus's forward progress.

"*Creo Chihuahua, este noche. Mañana a Zacatecas, y luego a*

119

México, la capital," replied Martín, pleased at the return of some semblance of fluency.

Julio bobbed his head. "*Ah, México.* "*Entonces*...please come Parral,
to my home? My daughter speak English."

Martín remembered that Hidalgo de Parral lay about 150 miles south of Chihuahua City, on the way to Mexico City. The thought of leaving the security of public transportation made him nervous, and he had no idea if he could trust Julio. In addition to the money in his wallet, he had $2,500 in traveler's checks, enough to tempt anyone in this poor country. At that moment, the seatmate of the large man behind the driver swiveled and looked directly at Martín. Dark and rawhide thin, his mustache and short beard failed to conceal a sea of pockmarks on his face. After a brief look, he turned and resumed his conversation with the man Martín was now sure was following him.

Martín made up his mind and said to Julio, "*Gracias, amigo.* How do we get to Parral?"

"I got *troca*...truck een Chihuahua. Parral three hour. You talk with my daughter. Her English good."

"*Muy bien, y gracias,*" said Martín, shaking Julio's hand.

That settled, Julio again placed his hat over his face and returned to sleep.

CHIHUAHUA

The sun descended toward twilight as the bus crawled through Chihuahua City's evening traffic. Twenty minutes later they nosed into a space behind the main bus station and rocked to a gentle stop, punctuated by a burst of deflating air pressure.

Martín followed Julio out of the station and down the street. The shabby neighborhood consisted mostly of cheap restaurants, tiny tourist shops, and uninviting bars. Martín glanced over his shoulder, but did not see the large man or his companion.

After two blocks, Martín asked, "Where's your truck?"

"*Adelante*," replied Julio, swinging his worn cloth bag forward.

Five blocks later, Julio turned into a small convenience store, whose door and windows were covered with beer and cigarette decals. Inside, Julio introduced Martín to the stooped, gray-haired proprietor whom he referred to as "*mi primo*," my cousin.

Martín accepted a frosty can of Tecate beer and soon wondered if the conversation, most of which was in rapid colloquial Spanish he could not understand, would ever end. He wandered to the shop's window and saw a late-model black Ford parked across the street. He couldn't make out the faces of the two men in the front seat, but the dim outlines resembled the large Latino and the man next to him on the bus.

The conversation between Julio and his cousin finally ended, and the cousin presented them with a six-pack of cold beer and a set of car keys held together with a piece of green yarn.

Martín pointed outside to the Ford. Not wanting to explain too
much and not knowing if he could trust his new acquaintances, he told them that he believed the occupants had followed him all the way from the bank in El Paso. He quickly assured Julio and his cousin that he actually had only enough cash for the trip to Mexico City.

The two men spoke briefly and then directed Martín to follow them through a storeroom stacked with canned goods and then out a door into a grimy courtyard that smelled of garbage. In it stood an old Ford pickup with a fresh coat of black paint and chrome exhaust pipes.

Moments later, following profuse thanks and goodbyes, the engine defied Martín's pessimistic assessment and rumbled to life. They entered an alley that delivered them to a cross street, where a block of two-story buildings screened them from the parked Ford. Nevertheless, Martín kept his gaze to the rear until he concluded they were not followed.

They turned onto the four-lane highway to Parral as the last vestiges of day lit the arid mountains in the electric pastels of a perfect desert sunset. The landscape reminded Martín of an unfinished version of New Mexico, as if God had not yet gotten to the final touches. Or maybe, he thought, He made this after New Mexico, wanting something even wilder and more powerful.

Entering the highway seemed to signify Julio's version of *the sun-over-the-yardarm*, and he wrenched a still cold Tecate from the six-pack. He opened it, spilled foam over the cracked, red upholstery, handed it to Martín, and then got one for himself. As Martín glanced nervously behind them, the man said, "No worry. Nobody there."

Martín nodded, beginning to discount his earlier alarm.

Only minutes had passed when Julio helped himself to another beer. That made four, including the ones he'd had in the store. Martín offered to drive.

"*No, gracias*," said Julio, taking a long pull at his beer and saluting his passenger with the now half-empty can.

Realizing only three beers remained, Martín quickly helped himself to another to keep it out of Julio's hands. Over the next half hour and the remaining two beers, Julio's driving became ever more erratic. After catching the shoulder and fishtailing wildly, he abruptly pulled to the verge and wiped his forehead. "You drive, okay?" he said.

Thanking God for the man's unexpected common sense, Martín took the wheel. Julio curled up by the passenger door and went into a deep sleep punctuated with barking snorts.

At the outskirts of Parral, Martín shook Julio's shoulder. The man awakened, yawned, and rattled off directions that took them to a rural road through rolling sandy hills covered with sagebrush. After another turn, they passed a lopsided, barbed-wire gate onto a rough dirt track. After two hundred yards, they pulled up in front of a large, two-story block home. Moonlight glanced off its metal roof into the sand and sagebrush, but the place was otherwise dark.

After being greeted by a pack of gleeful dogs that reminded Martín how much he already missed Pancho, Julio opened the door, switched on a light, and stooped to pick up something from the floor. As Martín reached him, he turned and held up a piece of lined notepaper. "My daughter go Juárez," he said, obviously disappointed.

ZACATECAS

The next morning, on the way to the bus station, Martín thanked Julio for his hospitality. As Martín got out, Julio produced a scrap of paper and handed it to him. "My phone number. Please come back when my daughter here." Martín was surprised to see that the number was virtually the same as his parents' in Santa Fe, except for the area code and the number two, his lucky number.

Inside the station, Martín checked carefully for anyone taking an interest in him. Nothing registered on his finely tuned senses, and he boarded a first-class coach. Nearly new, with airplane-style leather seats and small television screens showing a Steve Martin movie, it was a significant upgrade from the previous day.

As they wound through arid mountains, Martín wondered if the men had really followed him. The arguments against it said that Glendaring knew Martín was leaving town and presented no immediate threat, and the timing necessary to make the arrangements from Santa Fe seemed too precise to be likely. But not impossible. And how could he dismiss the coincidences? He had to also consider that if the men had really followed him it might be for the money he'd gotten at the bank and unrelated to Santa Fe. He concluded it didn't really matter; he was certain he'd lost whatever pursuit existed.

Then again, the previous day had taught him that he was now in a place where instincts honed in the United States could easily mislead him. He smiled. At least here people pronounced his name properly, including the accent: "MartEEN" rather than "Martin."

As late afternoon approached, the bus passed farms planted with alfalfa, grapes, and other crops and finally pulled around a corner to enter the outskirts of Zacatecas. At the station, Martín exited the bus and checked carefully, but again found no hint of pursuit. For a moment he thought about heading straight to Mexico City, but decided he needed to rest and stepped into a taxi.

The old city sat on the side of a steep mountain at an altitude of about 8,500 feet, and his artistic sensibilities marveled at the sights. Built with distinctive rose-colored *cantera* stone, the churrigueresque cathedral and surrounding buildings complemented the vivid sunset. After walking several blocks on winding, cobbled streets, he checked into a small hotel and fell onto the bed. He tried to nap but could not. For some reason he couldn't fathom, the closer he got to Mexico City the more nervous he became.

He ate dinner at a small bar and café near the cathedral. As he finished, a *mariachi* band began to play for a party of about twenty, crowded around several nearby tables that had been pushed together. Noticing his interest, the attendees of what turned out to be a birthday party urged him to join them.

He had never known such hospitality. At one point the band elicited cheers when they sang a distinctive ballad about a man called El Vengador. In response to his question, Martín was informed that El Vengador, which meant "The Avenger," was the charismatic leader of a new guerrilla movement fighting for peasant rights in the state of Oaxaca. During the next two hours, Martín drank a great deal more tequila.

Awaking with a brutal hangover, Martín showered, checked out, and took a taxi to the bus station. After

determining that no one except a group of giggling
teenage girls showed any interest in him,
he bought another first-class ticket, some Tylenol, and
sweet bread, the only thing he thought might stay
down. He looked carefully around again as he climbed
into the bus. *Am I becoming paranoid?* Then he smiled,
remembering the old joke: "Even the paranoid have
enemies." *And I sure as hell have a bad one.*

Martín dozed. As the bus entered San Luís Potosí,
he awoke. After the colonial magnificence of
Zacatecas it seemed just another sun-baked city
surrounded by desert. Although still feeling ill, as they
turned south, he managed to consume half a piece of
the sugar-glazed bread and some mineral water. He
wanted more sleep, but when the bus picked up speed
so did his restlessness.

MEXICO CITY

As the bus climbed onto Mexico's central plateau, afternoon brought a dramatic change of scenery and temperature. The land grew fertile and the air cool. Instead of the vast *ranchos* of the north, this new country was dotted with small farms. Row upon row of cone-shaped bales of hay and stacked cornstalks interspersed with traditional *milpas* of corn, beans, squash, and chiles, the land's ancient staples. Martín noted that while the scenery lacked the dreamy perfection of Oriental landscape it had much the same mystical ambiance.

Late in the afternoon, the bus crested a hill. Below stretched an immense valley drenched in yellow-brown fog, like a painting of *Dante's Inferno*. Martín had heard about the pollution in Mexico City, but what he saw outdid anything he'd imagined. The departure of his hangover made him feel as if he were emerging from a long illness, and his mind raced with expectation. He stretched, downed another piece of bread, and took a swig of water.

As the bus struggled through seemingly endless traffic-snarled streets, Martín realized he had no idea where he would stay. He had not made an appointment with the genealogist and only remembered his location in the Polanco district. It was too late to do anything today, and he decided to ask a taxi driver to take him to an affordable hotel in that part of town.

Although convinced he'd lost any pursuit mounted by Glendaring, Martín decided to make one more check. He walked around the station, stopped

128

suddenly, and reversed course, but detected no scrutiny. He decided he'd overreacted and shook his head at his angst.

Outside the station, darkness approached as he stood hesitantly on the busy sidewalk. The vast city felt like an enormous, unpredictable alien being, and he remained unsettled.

A dilapidated Ford sedan with a taxi sign in the window pulled up beside him. The driver hopped out and spoke in rapid Spanish. Martín's headache worsened as he tried to understand. "Do you speak English?"

"Yes, a little."

Martín asked the driver to take him to an inexpensive hotel near the Polanco district. The thin man had greasy hair, a weak chin, and a wispy mustache. His smile revealed numerous dental problems. He said he knew just the place and would take Martín for two hundred pesos, "Less than half the normal rate."

"Okay," said Martín, climbing into the back seat while the driver loaded his bag in the car's trunk. Five minutes later the cab suddenly pulled onto a side street and then lurched right into a narrow garbage-strewn alley. Looking back, the driver said, "Just one minute, I pick up something. No charge."

A swift movement from a recessed doorway sounded alarm bells in Martín's still aching head. Before he could act, the rear door jerked open, and the bulldog-jowled man he thought he'd lost was pointing a semi-automatic pistol at his head. His bushy mustache barely moved as he said, "You've been difficult. Now move over or I'll kill you right here."

Appraising the man's pistol and the revolver that

129

had appeared in the driver's hand, Martín could think of nothing but to obey. As he slid behind the driver, both weapons held their aim.

Keeping his distance and his pistol steady, the man handed Martín a pair of steel handcuffs and a black cloth hood and ordered him to put them on. The cab pulled from the curb as Martín snapped the cuffs on in front of him and slipped the hood over his head.

"What do you want?" asked Martín, his voice trembling with fear. "I have very little money, but you're welcome to it."

"*Cállate*, shut up," ordered the man next to him.

Martín forced himself to think calmly. From what the man had said, it seemed reasonable to conclude that Glendaring had hired him to kill the last and most troublesome member of the Cortés family. They would take him someplace and make it look like a robbery gone bad. That would provide his only chance to save himself in a last better-to-die-trying act. In the meantime, he must appear as unthreatening as possible. He began to whimper.

Something that felt like the side of a ham hit Martín's head. "I said shut up," growled the thug. Martín slumped into the corner and remained silent.

He guessed the cab twisted and turned for forty-five minutes before the traffic sounds dissipated and the cab pulled to a stop. The doors opened and powerful hands hauled him violently from his seat, and then pushed him, tripping and sliding across pavement. Soon the footing grew soft and uneven, like walking on piles of trash. That and the smell of garbage intensified his fear as he remembered reading that the city's murder victims often ended up in landfills. He stumbled often, and twice the man beside him swore and punched him in the kidney.

Eventually they slowed and steered him with more care. Then the same strong hands pushed him down as if to enter a low structure, and hurled him to the ground, knocking the breath out of him. "Take off the blindfold," commanded his captor.

Martín removed it slowly with his cuffed hands. He saw a tiny room built from scrap wood, chicken wire, and cardboard, lit by a battery-operated lamp. Beside him, the driver opened Martín's suitcase. The large thug loomed over him, looking bigger than ever. He bent quickly and flipped Martín onto his stomach as if he were made of papier-mâché and then snatched the wallet from his back pocket. Martín gagged from the stench.

After searching him quickly and efficiently, the big man kicked him in the side until he turned onto his back.

Through the pain he heard his captor sneer, "You come to Mexico with only a passport, a thousand pesos, and no bank cards? Find some more for us or you'll die screaming." For emphasis he cocked his pistol and aimed it at Martín's knee.

Realizing that his die-trying moment approached, Martín stammered, "Th-there's a wallet on my left leg."

The driver jerked up Martín's pants leg to reveal a bandage-like container secured with Velcro straps. Ripping off the fasteners, the man opened it and counted out $2,000 in American dollars and $2,500 in traveler's checks.

"That's better," sniggered the driver. "Maybe you got more?"

"No, that's all the money I have," stammered Martín.

"We will see." The smaller man unfastened Martín's belt, ripped his pants open, and then jerked them from his legs, pulling off his shoes and socks in the process. Next, he ripped off Martín's shirt, sending the buttons clattering across a piece of cardboard.

After a careful search the men conferred briefly, after which the big thug said, "Is that all?"

Scared but also becoming angry, Martín replied with frustration, "I told you, that's all the money I have. I don't even have a bank account."

The man spat and then grinned. "Now you have no family *and* no money. It's time to put you out of your misery."

The statement about his family—there was only one way the man could have known he had none—confirmed Martín's assumption. He was about to be killed by the same people who had murdered his brother and indirectly his mother and father. He tried desperately to conceal his panic and to find a way out. "Killing an American will be trouble you don't need," he said.

The driver shook his head and aimed a burst of Spanish at his companion. Looking disgusted, the big man nodded, never taking his eyes from Martín.

The driver quickly rolled Martín's clothing and other belongings into a ball and, clutching them, scurried out of the hutch.

Martín cringed, trying to appear on the verge of hysteria. Under the circumstances, it required very little acting. "It can't matter now," he said, stammering weakly. "Did Colin Glendaring pay you?"

"It makes no difference," said the big man, as he

slipped the pistol under his jacket and pulled out a long hunting knife. He caressed the blade lovingly and took a step nearer Martín.

"Then could you at least tell me how you found me?" begged Martín.

The man replied tersely, "Let's just say I asked the right people."

The man's face was now well lit, and Martín could see it was badly
pockmarked and wore a lustful expression, as if he were about to stroke a long-forbidden lover. Then he made his first mistake. He pulled his right leg back slowly enough to telegraph his kick.

Martín had practiced the defensive move hundreds of times in the *dojo*. He flipped his head to the side to avoid the deadly blow. At the same time, he raised his cuffed hands and deftly caught the man's foot. Instead of stopping the momentum, he allowed it to continue, raising his arms to full extension. Maintaining his hold, he sprang onto his knees and pushed the man's foot higher until he lost his balance and thudded onto his back.

Martín released the man's foot, but rather than following his instinct—trying to beat his adversary's head into the ground with his fists and the links between the handcuffs—Martín went for the knife. It was a risk. The man was strong but the knife posed the real danger.

Before the momentarily stunned man could recover, Martín's adrenalin-infused strength wrestled away the knife. He grasped the hilt with both hands and plunged it into his tormentor's exposed chest. He hit bone and the man screamed. Martín withdrew the blade and once more drove it downward, this time into the heart.

MEXICO CITY

Other than his single scream, the man died quietly. Even so, Martín thought the driver must have heard it. Although obviously too squeamish to remain for the killing, would he return with his revolver if he believed his payday was in jeopardy?

Martín's bloody hands fumbled through the dead man's clothing, searching for the handcuff key, but couldn't find it. Realizing he'd already taken too much time, he grabbed the pistol from the man's belt, checked it, and discovered it was cocked with the safety on. In an effort to remove evidence against him, he extracted the knife and wiped it on the man's bloody shirt and held onto it. He moved to the hutch's entry, and listened carefully. Hearing nothing, he lowered his head and stepped outside.

A few lights shone from where he imagined they'd left the car. Farther away, the night sky glowed with the reflection of city lights. Otherwise, he saw nothing but an expanse of shadowy filth. Gripping the pistol and knife, he moved away from where he believed the driver had gone. He went as quickly as he could, but broken glass and bits of sheet metal slashed his bare feet.

Soon, feeling like a contestant in some diabolical obstacle course, he crouched behind a mound of garbage. He desperately wanted to seek help but caution took precedence. The night was dark, and other than his boxer shorts and handcuffs he was naked. Not a good situation in this obviously dangerous place—except for those who might want to harm him. Too, the driver might have called for

additional muscle. He decided to move farther away and seek shelter
until first light.

A short time later, he heard voices and flattened himself in a depression of rotten fruit peelings and cooking grease. The moon was rising, and as the voices drew nearer, he craned his neck and made out two figures about twenty feet away. The voices seemed low but excited. They came yet nearer and suddenly stopped. He heard a hissing sound, then high-pitched laughter, and clearly saw two teenagers sniffing paint.

The boys passed within ten feet of him. One of them carried a hefty piece of pipe, which confirmed his decision to stay hidden in this dangerous place. Martín scrambled into another depression, both deeper and cleaner, and lay down to wait for dawn.

MEXICO CITY

Well before sunrise, a sharp pain in his foot awakened Martín. Lashing out with both feet, he heard scurrying and chittering. He choked back a scream and thrashed his entire body as he realized the source: rats. Forcing himself to be calm, he kicked again and grabbed the knife. The rats scampered off, and he lay shivering in the cold.

During the next hour, the rats returned several times, but he fended them off by hissing and lunging with the knife. Only the knowledge that morning approached allowed him to maintain some semblance of control.

At daylight he heard voices. He raised his head and saw two ragged little boys about ten or eleven coming toward him. Their hair was long and matted and their clothes so torn as to be barely intact. As he came shakily to his feet, they stopped and stared at him. "*Por favor ayúdame*," he said, remembering the words for "Please help me."

The boys came closer. The pain in his head and dizziness were so intense that he sat down. With gestures and broken Spanish, he explained that he had been robbed and ended with, "Need *ropa*, clothes."

The boys said something he did not understand and trotted away. When they returned, Martín had buried the knife and gun deep in the trash and again risen shakily to his feet. One of the boys carried a torn piece of burlap and a piece of string. Martín managed to secure the burlap around his waist and found that it would just serve as a very short skirt.

¿Teléfono? he asked. He had concluded that he had no

option but to contact the American Embassy.

The boys nodded in unison, turned, and motioned for him to follow. As he did so, he saw that the landfill resembled a vast sea of trash dotted with filthy islands of garbage that extended to buildings about five hundred yards in front of them. He stumbled uncertainly and looked down to see that his feet and legs were bleeding where he had been bitten by the rats and gouged by broken glass and other debris. The need to get medical attention energized him, and he limped after the boys, trying unsuccessfully to avoid further damage.

Eventually they came to a trash-strewn street lined with dilapidated buildings. His diminutive guides led Martín to an open doorway that turned out to be a small convenience store, tended by a scowling old woman. She shuffled over to meet them, eyes fixed on Martín's blood-caked, handcuffed hands. The boys explained what had happened, and he eventually made the woman understand that he wanted to call the American Embassy, and that he would pay for the call when help arrived. Reluctantly she found the number, dialed, and handed the receiver to Martín. The first thing he heard was a recording that said: "If you wish to continue in English, please press 1." He did, and the recording continued with several choices, none of which came close to describing his predicament. Finally, the message asked him to hold for an operator. He did so and was immediately cut off.

Swearing under his breath, Martín asked the woman to dial again. She did, but with even more reluctance. This time he refused to acknowledge he had a touchtone phone and just listened. Like the power and telephone companies, he hoped the embassy system would assume he had an old rotary phone and connect him with a human being. It did, and he explained his predicament to the female operator, who immediately put him on hold. After a long minute, a man came on the line. "Citizen Services, Jeff Crandall speaking. I understand you have a problem?"

"You could say that," said Martín, trying not to sound testy. Again, he explained what had happened.

"Are you physically hurt?" asked Crandall.

"I was bitten by rats and pretty badly cut up by broken glass, but I can function."

"Good. Then I suggest you make a police report, after which you can come to the embassy so that we can discuss any further assistance you may require."

Martín gritted his teeth. "Mr. Crandall, my only clothing consists of a tiny skirt made of discarded trash. I know nobody here. The person who has this phone is unlikely to let me use it for another call when she realizes no payment will be coming from you. How the hell am I supposed to get to the embassy? Can you not find a sweatsuit or something for me and give me a ride, or at least call the police for me?"

"Mr. Cortés. Do you have a relative or friend in the United States that can wire you money?" The voice was patient but unyielding.

"Yes, my attorney, but to receive money I'll have to have some ID. My wallet and passport are gone. I'll also need some clothes before I'm allowed inside a bank. Now can't you please help me with some of that?"

"Mr. Cortés, under the proper circumstances we are authorized to provide a voucher and repatriation loan to get you to the border."

Martín was livid, but somehow kept his temper. "Mr.

Crandall, you don't seem to understand. I do not want to return home. I just want to get some clothes and do what is necessary to contact my attorney and get some money sent to me. Specifically, what I need is something to put over my nearly naked body, a ride to the embassy, some help contacting my attorney, and some sort of ID. I will also need to see a doctor to inoculate me against whatever I might get from the rat bites and general filth." Finally losing his temper, he added, "I understand your desire not to waste your time and taxpayer funds on hapless citizens. I'm sure *that* money is better spent on diplomatic cocktail parties."

Suddenly afraid the man would hang up on him, Martín quickly continued, "Please listen very carefully; this is important for both of us. You may think New Mexico is a small, not-too-important state, and that may be true. But most experts predict it will be a critical swing state in the next election. The reason I say this is that my attorney, Herb Gonzalez, served as campaign treasurer for our current governor, is the personal attorney for our senior senator, and an important fundraiser in presidential politics. He is also much less patient and polite than I am. Now, can you please do something that will actually help me?"

After a moment's silence, Crandall said, "Mr. Cortés, if you will give me your location, I will inform the police of your situation."

Curbing the impulse to throw the phone through the store's window, Martín said, "Here's the storekeeper. Please ask her for directions."

As he waited to see what would happen, Martín realized he had consumed only a little bread and water during the last twenty-four hours. Without looking at the storekeeper he grabbed a tired-looking pastry from a bowl on the counter, wolfed it down, and grabbed a warm bottle of purified water. To eat and drink, he had to remove his still-handcuffed hands from the burlap skirt that was secured with a bit of frayed string and nearly lost it.

Although still upset at his situation, Martín gave thanks for his life and that he'd not had to exaggerate Herb's political connections.

An hour later, a light brown Ford followed by a police car pulled up to the curb. A young man with a prominent chin in a coat and tie got out of the Ford. Keeping his distance—probably to avoid the stench of garbage, guessed Martín—he identified himself as Jeff Crandall. Using his own key, the policeman quickly removed the handcuffs. Still at arm's length, and with the tips of his fingers, Crandall handed Martín a voluminous overcoat.

Martín gave his statement to the policeman, who spoke passable English but seemed angry. When Martín described killing his attacker and leaving the weapons in the dump but could not pinpoint either location, except to mention that the boys should remember where they found him, the cop looked like he would explode. To avoid complications that he believed would gain him nothing, Martín treated the incident like an ordinary robbery. The obviously hostile policeman ordered Martín to stay in touch with the embassy so that he could be called to identify the body.

Afterwards, Martín joined Crandall in the Ford, and they drove to the embassy. At Martín's urging, Crandall had paid the shopkeeper and handed ten pesos to each of the little boys.

An embassy nurse cleaned and dressed his wounds. She told him that the numerous cuts and abrasions did not require stitches. She expected them to heal quickly, and gave him a tetanus shot. The next few hours passed in a blur of bureaucratic absurdity: filling out forms, signing receipts, and trying to understand his options.

Fortunately, his call found Herb in his office. The canny lawyer mustered his considerable talents to provide for Martín, including a promise to send a review—good or bad—of Crandall's and the embassy's treatment of his client to the governor and senator.

Just as Martín was about to leave, Crandall said, "Forgive me but I must give you one last bit of advice."

Martín nodded curtly.

"In Mexico, appearance is extremely important. You're over six feet—tall for this country. With your long hair you may think you look a bit exotic. The truth is you do, but perhaps not in the way you think. To many Mexicans, and especially to the police, you look like someone involved in the drug business. That perception can lead to serious problems. Remember the cop who interviewed you? If I hadn't been there, things would have gone differently, and for you much less pleasantly. When the body is found you could still have serious problems."

"Thanks," grunted Martín, remembering his earlier conclusion that his US-honed instincts might be inadequate in Mexico.

By mid-afternoon, Martín found himself in a taxi—this one vouchsafed by the embassy—with a pair of sweatpants, a T-shirt, some extra-large flip-flops that fit over his bandages, a temporary passport, $100 in pesos, and a hotel reservation guaranteed by Herb's credit card. On the way, he stopped at the bank to which Herb had wired $2,000, after speaking with the manager and providing a credit card to guarantee receipt of the wire within forty-eight hours.

MEXICO CITY

Recommended by the embassy, the Hotel Polanco was a short walk from some of the city's most glamorous stores and restaurants in the upscale district of the same name. Martín found it simple but comfortable, tucked into a quiet corner where both time and super-premium rates had passed it by.

He collapsed onto his bed in the small room. Although more tired than he could remember and feeling feverish from the combination of stress and injuries, he knew that before sleep would come he had to evaluate his situation.

How had he thought that he could come to Mexico and enjoy discovering new relatives with no consequences from the recent past? Provoking the rich and powerful Glendaring made that impossible. Although the man he'd killed in the dump had not named his employer, Martín saw no other explanation.

Then what was really bothering him—in addition to having taken a human life—smacked him in the face. The pock-faced man also refused to say how they had located Martín. He said only, "We asked the right people."

Julio!" Martín exclaimed as he painfully arose.

Julio's phone number had been lost with his other belongings but, because of its similarity to his parents' number, he remembered it except for Parral's area code. The hotel operator provided that, and Martín was relieved when Julio answered. In response to Martin's question, in a combination of Spanish and broken English, Julio said that a man claiming to be Martín's lawyer had told Julio's cousin that he had good news for Martín and asked where he had gone. The cousin gave the man Julio's name and said he lived in Parral. Then he became suspicious and clammed up when the man refused to produce identification. Julio did not know how the man had found him, but speculated that he'd called all the Julio Castros in the area. Thinking he was helping Martín, Julio told the caller that Martín had gone by bus to Zacatecas and from there on to Mexico City.

Martín assured Julio that the man had lied and landed in jail after attempting to rob him in Mexico City.

His concern for Julio now put to rest, Martín began to relax. But again, he realized the difficulty of avoiding his Santa Fe problems while locating Mexican family members.

When Martín awoke, light—although now dim—still shone through the open curtains. Except for his headache, foot injuries, and a general soreness, he felt amazingly refreshed.

Out of nowhere came the revelation that he had received a gift that many people unconsciously longed for: the ability to begin life anew with no baggage from the past—good or bad—other than, of course, the damage from psychological trauma. Nevertheless, he began to feel reborn as a fully educated adult with a rare second chance.

Taking a piece of stationery from a bedside drawer, he made a list of everything he needed, except money, which he already had, at least in a temporarily sufficient quantity. The relatively small number of items amazed him: underwear, socks, two pairs of pants, a few shirts, a pair of shoes, a light jacket, toothbrush and toothpaste, a comb, a wallet, a watch, a pen—no, he had the hotel's, and the complimentary razor, as well. He could think of nothing else he needed besides a permanent passport and a suitcase of some sort.

The phone book produced the genealogist's number. His assistant's nearly perfect English enabled Martín to make an appointment for the following morning. According to her directions, Dr. Gallardo's office was only six blocks from his hotel.

Showering slowly and dressing in the embassy-supplied sweatpants, shirt, and flip-flops, Martín hobbled out of the hotel to return an hour later with everything on his list, plus a full stomach. He replaced the bandages on his feet with band-aids and dressed in a new pair of jeans, a long-sleeved khaki shirt, and soft running shoes.

For a moment he relaxed, thinking he could now disappear from Glendaring's radar. "Shit," he exclaimed, remembering he had told the so-called taxi driver to take him to the Polanco district. Canvassing the local hotels could have already revealed his location. He'd only checked in a few hours ago, but perhaps they'd already found him and planned to kill him at the first opportunity. In any case, he would have to redouble his precautions, at least until after he'd met with the genealogist.

He went to the front desk and asked to see the manager. After shaking hands with the slender, dark-suited man, Martín asked to speak with him in private. The man led him to a small office and invited Martín to sit.

"Thank you for your courtesy," said Martín. As you may know, the American Embassy sent me here after I was robbed and beaten."

The manager nodded.

"Because I identified my attackers, I'm concerned they may try to find me. Could you check to see if anyone has called the hotel asking
about me?"

"Of course, *señor*, we keep a record of all such calls." He picked up his phone, punched an extension, and gave rapid orders. Less than a minute later, he hung up. "No one has called since you arrived, and I just instructed the clerk to remove your name from the register."

"Thank you, I'm grateful. Can you recommend a reliable driver, one who speaks English? I'll need him tomorrow morning just before ten."

"We have several excellent and trustworthy drivers, and I will have one of them waiting for you."

"Thank you again! I'll check out at that time, so please charge the bill to my lawyer, Mr. Gonzalez's credit card."

MEXICO CITY

After a continental breakfast from room service, Martín rebandaged his feet, pleased to see no evidence of infection. He packed his belongings in a small soft-sided bag and went down to the lobby. As he approached the desk, the clerk motioned to a neatly dressed, clean-shaven man standing near the hotel entry. "Your driver is here."

In tolerable English, the driver politely asked for $100 a day and they quickly settled at $75. After the money changed hands, Martín said, "Yesterday I was robbed and beaten, and I'm worried the same people could come after me again. I want to leave quickly and make sure no one follows."

"No problem," said the driver, as if that were a normal request.

Martín hobbled after the man as quickly as his sore feet would allow to a yellow Fiat parked directly in front of the hotel. Before the passenger door shut, the driver accelerated onto the street. After several minutes of what Martín believed would qualify for a Hollywood chase scene, he happily agreed with the driver that there was no pursuit.

Dr. Gallardo's office was in a faded old house in an otherwise grand residential neighborhood. Although the two-story masonry building had the bones of a Mediterranean villa, its stucco had deep cracks, the paint peeled, and broken pieces of roof tile dotted a barren stretch of what had once been a lawn.

A spinsterish woman in her fifties ushered him inside, where he found the house's interior much better maintained than the outside. Oak floors and paneling gleamed with polish as did pearl-colored plaster walls with fresh paint. The woman showed him down a wide hallway and into an office with a threadbare but beautiful Oriental rug. Glass-fronted bookcases filled with scholarly looking volumes lined the walls.

Dr. Gallardo stood behind an ornately carved desk. Tall, thin, and about sixty, his narrow face sported a graying goatee, and he wore a shapeless, glen-plaid three-piece suit. Martín immediately thought of a disheveled stork. Completing the image, the man extended a long, bony hand and peered through small, round glasses. "Welcome, Mr. Cortés," he said in excellent English. Then eying Martín's bandaged feet, "I hope you had a good journey and that our directions were satisfactory."

"Well, the trip was certainly interesting, although I had an accident," said Martín, nodding toward his feet. "And your directions could not have been better." Then to change the subject, he said, "I'm anxious to learn what you've discovered."

The genealogist offered coffee and gestured toward an overstuffed wingback chair in front of his desk. Then seating himself, he glanced at an open file. "You have come a long way and must be tired, so I'll begin. The Conqueror had two sons named Martín, one by his wife and one by the Malinche. Do you know about her?"

"Vaguely, but please refresh my memory?"

"Of course. She was a slave girl given to Cortés by a Maya chieftain on one of his first landings on the coast of Tabasco. After recognizing her superb intellect and learning that she spoke several languages, Cortés took her for himself. Although her name was either Malinche or Malintzin, he had her baptized as

149

Marina." With a twinkle in his eye, he added, "Cortés had a strict rule prohibiting sex with non-Christians."

At Martín's chuckle he continued. "Although of uncertain origins, some believe she came from Tehuantepec on the coast of Oaxaca, a place known for its assertive women. She spoke both the Aztec's Nahuatl and the Maya language. She communicated with Cortés through Aguilar, a shipwrecked Spaniard whom Cortés had rescued on a former landing. Aguilar spoke Spanish and Maya. She had a keen insight into the thinking of the Indians and suggested tactics that enabled the Spaniards to defeat the Aztecs. Years later, after the birth of their child, and after she had otherwise served her purpose, Cortés gave her a dowry and had her married to another Spaniard. Because she helped the conquistadors, many Mexicans view her as a symbol of treachery and use her name in curses."

"Interesting," murmured Martín.

Dr. Gallardo continued. "Any history book has that information, but not the following details. Cortés became so despised that people destroyed a great deal of information about him. My research indicates that your ancestor descended from Marina's son, Martín, incidentally Cortés's favorite.

"So," said Martín, "our family began with illegitimacy."

Gallardo shook his head impatiently. "That was widespread in those days and is still common in Mexico. No one pays much attention to it. If it makes you feel more comfortable, at one point Cortés sent a group of Indian dancers to entertain Pope Clement VII. The pope must have enjoyed the performance because he subsequently issued documents declaring your ancestor, Martín, legitimate."

After a quick pause for effect, the genealogist continued. "Another point you may find of interest: while everyone knows that Mexico is a country of *mestizos*, people of mixed Spanish and Indian blood, most do not realize that your ancestor was arguably the very first one of them! My report has more details about his life, which ended tragically. Perhaps most important, I discovered you have relatives, descendants from the same union. The remaining member of one branch of the family lives here in the city."

Martín felt his heart begin to pound. He took a deep breath and had opened his mouth to speak when Gallardo continued. "I took the liberty of speaking to him on your behalf. He kindly gave me copies of notes from his family's private research that I found credible and that filled in some important blanks."

Gallardo paused to hand Martín a large box, and added, "It contains my report and the notes. The only problem is that, while this man said he would enjoy making your acquaintance, he just left for Spain and will be there for several months."

Martín's expression showed his disappointment, but Gallardo smiled again. "However," he said, raising his index finger, "there is another branch of your family—in Oaxaca."

Martín remained silent.

"After the Conquest, Cortés received the title of *Marqués de la Valle de Oaxaca*, and large amounts of land nearby. Although he never lived there, he did establish a home. Some believe he transferred a not inconsiderable portion of his wealth to the area in order to avoid the one-fifth royal tax. It was to Oaxaca that this branch of your family eventually went, and from there that a descendant of the original Martín Cortés journeyed to Santa Fe and founded your family."

Martin struggled to contain his excitement. Gallardo peered at him over his tiny round glasses. "Excuse me," he said. "It always surprises me how our ancestors leave their stamp on us. You have the white skin and hazel eyes of so many Spaniards and the black hair and prominent cheekbones of certain Indian tribes."

Not sure how to respond, Martín gave a little smile and said, "I've recently been advised to get a haircut."

Gallardo nodded, but Martín could not tell if in understanding or agreement.

"Well, never mind. Cortés's main home in Oaxaca was turned into a museum, but my information says the remainder of your family lives next to it. I haven't spoken with either the father, Hector Cortés, or his wife, Martha. They have a son named Trinidad and also a girl named Ilhui, the illegitimate daughter of Hector and a former Cortés family servant from Tehuantepec, coincidentally named Marina." He lifted his gaze from the report to Martín.

"Tell me her name again, the illegitimate daughter," requested Martín.

"Ilhui, spelled I-L-U-H-I and pronounced as you would say 'ee-loo-ee' with 'ee' as in your pronunciation of the letter 'e.'"

"Hector's mother, named Estela, also lives with the family. They call her *Abuelita*, "Little Grandmother." She keeps to herself and rarely speaks to anyone outside the family."

"How on earth did you discover all that? You said

you haven't talked to these people."

"I shouldn't reveal my secrets," chuckled Dr. Gallardo, "but I have a source, an old classmate who has lived in Oaxaca all his life. He works for the Bureau of Records. I have not spoken to anyone in the family, and my colleague, whom I assure you is trustworthy, agreed
not to communicate with them in any way or otherwise mention this matter to anyone else."

"Thank you—I value confidentiality," nodded Martín. "I want no one but you and members of the family to know about me." Not wanting to sound too eager, he said, "It sounds like it might be worth looking them up. Somehow it appeals to me to surprise them. What do you think?"

Gallardo narrowed his eyes and replied after a moment's thought. "Without previous notice you could arrive at an inconvenient time, and some people don't like surprises. Not knowing them, I can't predict their reaction. On the other hand, if you send them a letter introducing yourself and describing my research…" He tapped the box in front of Martín. "…you can establish credibility and possibly a more immediate welcome. I can easily make a copy of my report for you to send to them."

"Thank you," replied Martín. "Do you know if anyone in the family speaks English? My Spanish is poor."

"That, *Señor* Cortés, I do not know, but I have one other bit of information I should give you. The family has lived in the same house for many years—in fact, as long as anyone can remember. They were given it in exchange for turning over the original Cortés home next door to the museum. They live modestly but also quite well. Other than the son who owns a restaurant and the little convenience store the father keeps on the ground floor of their home, no one knows the source of their money. Gossip speculates that the family lives on remnants of the Conqueror's wealth, but they are tight-lipped, and nobody really knows. I think that's all I can tell you. Would you like a copy of the report?"

Stunned, Martín was unable to answer. The emerald and Aztec codices stolen from his safe deposit box, now presumably in Glendaring's possession, kept flashing in front of his eyes.

The genealogist repeated his question.

"Yes, of course," replied Martín, recovering his composure. "I can either send it to them or hand-deliver it."

Outside, Martín looked carefully around and then hurried to the yellow Fiat. Slamming the door, he said, "Can you take me to a travel agent in another part of town and then to the airport?"

OAXACA

Reaching for cruising altitude, the Mexicana airliner banked south toward Oaxaca. Disturbingly nearby, smoke belched from the snow-capped peak of Popocatepetl, the active volcano that had petrified the ancients and still threatened their descendants. As the plane sped away from it, Martín relaxed and loosened his seatbelt.

The flight cost a hundred dollars more than a bus but would save nearly a day's travel. More importantly, he hoped it would confuse his trackers. He had telephoned the embassy and learned that the police hadn't found the body of the man he said he'd killed. He could now leave the city. As an added precaution, he'd purchased the ticket for cash from a hole-in-the-wall travel agent.

Martín immersed himself in the report on the life of his forbearer and found the history as sketchy as Dr. Gallardo had noted. He also found it confusing because his ancestor, the illegitimate son of Cortés, and his younger legitimate half-brother shared the same name: Martín. However, penciling in his forbear as Martín1 and the younger brother as Martín2 solved that problem.

Born in 1522, Martín1 at the age of eight was brought to Spain by his father to serve the royal court. At nineteen, he joined his father in Algiers in a disastrous attempt to defeat the Islamic enemies of the Crown. After that fiasco, Martín1 continued soldiering in the service of the Holy Roman emperor. At some point, he produced an illegitimate son named Fernando, although details about the mother remain unknown, including even her name. Adding to the

155

mystery, all that is known about his later marriage to Bernaldina de Porras is that at one point she applied for permission to join her husband in Mexico and requested the company of their daughter, Ana, and the illegitimate Fernando, whom historians speculate she may have raised.

When the Conqueror died, he left his title and the majority of his estate to Martín2, but he also provided a substantial annual income to Martín1. In 1562, Martín1 sailed from Spain to return his father's bones to Mexico. His brother joined him there, and they were welcomed to Mexico City by a procession of two thousand men on horseback.

But Martín1's life soon went to the dark side. The King of Spain decreed that property taken by the conquistadors could be held for only two generations, after which it reverted to the Crown. The cunning Hernan Cortés had negotiated ownership in perpetuity for *his* family. The only other recipient of that favor was Isabel Montezuma, daughter of the deposed Aztec ruler, with whom Cortés had produced a daughter named Leonor in 1527. The problem arose when the envious sons of other conquistadors did everything they could to associate the star-power of the Cortés name with their efforts to reverse the decree. Soon, rumors circulated that the Cortés brothers were involved in a plot against the Spanish authorities. Martín1 was arrested and charged with conspiring with Martín2 to assassinate judges of the royal council.

The authorities did not believe Martín1's protestations of innocence and ordered him tortured. They used the infamous rack and a method similar to what is now called water boarding. Unlike the other men charged in the plot, he showed remarkable courage by enduring the torment and refusing to admit guilt.

The genealogist speculated that Martín1's military experience set him apart from the other accused men, who readily told the inquisitors whatever they wanted to hear and that his bravery induced the authorities to spare his life. In any case, in 1568, with his appeals exhausted, Martín1 was stripped of his inheritance, forced to abandon his family in Mexico, and sent to Spain to live in exile. There, he commanded a regiment in the War of Granada, where, according to his son, he died in 1569. Other than that, little else was known. Except that his son, Fernando, after a successful career as a soldier and marriage in Peru, returned to Mexico to become a judge and continue the family line.

At first, the present-day Martín found the lack of more precise details disappointing, especially the incomplete family tree. Then he remembered the explanation that the public hatred of the Conqueror caused the normally meticulous Spanish historians to delete or misplace many items relating to Cortés. Nevertheless, Gallardo asserted that the private research notes he'd so carefully considered convinced him that Fernando's offspring led to the Martín Cortés who had founded the Santa Fe branch of the family.

Martín had just reached this conclusion when the plane began to descend. It circled over tall, rugged peaks and then more rounded mountains surrounding the valley of Oaxaca, where clusters of terraced hills broke up crop-covered fields. Some had jagged, humped spines that from above resembled resting dinosaurs. Rough country not yet completely tamed.

As he buckled his seatbelt, Martín hoped that ignoring Dr. Gallardo's advice to announce his visit to his relatives in advance would not cause problems. He had questioned the reliability of the Mexican postal system and didn't want to risk staying in Mexico City waiting for a reply that might never come. He understood the risks. The family might think him an opportunist or imposter, or be out of town. If he had to cool his heels, he'd rather do it in Oaxaca, hopefully away from Glendaring's reach. He also preferred to deal in person with any confusion his relatives might have regarding his intentions.

He waited until after the last passenger disembarked, but while stepping off the plane he detected nothing suspicious. After the mega-terminal in Mexico City, he found the facility in Oaxaca more human in scale. Rather than incur the cost and risk of a taxi, he bought a ticket for a van ride to the city's central plaza or *zócalo*. According to Gallardo, the old Cortés home next to which his family now lived lay only a few blocks away.

A little after 4:00 p.m., Martín hoisted the bag with all his possessions and stepped from the van. Through the din of blaring horns and revving engines, the driver informed him that the city plaza was to his right. The Museum of Contemporary Art, housed in the old Cortés house, was to his left. A glance at a street sign confirmed he was on Macedonio Alcalá, the street name Dr. Gallardo had given him.

Martín thought about finding a hotel before calling on his relatives but decided that appearing at their door and asking them for a recommendation might better produce an invitation to stay with them, which could save him considerable money and keep his name off hotel registers. Of course, they might resent the intrusion and want nothing to do with him, but he had nothing to lose.

Most of the buildings on the street were two-story stone structures.

They looked either late nineteenth or early twentieth century, with small retail shops along the street with office space above. Glancing at an address over the doorway of a café, he estimated his destination was two blocks away.

He passed the first block, crossed the street, and stood in front of what appeared to be a school or university. Across the avenue sat a stone building, much older than its neighbors. A sign identified it as the Museo de Arte Contemporaneo, located in the house built originally for Hernan Cortés. On its far side rose a smaller, newer stone building with the address he sought. Next to a small shop at the front of the building, he saw an arched entryway.

Rehearsing what to say, Martín strode across the street to discover carved double doors set well back in the unlit entry. Seeing no doorbell, he knocked on one of the doors. As the sound echoed in the alcove, he thought he heard a noise from within, and the door opened to reveal an attractive light-skinned woman. She looked early fifties and wore a black silk blouse and skirt. Parted in the middle, her medium-length black hair had a spiderweb of gray strands.

Martín had just opened his mouth to speak when smile lines appeared around the woman's eyes. His jaw gaped further when she said, "*Bienvenido* Martín." Switching to English, she added, "Welcome. I am Martha Cortés; I hope you had a pleasant journey!"

OAXACA

Martín gaped at the woman for a moment as he realized that Professor Gallardo or his colleague must have broken the confidentiality agreement. Regaining his composure and encouraged by her use of English, he said, "Thank you, Martha, I'd hoped to surprise you."

"It's always a surprise to meet a relative for the first time," she replied. "Now please come in, and I'll call Hector."

Martín found himself in a spacious entry hall. At the far end, an archway led to a living area. To his right, a grand stairway curved up to a second level. The dark floor tile with its patina of generations of polish was set off by white plaster walls. The house immediately reminded him of his family's hacienda. The memory intensified as a door to his left opened and a solidly built man of medium height entered. Wearing a gray polo shirt and black pants, his graying hair, small mustache, and plump but firm face caused Martín's heart to race. The man was the image of Martín's father twenty years earlier.

Extending his hand, the man said, "Martín, I'm Hector. It's a pleasure, and thank you for coming." He engulfed Martín in an *abrazo*, causing him to drop his bag and awkwardly return the embrace.

"Come into the living room," invited Martha, leading the way into a large room with the same tile floor and plaster walls as the entry. It was filled—overfilled, thought Martín—with antique Spanish furniture that looked more like finely finished French furniture than the carved folk-art pieces he had grown up with in Santa Fe. At the other end of the room, he saw a door he thought must lead to a patio.

He seated himself in a brocaded maroon chair, while Hector and Martha sat on a nearby couch covered in velvet of the same color and smiled at him. Just as the silence became uncomfortable, a young man walked through the door from the entryway. Well over medium height, he carried a tray with a pitcher of blood-red liquid that looked to Martín like Kool-Aid. Mid-twenties and thin, noted Martín. Exceptionally handsome, albeit in a slightly effeminate way. His large dark eyes were lustrous, and his light skin gleamed like polished marble.

"Martín," said Martha, "this is our son Trini."

He approached Martín and placed the tray down on a coffee table. He extended his hand and said in a voice that was as musical as his face was beautiful, "It's a pleasure to meet you, cousin."

Noticing that Trini's English was even less accented than his parents. Martín rose and extended his hand. Although Trini's limp grip was no surprise, the calloused skin on his palm was. "Would you like a glass of *jamaica*?" he asked.

Martín had tried the refreshing tea, made with dried hibiscus flowers, in Santa Fe and quickly assented. Taking a sip, he tasted not just the flavor he remembered but also a hint of mint and something exotic he could not identify, possibly ginger. Noticing his reaction, Martha, said, "Trini is very talented with food."

"I can see that," smiled Martín.

Just as his mouth opened to confirm his suspicion that Dr. Gallardo or his colleague had somehow alerted the family to his visit, he heard the patio door open behind him. Turning his head, his mouth remained open when he saw the girl. She could not have been much under six feet and her posture was so perfect that she seemed even taller. Her nose, lips, and cheekbones were broad but finely chiseled, creating an effect that was both primitive and aristocratic. Her large, almond-shaped eyes shone like black opals. Unlike the other family members, her skin was not white. It wasn't brown either, more gold than anything else. Had the gleaming black hair that fell well below her shoulders been at all curly, Martín could have been persuaded that she had African blood. But other than a gentle wave it was nearly straight and appeared perfectly natural. She wore jeans and a sleeveless black T-shirt with a gold medallion embroidered over the left breast. On both wrists were stacks of silver bracelets that tinkled as she walked.

"Welcome, Martín, I am Ilhui," she said, in English more accented than the other family members. But it had a charming lilt, and her voice was resonant and husky, like that of a lounge singer accustomed to whiskey and cigarettes.

Martín had managed to close his mouth and, in an attempt to hide his embarrassment at Ilhui's impact, said, "I could not be more pleased to meet all of you. But I must ask you a question. I found you through a genealogy consultant. I had some problems in Mexico City and neglected to inform you I was coming. I wonder, did the consultant contact you?"

The room full of relatives looked at each other in what seemed to Martín genuine puzzlement. Then Martha said, "Abuelita, Hector's mother, told us about you, and that you would arrive this afternoon. Perhaps you can ask her how she knew. She's waiting to meet you on the patio." She gestured toward the door by

162

which Ilhui had entered.

Immediately, Trini rose and shook hands with Martín. "I must get
ready for work and look forward to getting to know you." He turned and disappeared through a door at the other end of the room.

Ilhui appeared silently beside Martín, bringing with her an exotic tropical scent and the tinkle of her bracelets. He guessed there were over twenty on each arm. She bent her head, and her lips and hair grazed his cheek. "I must go too," she said, straightening up, "but look forward to knowing you."

Trying to keep from blushing, Martín rose and turned toward the patio. He looked back at Hector and Martha. "Should I just go out?"

Hector nodded. "Of course, Martín. We will see you later."

What have I gotten into? wondered Martín, as he walked to the door and opened it.

For a moment he thought he'd fallen through the looking glass. The courtyard was about forty feet wide by sixty feet long. Stone pathways led from where he stood and also diagonally from the four corners to a large round stone area in the center. On it, water trickled from a faded green tile fountain t. Between the pathways grew a profusion of tropical trees, so thick that the grass below them was patchy and stunted from insufficient light. Some of the trees rose well above the second floor of the house, creating a canopy through which sunlight filtered to splash unevenly on the ground below.

Shorter trees bore fruits he did not recognize. Between them grew leafy plants and flowers, including orchids and bromeliads. In addition to the gurgling fountain, he heard a cacophony of bird songs. Though just a short distance from the busy downtown streets, he seemed to have stumbled into a jungle. To his right, stairs rose to a covered veranda directly above him that provided exterior access to the second-floor rooms.

On the pathway in front of Martín, a foot-long lizard sunned itself in a swatch of sunlight. Farther on, beside a glass-topped table near the fountain, sat an old woman. Stepping warily around the lizard, Martín moved forward. He neared the table and saw that Abuelita sat upright, her back straight in the wrought-iron chair. Her wiry frame was clad in a black skirt and white silk blouse. Luminescent skin, nearly devoid of wrinkles, stretched over strong cheekbones on either side of an aristocratic nose. Her hair was a mixture of very black and very white, as if it had been carefully frosted. It was pulled into a tight bun stuck through with what looked like a jade chopstick.

Raising her hand in a gesture of welcome, she waved him to a chair. "*Bienvenido, Martín.*" She gestured toward a pitcher of crimson *jamaica* and an empty glass.

"*Gracias, es un placer conocerle,*" replied Martín, thanking her for the welcome and acknowledging the pleasure of meeting her as best he could. Although the day was temperate, he found the patio uncomfortably humid. He poured a glass of *jamaica* and seated himself.

As he sipped the drink, the woman looked at him through bright hazel eyes and said in excellent English, "I have always known we had relatives in the United States and am glad you have come. Please tell me about your family."

Trying to put aside his astonishment, for the next fifteen minutes Martín summarized his family history, ending with an abridged description of the recent tragedies and the coincidence of his contact with Dr. Gallardo. When he mentioned the theft of the emerald and codices that his family believed came originally from Hernan Cortés, her eyes flickered as if in recognition, but she said nothing until he finished.

"Something has troubled me recently. Now I understand," she said.

Wanting to ask exactly what she understood, instead Martín said, "I assume Dr. Gallardo's colleague either contacted you or, in the process of collecting information, spoke to someone who did?"

She shook her head. "No, I haven't spoken to anyone outside the family for some time." Then smiling at Martín, she added, "Thank you for sharing your history. Now I shall tell you ours, much of which includes yours as well. But first, you must be hungry after your journey."

Rising with a supple grace that belied her age, she reached over and caressed a plant with large green leaves. "We call this *hoja santa*, 'holy or saint's leaf,'" she said. "We cook with it." She smiled and pinched off one of the giant leaves at its base. Moving to the fountain, she picked up a small bowl with other recently plucked plants and then turned to Martín. "I'll take these to the kitchen."

Martín watched her disappear through a door in the corner of the courtyard. In a few minutes she returned. "Please have some more *jamaica*, or would you like some beer or brandy? We'll have something to eat shortly."

"This *jamaica* is fine—delicious, in fact," replied Martín. Then not to be denied he added, "When you left, I was asking how you knew about me and when I would arrive."

The same puzzled look returned to the old lady's eyes. "As I said, I have always known about your family and recently realized that you would arrive today."

Martín's desire to press his questioning was delayed by the opening of the door to the kitchen. Carrying a tray was a slender girl in a tropical print dress. Tall and willowy, her hair was extremely short. She wore Ferrari-red lipstick, '50s Hollywood sunglasses, and medium-heeled white sandals that clacked on the stone walkway. Exquisitely beautiful, thought Martín, in a more dramatic but less earthy way than Ilhui.

"*Gracias princessa*," said Abuelita to the girl as she set the tray onto the glass table. Then to Martín she added, "Isn't Trini wonderful! Taking time before work to prepare some *botanas*."

Martín's feeling of disorientation surged as he realized that the girl was actually Trini, who gave a short bow, blew each of them a kiss, and returned to the kitchen with what seemed to Martín a little extra sway to his hips.

Trying desperately to break through his astonishment, Martín stammered, "Martha said that Trini is very talented with food. Is he a chef?"

"The best!" She gestured toward several bowls on the tray with small, steaming appetizers, some wrapped in *hoja santa* leaves, others enclosed in a thin bacon-like meat, and still others that resembled tiny *empanadas*. "Try these and you'll be convinced."

The aroma of the just-cooked delicacies reminded

166

Martín how hungry he'd become, and he immediately helped himself. Most of the items had fillings of finely chopped vegetables and cheeses, each one superb. He detected the bite of smoky chile, the succulence of pork fat, the surprise of various herbs, invigorating splashes of lime juice, and a spicy syrup, all seemingly designed to pair with something he could not identify that was slightly bitter but mysteriously tantalizing. Martín's main task was to refrain from making a pig of himself. Sitting back and taking a sip from his glass he said, "These are incredible."

I knew you would appreciate them," she replied. "By the way, please call me Abuelita. You belong to this family and, in that regard, let me give you some of our history."

She began with essentially the same story of Cortés's acquisition of the slave girl, Malinche, that Dr. Gallardo had given him the day before. As the story progressed, Martín felt dizzy. By the time she got to the generation after the birth of the illegitimate Martín, the present-day holder of that name realized he was losing his equilibrium, and his limbs seemed to be made of lead. Abuelita's voice seemed to come from behind him and then from above him. As his head swam, the filtered sunlight combined with the shapes and colors of the trees to form a kaleidoscope that began to whirl into a vortex. The patio walls disappeared and he floated above the earth, traveling back and forth between centuries, for the first time in his life seeing the world as he instinctively knew it ought to be. Through it all, he could clearly make out Abuelita's voice describing one forebear after another, until at some point everything stopped.

OAXACA

Martín awoke slowly from a strange but comforting world. A vaguely familiar scent penetrated his consciousness, followed by a musical tinkle. Opening his eyes, he focused on a figure standing over him.

"Martín, you are all right?" exclaimed a voice in the rich, husky tones he recognized as Ilhui's. At the same time, he identified the scent as hers and the sound as coming from her bracelets. He propped himself on an elbow and found himself on a bed in a room illuminated only by a candle burning on a table to his left. Holding the sheet to his chest to cover his nakedness, he shook his head. "I...I guess so. What time is it?"

"Eleven o'clock—on Saturday night."

After a quick calculation he exclaimed, "I've slept for over twenty-four hours?"

"Yes. We should have warned you about Abuelita's...I think you call them magic mushrooms. She believes they reveal a person's true character."

"How did I get here?" As his head cleared, he added with a hint of irritation, "I hope I passed whatever test that was supposed to be."

After a few bars of musical laughter, she replied, "You walked, with some help from Hector, and Abuelita seemed pleased. Anyway, we hoped you would sleep well and it seems that you did. Now, how soon can you be ready?"

"Ready for what?" he replied, raising himself to sit with his back against the headboard.

"To go dancing," she laughed. "Isn't that what you

168

do in Santa Fe on Saturday night?"

He regained some of his composure. "Only when you're very young."

"Then that includes you. How long?" Without waiting for an answer, she raised her hand to the wall and a muted click produced light from a stained-glass ceiling fixture. "The bathroom is through there," she said, gesturing to an opening in the wall about ten feet in front of the bed. She strode to a pair of French doors opposite the entry, which Martín assumed led to the portico over the patio where he'd met Abuelita. She opened one of them and left the room without closing it.

After a moment's annoyance, Martín smiled. He felt rejuvenated, and definitely preferred waking up to a beautiful girl asking him to go dancing than fighting rats in a landfill. *And surely, things couldn't get any stranger.* He swiveled off the mattress and was surprised to discover he was not at all unsteady. Grabbing his bag from the floor, he headed for the bathroom. After showering, he rebandaged his feet. The embassy nurse had been right; they were healing well. Walking was no longer painful.

Fifteen minutes later, he stepped onto the second-floor portico to find Ilhui leaning on the balustrade, gazing into the patio below. It was unlit, and through a curtain of vines spilling from the roof he could see only the dark shapes of plants, some of them rising well above him to block any glimpse of the moon or stars.

She motioned him to follow her downstairs. Although the ground floor was fully lit, no one was about. Seeing her in the light, he realized she was dressed simply and elegantly in a black linen dress, set

169

off with her bracelets and a necklace that looked like it was made of silver nuggets. Martín followed her out to the street where she hailed a taxi and said, "You must be hungry. We'll go to Trini's restaurant."

He had not eaten in over twenty-four hours and did not argue. "Are taxis safe here? I had a bad experience with one in Mexico City."

"Oaxaca is different."

As they twisted through narrow streets, Ilhui seemed content with silence, and Martín decided to defer the questions that raced through his brain. After about fifteen minutes they entered a particularly seedy neighborhood, and shortly the driver pulled to the curb by two low buildings with peeling stucco. Between them was a wide entry with an open gate.

As Martín opened the car door, he heard strains of music and asked, "Where are we?"

"El Pueblito, the little village," replied Ilhui. "It's where Trini has his restaurant and where we can dance."

Noticing two men preceding them past an obese policeman with a large pistol strapped to a belt as wide as a saddle cinch, Martín realized what El Pueblito was. "Is this what we call in English a red-light district?" he asked.

"Red Light," repeated Ilhui. "El Foco Rojo. There is actually a club by that name in another place that is much more expensive. But yes, you're correct." She turned and walked by the policeman, whose eyes were now stroking her body. Martín followed, trying not to show his uneasiness.

Inside, he found that the place did resemble a small village.
Pedestrian walkways at odd angles fronted ramshackle

buildings, many of them in the style of *palapas*, the round structures with tall, central poles supporting conical roofs of palm fronds. Others were assembled with obviously scavenged materials: odd pieces of two-by-fours, concrete block, broken tiles, and corrugated metal roofing. Old-fashioned lampposts poorly illuminated the dirt streets.

Martín followed Ilhui to where two streets came together in a triangle. At its tip stood an open *palapa*. The thatched roof sheltered a small kitchen and serving area, and around it sat metal tables and chairs advertising Mexican beers.

A line of people by the counter waited to be served. Behind it stood Trini in his female persona, flirting with his customers. Martín grinned sheepishly as he admitted to himself what an attractive sight the young man was. He could find no sign identifying the restaurant. The aroma of wood smoke reached him, mingled with an enchantingly complicated scent of exotic spices and herbs, and he quickened his pace toward the counter.

Trini waved them to the front of the line, and without protest the queue opened to make way. The sounds of music coming from nearby clubs made it difficult to hear Trini's "Welcome!"

Martín returned the greeting, surprised to see that the kitchen consisted only of a brick barbecue, two ancient refrigerators, and a galvanized metal sink. On the barbecue sat a large stainless-steel pot and a round clay griddle. Behind it stood a young girl preparing corn tortillas. Nowhere could he discover anything resembling a menu. *No name and no menu!*

As if reading his mind, Ilhui said, "There's only one dish." She waved her hand at the noisy group around them and added, "I'll tell you about it while we eat. There's a free table. I'll get some beer."

A minute later, Trini handed them two identical plates with portions of meat in a glossy, brick red sauce, garnished with toasted sesame seeds, and a small stack of corn tortillas. He curtsied and exclaimed, "¡*Buen provecho*!"

After thanking Trini, Martín seated himself, scraping his steel chair across the uneven slab. He looked at his steaming plate and then at Ilhui. She had put on lipstick that was red with a tinge of purple, the exact color of the bougainvillea that each summer grew outside his parents' home in Santa Fe. It always appeared after his mother scraped off the winter mulch and nursed the dormant plants back to life. He jerked his mind back to the present. "You were going to tell me about this dish?"

"Of course," she smiled, light flashing in her dark eyes. "Oaxaca is called 'The Land of Seven Moles.' *Mole negro* is the best known and is better than Puebla's more famous *mole poblano*. Trini invented this very special dish, a *mole* made of lamb cooked with smoke and many spices. He calls it the Eighth *Mole*. If there is any justice, it will soon be the most famous dish in Mexico. Of course," she shrugged, "in this country, things are rarely just. Anyway, please try it."

Martín dipped his fork and took a bite. As the flavor hit him his eyes opened wide. Certainly, the heat indicated chiles, but it was a mysteriously elusive heat. The smoky, falling-apart lamb blended perfectly with a host of spices and herbs to create a taste he had never experienced, but one that he knew he must have again and again. "You didn't exaggerate—this is fantastic!"

As he ate, Martín noted the area was filling up. More

and more men cruised the various establishments, alone and in small groups. In the doorways, touts and garishly clad prostitutes made their pitches. The volume of music went up and down as doors opened and closed.

As Martín and Iluhi finished their beers, she pushed back her chair and lit a long cigarette with a gold filter, causing the line of bracelets on her forearms to jingle. "Now we can dance," she said. She stood and walked away.

Martín waved to Trini and exclaimed, "¡*Increible*!" Then he made the universal scribbling sign, asking for the check.

Trini shook his head, gave a dazzling smile, and again curtsied.

OAXACA

When Martín caught up with Ilhui, her long, golden legs had taken her to the arched doorway of the largest club in the area. Although the men she had walked by stared at her, no one made a pass. Above the establishment's door was a neon sign in the shape of a large spider. Below it, rainbow-colored lettering proclaimed: Club Araña, Ladies Bar. *Club Spider*, translated Martín to himself, realizing that his Spanish vocabulary was coming back.

He followed her past a fat doorman in a threadbare black suit and bow tie into a large, low-ceilinged room. Directly to the left was a long bar where about ten obvious prostitutes of different ages were seated. Their costumes ranged from low-cut evening gowns to fishnet bikinis. In front of them was a dance floor filled with couples circling to the repetitive beat of *cumbia* music blaring from ceiling-mounted speakers. A sea of tables and chairs, about half of them filled, surrounded the dancers. As usual, Ilhui caused heads to turn, and Martín noticed five men in military uniforms at a table about twenty feet away who took particular notice of their arrival.

Seconds after they seated themselves at a table near the dance floor, a waiter in black pants and a white *guayabera* shirt arrived. Soon he placed a tray with a small carafe of clear liquid and two tall shot glasses in front of them. "This is the best mezcal in Oaxaca and that means the best in Mexico," said Ilhui. "It's smooth but also strong. I hope that makes up for not warning you about Abuelita's mushrooms."

"Thanks. With the problems I've had, I need all the

help I can get."

Ilhui frowned. "Abuelita said you've had a tragedy....
But we can discuss unpleasantness later; let's have fun
and get to know each other."

"In that regard," said Martín, "I understand why we
came to Trini's, but why did you choose this place to
dance?"

Her expression turned serious. "This place is
authentic, full of real people, living real lives, not some
silly club created for the amusement of spoiled
children." She stubbed out her cigarette, lit another,
and poured mezcal to the top of each glass. Martín
saw that his was smudged with lipstick from some
previous patron. "*Salud*," he said, raising it.

The liquor was as smooth as advertised. As the
music changed from the formulaic *cumbia* to
something slow and romantic, Ilhui said, "Now we can
dance. I think you will be more comfortable with this
music."

As they rose, Martín noticed that one of the men at
the table of soldiers who had paid particular attention
to their arrival had also risen and seemed to be coming
their way. As Ilhui stood and walked toward the dance
floor, the man stopped and glared at Martín.

He meant to question Ilhui about the man, but as his
arms went around her, she pressed against him, and all
he could think of was the silkiness of her cheek and
the perfume in her hair. They danced two dances and
then the music changed to a tropical beat. Ilhui was as
good as her word and began to return to their table.

Coming up beside her, Martín said, "Don't look
now, but a man at the table of soldiers in front of us is
staring at you and looks angry."

Without looking directly at the table, she gave a

throaty laugh.

"That's *Capitán* Raul Rodríguez and some of his men. He thinks, how should I say it...that I belong to him. Pay no attention."

Again, they toasted each other, and this time Martín refilled their glasses. During the next twenty minutes they danced again, finished the carafe, and ordered another. Martín tried to relax but felt disoriented. *Here I am dancing with a beautiful relative in a whorehouse.* He could not help glancing at the soldier's table—and noticing signs of increased hostility. At that moment, Ilhui excused herself to go to the restroom.

The bathroom was on the other side of the bar, to their left, while the table of soldiers was to their right, so she would not have to pass by them. But as she approached her destination in her erect, supple stride, the captain, who was over six feet with broad shoulders, rose and walked toward the bar. His companions had obviously been chaffing him, and his mouth, below a well-groomed pencil mustache, looked grim. Martín realized he had drunk more mezcal than was good for him and decided he had best monitor the situation.

He did not have long to wait.

As Ilhui exited the women's room, the soldier placed himself directly in front of her, blocking her way. She tossed her head and motioned with her hand for him to step aside. He reacted by grabbing her by both arms well above the stacked bracelets and gave her a less than gentle shake.

Like a shot, Martín was out of his chair and across the room, adrenalin overcoming the remaining soreness in his feet. Rather than start a fight, he preferred to confront the man verbally, but he could not think of the words in Spanish. Improvising, he placed his forefinger a few inches in front of the man's nose and shook it. "No," he said, as if scolding a child, and gestured for the man to back

away. The captain complied but said something obviously insulting to Martín.

"*Gracias*," said Martín, choosing to ignore the words he didn't understand. Turning to Ilhui, whose expression reflected both shock and indecision, he said, "Let's go." She looked toward the entrance but didn't move.

The music had stopped, and nearly everyone in the club had turned toward them, like a pack of animals sensing danger. The drinks were paid for, so there was nothing to keep them. Taking a last look around, he saw the army officer still glaring at him. Shifting his gaze, he noticed that the table where the man had sat with his companions was now empty. Martín said firmly, "Let's go."

"*Sí, señor*," said Ilhui. He detected more respect than sarcasm in her tone.

Outside, she said, "Martín. I'm sorry. Sometimes my judgment... Shall we go somewhere else, or would you rather go home?"

Martín noticed that Trini's business was still brisk. Rather than diminishing, traffic in the area was increasing. Although inclined to stay—now that the ice had been broken, he thought he could now speak with Ilhui on a more intimate level—but something about the empty table at the *Club Araña* bothered him. "Ilhui, I would love to spend more time with you, but I've had enough excitement."

She nodded and turned toward the entrance to *El*

Pueblito. As they passed through the entryway, the fat policeman nodded to Martín but averted his eyes. Although there were hundreds of people behind them, as they stepped onto the sidewalk outside the gates, Martín saw nobody, no traffic, and no waiting taxis. That unlikely situation combined with the empty table and the guilty-acting policeman set off the same alarms that had come too late when he had been kidnapped in Mexico City.

The soldiers came from the doorways of the buildings on both sides of the entry. Martín counted four in all, two on each side. One of them growled an obscenity as they approached. Another swung what looked like a foot-long piece of rubber hose but seemed much heavier. Although he saw no other weapons, he was not reassured; an experienced knife fighter would keep his blade hidden until the last second.

Realizing it was too late to retreat, he took the only course he could think of. He pushed Ilhui into the street and yelled, "Run!" In the same motion he spun and slid toe to heel toward the two soldiers nearest the gateway. His first move brought him within six feet of his adversaries. Surprised, they stopped. Quickly sliding forward again, Martín vaulted off his rear leg, cocking the other one in midair. As he reached the maximum height of his trajectory and started down, he drove a flying side-kick into the solar plexus of the nearest man, who was thrown violently backward.

Landing catlike, he immediately spun and released a reverse side-kick into the other man's ribs, doubling him over. *Two down,* he thought as he spun again toward the remaining two soldiers.

But there was only one, and the man was nearly on

him. Taking a long step back, Martín swiveled his head to the right until he could almost see his opponent, and his own body was wound like a spring. Shifting his weight to his front foot, he executed a lightning-fast spin to the right, releasing the cocked tension. As he did so, he straightened and raised his rear leg so that the heel was leading. His perfectly executed spin-heel kick connected with the man's head, sweeping him off his feet.

Even as he regained his balance, Martín's stomach sank. Where was the last man, the one with the obviously weighted hose? His alarm came a second too late as the blackjack crashed into his skull from behind, sending him to the pavement where he lay still, oblivious to Ilhui's screams.

OAXACA

When Martín awoke, a girl in a nurse's uniform said something in Spanish he did not understand. Then she turned and left what he assumed was a hospital room. His watch told him it was 7:30 a.m., Sunday.

Minutes later, the girl returned with a middle-aged man in green scrubs. In excellent English he introduced himself as Dr. José Aguilar. He announced that Martín had a slight concussion and badly bruised ribs, but that a little rest would make him reasonably fit within a week. He could leave whenever he wanted, but should take care not to injure his head again.

Moments after the doctor left, the tall army captain, identified by Ilhui as Raúl Rodríguez, filled the doorway and then slowly approached Martín's bed. Martín noticed a gash on the man's cheek that was barely covered with a piece of gauze.

"*Señor* Cortés," he said in good English, "I'm glad to hear your condition isn't serious and want to apologize. I've already paid the hospital for your treatment, and the men who did this will be punished."

"Ilhui?" exclaimed Martín, trying to sit up, but slumping back as pain flashed through his head. "Is she all right?"

"She's fine," replied the man. Smiling ruefully, he touched his bandage and added, "Yes, she's fine. What happened last night was inexcusable. You've certainly heard that Mexico is corrupt, and this must confirm that. Rough methods are sometimes necessary, but I assure you the word *corrupt* does not describe me.

That's why I'm
here."

"Then why am *I* here?" asked Martín, grimacing at
the pain in his head.

"You were being taken to jail. Ilhui found me, and I
made sure you were brought here."

"I guess I should thank you for that, but why was
this necessary?"

"This won't seem adequate and is certainly no
excuse—an explanation with your permission?"

Martín nodded and the captain continued. "There
was a misunderstanding. I...we thought you were
someone else. We drank too much mezcal, and after
what happened at the *Club Araña* my men decided to
take action. Your appearance...you looked like
somebody you're not. Again, that's no excuse, but I
knew nothing of their plans."

Wondering if the pain in his head was the cause of
his confusion, Martín said, "I don't understand."

"I am responsible for stopping the terrorists
operating in Oaxaca before they spread to other parts
of the country. I also like Ilhui…very much.
Unfortunately, according to my reports, she's involved
with the terrorist's leader. I thought you were one of
them. It was too late when I found out that you're her
cousin from the United States."

"What do you mean she's involved?"

"She spends time with him—too much time. She's
idealistic and often thinks emotionally." Again, he
touched the wound on his cheek and added, "And
she's very determined."

Remembering the *mariachi* ballad at the birthday
party in Zacatecas, Martin asked, "What is this
terrorist's name?"

The captain hesitated a moment, then replied. "Nobody knows his real name, but he is called El Vengador, The Avenger. That's all I should say, except once again to tell you that I regret what happened, and that I take full responsibility."

With a disarming smile, he added, "My men said you are an excellent fighter and they won only by luck. Perhaps you will become an ally in my concern for Ilhui, although I suspect we may become rivals in a more common way." His smile widened, and he concluded with, "Now I should leave before she makes me your roommate."

Bending over Martín, he held out his hand. Martín raised his from the bed, and as they shook, he said, "I was recently told I look like a drug dealer. Now it seems I also resemble a terrorist?"

The captain's expression grew serious. "Perhaps a haircut."

As Rodríguez left the room, Martín heard a torrent of Spanish delivered with the passion that can only come from an angry Latina. Moments later, Ilhui burst into the room, her crimson cheeks indicating she remained furious. She bent down and kissed Martín on the forehead. Rising up she clenched her fists in front of her. "Martín, I'm so sorry. This is my fault."

Martín raised himself carefully to a sitting position. Although his ribs ached, the agonizing pain in his head had begun to subside. "Thanks. But it was their fault, not yours. The doctor said I could leave, and I'd like to, as soon as possible."

"Of course," she said. "You are too kind. This happened because I made a mistake, something that seems to happen often. Now, how can I help you?"

"My clothes are hanging beside the door...if you'll

just give me a minute."

An hour later, Martín found himself once again in the second-floor bedroom of the Cortés home and quickly fell asleep.

OAXACA

The next morning, Martín's head still ached but not as badly. While showering, he realized that without invitation or acceptance he had become a houseguest. He dressed and made his way to the living room where he found Martha alone on the red velvet couch.

"Martín, we've been worried about you," she exclaimed, looking at him closely.

"I'm much better, thank you."

"Ilhui told us what happened. So many times, we've advised her to be more careful."

"It was a misunderstanding. Perhaps Ilhui should pay more attention to you. The soldiers thought I was someone else—a terrorist."

"Too often she makes unfortunate choices. Can I bring you some tea?"

Martín had hoped to learn more about Ilhui but felt uncomfortable pursuing the subject. "Yes, thank you, but no mushrooms!" he joked.

Martha returned a few minutes later with a silver teapot. "*Té de manzanilla*," she said, and dead-panned, "no magic, just very relaxing. Now, I must go shopping. Please join us for supper at eight o'clock."

"Thanks. By the way, I was surprised to find that Abuelita speaks excellent English."

Martha considered for a moment, and then gave what seemed like a secret smile but said nothing as she turned to leave.

Martín drank the tea, which he recognized as chamomile, and then
took a nap. As he dozed off, he considered that he had

spent most of his time in Mexico either in serious trouble or recovering from it.

At 8:00 p.m. he found the family in the dining room at a long table spread with a lace cloth. Hector and Abuelita were at either end. Ilhui, in black jeans and a honey-colored top with blue embroidery, and Trini, who now wore khaki pants and a polo shirt, sat in high-backed chairs on one side. Martha sat across from them next to a vacant chair.

"Our famous *estofado de pollo*, rice, and *nopalitos*," said Martha, gesturing to three steaming Talavera bowls on the table.

As Martín took the empty chair and served himself, Abuelita, her carefully coiffed black and white-streaked hair stuck through with the same jade piece, said, "Hector just returned from Mexico City and hasn't told us what happened."

Looking up from his now filled plate, Martín appreciated her courtesy in using English.

Hector grimaced. "There isn't much to tell. The offer was too low, and I've decided to look for another dealer."

"But," replied Abuelita, now all business, "Gomez has always been fair and discreet."

"I know, and we can always go back to him if we can't get a better price."

Sensing Martín's puzzlement, the family members glanced at Abuelita. She nodded to Hector. He pulled a small silk bag from his pocket, drew the string, and plucked out two huge emeralds. Although uncut, the sheen and rich dark-green color indicated great value. Martín drew a quick breath. They were nearly identical to the stone that had once resided in his father's safe, before its theft from his safe deposit box.

"We live by selling things like this. Our family has always done so," said Hector. Then he lowered his voice and added, "You understand, this must remain within the family."

Martín's heart pounded. "I understand. As I told Abuelita, my family had a stone exactly like those and some codices that belonged to the original Cortés. Our problems began when their existence became known."

The family nodded in confirmation.

Abuelita said, "Trini, please bring some brandy to celebrate our finding Martín."

Trini quickly returned with a dusty bottle of Cardinal Mendoza brandy in one hand and a tray of snifters in the other. After a toast, Martín sampled the *estofado de pollo*, a stew of chicken, with olives, raisins, cinnamon, and almonds in a fresh-tasting tomato sauce. Looking up from his plate, he said, "Truly delicious, but nothing can compare to the *mole* I had last night. Trini, what is in it? There's lamb, but what else?

Trini bowed. "Thanks, Martín. But that's *my* treasure, the one recipe I won't reveal, at least as long as other treasures remain secret." He glanced at Abuelita and the table fell into an uncomfortable silence. "But thank you," he concluded.

Coming to the rescue, Hector said, "Martín, we're going to our *finca*, our country home, on Thursday and hope you'll join us. The house is primitive but comfortable."

"You're very kind. I'd love to."

After supper, Ilhui and Trini removed the dishes to the kitchen. Although his head still ached, Martín offered to help. Several times

he had wondered why there were no servants in the

186

house. Now, he thought he knew but decided to ask Ilhui. When the dishes were done, Trini said he was going out to see some friends. Ilhui gave Martín a soft kiss on the cheek, apologized again for what had happened and said, "If you have forgiven me, could we talk for a few minutes?"

"I'd like that." He followed her to the living room.

When they were seated across from each other, she cocked an eyebrow. "I assume you realize that you've been accepted as a member of the family."

"I gathered something of the kind, but you really know very little about me and, I suppose, vice versa."

"Abuelita already knows whatever she thinks she needs to know."

"Okay, but just one thing," said Martín. "I'm curious at the absence of servants. Does it relate to privacy and security?"

"Yes. We're very careful. Abuelita said that you're an artist? Art is one of my passions."

Martín described his work, telling her that although he made a meager living, his art had never caught on, and he'd never been satisfied with it.

"Maybe you lack the right inspiration." After a moment's thought, she added, "I hope you will paint while you're here."

"I don't know. I don't even know how long I'll be here."

"You've seen nothing of Oaxaca, except, unfortunately, *El Pueblito*. Let me show it to you. It's pure inspiration, and we can get to know each other."

"Great, how about tomorrow?"

She rose and glanced at her watch. "Sometime in the morning; I'll let you know. Now I must go." Moments later Martín heard the front door close.

Upstairs, he lay on the bed and placed his head gingerly on the pillow. *So many questions. Maybe tomorrow will provide some answers.*

OAXACA

Next morning, Martín found a note from Ilhui under his door asking him to meet her in the *zócalo* at ten-thirty. The large town square, surrounded by shops, hotels, restaurants, and municipal buildings lay just a few blocks from the house. Pleased to discover that his feet no longer hurt and, other than a tender lump, neither did his head, he decided to leave early. He stopped at a barbershop. Before he left, the mirror told him he no longer looked like a drug dealer or a terrorist.

He found Ilhui alone at a table in a sidewalk café under one of the hundred-foot laurel trees that shade the plaza. She wore jeans and a pink T-shirt embossed with pre-Hispanic designs. As he sat across from her, she frowned and then burst out laughing. "I hardly recognized you!"

"I decided to take Captain Rodríguez's advice and try to look less like a terrorist. What do you think?"

Her laughter vanished into another frown. "You look fine."

She ordered without consulting him, and soon steaming packets wrapped in banana leaves and mugs of fragrant hot chocolate arrived. "Our special tamales," she explained, "with chicken in *mole negro*."

The sweet, earthy taste of corn mingled with the bold but sophisticated inky-black sauce and shredded chicken. Martín thought the hot chocolate complemented the tamale's flavors.

After breakfast, Ilhui said, "We'll start with Oaxaca's heart and soul."

Rather than ask the obvious question, Martín

189

decided to let her show him the answer. She led him one block past the plaza into a huge indoor market. Stands on the concrete floors were piled high with chiles, herbs, spices, vegetables, and cuts of meat, most of them unfamiliar. Beyond it they entered another market hall filled with tiny restaurants, like stalls at a county fair, and he discovered more unusual foods.

"Try the *chiles rellenos* made with our smoke-dried *pasilla de Oaxaca* chiles."

He did and they were as exotically delicious as the tamale. *If everything in Oaxaca is like what I've just experienced…*

Outside, his delight grew as the captivating smell of roasting cocoa beans led them to a street of small chocolate factories. "They roast the cocoa beans and grind them with sugar, cinnamon, and sometimes almonds to order," she said.

Martín noticed that many among the throngs of people were Indians, mostly women dressed in *huipil* blouses and voluminous, bright-patterned skirts. They seemed to be everywhere, a quiet almost otherworldly presence that reminded him of Santa Fe's plaza, but more touchingly authentic.

At first, he thought the buildings flanking the crowded streets looked old and tired, like royalty reduced to one set of threadbare clothes. But as he caught glimpses of perfectly restored interiors and courtyards as lush as that of his family, he realized the shabbiness was mostly on the outside.

Later, they walked back toward the Cortés home and Ilhui pointed at a bandstand being erected in the middle of a street near the *zocalo*. "In the evenings musicians from all over Mexico come here to play, free of charge. They set up on different streets, but never

far from
the plaza."

They walked for another twenty minutes and then
hiked up a steep hill to the Hotel Victoria, where they
ordered drinks and a snack in a dining room with a
panoramic view of the city. Afterwards, they walked
around the grounds, enjoying the afternoon sunshine.

On the way back, they stopped at a huge park,
dotted with tall trees and wrought-iron benches, where
old men fed pigeons, mothers wheeled their children
in prams, and lovers stole precious moments. Martín
felt as if something exciting were growing inside him,
something that would soon demand release

"Let's sit." Ilhui motioned toward an empty bench.

Martín welcomed the invitation. *So far, we've spoken
only about the sights. Maybe we can get to a more personal level.*

Once seated, Ilhui clasped her hands in her lap and
gave him an uncharacteristically shy smile. "Tell me
everything...how you find yourself here."

"Okay, but remember it goes both ways."

Receiving no reply, he began. "With everything that
happened during the last year I felt disoriented, almost
like I was dreaming. I hoped coming to Mexico would
allow me to clear my head, but it's only gotten worse,
at least maybe until today."

"I'd like to help, but all I know is that your mother,
father, and brother died."

"I told Abuelita some of the story. I thought she
would have..."

"Abuelita only tells people what she thinks they need
to know."

"I suppose I've been trying to bury the memories,
but that's impossible. Do you have a little time?"

She squeezed his arm. "Of course, and there's always

tomorrow."

Martín began by describing how Abel's desire to prove himself and his resulting missteps led to the death of his entire family. When he finished, Ilhui threw her arms around him and held her cheek next to his. After a moment she moved back, clasped her hands together, and stared into her lap. "I've never had such a loss. I can't imagine... I'm so sorry."

Martín felt drained. "That's the worst of it," he said, wiping away a tear. "But it's not all, and I still know almost nothing about you. It's getting late, so maybe we should finish tomorrow?"

"That's a good idea; I have some work to do."

Martín wondered what work she meant, but something in her manner told him not to ask.

OAXACA

The following afternoon, Martín and Ilhui joined the throngs of Oaxacans in the market for the *comida*, the main meal of the day. They sampled items from different stalls, and Ilhui promised him that this afternoon would be the highlight of their tour.

After the meal they walked to the ex-Convent of Santo Domingo, part of which housed a museum of Oaxacan artifacts. Most impressive to Martín was the jewelry from Tomb 7 in Monte Albán, much of it beaten gold, similar to a piece Abuelita wore, and rendered in patterns nearly identical to the ones embossed on Ilhui's T-shirts. Those connections combined with their beauty rekindled the excitement he felt yesterday.

From the museum they took a cab to the top of the mountain behind the city, where the ancient ruins of Monte Albán overlooked the valley. Pools of mist swirled around the ceremonial center, as if to emphasize the mystery of its murky origins. Above the grassy mesa, huge flat-topped pyramids rose like the first steps of a stairway to the gods. For half an hour, they wandered the grounds, occasionally brushing off furtive men offering artifacts for sale. Maybe it was the altitude, but Martín felt as if he were in a trance-like state and could not shake the eerie feeling that he had been transported into a previous life.

"They're mostly selling fakes," said Ilhui, "but not always. It's a serious crime to possess real ones."

Martín marveled at the architectural perfection of the ancient city and asked Ilhui about the civilization that had produced them. "We know a few things, but

I'm afraid the most important mysteries will remain."

As late afternoon approached, like tiny dolls they perched on the edge of an immense stone wall and looked into the valley and to the other side where yet more mountains disappeared into the darkening sky. Martín's excitement increased as he tasted the grandeur of the sight and was certain he felt something of what those first Oaxacans had experienced.

Ilhui placed her hand gently on his arm. "Do you feel like finishing...from yesterday?"

"If you can bear to hear more."

She slid nearer, her glossy hair brushing his shoulder.

Martín explained how, after his parents and brother died, the bank, the family hacienda, the emerald, the codices, his bonds, and gold had also been stolen. Then he described the attempts on his life in New Mexico, ending with the destruction of his home and the near fatal attack on his dog, Pancho. He said he believed the theft of the hacienda and historical items had been part of Glendaring's original plan, at least following Abel's announcement of his intention to dissolve their partnership.

"Things like that are common in Mexico," she said. "But in the United States? I can't believe it!"

"Me too, but it happened."

A uniformed guard approached and told them the site was closing.

As they stood, Ilhui peeked at her watch and hugged Martín. "I have to go anyway. We can finish later, maybe at the *finca*," she said. "My God, Martín, I never dreamed...I..."

He hugged her back. "Neither did I." Then, holding hands for the first time, they left the site.

In the taxi, Martín asked, "Do you have to work this

evening? And I've been meaning to ask what you do."

"Something that's important to me. Maybe I'll show you sometime." Her tone made it plain that was all she was going to say.

As they got out of the taxi in front of the Cortés house, Martín felt a strong connection between himself, the ancient ruins, and the family home. It was as if the two places had similar magnetic poles that were the opposite to his, exerting an inexorable pull on him.

In his room, he lay down and tried to analyze his feelings. Were they due to the attraction he felt toward Ilhui? Only partly. There was something special about Oaxaca. The culture, the history, the art, and most of all the people infused the place with a mystical energy. But something warned him that it was not all benign. Although the place exuded a pastoral calm, the alien foods, the tropical landscaping, the quiet Indians in native dress, and the brooding ruins on the mountain above the misty valley gave it an otherworldly ambiance. He had the distinct impression that things could quickly veer well beyond the ordinary and not necessarily in a pleasant way. There was incredible power, but one that seemed temporarily passive, like a dormant volcano. Whatever it was, he knew it had captivated him.

It struck him that he had reached the saturation point. Some of what he had absorbed demanded release. A compulsion to paint came over him, beyond anything he had previously experienced. Ilhui was right. Oaxaca *was* pure inspiration. But that would have to wait. He needed to learn more about his new family and decide how long he would stay here and how to resolve the situation in Santa Fe, assuming the legal system failed to punish Glendaring.

Then he remembered the nearly constant criticism aimed at him by his artist friends. "Martín, why don't you stop thinking, listen to your heart, and just create something?" *Maybe it's time.*

When Martín came downstairs for supper, he found the house deserted. As he looked around, Martha appeared behind him. "I forgot that you didn't know that each Tuesday we dine in the old house, when the museum is closed."

She led him through a small door in a corner of the kitchen that connected with one in the museum next door. They passed through a room full of art objects in display cases into a grand courtyard where a table was set with fine silver. Around it sat the rest of the family. When Martín was seated, Abuelita whispered a grace, and Trini served his special *mole*.

After dinner, Martín walked through the museum, gazing at works by Nieto, Gutierrez, Morales, and what he thought was Mexico's greatest contemporary artist, Ruffino Tamayo. Surrounded by the splendor of the ancient home built for Hernan Cortés, Martín was swamped by a sense of belonging that nourished his soul.

Back in the family's home, Martín joined Ilhui in the kitchen to help with the dishes. She said, "I'm going out to the *finca* tomorrow afternoon, a day early to make sure everything is ready. Will you join me? The work will be easy for two."

Martín tried unsuccessfully to control his grin, and they decided to leave the next afternoon at three-thirty. He noticed Abuelita smile as she overheard the arrangements. He meditated on that smile as he listened to the rain drumming on the roof tiles, but at

last he drifted
into a deep, untroubled sleep, anticipating the next
day.

OAXACA AND CORTÉS FINCA

At the appointed time, Ilhui found Martín in the living room studying a Spanish textbook he had found at a nearby bookstore. She wore her bougainvillea-colored lipstick, low-cut jeans, and a black cotton tank top that accelerated his heart rate. He grabbed his bag and followed her outside to find a tan Volkswagen double-parked. "I didn't know you had a car," he said.

"I don't use it often." She nodded to a small suitcase and several large mesh bags filled with provisions in the back seat. "I think we have everything we need, except ice."

"Where exactly are we going?" he asked as she pulled into traffic.

Lighting one of her gold-filtered cigarettes, she said, "We go northwest about fifteen kilometers to a small village, then another five to our property. Like the house next door, it was built for Cortés, but is mostly unknown outside the family."

They left the outskirts of the city and entered a country of rolling hills dotted alternatively with cactus and lush crops, a mixture of desert and oasis. The narrow road twisted upward through hills that gradually became steeper and rockier. As they approached a village, the terraced fields disappeared to be replaced by hardscrabble soil and brush. There was no sign with a name or population, only a dozen or so adobe and stone buildings around an ancient plaza. The few people they passed either stared at them or ignored them. They stopped once to avoid a huge sow with several piglets drinking from a rain-filled pothole. Ilhui pulled in at a small grocery store next to a donkey piled high with flattened cardboard. "Just ice," she said.

"Let me get it," said Martín. "I need to practice my Spanish. *Hielo,*

isn't it? Besides, I've been here nearly a week and haven't paid for anything."

"You may actually speak Spanish better than these Indians, and you're part of the family, so you don't need to pay." When he stepped out of the car, Martín was surprised to find that the moist warmth of the city had been replaced with dry cool air.

With three bags of ice stowed in the trunk, they drove out of the village. After two kilometers, the paved road became a rough dirt track, and Ilhui slowed to a crawl. After another rugged kilometer, which took over five minutes, the road ended at a solid, six-foot-high iron gate, topped with barbed wire and attached to a stone wall crowned with broken glass. A sign on the gate said *No Entrada.* Ilhui got out, removed the padlock from its heavy chain, and pushed the gate open. As they passed through, Martín said, "Should I close and lock it?"

"I always lock it when I'm here alone, but it seems safer with you here."

"You mean because I was so successful last Saturday?" joked Martín. "I'll lock it."

They continued up and over a ridge. A hundred yards away, the house sat beside a clearing, surrounded by the only trees in the area. Behind it towered a mountain with boulders protruding from its sides, like the bumps on an oversized tropical fruit. The sprawling two-story structure of stone seemed held together with bits of cracked adobe. *Not a ruin but well on its way.* However, Ilhui easily turned the key in the massive front door, and it swung smoothly on well-oiled hinges.

Although cold and musty, the interior was in reasonably good shape. Dark tile covered the floor, and the living room was furnished with plain but well-crafted furniture. On the other side of it, through an arch lined with indigo tile, he saw a dining room, and beyond a similar arch was the kitchen. Inside it stood a massive stone hearth, covered with blue and white Talavera tile in diagonal patterns. A gas burner rested over one of four cavities that had originally held live coals. Between the stone supports of the hearth were stacks of logs and kindling. To one side stood a huge iron oven. At the other end of the room, Ilhui shoved the sacks of ice into an old-fashioned oak icebox lined with tin.

Turning to Martín, she said, "The kitchen is Abuelita's favorite room. When she's here, she allows no one but Trini to use it."

Instead of voicing his thought that the place reminded him of genteel decay approaching ruin, Martín said, "Looks like something out of a museum. What do we need to do?"

"Clean the floors and *despolver*...dust. Upstairs...the roof...well, you'll see." She walked back into the living room and made for a stone stairway at the other end.

Upstairs, a central hallway provided access to the bedrooms. Martín counted six in all. "Each one has a small bathroom that Hector added a few years ago," said Ilhui, opening one of the doors. "Now you see," she added, stepping aside. "He should have also fixed the roof."

The tile floor was spattered with mud and other

200

debris from the disintegrating roof. "What about water?" he asked.

"It comes from the *tinoco*." She waved at a stone tower outside the window. It's rainwater, but, how do you say it: *no es potable*."

"Unless, I suppose, you like your water flavored with dead rats,"
muttered Martín. "Give me a mop and I'll do the upstairs."

An hour and a half later, he replaced a large broom and a mop in a closet and went downstairs to find Ilhui doing the same. The house now smelled clean and fresh.

"That's done." She rose to her full height in a stretch of satisfaction. The material on her tank top pulled tightly against her full breasts and rode up over her navel. Martín looked away, as the now familiar increase in his heart rate returned. "It's getting dark—I'll light the lamps," she added.

Martín had noticed there were no electric outlets and that each room was fitted with oil lamps. As she moved from one fixture to another, the living area took on a warm glow.

"Time for a bath, then something to eat. You've seen the water heaters?" she asked.

Martín, having discovered the on-demand propane heater in his bathroom and the butane lighter on a nearby shelf, realized the house was in better shape than he'd thought. He savored the thought of a warm bath and rejoining Ilhui.

CORTÉS FINCA

A half hour later, Martín returned to the living room to find Ilhui already there. The gaslight flickered about her like candlelight in a draft as she stood to hand him a glass of amber liquid. She wore a short skirt of rough white cotton, and a *huipil*, similar to the embroidered Indian blouses he had seen on women at the market. Although the skirt might not be called tight, Martín could detect no visible slack in it either. Earlier, she had pulled her hair back into a ponytail; now it hung free over her shoulders and well down her back.

"You look terrific!"

"Thank you. Are you hungry?"

"I could certainly eat," he smiled.

"I never learned to cook, but I wanted to have something special for you, something to remind you of home, something that would not spoil without refrigeration. I spoke to a friend who lived for a year in the United States. She suggested something…. Just sit down at the table and I'll bring it to you."

Ilhui disappeared into the kitchen, and Martín seated himself at the newly polished table under the flickering lights. Moments later she returned with a bottle of Mexican rosé wine from Fresnillo, and a clay plate piled high with sandwiches. "Peanut butter and jelly," she exclaimed with delight as she put them on the table. "My friend said it's a favorite food in the US."

"She's right," said Martín. "That's what got me through college."

"I even used *Pan Bimbo*. She said it's like your Wonder Bread."

Martín was so touched that he had an almost

202

uncontrollable desire
to hug her, but restrained himself.

As he took his first bite, his delight turned to surprise. These were indeed peanut butter and jelly sandwiches, but rose to heights he'd never imagined. "These are incredible!" he said, "What's in them?"

Ilhui blushed happily. "Peanut butter ground fresh in the market this morning, jelly made from guava and smoked chiles, and some very special honey that's sold only at this time of the year. I also added some banana."

"What do you mean you can't cook!" he exclaimed.

When they had finished the sandwiches and most of the wine, Martín asked if she wanted to hear the end of his story.

"Yes." She lit a cigarette, and moved to a couch in the living room not far from the huge fireplace. She shivered slightly. "It's chilly, but too late to make a fire."

"Never too late," he said. "Is it okay to use the wood under the stove?"

"Yes."

When he had a fire going, he brought the brandy bottle and two glasses and sat next to her on the couch. Pouring a little brandy into each glass, he raised his own. "Here's to peanut butter and jelly!"

"Thank you!" she laughed and took a sip.

Martín told her how he had found Pancho bleeding and near death by his adobe house and rushed him to the vet. He described returning just as the bomb exploded, killing the sheriff's deputy, and how the series of events had been so cleverly planned that, despite their suspicions, law enforcement including the FBI could do nothing.

He told her it was then that he decided he would have to leave Santa Fe or kill Glendaring. He described his confrontation with the man and his German thug at the Hilton. He concluded by relating the events since he'd been in Mexico, including killing one of his kidnappers.

Ilhui drained her brandy. "I don't know what to say, except thank you for telling me. I know how difficult it was."

Martín felt a weight lift, as if he'd returned to the surface from a deep dive. "Thanks for listening."

He was exhausted, but still highly charged, and did not want to break the mood. "Now that you've heard my story, I want to hear yours. All I know is that the genealogist said you were a half-sister to Trini, but nothing about your mother. I know it's late, but..."

She looked into the fire and then turned to face him. "It is, but I'll tell you." Then she stopped and cocked her head. "Did you hear that?"

Martín had. He thought it sounded like the type of predator call that imitates the death throes of a small animal. "Could be a rabbit," he said, "but it sounded more human to me. Maybe some Indians?"

"No. Indians never come here. They think it's, how do you say it, a bad place?"

"Is there a gun?"

"Hector has...*un escopeto*, the gun for killing birds. But it's in the city."

"A shotgun?" said Martín. "Let's just listen for a few minutes."

Several minutes passed with nothing but the wind sighing in the trees. He went to make sure the doors and windows were secure.

"A little more brandy?" he offered when he

returned.

"No, thanks." She clutched her hands tightly in her lap. "I'll tell you my story. "I never knew my mother and have only one picture of her.
She came from somewhere on the Gulf of Tehuantepec. She needed work, and Hector hired her. That was over twenty-six years ago. They were attracted to each other, and I was conceived. My mother disappeared just after I was born, and I was raised by Hector and Martha as their own daughter. How and why she left I don't know. My guess is that Abuelita told her something like, 'Raise her by yourself with no money and no job, or leave her with us to be loved and cared for by a secure family.' I don't know for sure. They won't say."

"Have you ever looked for her?" asked Martín.

"Several years ago, I took a photograph I found in an old family album—my mother was holding a tray of food in the background—and went to the Gulf. I spent three weeks going from one village to another, showing the picture and repeating her name, Marina. I guess too much time had passed, or maybe I didn't go to the right places. All I know about her is what she looked like—very much like I do now. I know I sound like a spoiled child, but I realize I'm lucky. Everyone in the family has loved me and treated me as if I were their legitimate child. And I often make mistakes, like the other night at El Pueblito."

Martín gave her a hug, perhaps holding her a moment longer than he should have. As he pulled away, she looked surprised.

Trying to cover his lapse, he said, "Don't worry, you seem to have your share of common sense. Anyway, it looks like we've finished the most difficult parts,

205

except for one important thing, which I want to discuss some other time. Please go on."

She eyed him questioningly and then poured more brandy into her glass, lit another cigarette, and said, "Yes, I'm lucky. I'm part of the Cortés family. That means I have more money to spend than most. If I want more, I can take a job or start a business, like Trini with his restaurant. Sometimes I make designs for a silversmith. In return I can afford..." She raised and twirled her forearms, showing off the stacks of silver bracelets.

She looked directly at Martín. "You said we had finished the difficult parts of our stories, except for one important item. What is it?"

Martín thought for a moment. "When Captain Rodríguez came to see me in the hospital, he said he was concerned about you. I asked him what he meant. He said you had a relationship with a man he called a terrorist: El Vengador."

Ilhui clenched her fists, her face suddenly a mask, and stood up. "I need to think about it. Maybe tomorrow before the others come... Now I should go to bed, but first I need to use the bathroom. I'll be back in a minute." She turned and went into the dining room.

Disappointed at the turn of events, Martín placed a small log on the fire. As it dropped into the bed of glowing coals, he heard a scream and seconds later a crash, then another.

By that time, he'd reached the dining room and saw Ilhui clutching something near an open door at one side of the room. She had a shovel in her hands and was staring into the tiny, unlit bathroom. He moved closer and identified the cause of the outburst: a huge rattlesnake, now mostly uncoiled but still writhing in death. It must have been five feet long with a large girth. But it would cause no more problems. Its head had been smashed into the tiled floor, and its body and rattled tail twitched, making a sound like dry leaves in the wind.

"Are you all right?" he said, looking at her carefully. "Did it strike you?"

"It tried," she said matter-of-factly and motioned with the shovel at a vent at the base of the outside wall. The cover was missing.

"Good work!" he said. "I don't think I know another woman who would have done what you did."

"I'm part Indian."

"I understand. But don't forget I come from Santa Fe, where there are probably more full-blooded Indians than in most of Mexico."

"That's because your founders kept the races separate, unlike ours," she snapped.

Gently prying the shovel from her fingers, he kissed her on the cheek and said, "Could that have anything to do with what we're going to discuss tomorrow?"

The blood drained from her face, but she managed a smile. "Perhaps. Good night."

As she turned, Martín asked, "Could there be more snakes?"

"I don't think so," she replied. "That's the only place I didn't clean."

Not wanting to leave things on that note, Martín said. "I've been meaning to compliment you on your English. It's excellent. Where did you learn it?"

Some of the color returned to her face. "Thank you. I studied English in school. Then for several years I taught Spanish at the *Instituto Cultural*. Most of the students were college girls from the United States, about my age, and it was good practice. We were supposed to speak only Spanish, but I always used some English, especially when we went out together."

She went upstairs, and Martín sat by the dying fire listening intently. Hearing nothing unusual he went up to his room.

He lit the oil lamp, and in spite of Ilhui's confidence he looked carefully under the bed. His experience with rattlesnakes reminded him that where there is one there are usually more. Reassured, he turned off the lamp and lay down.

It was cold, and he pulled the coarse blanket to his chin.

OAXACA

Martín scooped the dead snake into the shovel and tossed it into the grove of trees early the next morning. Near where it landed, he spotted footprints clearly defined in the rain-dampened earth. He held his own size ten next to one of them and guessed it was a size nine. He wondered if they might explain the noise they heard last night.

Back in the kitchen, he found Ilhui in her low-cut jeans and another black T-shirt, boiling water for coffee. When he described the footprints, she said, "Even though no one outside the family knows the treasure exists, there are rumors and sometimes people come looking for it. Hector usually fires his gun into the trees and they run away."

Martín felt suddenly queasy as he recalled his near death in the Mexico City landfill but quickly dismissed any connection with the footprints, convinced he had long ago disappeared from Colin Glendaring's radar.

"It may not be proper to ask, but does the treasure consists of emeralds like the ones Hector showed us the other day and perhaps gold and other valuables?"

She arched sculpted eyebrows. "Proper? You saw Abuelita authorize Hector to show you the stones. She must be thinking of making you *un guardián de la fortuna*. Before her, it was always a man in the family who could carry on the name. She made Hector a *guardián* many years ago, and he produced me and Trini. She knows that I can't pass on the name and Trini's unlikely to. As for the treasure, I really don't know any more about it than you."

He nodded. "The word *guardián*, what does it really

mean in this situation?"

"You would know where the treasure is, so that if anything happens to the senior *guardianes*—Abuelita and Hector—you could find it." Without changing her expression, she added, "I suppose it also means that you have an obligation to carry on the family name."

"I'm flattered," said Martín, as he filed her last statement away for further consideration. "But she—none of you—know me well enough for that kind of trust."

Ilhui shook her head impatiently. "No one knows how Abuelita thinks. You still don't know how she knew you were coming, do you? Never underestimate her, and don't bother trying to understand her. Now, I've thought about what we discussed last night, and we need to talk. The others arrive this afternoon, so let's go for a walk. I'll bring the leftover sandwiches if you'll carry some water."

The prospect of learning something significant about her excited Martín. When they were outside, he glanced at the grove of trees and up at the towering mountain. "How big is the property?"

"I'm not sure, but it includes the entire mountain, so it's many hectares." She glanced upward behind the house and through the trees to where, above a short cliff, dense brush and huge rocks rose steeply into another cloudless blue sky. "It's rough, and there's a fence on top of that cliff so we always stay on this side."

He followed her through the trees to the cliff. As they turned left, he had the uncomfortable feeling of being watched. He looked around several times, scanned for footprints but saw nothing. After skirting the mountain for ten minutes, they arrived at a huge shelf of nearly flat rock that overlooked the valley below. Martín still felt the eerie presence of unseen eyes but decided to ignore it, at least for the moment. They sat, legs dangling over a twenty-foot drop, and he cast his eyes over the far-off terraced fields, hoping that at least some of his questions were about to be answered. He said, "It's so beautiful and still so wild, in spite of the efforts to tame it over many centuries."

She gave a faint-hearted smile. "I guess you're right; it seems so familiar to me. Now, shall I begin?"

He nodded, his heart beating like a snare drum.

While lighting a cigarette, she cleared her throat and turned to face him. "I don't think I'm much different from other people; my beliefs come from my experiences. I told you that twenty-six years ago the family hired my mother as a servant. She came to Oaxaca from the Gulf. She had no money and knew nobody, but eventually Abuelita hired her to do housework. A common story, so far. Before long she had an affair with Hector. Still nothing unusual. But after I was born, she was denied me and I her. She simply disappeared. Why? No one will say. But as I mentioned last night,
I think it was because she was inconvenient and the family was in a position of power. Again, I asked myself the question: *Why?*"

She began to speak faster, her words a torrent, like snowmelt in spring. "The answer is because they had money. The fact that it came from the Conqueror, who left some of his stolen wealth buried somewhere, makes no difference. What is important is that it existed. The lesson for me is that power comes from money; its source doesn't matter, and those without it will always be treated unequally and often badly."

In spite of her size, she seemed suddenly small and vulnerable. Martín touched her hand. "That's a reasonable conclusion. Under the circumstances it would be difficult for you to think otherwise, but what does it have to do with this terrorist?"

She ran her hands along the top of her thighs as if to smooth the material of her jeans. "It was important that you first know a little about me, and then maybe you'll understand."

She stared at him. "You've walked the streets of Oaxaca and know that most of the people are poor. That doesn't mean they're less happy than rich people. They laugh just as often, perhaps more, because they've learned to enjoy what little they have. The problem is, they have no choice, no power, not even a little." She stubbed out her cigarette and put the butt in the pocket of her jeans.

"Just a moment," said Martín, taking a sip of water and offering it to her. She took some and handed it back. "I haven't followed the news in Mexico closely, but don't the recent elections prove that the people have at least some power?"

"Of course," she snapped. "But it took decades of corruption and mistreatment before anything happened. An abused dog would never have taken so long to turn on its owner. One thing I've learned is that democracy never works unless the people are educated. Only then can they understand that opportunity is available and how to use it. But education and opportunity is still not a priority. Good education is mostly for the rich. The single opportunity for the poor is to go to the United States and wash dishes or pick grapes. The one percent of

212

people in Mexico that have almost all the money and power are interested only in keeping those things. They'll do anything
to prevent competition for what they have and to keep the cost of labor cheap." Her eyes narrowed. "No, I'm not a communist! I can see that's what you think. Communism just creates another ruling class, but with less prosperity to go around. I want the entire country to be educated so that membership in the ruling class is based on achievement instead of some inherited privilege that no one else can have."

"I...," he began. She clenched her fists so tightly her knuckles turned white and shouted, "Let me finish! About a year ago, I discussed these things with a friend. She's a professor at the University and also taught at the Cultural Institute during the summer. She said she admired my passion and told me about a man who is doing something about it: organizing peasants. I told her I wanted to help. She invited me to a meeting, and I agreed to come." Ilhui flashed a quick smile. "See, I'm telling you!"

Her cheeks glowed and Martín, despite his confusion, decided she was the most beautiful woman he'd ever seen. Again, he patted her hand.

Smiling with pleasure at the gesture, she continued. "The meeting was in a room behind one of the bars in El Pueblito. El Vengador told us that his father was found shot to death a week after the massacre in Tlatelolco plaza in 1968 where killers working for the President dressed in army uniforms. They wore one white glove to identify them and murdered over three hundred students to silence their legitimate protests. Two soldiers were killed because they were so stupid they shot each other. Although it was obvious what happened, El Vengador's father and several hundred students were accused of killing them. Many of the students were later killed or just disappeared." She snapped her fingers with finality.

"El Vengador is the only name I know, and don't ask me who he really is. What I do know is that he grew up hating the government. He's organizing peasants, the way Subcomandante Marcos did in Chiapas. He asked us to help by supplying information—printing notices, things like that. Nothing dangerous, nothing violent. I said yes, even though I didn't agree with what I'd heard of his methods: the kind of violent guerrilla tactics that are never successful for long. That's why Raul calls him a terrorist. Since then, I've been with him several times and done a few things to help...until recently."

"What happened?" asked Martín, wondering what she meant by "been with him."

"You probably haven't heard—the government conceals the news—but there've been a lot of killings in remote villages in addition to those committed by the drug cartels: politicians connected to the government and some soldiers that were sent to investigate. El Vengador was responsible for those, and that was wrong, so I refused to continue working with him. But he is very persuasive. He's convincing when he talks about justice, but he's also dangerous, and his violence frightened me. Two weeks ago, he told me to think about my decision very carefully and asked me to reconsider. The way he said it, I was sure it was a threat."

Martín thought carefully. This was a situation he wanted to handle well. "Is there any possibility El Vengador could be responsible for that noise last night or the footprints?"

"I still haven't given him an answer, and I don't think he knows about this place."

"If you truly believe what he's doing is wrong and that he's
threatening you, isn't one option to make certain he can't hurt you or anyone else?"

"I'm listening," she said, obviously skeptical.

"Raul Rodríguez, the army captain, told me it was his job to find and capture terrorists, and that he believes you are somehow connected with this one. He asked me to intercede with you. Why don't you tell him what you've just told me and let him take it from there?"

Ilhui laughed harshly. "Of course, it sounds that easy to you. I provide the evidence and location. Raul captures El Vengador and kills him or puts him in prison. In your country, under the same circumstances, you could probably do that. But Mexico isn't like that. I have no idea who El Vengador or his benefactors bribe—some judges, maybe the governor of Oaxaca. Maybe even Raul's commanding officer. Because of those very real possibilities, there's no guarantee that anyone would do anything—except kill me! I do know there's a lot of money involved, and because of that I'm as powerless as the poorest *campesino*. It all comes back to money!"

Deflated as he realized he'd miscalculated, at least in Ilhui's eyes, Martín raised his hands in frustration. "Then what do you suggest?"

She lit another cigarette and expelled a thin stream of smoke. "In Mexico we have to solve our own problems. We can't trust the government. Maybe if you help me, we can show this man I'm not just a helpless woman, that I'm not alone in the world and actually have some power."

Although he could not see how he could help and still thought it sensible to contact Rodríguez, he said, "Ilhui, I'll do whatever needs to be done. You can't live in fear; I know that from my own experience."

"Perhaps I should follow your example and go to the United States?"

His smile evaporated and he rounded on her. "You think I came here to run away from my problems!" He lowered his voice. "I'm disappointed if that's what you think. I came here to keep myself from doing something stupid, to find my relatives, and come up with a solution. When the time's right, I'll return and do what's necessary."

Ilhui threw her arms around him. "I didn't mean anything like that. It was a stupid thing to say. Forgive me!" She burst into tears. Then pulling back she looked pleadingly into his eyes. "Please, Martín, I've just found you, and..." She closed her eyes and kissed him hard on the lips.

Martín was so surprised he nearly fell off the rock. Trying to recover, he put his palms beside him on the rough surface and stared at her. She slowly removed her arms from around his neck and returned his gaze, her anguish obvious. "I mean it, Martín, I'm sorry. I didn't think, which is the reason I have so many problems." Again, she burst into tears.

Martín cleared his throat, now desperate to smooth things over. "The truth is that I'm so anxious for you to like me that when you said what you did, I took it the wrong way, lost my temper in frustration. I'm sorry. It wasn't your fault. Also, perhaps I'm not entirely at peace with how I've handled my own situation."

She cocked an eyebrow and gave a shy smile. "Now that we're both sorry, maybe we should eat and then make sure the house is ready."

Martín felt he'd been close to breaking through her defenses—his own had certainly been demolished—and wanted to continue the conversation, to find out how she thought he could help her. However, he intuited that another barrier had surfaced and that he'd best tread carefully.

As they shared the remaining sandwiches, he could not take his mind from the taste and feel of Ilhui's lips and the question marks that still surrounded her, particularly regarding her relationship with El Vengador. He had to know more about her. "Twice you've promised to tell me about your work."

"I shall. Even better, I'll show you when we're back in the city."

Another dead end? I'd better let it go.

On the way back to the house, they had just stepped from the rocky base of the mountain onto a small trail through the trees when Martín jerked to a halt. "Look," he said, pointing to footprints in the still soft soil. "They're bigger than the others. I'm pretty sure they weren't here when we came. I had a feeling we were being watched."

Ilhui seemed preoccupied. "Better show them to Hector."

OAXACA

So far, Martín considered Hector and Martha mild-mannered and always ready with a kind word and hug, like some '50s sitcom couple. Not now. That afternoon when they got out of their white Jeep Cherokee, Hector led a huge German shepherd into the house. Martha's face was drawn, and Abuelita all business, the dreamy otherworldliness gone.

Ilhui sensed the change. "Where did you get the dog? Is something wrong?"

"Not yet," Abuelita replied. "But it will be. How serious, I don't know, but we have to prepare for the worst. The dog has special training."

"Martín," said Ilhui, "tell them about the noise last night and the footprints."

After Martín did so, Hector motioned him outside. He popped the back of the Jeep and pulled out a pump-action shotgun. "Show me," he said, "but first meet Dragón."

Stepping to the dog, Martín gingerly held out his right hand, palm down. The hyper-alert animal sniffed him carefully, like a king's food taster. After a few moments of consideration, the dog gave him a friendly push to the leg with his nose.

"Let's go," said Hector. "This sort of thing has happened before, but this time Abuelita predicts that something terrible will happen. She's never been wrong."

Martín showed Hector both sets of tracks, and he directed the dog's attention to the most recent ones. Hector released Dragón from the leash and gave him a command. The dog made ever widening circles around the tracks and took off at a smooth, ground-covering trot through the trees, heading up toward the heavy brush at the base of the mountain. Martín and Hector scrambled after him as quickly as they could, making considerably more noise.

In less than a minute they heard two sharp barks followed by a scream. Moments later, Hector and Martín plowed through the thick brush and found a slender young man pressed against the trunk of a tree, frozen in place, clutching his bleeding forearm. The dog stared up at him menacingly.

Hector said, "The dog is trained to attack him if he moves." He aimed the shotgun at the man and gave the dog another command. It sat down, but kept its eyes fixed on the man.

"Who are you; what are you doing here?" demanded Hector, the kindly father figure a distant memory.

"Please," whimpered the man, whose wispy mustache and receding chin made him resemble a gangly, two-legged rodent. "I meant no harm. I'll never come back."

"Tell us why you're here," snarled Hector, "or you'll never return anywhere."

"Please, *señor*, pleaded the young man. I heard there was a treasure hidden on the property. I was looking for it."

"You're a fool," said Hector. "What treasure this family has is in a bank. Now, we know you're a thief. How do we know you're not something else, maybe one of those guerrillas?"

Martín detected a flash of surprise in the man's eyes. "No, *señor*. I only wanted to find the treasure and return after you left."

"Only a fool would leave anything of value unprotected for someone like you to steal," snapped Hector. "Do we look like fools? Where's your *compadre*, the one you signaled last night?"

"Please, *señor*. I apologize. I meant no harm. My friend left."

"Meant no harm! You meant to take something that doesn't belong to you; that's called stealing. The fact that it doesn't exist is no excuse. Listen carefully! You can go, but if you ever come back your bones will stay here forever. I won't have scum like you putting my family in danger. *¿Me entiendes?*"

"*Sí, señor. Nunca volveré.* I'll never return."

Hector leashed the dog, and they followed the intruder to the wall where a heavy tarp covered the broken glass. They watched him climb over and disappear down the dirt track, wrapping his injured arm in his torn shirt.

When Martín and Hector returned to the house, they told no one what had happened. Abuelita nodded as if she already knew, Trini stood in the kitchen preparing a meal, and Ilhui and Martha had gone to their rooms. Martín decided to do the same.

Lying on his bed, he considered El Vengador's threat to Ilhui. *Could be serious.* Then realizing he didn't know enough about Mexico to suggest a practical solution, he clenched his jaw in frustration.

Learning he had relatives after losing his own had aroused deep feelings. The existence of the treasure somehow validated and compressed the relationship begun by the Conqueror's illegitimate son, Martín, not too far from five hundred years ago. He decided that he could always decline whatever was offered and leave. Then he shook his head as he admitted the truth. *Family and treasure are important, but when Ilhui's added to the mix, I'm helpless!*

CORTÉS FINCA

As if by prior agreement, after dinner Martín and Abuelita were left alone in the dining room, still seated across from each other.

"Martín," the old lady began. "You've seen a little of the treasure, and this afternoon you've seen something of what it can cause. The family has had it for nearly five hundred years. It's grown smaller, but will still be sufficient for several more generations. With the temptations involved, it's a miracle it exists at all. It does so only because of the integrity of the people who have taken care of it. We call them *guardianes*. Except where necessary—as in my case, because Hector was too young—the *guardián* is always a male so that both the treasure and the family name will continue."

She rose from the table and he saw she had on dark pants, the first time she'd not worn a skirt or dress. She bent, placed her hands on the table, and gazed into his eyes. "I now realize that your coming, which was foretold to me, means danger is approaching."

She raised a warning finger. "Don't ask me how I know. I'm never wrong about these things. The treasure and the family must be protected. Hector is already a *guardián*, but he and Martha will have no more children. Trini has all the qualifications except an interest in producing a family. Your coming signals both the approaching threat and an opportunity. You're a young man, intelligent with good judgment, and you'll want a family. Most importantly, you're honest. Before you tell me you can't make any commitments—that you might decide to leave tomorrow—let me tell you that the only pledge you

222

need to make is to never reveal the location of the treasure, no matter the circumstances."

Martín made his decision with the same speed he had decided to come to Mexico. "That I can promise you. But before I agree, I must know how Trini and Hector feel about including me in this, or do they even know?"

"Both agree."

"Then so do I."

"*Muy bien*! Now I have something to show you, and I'm not sure how much time we have left. We'll take the dog." She picked up a flashlight and motioned for him to follow.

Hector met them at the door and handed Dragón's leash to Martín. No words were spoken, but Hector smiled and patted Martín's arm. The dog rubbed his muzzle on Martín's leg and looked up at him expectantly.

The night was moonless with only a dusting of starlight penetrating the clouds. Martín followed Abuelita through the trees and then to the left, the way he and Ilhui had gone that morning. He had no idea how old she was—at least seventy-five, maybe eighty, he guessed—but she moved with a wiry energy that made her seem much younger. As they came to the rock shelf where he'd sat with Ilhui, she turned abruptly to the right and walked slowly up to the brush-covered cliff at the base of the mountain. "*Ven aca*, come here," she whispered.

Straining to see in the dark, Martín watched while she lifted a rock the size of a small melon from the side of the cliff, revealing a dark hole. She placed the rock on the ground and took the leash from him. "You'll find a key," she whispered. "Take it out and put it in your pocket."

His fingers wrapped around a piece of metal the size of a pencil
and slipped it into his jeans. "Now reach to the back," she said. "You'll find another piece of iron. Turn it to the right and then step back."

Finding it, he did so. It turned easily and he heard a grating click. Withdrawing his hand, he waited for further instructions. She patted a protruding rock at shoulder level and said, "Grab this and pull carefully back to open the door."

At first nothing happened, but then the wall began to move. Dirt and pebbles scattered as the rocky face opened just far enough to allow entry into a very dark space. "This will get us past the cliff and under the thick brush. Follow us inside and close the door."

When that was done, the flashlight illuminated a cave at the far end of which was a tall, stone stairway leading to the ceiling.

"Climb to the top, and push the piece of iron you will find above you up and to the left."

Martín glanced back to see the old woman and dog watching him expectantly, and for a moment he felt like a character in a Harrison Ford adventure movie. Looking upward, he saw that he needed to ascend only a few feet before he could touch the roof. He stepped high enough to allow himself leverage and pushed upward on the two-foot diameter iron disk he found. Like the door, it stuck at first and then broke free, releasing a small cascade of dirt onto his head and shoulders. With some effort, he managed to shift it all the way to the left, leaving a hole through which fresh air immediately poured in, freshening the musty air in the cave.

Martín knelt beside the uncovered hole and whispered, "Dragón." The dog scrambled up and out. Then he reached down and helped Abuelita through the opening. As he brushed off the dirt and oriented himself, he guessed they were on the other side of the thick brush and stone barrier at the base of the mountain.

Abuelita took the leash and began to pick her way upward over the rocks. After a few minutes they came to a crude pathway, and she began to climb, twisting and turning up the mountain. They stopped to rest only once. Panting and sweating with the exertion, Martin was amazed at the old lady's stamina; she seemed to be part mountain goat. They had climbed for thirty minutes when Abuelita suddenly disappeared over the crest. Martín followed and found himself on a flat-topped mesa, where they moved through shadowy boulders toward a tall formation near the other side of the mesa. When they reached it, Martín saw that it was solid rock. At that point, Dragón began a low-pitched whine and pushed his body against Martín's leg.

"What's that mean?" Martín looked quickly around but saw little in the darkness.

"I don't know. When he senses danger, he's supposed to growl. But let's hurry." Abuelita pulled Martín's hand to the wall of stone and whispered, "Remove this rock and you'll find the lock. Put in the key and turn it to the right."

Martín carefully removed the football-sized stone, felt inside, and found the keyhole. After a few fumbles, he inserted the key and turned it. At first it resisted and then gave way, producing a noticeable click.

"Grasp the side and pull, just like the door below,"

she said.

A door about two feet wide and five feet high swung open, causing another rain of pebbles and dirt. When they were inside, Abuelita pulled the door closed behind them and turned on her light. The interior of the cave was about twenty feet wide and went back nearly forty feet into the rock. As the old lady swung the beam of the flashlight, Martín saw stacks of containers lined along the walls of the last six feet. As they drew near, he observed that about a third of them consisted of wooden crates filled with flattened paper and a few wooden casks of glittering coins that could be gold or silver. He saw nothing that looked like emeralds.

"Here it is," she said. "Can you find it again?"

"Yes," he said. He did not voice his surprise at how relatively little there seemed to be. Certainly, if the coins were gold, there was enough for a good-sized family to live a very comfortable lifetime, maybe two or three of them.

As if reading his thoughts, she said, "Don't be deceived. The treasure is far greater than it appears."

Dragón had continued his soft whine. Hackles now raised, he looked back and forth from Martín to Abuelita. Abuelita watched him a moment. "This is where Cortés's men were trapped and died of thirst as they brought the treasure to Oaxaca. I think that's what he senses." She paused and then shrugged. "Anyway, the Conqueror saw no reason to move it and commissioned the door when he decided to build the house. Over the years, the family added the entry below and modernized the doors and locks. During the early years, anyone who came near was killed. In Indian legends this is forbidden land. They never trespass. We try to use secrecy, but as you've seen, sometimes force is necessary. Now let's go."

When they were about twenty paces from the cave, Dragón stopped whining and otherwise returned to normal. They went back to the house, reversing the procedures. As they descended, Abuelita paid particular attention to the dog, but it gave no further sign that it sensed anything amiss.

The next two days passed without incident. Ilhui seemed preoccupied and avoided Martín. Abuelita sat for hours in a lawn chair behind the house, seemingly lost in her own world. Trini told Martín that he had temporarily closed his restaurant. "Why not, I'm the only one who can make the *mole*, and the customers will return." He appeared to be at peace with Martín's new status in the family.

In one respect, Martín shared that peace. After feeling adrift for so many months, he again felt part of something vital, like an unemployed man who suddenly finds a job. But in another way, the ambiguity of the situation made him uneasy. He lacked a real understanding of the family, especially of Ilhui. She was the most exotically beautiful woman he had ever known. She was intelligent and obviously had depth, but she had allowed him to peek just below the surface, then no further. The potential was so intriguing that he would be a fool not to proceed.

On Sunday afternoon they packed the cars and returned to the city in a caravan of two. Martín was disappointed when Trini decided to ride in the VW with Ilhui, and politeness dictated he take the young man's place in the Cherokee with the rest of the family.

That night in bed, he tossed and turned as his mind

whirled with unanswered questions. He was finally able to drift off, only after the details for a painting that had apparently been forming in his subconscious suddenly manifested themselves. The knowledge that he was once again open to inspiration acted like a sedative, and he fell into a deep, dreamless sleep.

OAXACA

The next morning Martín walked downstairs from his room in the Oaxaca house to find Ilhui in the living room, wearing her usual jeans and T-shirt. "A walk before breakfast?" she asked.

Relieved at her apparent mood change, he followed her out to the street. "Would it spoil a surprise if you told me where we're going?"

"Yes." She patted his cheek. "Actually, there are two surprises."

"Before we go," he said, "when we last spoke you suggested that maybe I could help with your problem, but you never said how."

"I've decided to see what happens next. I'll let you know. Now please don't spoil my surprises!"

They walked two blocks, turned left, and continued uphill for six more blocks to where the road dead-ended at a cross street at the base of a hill, lined with nicely kept two-story stucco homes. Ilhui ducked into a narrow alley that zigzagged up between them. After a hundred yards, the alley ran into a street on which sat a row of grand homes, nestled into the steep hillside. Ilhui entered the gate to the nearest one and began climbing the stairs leading to the entry. As he followed, Martín could not help focusing on the rhythmic sway of her jeans.

At the top of the stairs, she stopped before a set of double doors, and turned to him. "After I realized the mistake I made with El Vengador, I became angry and desperate to do something that couldn't possibly be wrong. I had read about an organization that helps poor children. Some of them have only one parent and some are orphans. The ones with parents are brought here so volunteers can help them with their lessons while their parents work. The orphans live in houses with volunteer families. Volunteers help with everything from cleaning and cooking to schoolwork. That's mostly what I do."

Martín shook his head. "Why the secrecy?"

Ilhui's eyes flashed with resentment. "Abuelita doesn't approve of charity. She says it's wasteful." She turned to the doors and twice rapped the iron knocker.

When the door opened, a stern-looking old woman in a starched white nun's uniform looked out at them. Ilhui introduced her as Sister Beatriz, and the woman's face creased into a smile. Martín and Ilhui followed her into a large living area.

As if triggering an alarm, boisterous shouts of "Looie, Looie, Looie" filled the air, and about fifteen children rushed toward them. It seemed that Ilhui had become the object of a game of tag, as the children, aged from about five to nine, mobbed her. Some climbed over each other to get closer, as if she'd just scored the winning touchdown at the Super Bowl.

Several times the nun barked an order. The only effect was to reduce the mood to a slightly milder hysteria. Ilhui turned to Martín and raised her voice to introduce him to the children. At the sound of his name, they clapped and shrieked. Most of them kept their distance from him except for one little girl of about eight with saucer-sized eyes. She stepped close, looked up at him, and said something he could not understand. Ilhui said, "That's Ana. She wants to know if you'll be her cousin too."

Martín smiled, patted her on the head, and said, "*Sí, ya eres mi prima!* Yes, you are now my cousin."

The little girl clapped her hands and kept her large eyes glued on Martín. Then Ilhui rattled off a few phrases that quieted the room. Turning to Martín, she said, "I told them we must leave now, and they have to be good if they want Sister Beatriz to give them the candy I brought."

As they left, Martín saw that the little girl, Ana, was about to burst into tears so he once again patted her head and told her he would visit her again soon. She nodded but seemed unconvinced.

Outside the house, Martín said, "The kids love you. What a wonderful thing you're doing. Thanks for showing me."

Her smile had never lasted so long, and she hugged his arm. "Most of them have at least one parent, but some are orphans—like your new cousin."

Understanding what it felt like to be an orphan, Martín said, "I don't know what to say."

"Then say nothing and come with me." She turned and headed down the steps.

Four blocks from the Cortés home, she stopped at the door of a shop Martín recognized. It was an art supply store, and he remembered being surprised at the depth of its inventory. His pulse began to race.

"I'll buy whatever you need," said Ilhui, "and help you carry it. The room next to yours is empty and can be your studio."

Remembering the previous night's inspiration, Martín put his arms around her and kissed her tenderly on the cheek. "First those lovely children, now this," he said. "Painting is exactly what I've wanted to do, and I'm ready."

Forty-five minutes later, after arranging his purchases on a large table in the upstairs bedroom next to his, Martín began to sketch. Suddenly, he began to panic. *Can I do it?* He held his hands out and stared at his fingers. They seemed somehow different, as if he had borrowed them from someone else. *We'll soon see.*

OAXACA

For Martín, the next week passed in a haze. At its end, he examined the completed canvass and beamed with satisfaction. He had never painted so well! He looked for Ilhui, but she wasn't home.

An hour later she came in the front door and found him pacing. "Come," he said.

When they stopped by the door to his little studio, Illhui's hands wound tensely together, as if she were kneading dough. Opening the door, he stood aside to reveal the painting, which sat on a small table propped against the white wall. She put her hand to her mouth and then stepped nearer, moving around to view the painting from all angles. It depicted the home's courtyard. On the pathway was the familiar lizard and farther back, seated at a table by the green-tiled fountain, sat Abuelita, dressed all in black. Her eyes seemed to be everywhere and nowhere, like a fortune teller viewed from the other side of a crystal ball, and her lips formed a Mona Lisa smile.

"Ahi!" exclaimed Ilhui, "you've done it! That's Oaxaca, the beauty, mystery, and magic." She threw her arms around him. "Simply fantastic! I don't know what else to say."

Martín looked into her eyes "I'm just as surprised as you are. I've never been able to express myself so well. Maybe it's because I've never felt so strongly about something. I..."

"Surprised? Not me. I knew you could do it."

They stared at each other for a few moments, and then he kissed her on the lips. She kissed him back, her tongue probing his. Her strong body began to melt into him but suddenly stiffened. Quietly she stepped back and continued as if nothing had happened. "Martín, this is fabulous. A friend of mine owns the best gallery in town; you must let me show it to her."

"Okay, but we better wait for one or two more. He reached for her again, but she stayed just out of range. "Is something wrong?" he asked. "Anything new from El Vengador?"

"No, nothing. Please be patient with me."

OAXACA

Desperate not to lose what he he'd found with his first painting, Martín worked constantly for the next two weeks. Now convinced that his work had reached a much higher level, he felt the need for a break and longed for Ilhui, who had remained withdrawn since their kiss.

After supper, he said to her, "Please forgive me, but can we finally talk about your situation? And afterwards, I'd like to show you what I've done."

"Yes," she said, looking pleased. "Let's go out; there's a band from Guadalajara playing outside the cathedral." Her smile and expression sent an electric-like pulse through him.

The area surrounding the cathedral was packed, and they were constantly jostled by the crowd, excited to hear one of Mexico's premier mariachi groups. Martín bought ice cream cones, and they grabbed a seat on a suddenly vacant bench just as the band took a break.

Trying to banish the guilt he felt at his recent self-absorption, Martín said, "Has anything happened with El Vengador?"

"Nothing, and I hope that continues. Let's talk about something else. Are you pleased with your work?" Her bracelets jingled as she licked her cone.

"I'm thrilled with it, but I thought discussing your problem is one of the reasons we came here?" When she didn't respond, he shrugged and said, "I've finished another painting."

"Then let's go see it."

As they stood, Martín's eyes met those of a well-built young man with a thin mustache on the other side of the plaza. He had been watching them, but at Martín's gaze he turned and melted into the crowd.

Martín grabbed Ilhui by the arm. "I just caught someone watching us." He described the man. "I haven't been out much, but I've seen him before. In fact, the last time I left the house for a walk. I assumed he was a student killing time between classes, but now…"

Ilhui arched her eyebrows. "And you're sure he was looking at you?"

Martín laughed. "When you put it that way…if I worried every time a man stared at you… Maybe he *is* a student." Nevertheless, Martín felt unsettled and glanced over his shoulder several times on the way home.

As they walked into the house, they found Hector in the entry hall. "*Bueno!*" he exclaimed to Martín, sounding relieved. "You have a telephone call."

As he followed Hector into the living room, Martín wondered who it could be. No one knew he was here, not even his lawyer and closet friend, Herb Gonzalez.

Fearing the worst, he picked up the phone and said, "Hello, this is Martín Cortés."

"Mr. Cortés, Felipe Gallardo, the genealogist, speaking. I hope you'll forgive me for disturbing you, but I have information that you should know."

"Yes, Dr. Gallardo, no bother at all." Martín felt relieved.

"When we met," began Gallardo, "you seemed concerned with security, so I thought I should contact you. I just spoke with my friend in the Bureau of Records in Oaxaca. Another genealogist looking for information on your family contacted him. I thought you would like to know."

Suddenly apprehensive, Martín asked, "Any idea who's making the inquiry?"

"The man is a good friend, so I asked him. He didn't want to tell me but owed me a favor. His client is an American named Colin Glendaring."

MITLA, OAXACA

Inside the walled compound of a recently restored nineteenth-century hacienda, El Vengador stepped out of a taxi. The estate, leased by Colin Glendaring, lay twenty-four miles south of Oaxaca City and about four miles north of the famous ruins at Mitla. The slender guerrilla leader, who looked to be in his forties, had a handsome face framed by a mass of wavy black hair. On it he wore a mustache that ended just above a short beard. Had he worn a beret, he could easily have been mistaken for Che Guevara, a resemblance some of his followers had accused him of cultivating—but never to his face. A petite blond girl followed him out onto the cobblestone drive. A well-used bomber jacket swallowed her anorexic body, and the luminous eyes of a renaissance angel dominated her exquisite chalk-white face.

Speaking in French, El Vengador said, "Remember, Karin, I'll meet this man alone."

"I understand," she replied in the same language.

At the entry, a blond man with a decided limp greeted them in German-accented English. "Follow me."

El Vengador motioned the girl into the adjoining living room and followed the blond man up a wide staircase. At the end of a hall flanked by antique doors, the German waved him into a spacious study.

From behind a highly polished marquetry desk, Colin Glendaring rose to his feet. His lanky frame and uncommonly wide shoulders accentuated his height. His shoulder-length graying hair was pulled into a ponytail, secured by a turquoise-studded silver clasp. As he extended a large, bony hand, his craggy features creased into a smile, but no sign of pleasure reached his eyes.

"Welcome," he said. "The last time we convened, you looked like Che Guevara. Now you look like a Frenchman trying to look like Che Guevara. And I understand you now call yourself El Vengador! You Mexicans are certainly adept at nicknames."

The man who some called a terrorist smiled thinly. "No one pays attention to French tourists as long as they don't complain too loudly about the wine. It's a pleasure to do business with you again, but we must be quick."

"My sentiments exactly; we needn't even be seated. The relics?"

"If the payment is in order, they'll be delivered to you tomorrow, hidden in a produce truck with the pistols."

Glendaring retrieved a bulky manilla envelope from his desk and handed it over. "Thirty thousand dollars in pesos. You may count it."

"I will—before the delivery."

"Did you get the silencers?"

"Don't be ridiculous! This isn't the United States. Large-caliber pistols are difficult enough, particularly on short notice, except for the cartels."

"And the other matter?"

"The Cortés family," said El Vengador, confirming his decision not to tell Glendaring of his own interest in the subject. "The American, Martín, arrived several weeks ago. He's done nothing of interest. At first sightseeing, and more recently he stays in the house." El Vengador had also decided not to describe how one of his men had been surprised at the Cortés *finca* by the dog.

"You have certainly outperformed the genealogist I hired," chuckled Glendaring. "All I have from him is the location of the family home in Oaxaca City. You will continue surveillance?"

The younger man smiled. "We did not discuss financial arrangements."

Glendaring picked up a sealed business envelope and passed it over. "This should be satisfactory."

"If you are correct, the reports will continue. Now, I think this concludes our business. *Señor* Glendaring, you know how to reach me. Next time we'll meet on my terms."

The men shook hands and nodded to each other, their eyes remaining locked like martial artists bowing after a match.

As the man and the girl left, Glendaring said to Gabel Rausch, "Please dispatch Dennis and Luke to report on what is happening at the Cortés home. In such matters, a second opinion is always desirable. But they must be circumspect—and allowed no drugs!"

Outside in the hacienda's courtyard, El Vengador mounted a mud-spattered dirtbike that had been left there earlier in the day by one of his men. As he kicked it into life, Karin wrapped her arms around his waist and snuggled into his back. "Did it go well?" she asked.

"Yes," came the curt reply. His attention was now focused entirely on the arrangements for his upcoming meeting with the two Iranians.

OAXACA

After hanging up the phone, Martín tried to compose himself. The genealogist's mention of Colin Glendaring's interest in the Cortés family confirmed the man's continuing interest in removing him. Not to mention the possibility that the former archeologist had heard about the treasure and had it in his sights. He might even have sent the trespassers to the *finca*. Worst of all was the danger to Martín's newly discovered family.

After Martín's confrontation with Glendaring and his German thug just before he left Santa Fe, he'd relished making a commitment in front of his enemy. By disabling the German, he had also demonstrated that his threats had teeth. And, truth be told, he'd enjoyed a scrap of revenge. He had assumed Glendaring would eventually celebrate his departure and go on to more important things.

How foolish! What could be more urgent than eliminating someone who had sworn to destroy you, someone who had just demonstrated the capability to do so?! As for the treasure, Glendaring had a sample in the form of the Cortés family emerald and codices taken from his safe deposit box, and he surely suspected the existence of more of the same.

When Martín took the call, Hector and Ilhui stood next to him. Now, Martha and Abuelita joined them.

"It's bad news," said Abuelita.

"Yes," said Martín. "Please, everyone sit down."

After explaining the situation, he said, "If I'd even suspected this could happen, I would never have come. Now you are all in danger."

"Don't be silly," snapped Abuelita. "That man would have followed the treasure to us no matter what you did. At least now we're warned."

Although Trini usually stayed on the sidelines, he chimed in.

"Martín, we live better than most because of the treasure. But nothing's free. We just have to ensure that we pay as low a price as possible."

Resuming her role as family leader, Abuelita said, "We could leave for a while, but that would only postpone the inevitable. Our individual safety is important, but the treasure and the continuation of the family is paramount. We'll remain here and take precautions. Dragón should be left loose in the house, and the gun should be kept loaded and accessible."

"How about hiring some guards?" suggested Martín.

"No one's trustworthy," snapped Abuelita.

"I'm sure you've thought of it, but why not put at least a portion of the treasure in a bank?" asked Martín.

Abuelita shook her head. "Much too risky. Because of its origin, the government would love to claim it's national patrimony and confiscate it."

"What about at least getting some more guns, perhaps some pistols? We only have the shotgun."

"Too dangerous," replied Abuelita. "In Mexico, possession of such weapons carries a long jail term and could be used against us." Then she added, "It's possible that the jewel dealer, Gomez, broke confidence. Hector, call him and find out if he's spoken out of turn."

Hector found the number, dialed, and spoke for nearly five
minutes. When he hung up, he turned to the family.

"He admits that after being assured any dealings would go through him, he told a dealer in Thailand about the stones and provided our names, but no address. I'm sure they bribed him."

Abuelita shook her head in disgust. "*Así es la vida en México*. That's life in Mexico. Now see to the arrangements."

OAXACA

The Tonhamani brothers arrived in Oaxaca at noon, following a grueling trip from Tehran and fervent requests to Allah to allow them to replace the stolen emeralds before their theft was revealed by the impending inventory. As part of their cover reason for coming to Mexico, Reza had arranged to meet with a potential supporter of the Islamic Republic. After contacting El Vengador to arrange a meeting for that evening, they spent the remainder of the day napping in their room at the Hotel Presidente.

At 7:00 p.m. Parwis arose and said, "I think we have time for a meal before the meeting."

"Yes," said Reza. "Let's find a restaurant less expensive than this hotel."

"Indeed," agreed Parwis. "It would be stupid to inflate our expenses."

The hotel's concierge recommended a *taquería*, and within minutes they found it just off the plaza.

When they were seated at the counter, behind which stood a small tiled kitchen with a large pit of glowing coals, Reza said, "I did some research, and tacos are made by enclosing meat in flatbread made of corn or flour. Something familiar to us. And this word, *alambre…*" He pointed at the menu. "…means shishkabob. We should have no problem finding something appropriate."

"This here," pointed Parwis, *"tacos alambres arabes,* sounds like just the thing."

"Arab tacos, a gift from our Muslim brothers!" agreed Reza.

When the plates arrived, the brothers ate heartily,

wrapping the char-broiled chopped meat, onions, and mild chiles in the tortillas, even adding a few drops of fiery salsa. As they finished, Parwis said, "Delicious, but it didn't taste like lamb or chicken—or even beef."

"You don't suppose...," said Reza, rolling his eyes.

"*Sí, señor*," replied the waiter to Reza's question. "*Es carne de puerco.*"

"Pork!" choked Parwis.

For a moment Reza looked equally concerned but then smiled and said something in Farsi that is best translated as, "Fuck'em if they can't take a joke."

Parwis's eyes met his brother's. "Remember, we want Allah to look with favor on our endeavor. Not a good beginning."

Reza shook his head. "Parwis, pork became unclean when it *was*; that situation no longer exists, and Allah knows it!"

An hour and a half later, Reza and Parwis's rented Toyota crept along highway190, halfway to Mitla. "That must be it," exclaimed Parwis.

To their right sat a dilapidated stucco building with a faded sign that said, *Mezcal La Guadalupana*. As instructed, Reza pulled the car behind the unlit building and up to a porch covered with a thatched roof. The figure sitting at a table under the awning was unrecognizable in the dim light.

They approached with caution, but after introductions were made, the three men sat at the table. Reza said in English, "Thank you for coming. I know it's dangerous."

El Vengador remained silent.

Reza continued. "As you know, we wish to explore mutual assistance. Our goals are much the same: destruction of the western ruling classes. We ask that you do nothing you would not already be doing. In return we offer financial support."

"I think I understand," said El Vengador. "But could you be more specific?"

"Of course," replied Reza. "I understand your name means vengeance. But I assume you are also seeking change, and what you've already done shows you have the courage to use force. I know you received training in Libya and are skilled at everything from explosives to unconventional warfare. We're prepared to provide you with $5,000 each month. The money will come from our embassy in Mexico City. If you're successful, that amount will be increased, perhaps substantially. From time to time, additional payments may be made for certain mutually agreeable favors."

"That's generous," replied El Vengador, suppressing his impulse to bargain.

"Good," said Reza. "Now, in regard to additional payments, I'm authorized to offer you $2,000 for your assistance in a small but extremely important matter."

El Vengador again said nothing.

"Specifically," continued Reza, "we have business with a family in Oaxaca. It's an old family, named Cortés. We want to speak with Hector Cortés. We have his telephone number, but we need his address, and some background information."

Trying to conceal his surprise, El Vengador said, "Cortés is a common name, as is Hector."

"As I said," replied Reza, "they're an old family. That should help."

"I'll do what I can and call you tomorrow at your hotel."

Reza said, "We're grateful for your help." He handed over an envelope. "Here is the first payment, plus one-

246

half for the special situation."

Unable to contain himself, El Vengador, said. "Please consider one thing you could do to further our mutual cause."

"Yes," said Reza, taking his turn at being noncommittal.

"I may have need of some plastique, enough to fill a briefcase."

Reza pondered a moment. "That may be possible. I'll let you know tomorrow after we receive your report."

After the Iranians left, El Vengador remained seated at the table. An undefined nagging doubt had plagued him for several weeks, but in spite of this he smiled. *Glendaring and the Iranians are both interested in the Cortés family. They may prove even more profitable than I'd hoped.*

The next morning, he called and gave the Iranians the Cortés family's background and address. In return Reza told him to expect the explosives within a few days.

OAXACA

Martín thought the news of Glendaring's reappearance would suppress his motivation to paint, but instead it became more intense. Ilhui knocked on the door while he examined a newly stretched canvas. Through the door, she said, "Hector just received a phone call, and Abuelita wants to see you."

Moments later Martín arrived in the living room to find the rest of the family already seated.

Although they increasingly used Spanish with Martín, English was still the lingua franca for anything significant, and Abuelita began in that language. "Hector just received a call. A man claiming to be from Iran said a Thai gem dealer suggested we meet to discuss an item of 'mutual interest.' That coincided with what Gomez, the jewel dealer said. Hector invited him here at seven this evening."

She looked directly at Martín. "Of course, I'm suspicious, but probably nothing to do with this Glendaring. If these men really want emeralds, we can use the money, especially now. However, I want you to wait in the dining room with Dragón and the gun. If it seems safe, please join us; Trini will be at work and Ilhui in her room. The rest of us will be here."

The doorbell rang at seven. Martín sat in the dining room, Dragón by his side. When the sound of voices reached them, the dog's ears levitated like launching missiles, and he began a slow growl. Martín held up a hand for silence, grabbed the shotgun from the table, and went to the double French doors where he could see most of the living room through the lace-curtained glass panes.

Two portly men of Middle Eastern descent were taking seats on the couch. As planned, their backs were to him. The family members sat beyond them, facing him so he could read their expressions. They spoke in English, and as the conversation progressed from pleasantries to business, Martín saw nothing to arouse concern. Abuelita reached the same conclusion. "Martín must not have heard us," she said. "Martha, will you find him?"

As Martha arose, Martín stepped away from the door. A minute later, he and Martha returned to the dining room.

"Excuse me," smiled Martín to the Iranians, "I didn't know you had arrived."

One of the Iranians explained that they wanted to buy two emeralds. A dealer in Thailand had assured them the Cortés stones might be just what they sought and within their price range. After some haggling in which Hector pointed out that stones of that size were extremely rare, the Iranians agreed to pay $200,000 US for each stone, if all was as stipulated.

"We don't keep the stones here," said Hector, "but we can have them by late tomorrow."

"Tomorrow night, at the same time?" queried the Iranian who had done all the talking.

Abuelita nodded. The Iranians refused refreshments and left immediately after handshakes.

"Tomorrow," said Abuelita, "will be the dangerous time. They know we'll have the emeralds. If they're criminals it will do no good for Martín to hide with the gun; they'll have others waiting outside. To ensure the family's survival, I want Martín to stay away. With everything that's been happening, this would be a good time to check the *finca*. Trini will be at work, and there's no reason for Ilhui to be here. She should go with Martín. They can return later in the evening or the next day."

Martín jumped in. "Abuelita, only one of us needs to be in danger and that should be me. The danger is probably my fault, and I should deal with the consequences."

"That's the right thing to say but the wrong course of action for the family's future. I assume you studied biology in school?" She raised an eyebrow and glanced at the aging Hector and Martha.

Trini entered, carrying a folded newspaper. "Not much business, so I closed early. I thought you'd want to see this." He handed the paper to Abuelita, and added, "Did everything go well?"

"So far," muttered Abuelita, scanning the page. She read for a moment and then looked up, pursing her lips. She handed the paper to Martín, indicating the article with her thumb.

Martín translated the headline: "Is Canal Dream About to Come True?" The article reported that "The American businessman, Colin Glendaring, announced today he is the lead partner in a group that intends to develop a canal from the Pacific Ocean on the Gulf of Tehuantepec to the Gulf of Mexico, near the border of the states of Veracruz and Tabasco." It went on to recount the failed history of similar projects, but highlighted the developer's claim that modern technology and sufficient capital would ensure success. It also noted that partners in the venture included the government of Oaxaca as well as individual investors.

"Worse than I thought," said Abuelita. "He has the authorities in his pocket. Nothing changes, except we

250

must take even more care."

While that conversation was taking place, one of Glendaring's

employees, Dennis Craddock, drove as fast as seemed prudent from Oaxaca to the hacienda. For once, he and his brother, Luke, had obeyed Gabel's orders to stay clean, and his unusually lucid thought process told him to report the recent development in person rather than by cell phone. Martín would have recognized him as one of the two hippie-like Sikhs who had twice tried to kill him in New Mexico.

Half an hour later, Glendaring regarded Dennis with distaste. Like his brother, he had scraggly shoulder-length hair, an unkempt beard, and teeth so bad he looked like a cross between a '60s hippie and a disheveled rodent. Also like his brother, he affected the speech patterns of the former. "Yeah," he said, "like these two foreign guys went in the house, stayed for half an hour, then split."

After learning that the visitors appeared Middle Eastern and prosperous and that the other watcher, undoubtedly El Vengador's man, remained in place, Glendaring instructed Dennis to return to his post but asked Gabel to stay.

"Gabel," he said, rising to his full height. "I hope I have not waited unduly long. The appearance of these foreigners makes me nervous. We must conclude this matter with the Cortés family quickly. Tomorrow night, I think."

El Vengador got the report of the meeting between the Cortés family and the Iranians from his watchers by cell phone and decided that his best course was to await events.

MITLA

With barely concealed excitement, Colin Glendaring received his delivery from El Vengador the next morning. When the boxes were safely stowed in his study, he carefully opened each one. Nestled in straw and crumpled newspapers were clay figures and pots that caused his pulse to race. *Incredible, and they're all mine!* He showed no emotion as he noted the four nine-millimeter semiautomatic pistols and several boxes of cartridges.

Afterwards, he completed his plan of attack and advised Gabel Rausch to be ready to leave the hacienda for the city at 6:15 p.m. That would bring them to the Cortés home about forty-five minutes later. He pointed to an aerial photograph of the home. "Dennis and Luke will enter by the front door. You and I will go through the back from this alley. There appears to be a garage through which we can reach the courtyard. Much more private than the front door." He frowned at the German. "I hope those two have been watching the back as well as the front?"

The German hated making mistakes, but when he did, and adverse consequences resulted, he always made it appear that he was one of the victims. "So do I," he said. "Someone could leave that way before we get there." Seeking to change the subject, he quickly added, "You've always stayed well away from unpleasantness. Why change now? We can handle it."

"Gabel, Martín Cortés's continued existence disproves that statement. This is a matter of considerable consequence to me. To someone with my background, the Cortés treasure—if it exists—is

252

far more important than its monetary value. Be certain Dennis and Luke understand. In fact, tell them that you will slit their throats if they display their usual carelessness."

CORTÉS FINCA

Having indeed abandoned abstinence, Dennis and Luke took turns going between a café with a view of the front of the Cortés home and their nearby van, where they smoked one of the more potent offerings from the local underground economy. As the late afternoon sun set, they failed to see the black Volkswagen emerge from the alley behind the home and turn north.

As he and Ilhui left the city, Martín said, "I still think it's a mistake for me not to be there."

Ilhui glanced at him, switched on the headlights, and returned to her own thoughts.

When they arrived at the *finca's* gate, Martín got out and unlocked it. As he turned back, the early moon illuminated the rear passenger-side tire. "Shit, it's almost flat!" He quickly discovered that the spare was also flat. "It's nearly six o'clock," he said. "What do we do now?"

"There's a *vulcanizadora* in the village," said Ilhui, "but it'll be closed. We'll have to stay over and walk in tomorrow morning. That's okay. Remember, Abuelita suggested we come back tomorrow."

"We should have a cell phone," said Martín. "Why don't you carry one?"

"There's no service out here." Then after a moment she added, "I did have one once, but I always forgot to recharge it. It either rang when I didn't want it to or it didn't work, and it was expensive."

Deciding not to dispute feminine logic, Martín grumbled, "I don't like it. We won't know what happened. Is there a public phone in the village?"

"Yes, but I'm not going to walk in at night."

Any other time, Martín would have jumped at the chance to spend an uninterrupted evening with Ilhui, but he could not shake the feeling of foreboding. Keeping his silence, he grabbed their overnight bags, and Ilhui followed with a sack of groceries. A minute later they topped the rise and approached the moonlit house.

OAXACA

Inside the Cortés home, Abuelita, Hector, Martha, and the Iranians sat in the same places as before. In a show of good faith, Reza opened his briefcase, showed the stacks of neatly banded hundred-dollar bills, and then left the case on the coffee table between them. In return, Hector handed over a bag with the two emeralds.

Mindful of the emerald copies he had so recently made, Reza carefully examined the huge stones. As he ticked off the Thai dealer's instructions, he became certain the emeralds were real. The warm glow of their deep green color and the number of inclusions seemed right. Just as important, they were similar to the ones he and Parwis had stolen.

While Reza examined the stones, Colin Glendaring sat in the passenger seat of a black Jeep Cherokee three blocks north of the Cortés home. In the rearview mirror he caught sight of Gabel returning, his luminous, close-cropped blond hair covered with a black leather cap.

"Well?" demanded Glendaring, as the German entered the car.

"Dennis and Luke said the family is still there, and the same two foreigners went in about ten minutes ago. One of them carried a briefcase."

"I was afraid of that," muttered Glendaring. "The first visit was likely a negotiation. If so, the transaction will be consummated tonight. Of course, it could be something else entirely, but I dare not risk losing something so potentially valuable. In any case, the puzzle's solution should prove interesting!"

He looked sharply at Gabel. "I've changed my mind about the tactics. Our violent but stupid colleagues should not be left to their own devices. For them to enter from the front is too risky. Also, they reported hearing a dog bark. It may be in the courtyard. If so, we will need to deal with it. Fetch Dennis and Luke, and join me in the rear."

"I mean no disrespect," said Gabel, "but this is risky. The canal project publicity is just beginning. Are you sure you want to involve yourself?"

Glendaring glared at his assistant. "Thank you for your concern. Now go."

Glendaring said no more, fearing he had already revealed too much of the importance he placed on the historical treasure, a value that went beyond any amount of money and for which he had already risked so much.

Minutes later, he stood in the alley behind the Cortés house, Gabel, Luke, and Dennis by his side. In front of him were two wooden double-doors to the garage through which he proposed to enter. Both were secured by padlocks. Without being told, Gabel took bolt cutters from a canvas bag and quickly severed them from their hasps.

CORTÉS FINCA

Martín and Ilhui sat together on the couch near the *finca's* fireplace eating *tortas*, bought earlier from a stall in the market. Martín praised the crusty French rolls, stuffed with cured ham, a string-like cheese, and pickled onions, carrots, and chiles. But his uneasiness never left him. "Glancing at his watch, he said, "The meeting should have started fifteen minutes ago."

"Do you know why Abuelita wanted us here?" asked Ilhui.

"She said for the sake of the family. Just in case."

"But why do it this way?"

Martín considered a moment, realizing she was trying to make a point but missing it.

Ilhui flushed. "Isn't it obvious? Abuelita didn't just want us safe; she wanted us together—and alone. She knows as well as anyone that people who share stressful events often develop feelings for each other."

Martín's eyes lit up. "Is that so bad?"

"That's the problem; I don't know. There are so many things you don't know about me. Everything is so confusing." She lowered her eyes and twisted her hands together as if wringing water out of a towel.

"Maybe that's why we're here: to learn about each other and sort everything out," said Martín.

Raising her eyes to his, she took his face in her hands, leaned forward and kissed him tenderly on the lips, and then pulled slowly back. "Just give me time. When this is over and things are back to normal..." *If they ever return to normal,* thought Martín, but he nodded in agreement.

"Thank you. I'll be right back."

While she was gone, Martín tried to order his thoughts. For a while, the paranoia caused by the chain of events culminating with the attempt on his life in Mexico City had all but disappeared. Now it was back at full throttle. When Ilhui returned, he stood up. "I'm going into the village to call," he said. "It can't take more than twenty minutes each way. There was no warning for what happened to my family in Santa Fe. But now...I won't ignore my intuition."

Ilhui nodded glumly. "I'll come with you."

OAXACA

"No noise," warned Glendaring, as Gabel Rausch opened the garage door. "We need to see if the dog is here. And remember, absolutely no violence without my orders. Now, the masks, please."

Each of the men pulled a ski mask from his pocket and put it on. The German's flashlight probed the space that was big enough for two cars. There was only one, a white Jeep Cherokee.

"As I feared," whispered Glendaring. "The Volkswagen our informant said the girl drives is gone, possibly with Martín."

Gabel Rausch remained silent as he moved to a locked door at the back of the garage. Going down on one knee, he aimed the light into the old-fashioned keyhole. "The key's in it," he whispered. Bring me one of those newspapers." His light flicked to a stack of them against the nearby wall.

Luke brought one of the papers, and Gabel slid several sheets under the door. He then pushed a screwdriver from his toolbag into the lock. Outside the door, there was a barely audible thud as the key landed on the newspaper, followed instantly by the distant bark of a large dog. Gabel quickly pulled the newspaper back under the door. On it was the key, and he slipped it into the lock. The dog barked again, this time much closer.

"Hurry," whispered Glendaring. "Stand on either side of the door and dispatch the dog when it enters."

Gabel turned the key and flung open the door. As Dragón charged in a blur, Gabel brought the heavy bolt cutter down in a powerful arc that struck the dog's head a glancing blow. But it was enough, and Dragón fell motionless without a whimper. As Gabel raised the bolt cutters for another blow, Glendaring shoved him toward the door and hissed, "There's no time. We must go in *now*!"

When the dog barked, the Iranians were greedily examining the emeralds, and Abuelita was counting the money in the briefcase. She jerked her head up at the sound. "Hector, go and see what's wrong," she said, trying to sound unconcerned. A glance at the nearly gleeful Iranians convinced her they were not involved in whatever might have caused the barking.

Hector went to the French doors that opened onto the patio. He longed for the shotgun, but he had placed it under the couch in case the Iranians proved troublesome. Taking it out now would only frighten them. The bark was undoubtedly due to nothing more sinister than a cat fight. He opened the door just enough to put his head out, and yelled, "Dragón, *hier*."

The iron grip on his hair and the cold steel that pressed against his forehead informed him he had made a big mistake.

Gabel shoved Hector back into the room, spun him around by his hair, and pushed him forward with such force that he lost his balance and sprawled face forward in front of Abuelita. Luke and Dennis rushed in, and Glendaring followed at a more leisurely pace. Each intruder wore a ski mask and dark outfit, and held a nine-millimeter semi-automatic pistol.

"Nobody move," ordered Gabel in English, and everyone obeyed.

"Good," said Glendaring. "You will find that

obedience is the best course. Resistance and lies will be dealt with severely. Now we shall see if you understand. I assume the young man, Trini, is working, but where are Martín and Ilhui?"

"They aren't here," said Abuelita.

Glendaring nodded almost imperceptibly to Gabel. He stood beside Hector, who had just risen from the floor to his feet. In a flash, the German smashed the barrel of his pistol into Hector's mouth. Blood and broken teeth flowed down his chin, and Martha screamed.

"Quiet," boomed Glendaring. If there is one more sound, someone will die." For emphasis he aimed his pistol at Abuelita's head.

Silence descended, and he continued. "You apparently did not understand me when I suggested obedience. I asked you where Martín and the girl were. You told me they were not here. That was undoubtedly truthful, but not the answer to my question, therefore disobedient. You have one more chance." He kept his pistol aimed at Abuelita.

"I don't know where they are," she said, her voice remarkably steady. "I told them to stay away because of the possible danger. They probably went out to dinner. I expect them back before long. That's your answer, and it's the truth."

"We shall see," muttered Glendaring. "Now, I would like to know the purpose of this meeting." He turned to face the Iranians. "Perhaps one of you will tell me?"

When the trouble began, Reza's first reaction had been to hide the emeralds. The best he could do was slip them between his right leg and the side of the couch. "We came to purchase two stones," he said.

"The details—what stones, the price, where are

they?"

"The stones are emeralds," said Reza, his voice quavering. "They are here beside me. May I...?" He nodded to his right side.

"Carefully," warned Glendaring.

Reza slowly extracted the emeralds and placed them on the coffee table.

"And I assume that is the payment?" Glendaring gestured toward the open briefcase. "How much?"

"Four hundred thousand American dollars," whispered Reza.

Even though partially obstructed by the mask, the gleam in Glendaring's eyes was unmistakable. After finding out about the treasure, he had originally planned to kill the entire family in a manner that would place the blame on Martín—a simple riff on the way he had disposed of Martín's brother. The American's absence made that impossible, forcing him to improvise.

He scooped up the emeralds with his left hand and motioned with the pistol in his right to the Tonhamani brothers. "You two, come with me. The rest of you remain silent." He led the Iranians into the dining room and closed the doors behind them.

Turning to Reza and Parwis, Glendaring said, "If you do as I say you can leave this affair both alive and wealthier than you hoped. But first, tell me where you are from."

"Iran," said Reza.

"There is no time for more details, but I suspect that your business would no more endure scrutiny than mine."

He allowed his words to sink in and then said, "I have two objectives: first, I want the Cortés treasure, if it exists—and these stones make that appear likely. Second, I intend to ensure that Martín Cortés never bothers me again."

"What do you expect of us?" asked Reza.

"Simply that you place the blame for whatever happens here tonight on Martín Cortés and the girl; Ilhui is her name. I will show you photographs so you can describe them accurately to the police. You will say that you were here to negotiate the price of the stones. When you and the old lady reached agreement, Martín and Iluhi became angry and would not stop shouting. They spoke Spanish, and you couldn't understand what was said. The woman told you everything would be fine, but that you should leave immediately and come back tomorrow at the same time. As you left the room, the shouting became even more heated. When you closed the front door, you heard gunshots. You don't remember how many. That's all you know. In return for doing this, you may keep the emeralds, your money, and most importantly, your lives."

Reza nodded. "That sounds reasonable. May we confer briefly?"

"Very briefly," snapped Glendaring.

The brothers moved to the other end of the room and whispered in Farsi. Reza began, "What the man proposes is the only possible way out. If we don't do it, he'll surely kill us. He may anyway. Even if we don't die, we still have serious problems, especially the publicity. Our masters in Tehran will hear the news, and they're smart enough to figure out what we've done."

"Of course," said Parwis. "We can't return to Iran, and our families will be punished. And even if we get the emeralds and money, there won't be enough for a comfortable western lifestyle."

"I understand, brother, but we must do whatever we can to play for time. Here is what I propose: We agree to help and accept the emeralds and the cash in return. After they leave, we also leave, but without calling the police. We can ask our terrorist contact for protection and then quickly leave Mexico. Back to Iran if there is no publicity and somewhere else if there is. Our diplomatic passports make that possible."

"What if they hold on to the money and the emeralds? And what if they blame the killings on us when they discover we deceived them?"

"As to the stones and the money, we'll have to trust to luck and Allah's mercy. As to the rest, with or without them, we should leave before they discover what happens."

Agreement reached, they returned to Glendaring. "We will do as you ask," said Reza.

"Then take this as a demonstration of good faith." Glendaring handed one of the emeralds to Reza, knowing he could retrieve the stone before they left the premises.

Back in the living room, Glendaring surveyed the scene. Abuelita sat in the same chair facing the couch. Across from her was Martha and beside her sat Hector, holding a handkerchief to his mouth. Standing around them were Gabel, Dennis, and Luke, pistols held steady.

As Reza and Parwis resumed their seats, Glendaring spoke. "We shall begin again and try to avoid any further tragic misunderstandings." He waved his pistol toward Hector. "Listen to me carefully, all of you, and take care with your responses. I have heard that you live off the treasure of your illustrious forebear. The emeralds we have seen tonight and the fact that you have no other visible means of support confirm those rumors."

He took a deep breath. "Like all noble causes mine is simple. I want to know where the treasure is. Once the accuracy of your information has been confirmed you will be released. I do not fear your going to the authorities. You would be foolish to report the loss of something you should not have in the first place. Your response?"

After a moment's pause, Abuelita said, "Other than some gold coins and jewelry that are in my bedroom, those emeralds are the last of the treasure. After nearly five hundred years...I'm sure you understand."

Glendaring said, "That is not the answer I wanted." He nodded to Gabel. "Perhaps you can help."

The German slipped his pistol inside his black leather jacket, then removed a razor-sharp commando knife from a sheath on his belt. He moved behind Martha and patted her head with his left hand. With his right, he caressed her cheek with the curved, serrated side of the knife's blade. All eyes were glued on the German.

"Please, no," begged Hector, removing the handkerchief from his mouth.

Ignoring him, Glendaring said to Abuelita, "Notice that I did not call you a liar. I merely informed you that was not the answer I desired. I will give you one more chance to tell me what I want to hear."

Martha cried out as Gabel grasped her hair with his left hand and jerked her head back, exposing her throat.

"Please stop—I'll tell you what you want to know!" pleaded Hector.

"Very sensible," said Glendaring.

"Don't be a fool," yelled Abuelita. "They're going to kill us anyway."

The room went still as Hector's agonized eyes darted between Martha, Glendaring, and Abuelita. Making his decision, Hector lowered his eyes.

"Last chance," said Glendaring.

Hector remained still, eyes downcast, heaving with sobs.

Glendaring nodded to Gabel. With one lightning stroke he slashed Martha's throat. Her eyes opened wide in horror as the blood gushed from her body and pooled on the floor.

Gabel stood smiling with the bloody knife in one hand, like a performer preparing to take a bow. He had assumed that Hector was completely cowed, but he was wrong. With an earsplitting shriek, Hector rocketed from his seat like a demon on steroids. The fingers of his left hand locked around Gabel's wrist above the knife, while his right hand grasped the German's throat. An inhuman cry escaped Hector's lips as the force of his charge buckled Gabel's bad knees and sent both men to the floor. Hector emerged on top, and with the strength born of insane rage, he slammed Gabel's head into the floor. He brought his right hand to join his left on the wrist above the knife. Partially stunned, Gabel allowed the knife to be twisted from his fingers.

Just as the bloody blade reached the German's throat, a deafening explosion shook the room. The nine-millimeter bullet from Luke's pistol drilled a whole in Hector's forehead, and the knife dropped from his fingers to clatter on the floor.

"Fools," screamed Glendaring. He slammed his pistol into Luke's cheek and then brought it down on the man's wrist, knocking his pistol to the floor. "I told you no violence without orders. And you..." He looked down at Gabel, who was just rising from the floor. "Did you think he would just sit there after you killed the woman? Now there's only one left!"

Adrenalin and the realization that she had but one slim chance overcame Abuelita's horror at the massacre of her family. While Glendaring was distracted, she dove for Luke's pistol, which had come to rest four feet from where she sat. She landed on her stomach and grasped the pistol in both hands. Rolling onto her side, she pointed it at Glendaring and pulled the trigger. As he screamed in pain, another shot cracked, and Abuelita slumped to the floor before she could pull the trigger a second time.

"Sorry," said Dennis, shrugging his shoulders and pointing his pistol toward the floor, anxious to avoid the wrath that had been visited on his brother.

He needn't have worried. Glendaring was examining his side. Concluding it had only been grazed, he regained his composure. He turned to the Iranians, who had not moved. "The son and daughter and the American are not here. Do you think they know about the treasure?"

Reza answered promptly. "The old woman said the son and daughter don't know the details, but the American was in the meeting with us and seemed fully involved."

Glendaring considered a moment. "We could await his return, but someone may have heard the shots. The only alternative is to make certain Martín and

Ilhui are blamed for these killings." He motioned with his pistol to include the nearby bodies. "Once they are captured, I have contacts that will allow me to get to them."

He gestured at the Tonhamani brothers. "This is what you must say..."

When he had finished, Reza said, "The publicity from this will prevent us from returning to Iran. We will need more than just the emeralds and the money. Without that, it will be difficult for us to help you."

Glendaring glared through his mask. "You have just seen what happens when I'm crossed. And don't forget that you told me that Martín met you yesterday. He is aware of this meeting and will certainly blame you for the killings unless you accuse him first. And lest you consider double-crossing me, I will hold onto the emeralds and the money until you've completed your task." He motioned to Reza, and the Iranian immediately handed over the emerald.

Glendaring turned to Dennis. "Give them the photos of Martín and the girl."

When that had been done, Glendaring said to the Iranians, "If we're ultimately successful and you have done your part, I will provide you with a considerable bonus. Now, where can I reach you? And don't worry, I'm aware that you can still cause me a great deal of trouble, so in this case there *is* honor among thieves."

Later that night, El Vengador received three telephone calls. The first call came from Colin Glendaring. He reported that his project was not going well and that he needed two people found. He was given instructions as to where he would be picked up and brought to a meeting.

The second call came much later. Reza Tonhamani said he had a serious problem and asked for a meeting to explain his needs. By this time, El Vengador had already met with Glendaring and concluded that the situation with the Cortés family was what his gut had been warning him about. But after a moment's calculation, he decided there might yet be profit for him. Although he was unable to immediately form a plan, he arranged to meet the Iranians.

The third call, the one that would make his course of action obvious, was yet to come.

OAXACA

After a twenty-minute hike into the village, Martín and Ilhui found a public phone at one side of the plaza. He told Ilhui he wanted to make the call, so she inserted her debit card, dialed, and handed him the receiver. After the second ring, a male voice that Martín could not identify said "¿*Bueno*?"

Martín froze, and then dizzy with apprehension and shaking his head, he shoved the receiver into Ilhui's hand.

Hyperventilating, she managed to say, "Who is this, please?"

She listened a moment, seemed to regain control, and said, "This is Greta. I would like to speak to Iluhi. And who are you?"

After another pause, she said, "I'm a friend, and I haven't seen her since last week. I'm just calling to catch up. What's going on?"

She listened again and then abruptly hung up. Facing Martín, she stammered, "It's the police. They wanted to know who I was. I don't know why I lied. He wouldn't tell me what happened. I'm scared!"

"Me too; we've got to get back!"

Down a side street they found a yard walled with adobe. On its gate hung a faded sign depicting a stack of tires and the legend: *Vulcanizadora*. At the back of the cluttered courtyard, they found a tiny apartment with light glowing through a grimy window and the sound of a radio. Ilhui's obvious distress bolstered by an offer of five hundred pesos convinced the old man who answered the door to help. Throwing a worn wool jacket over his undershirt and slipping into leather sandals, he led them into the courtyard. He sorted through a pile of tires and tossed one already mounted on a wheel into the bed of a battered little Japanese pickup truck.

"He has a Volkswagen tire already on a wheel. It'll be much quicker than fixing ours," explained Ilhui.

Thirty minutes later Martín and Ilhui were in the VW, bumping down the dirt track from the *finca* back toward the village. Ilhui glanced at her watch. "It's almost ten o'clock. Let's see if there's anything on the news."

"This just in," began the announcer. Martín could not understand the rapid Spanish until a distraught Ilhui cried out, "They say that after gunshots were reported at the Cortés home, police found several bodies. They're searching for two family members, a man from the United States and a woman. My God, Martín, what's happened? When Abuelita mentioned danger, I never dreamed..."

Desperate to remain calm and prevent the all too familiar horror at what he had just heard from overwhelming him, Martín shook his head. "Whatever's happened, it sounds like we've been blamed for it. We've got to talk to Trini. He should still be at work unless he's heard the news. Can you reach him?"

"Oh my God, I…I!" After taking a moment to collect herself, Ilhui said, "There's no phone in the restaurant, but if he's still there maybe someone from the bar next door will get him. I have the number in my purse."

When they reached the village, Ilhui parked in front of the public phone and fished a small leather-bound notebook from her purse. As she got out, Martín said, "Hurry, the tire guy's radio was on. He may have heard the news and called the police."

Martín shifted to the driver's seat and left the passenger door open. His eyes moved constantly between Ilhui and the surrounding area. As the minutes ticked off, he became increasingly nervous. Just as his

desire to grab Illuhi and flee was about to win over the need to complete the call, she spoke again. Less than a minute later she hung up and dashed back to the car.

"He hadn't heard the news and is on his way home. He said he would tell the police that Abuelita was selling a collection of Spanish gold coins. Anticipating danger, she ordered us to stay away." She reached over and turned up the radio. "Maybe there's more news."

After two energetic *tropicale* instrumentals, they heard the same news bulletin, with the addition of, "Police report discovering three bodies. Based on an eyewitness account they are searching for Martín and Ilhui Cortés." The commentator then gave a brief description of the fugitives.

"Eyewitness," exclaimed Martín. "What the hell's that mean?" Then he added, "Trini should be able to clear us."

Ilhui waved him to silence, her attention still focused on the radio. After a moment she turned down the volume. "In a new broadcast, they just said that the Governor's office announced that on Wednesday there will be a ceremony at Monte Albán to inaugurate the *Golfo al Pacifica* canal project."

Martín blanched. "Shit," he said. "That means if Glendaring's responsible for whatever happened. Nothing Trini says will matter. As Abuelita said, he'll have the authorities in his pocket."

ILhui nodded. "You're beginning to understand

273

Mexico." She put her head in her hands and burst into tears. Moments later, she looked up, her face contorted in anguish. "How can everyone you love be there one moment and gone the next? This must be how you felt."

"Now even worse!" exclaimed Martín, tears streaming down his cheeks. "It's all my fault. I should have known. I should never have come."

"Stop it! It may have been the Iranians, and we have to decide what to do."

"If the police catch us, we'll spend the rest of our lives in jail. And if Glendaring didn't learn where the treasure is, he's looking for us too. We've got to find somewhere to hide until we can get more details and make a plan. Any ideas?"

"No. They'll distribute photographs of us and a description of my car. We have to get rid of it and find someplace safe. But there's no one I can trust except Trini, and he'll be watched, impossible to contact. My God, what will Sister Beatriz think?

"What about your admirer, Raul Rodríguez?"

Ilhui shook her head. "He's an important law enforcement authority. We might as well call the police."

"Couldn't we try to get out of Oaxaca? Maybe head into Chiapas? I understand it's pretty wild."

"No," said Ilhui. "Every highway has police checkpoints that will have our descriptions."

Martín considered the possibility that the tire man could provide an alibi but dismissed it. For the news to get on the radio when it did, the murders must have occurred early enough for him and Ilhui to have committed them before arriving at the *finca*.

Ilhui said, "This sounds crazy, but it's the only thing

I can think of. El Vengador has been a fugitive for years and knows how to hide. He hates the authorities, and we could offer him money. He might help us."

Martín had considered their options and come up blank. His first thought, returning to the United States, was obviously not feasible. In hopes of obtaining reciprocity, the U.S. government was anxious to cooperate with Mexico on the subject of extradition. He didn't know anyone he could ask for help. Reluctantly he agreed with Ilhui. He still had some money that Herb could wire to the guerrilla leader. "It's an awful risk, but I can't think of anything else. Can you contact him?"

"I've never used the telephone number he gave me, but I can try."

They were at the outskirts of Oaxaca, and Martín saw a public phone in front of a closed pharmacy. He pulled around and parked behind the building. "Try it," he said. Ilhui grabbed her notebook and got out.

Ten minutes passed, and Martín's nerves were redlining when she jogged around the building. Back in the car, she said, "It's all right. I called and a man answered. I gave him my name and the number of the telephone. El Vengador called back. I explained what happened, and he agreed to help. He said to wait here. Someone in a brown...how do you say it, a vehicle used for deliveries?"

"A van?" prompted Martín

"Yes, two men in a brown van will pick us up, and one of them will get rid of this car."

"So far so good," said Martín.

After he spoke to Ilhui, El Vengador gave a rare grin. Colin Glendaring was already with him at his headquarters, and the Iranians were on the way. The

275

call from Ilhui told him exactly what he needed to do.

BELOW AN ANCIENT CITY

Martín and Ilhui waited in the Volkswagen, both lost in their own thoughts. Martín's ricocheted erratically like balls in a pinball machine. But with the inevitability of gravity, they always returned to where they had begun, without producing a scrap of inspiration. For a while he thought he had escaped the pattern of violence that had destroyed his life in Santa Fe. He had even begun to believe he could start anew in Oaxaca. This day signaled that was not to be. Mexico had beckoned with the siren promise of a new family, but now seemed to have become the deadly end of a diabolically constructed maze.

Sensing his mood, Ilhui held his arm and put her head on his shoulder. "Don't blame yourself. The treasure has attracted this evil, not you. You're simply the good that stands in its way."

Martín shook his head. "So far I haven't been much of a barrier."

Her voice sharpened. "The two of us and Trini are still alive, and the treasure is still safe. It's not over yet. Now I'm going to do something I haven't done for a long time."

She folded her hands in her lap and bowed her head, tears glistening on her face. Although her lips moved, Martín heard no words. Eventually he too bowed his head, realizing he'd tried everything else.

An hour later, a brown Ford van pulled into the lot and parked beside them. Two young mestizo men dressed in jeans, dark sweaters, and wool caps got out. Following instructions, Martín and Ilhui left the Volkswagen key in the ignition and climbed into the back of the van. It smelled like rotten produce, and there were no windows. The only opening was through a steel-mesh barrier behind the front seat. Several wooden crates filled with oranges served as seats. One of the men tossed them two knitted caps then slammed the rear doors. Martín heard a click as they were locked. From behind the wheel the driver turned. "For security, you must face the rear and pull the caps over your eyes. That will be strictly enforced."

"Certainly," replied Ilhui. "How long will it be?"

"A little over an hour."

From time to time, they reached out and squeezed each other's arms. Martín was reminded of the taxi ride just before he was nearly murdered in Mexico City, and hoped this was not a reprise.

Soon the van left the city and settled into highway speed. After forty-five minutes, it suddenly slowed, throwing Martín and Ilhui against the mesh divider. Then it swung to the right, almost landing them on the floor. They began to climb at a steep angle, twisting upward over a rough road. Another fifteen minutes passed before the van finally creaked to a halt.

"Remove the caps," said the driver as he got out.

Moments later, the back doors opened. Martín and Ilhui climbed stiffly down, stretched, and took deep breaths. The moon was nearly full and illuminated the end of the lonely, rugged dirt track where they had parked. To the right and directly in front of them a steep hillside rose into the night. On the left was a drop that was also too dim to measure but seemed considerable.

"He'll take you to El Vengador." The driver nodded to a man who had materialized from the nearby shadows.

"It's only a short distance," said the short, thickset man with dark Indian features, turning toward the edge of the cliff.

They followed him to the side of the drop-off and then over the edge onto a previously invisible, rocky pathway that continued upward in the same direction as the road. They twisted higher around the mountain and were soon gasping for breath. "Altitude," wheezed Martín. "It feels like Santa Fe."

"*Cállate*, be quiet," hissed the Indian.

The rocks soon gave way to a sandy surface, and in the moonlight Martín detected narrow tire tracks. A motorcycle, he guessed. After another ten minutes, they had circled much higher and nearly to the other side of the mountain, and their guide motioned them to halt. To their right, a door-sized rectangular piece of the mountainside swung open. It was perfectly camouflaged and set at the same angle as the hill. A young Indian stood by the door and motioned them inside.

Martín and Ilhui found themselves in a rough-hewn passageway that resembled a mine shaft, about the same height and width as the door. The air had the dank chill of a cave, and the only light came from where the passageway ended about thirty feet ahead. They followed the young man to where the tunnel opened onto a large space that seemed carved from the center of the mountain. It was about 150 feet long by a hundred feet wide, and the ceiling was at least twenty-five feet above them. Light came from flickering torches and a few electric lights clipped to small projections on the walls. Martín detected the hum of a generator. Nearby, he saw what looked like doors to rooms, but the far side was too dimly lit to make out details. Although he wore a light jacket, he shivered in the clammy air.

The most striking feature of the space was directly in its center. A huge slab of rock had been carved into a rectangle, about twelve feet long by six feet wide and three feet tall. The sides tapered gently to the top, making it resemble a small stage shaped like a flat-topped pyramid. It was illuminated by a shaft of moonlight knifing through an opening in the ceiling. The place looked like a movie set where people died horrible deaths in the quest for some priceless relic.

From a small group near the stone stage, a man approached them. Martín was sure it was El Vengador. Clad in khaki pants, shirt, and bush jacket, he rose nearly to Martín's height, tall for a Mexican. His European features, light skin, and long brown hair, as long as Martín's before his recent haircut, set him apart from his Indian followers. He looked at least late thirties, older than Martín had imagined. Behind him followed another young Indian.

"Ilhui...and Martín, I presume. Welcome," he said in near perfect English. Martín noted that while he tried to inject some warmth into his tone, his eyes were so expressionless they seemed almost dead.

El Vengador stepped back and scrutinized them. "You must be tired. I'm sorry to confirm that your mother, father, and grandmother were indeed murdered, and that both of you are wanted for questioning. That's all I know, but I should have more information later today."

Sensing the unspoken questions, he said, "We're below the ruins of a ceremonial city, much smaller than Monte Albán. It was completely destroyed and looted. This space probably began as a series of caves painstakingly expanded by the people who lived above. Nobody but a few local Indians know it exists. The underfunded antiquities authorities never discovered it and abandoned the site above us. We constructed the hidden door, and it serves me well."

"I'm impressed," said Martín, "but how do you stay in such close touch with the world outside?"

For a moment the man's eyes flashed as if in anger, and then he said, "A guard outside receives calls and notifies me." Glancing at his watch, he added, "It's almost daylight, and you must be exhausted. Please rest; we'll meet for supper this evening." He waved to an open door about twenty feet to their right. "You'll find water and a crude toilet. The door will be locked from the outside; I'm sure you understand."

Ilhui remained silent, eyes fixed on El Vengador.

Martín said, "Of course, thank you."

El Vengador nodded, and Martín felt a chill as he noticed the man's eyes become even more lifeless. He and Ilhui turned and followed the young khaki-clad Indian to the doorway.

Two cots, covered with threadbare gray blankets, took up most of the space on the packed dirt floor of the small room. At the back was an alcove with a table that held a bowl, two large pitchers of water, a sliver of soap, and a cracked mirror. The door closed behind them, and a padlock rattled in its hasp. Martín said, "What's wrong? You didn't say anything."

Ilhui whispered into his ear, "Be careful, we may be overheard." Then she continued, "Something's different. Before, he seemed so human. Now he's cold, like a machine. I'm afraid that what I saw was an act, and now he doesn't bother with it, doesn't care what we think. That's what scares me. What can we do?"

Martín put his arms around her and whispered, "I imagine most people in his business are what you describe. We've no choice but to wait until we know what we face. We're like someone who knows he's sick but not how serious it is. We're waiting for the test results. One way or the other we should find out before long. Now we better get some rest."

Ilhui returned his embrace and kissed him softly on the cheek, then turned and lay on one of the cots. Within minutes she was asleep.

Martín was not so lucky. He'd faked confidence he didn't feel, and he couldn't help wondering how intimate Ilhui had been with the handsome guerrilla leader. But he finally succumbed to exhaustion and drifted into a world of troubled dreams.

BELOW AN ANCIENT CITY

Martín and Ilhui slept on and off for most of the day. At six-thirty, a tap on the door was followed by a voice that informed them they were expected for supper in half an hour.

The alcove had no curtain, so Martín turned his back while Ilhui took an abbreviated sponge bath. When she finished, he washed in the ice-cold water. Feeling the stubble on his chin, he wished he'd asked for a razor.

They had just finished when they heard the lock being removed. Martín put his arms around Ilhui and whispered, "I wish I could turn the clock back twenty-four hours. Just know that I'll give this guy anything he wants to keep you safe."

Ilhui's expression of disbelief shocked him into remembering his vow to Abuelita to never disclose the location of the treasure. He shook his head. "No treasure is worth the lives already lost!"

"Except that handing it over would probably not have saved anyone."

Did Abuelia or Hector disclose the location of the treasure? Is it already gone? Martín kept the thought to himself

They opened the door to find a large table placed near the stone stage. Approaching it, they saw three places set with empty plates and silverware.

Their host appeared from the other side of the stage and greeted them with handshakes. "Please be seated," he said. He wore the same khaki outfit, and his wavy brown hair cascaded nearly to his shoulders. Martín noticed that he now wore a pistol on his belt.

Martín and Ilhui took the two seats facing the stage, with Martín on the left. El Vengador sat opposite them. "I hope you could rest?" he said, but his tone conveyed no interest in the answer.

As he spoke, a young Indian approached with a large serving tray and placed a bowl of stew and a basket of tortillas on the table.

"We eat well, but not elegantly," said El Vengador. "Probably not what you're accustomed to."

Martín had noticed the man's almost perfect English and at first wondered if he had lived in the United States. But his speech was not colloquial—perhaps a previous career in academia? Martín said, "May I ask you a question?"

"Certainly."

"Ilhui told me about you and what your father unfortunately experienced at the hands of the government. But what exactly are you really doing, and why? Your name means avenger..." Then he quickly added, "I'm new to Mexico and truly want to understand. I also want to compliment you on your English. You sound like a professor."

El Vengador considered a moment and then scornfully said, "A professor?" Eyes flashing with anger, he added, "What I do and why I do it aren't important. What is important is that I do it—and how I do it. We'll come to that. Now please eat."

Martín tried to mask his concern as he ate the spicy pork stew. Most people could not resist the opportunity to talk about something they believed in passionately. Nor did the man's statement, "We'll come to that," bode well, and he desperately needed clarification. "With all due respect, sometimes an outside view can be helpful. In spite of the circumstances, I'm glad of the opportunity to speak with you. After Ilhui told me about you I did a fair amount of reading and thinking about Mexico. You'll probably call me naive and stupid, but may I please tell you some of my conclusions?"

"Why not?" came the reply, laced with a healthy dose of sarcasm.

"First," said Martín, "I can't think of one successful recent revolution that has not become a tyranny of some sort: the Soviet Union, China, Cuba, and Venezuela come to mind. The ones that benefit the people seem to be those led by leaders seeking only democracy, using mostly nonviolent tactics. Until recently, anything like that had no chance of success in Mexico. Your father's experience is proof of that. But now, partly because of the scrutiny of the international community, nonviolence might just work. It seems to me that killing people, no matter how bad they are, only provides the justification for brutal retaliation that few outside of Amnesty International will complain about."

When he finished, he saw that Ilhui was staring at him, eyes wide and fearful. Martín knew he had taken a risk, but what he had done was the only way he could think of to find out what kind of man this was. He didn't have long to wait.

El Vengador's face flushed and his eyes became slits. "You *are* naive and stupid. You don't understand these things and they're none of your business."

The rest of the meal passed in silence, but Martín noticed that El Vengador barely touched his food. Ilhui said nothing, nor did she make eye contact. When they finished, three of the Indian subalterns piled the dirty dishes and silver onto the serving tray. Like their leader, they also wore pistols.

El Vengador pushed his chair back and crossed his

legs. "I'm sure you're anxious to settle the business between us," he said.

"Yes," agreed Martín. "As I said, we're extremely grateful for your help. I lost nearly everything before I came to Mexico, but I can still arrange for some money to be wired to the bank of your choice."

El Vengador smiled for the first time. But it did nothing to reassure Martín, as the man's words became a sneer. "How very generous, *Señor* Cortés, but I had something more significant in mind." Out of the corner of his eye, Martín saw Ilhui's hands begin to tremble and then watched her clench them together in her lap.

"For many years," continued El Vengador, "I've heard rumors that your family lives on a vast treasure amassed by Hernan Cortés, the man who destroyed the finest civilization the world has ever known. That explains my original interest in Ilhui."

"Ilhui," he snapped, all pretense of civility gone. "Look at me when I'm talking to you." Then he shrugged. "No matter, this will get your attention." He pulled something from his pocket. "I have recently received evidence that the treasure exists." He placed the object on the table.

Ilhui gasped as she saw the huge emerald. "Where did you get that?" she snapped.

"Oh, so now you're paying attention!"

BELOW AN ANCIENT CITY

Martín's heart rate slowed, and he felt his head clear, the way an experienced fighter settles down once the first blow has landed. From the corner of his eye, he saw the two Indians move their hands to the butts of their still-holstered pistols.

"We can still avoid any serious unpleasantness," snapped El Vengador. "The location of the treasure, please."

Ilhui spoke for the second time and spat out her words. "You claim to fight for the weak. How can you use the same tactics used against them since time began? Liar!"

"I'll humor you this once," grimaced El Vengador. "The worst mistake a revolutionary movement can make is to not have enough money and to flinch from destroying anyone who can harm it by informing the authorities. Both of those apply to you. I use the methods used against me. Until this moment you belonged to the privileged class, making you anything but weak. Now, the location of the treasure!"

Knowing he would not have another opportunity, Martín whirled to his left, and with the edge of his palm, he swept the Indian guard's hand from the butt of his pistol. With his right, he snatched it from its holster. As he swung back there was a deafening explosion and something stung him on his right side. He froze when he saw El Vengador's pistol aimed steadily at his chest. The shot had hit the table, sending splinters into his side.

"Drop it, you fool!" yelled El Vengador. Then more calmly he said, "You disappoint me. I had hoped to avoid this. Put your hands behind your backs!"

The Indian retrieved his pistol from Martín, and he and his compatriot roughly handcuffed Martín and Ilhui's hands behind them.

Again, El Vengador nodded to the man nearest Martín. "*Andele* Rico."

"*Sí, Comandante.*" He took off at a trot around the stage-like platform toward the other end of the dimly lit space.

A minute later a group of men appeared from the shadows. Martín's stomach fell and his mind whirled as he recognized Colin Glendaring, Gabel Rausch, the German he thought he had disabled, and two unkempt, bearded men, one of whom was the Sikh who kidnapped him in Santa Fe. Behind them were the two Iranians.

When they reached the table, El Vengador said, "I believe you are familiar with my new colleagues. We recently discovered that our interests coincide. He turned to Glendaring and said, "*Señor?*"

Glendaring wore his fringed, buckskin jacket, and the silver and turquoise clasp pulled his graying hair into a ponytail that looked to Martín like a rotten swamp root. He rose to his full height and stared down at Martín

"Good evening, Mr. Cortés. It appears that you are a slow learner, but you must realize that obstinance will not serve you well. Time is short and our business urgent. The location of the treasure, please."

The stilted language sent a shiver down Martín's back. Even though he knew the answer, he said, "You're going to kill us anyway. Why should we give you the satisfaction? The truth is, the treasure isn't enough to waste the time of even a petty thief, which you are not."

Glendaring smiled. "Thank you for the compliment. That the treasure is depleted is what your late relatives said, and you know how well that served *them*. Now enough of this." He nodded to El Vengador.

"Rico," snapped the guerrilla leader, "bring the woman."

The man again disappeared into the shadows. Soon he returned pushing a hospital gurney. Although well packed, the floor of the cavern was uneven, and the body on the conveyance bumped from side to side.

As it came into the light, Ilhui gasped. "Greta," she exclaimed, recognizing her friend, the professor who had introduced her to El Vengador. She was dressed in a white hospital smock.

"Like you," said El Vengador to Ilhui, "she decided to renege on her commitment. She was even stupid enough to threaten to contact the authorities. What is about to happen will provide a lesson to you both. Karin!"

From behind them appeared a waif-like blond girl who slowly walked to the stone platform. Martín saw that although her body was concentration-camp thin, her face was exceptionally beautiful, and her blue eyes shone with an otherworldly radiance that he suspected was drug induced. Her most striking feature was her outfit. She wore a floor-length robe made entirely of colorful feathers, and her nearly white hair was bound with a tooled leather headband. In her hand was a small, razor-edged scimitar made of gleaming black stone.

El Vengador said, "This is how our ancestors should have dealt with Cortés: with an obsidian blade." Then he added, "We found it in the ruins. Its use in this setting will remind my men of their history."

As the two Indians lifted the obviously drugged woman onto the stage, a group of at least thirty more came from the right side of the cave to form a semicircle around the back and sides of the pyramid-shaped platform.

"No!" screamed Ilhui.

El Vengador moved quickly to her side and slapped her so hard that her chair nearly went over backwards. He nodded to one of the guards, who produced pieces of duct tape. He stretched one over her mouth and then did the same to Martín.

In spite of the white-hot rage that possessed him, Martín realized there was nothing he could do.

His voice harsh, El Vengador said, "I'm not without compassion. She's been sedated."

Indeed, the woman appeared tranquil, except for her eyes, which darted fearfully from side to side.

El Vengador nodded to the blond girl. Her lips arched into an angelic smile as she stepped to the side of the stage-like platform. One of the Indian guerrillas moved beside her and pulled open the smock to expose the prone woman's breasts. Like some ghoul in a horror movie, the blond girl hovered over the helpless form, intoned a few words in a language Martín did not recognize, and slowly lowered her blade.

Ilhui's body began to heave and muffled sobs came from behind the tape on her mouth. Chained to his chair, Martín felt more desperate and useless than ever before in his life. He strained to break the grip of his handcuffs and tried to close his eyes, but could do neither. As the blade touched Greta's left breast and began a sawing motion, her eyes moved frantically and her lips twitched as her drugged mind struggled to make speech. At the last moment Martín turned his head to the side and shuddered as he heard a deep, inhuman wail burst through the girl's sedation.

A minute later he forced himself to face forward. He knew that what he saw would stay with him for the rest of his life. High above her head, in a grotesque victory salute, the blond in her bizarre costume held the still-beating heart clutched in her left hand and the obsidian knife in her right. Her expression was twisted into a rapturous grin, as depraved as anything he had ever seen.

Iluhi continued to sob uncontrollably and Martín longed to comfort her. Instead, he focused on the men responsible for this monstrosity, vowing that somehow he would destroy each and every one of them.

"Mr. Cortés," said Glendaring, "I hope you found that instructive."

"Time's short!" broke in El Vengador. "I understand that Ilhui does not know the location of the treasure. Therefore, she is only useful to gain your cooperation. What you just witnessed will happen to her if you don't cooperate immediately, and you will be made to watch."

Martín saw that the blond girl had thrown open her feathered robe and, like a delighted child, was using the now still heart as a paintbrush to draw patterns on her naked body. One of the Iranians moved to one side, bent over, and threw up. As bile rose in his own throat, Martín exerted every shred of willpower he possessed. He knew the tape on his mouth would cause him to drown in his own vomit.

"We'll see if you've learned your lesson," said El

Vengador. "I could tell you that if you cooperate we'll release you, but you wouldn't believe me. What I will promise you is that you will be treated humanely. So, tell us what we want to know. Now!" He motioned to one of the Indians. "Remove the tape."

Quickly, the young man tore the silver strip from Martín's lips. Pain flashed as the tape tore at his unshaven face and lips, but he barely noticed. Seeing that all eyes, including Ilhui's, were on him, he made a desperate effort to think clearly. He knew that throughout history hopeless situations had been reversed by freak accidents—some said miracles. He had to play for time. As long as he and Ilhui were alive there was a chance, no matter how slim.

He nodded to El Vengador. "I will do what you ask. The treasure is hidden in a cave on the Cortés property, about forty kilometers north of Oaxaca, but I honestly cannot give you directions."

"We know where the property is," broke in El Vengador. "That was one of my men your dog attacked."

"I'm talking about the location of the treasure, not the property," responded Martín. "I was only there once, and it was very dark. Getting to it requires going through an underground passage with a hidden opening mechanism and finding a well-hidden key. I think I can find them, but it won't be easy. And there's no way I can give you directions."

Looking suspicious, El Vengador said, "Try."

Martín knew that if he told them the treasure was in a cave inside the only prominent outcropping on top of the mesa, they could easily find it by themselves. That was something he could not permit. Getting away from the guerrilla hideout and onto something approaching home ground was his only chance.

Trying to be accurate but vague, Martín said, "The key is hidden behind a rock on a cliff that is itself behind some brush not far from a large stone ledge that overlooks the valley, a little less than a quarter mile around the mountain from the house. The treasure cave is a good twenty- minute walk up and around the mountain."

"Where on the mountain is the cave?" snapped El Vengador.

"I'm honestly not sure enough to describe it," said Martín. "I told you, it was very dark the one time I was there, but I think I can find the path that leads to it."

"One other question," said El Vengador. "Is it possible that the police could be watching the *finca* in case you return?"

"I was told," said Martín, "that no one outside the family knows it exists."

Although he still looked suspicious, El Vengador motioned to the others. They followed him to a point about fifty feet away and conferred for several minutes. When they returned, the guerrilla leader said, "You'll be taken there. I'll stay here and be in close contact. The moment you become uncooperative Ilhui will be tortured. Our phones have speakers and you'll be able to hear the screams."

Martín nodded, and El Vengador looked at Glendaring. He stepped forward and slapped Martín. The heavy ring on his middle finger left an angry welt. "Gabel, Dennis, and Luke will go with you," he said. "You know what will happen if you misbehave."

El Vengador motioned to the Tonhamani brothers. They appeared to realize that they could only play along and hope to stay alive, maybe get a share of the spoils. Reza said, "My brother and I will go."

El Vengador nodded agreement. "Four of my men will go on my behalf."

Turning toward Ilhui, El Vengador said, "Lock her in the room."

Two of his men jerked her roughly to her feet and started to drag her toward the room she and Martín had shared. Martín rose to his feet.

"Just a moment. May I speak with Ilhui?"

"Certainly," said El Vengador, smiling. He stepped to Ilhui, and ripped the tape from her mouth. "Go ahead."

Martín looked at the group. "Alone," he said.

El Vengador shook his head. "Take her away," he said. But for the first time Martín noticed a change in the man's eyes. Was there a tiny hint of regret? Whatever it had been, it turned to rage as Ilhui spun free of her escort and spit full in his face. "*Cabrón!*" she screamed, and her kick just missed his groin.

As the Indians once again grabbed Ilhui, El Vengador regained his balance. Enraged, he stepped toward the girl with his fist raised.

"Stop!" screamed Martín. "Touch her and you'll never see the treasure, even if both of us have to die right now."

El Vengador slowly lowered his fist but said nothing.

"And," said Martín, "I will need the use of my hands. To get through the brush, find the keys, and climb the mountain."

Glendaring said, "Cuff him to Luke. That will keep him out of trouble. Luke, keep your pistol on the opposite side and the safety strap secured. As we have learned, Cortés is rather skilled at hand-to-hand combat."

When that was done, the group moved to the short flight of stairs that led to the exit passage.

The descent to the road from the mountain hideaway was more difficult than the ascent. Dark clouds curtained the moon, and the trail was too narrow for the men to walk abreast. Martín's right hand was cuffed to Luke's left, so they had to descend in an awkward crab-like manner. To make matters worse, Luke had obviously not bathed recently.

Gabel Rausch was in front of them. He stumbled often and was obviously in pain. At one point he turned to Martín. "I'll soon repay you for these knees."

When they reached the road, two of the guerrillas got into the front of the van, and the other eight men piled into the back, where they arranged themselves uncomfortably on the floor.

No one spoke to Martín, so he assumed that the driver was familiar with their destination. That allowed him to focus his mind on his predicament. Over and over, he replayed the route to the treasure cave on the mesa, scrambling for a plan. The situation seemed hopeless, and he was about to despair when suddenly the unformed shadow of a possibility presented itself. He knew that whatever it turned out to be would require both luck and perfect timing, but in spite of the impossible odds he felt a glimmer of hope.

CORTÉS FINCA

Gabel Rausch's bolt cutters quickly severed the padlock on the gate to the Cortés *finca*. Moments later the van jerked to a stop in front of the old house. One of El Vengador's men stayed with the vehicle, while the rest of the group got out and formed behind Luke and Martín. The German lit the way with a powerful flashlight, his pistol in the other hand.

There was still no moonlight, but after a few false starts, Martín found the hidden opening in the cliff. Following his directions, Dennis pocketed the key and opened the door to the small cave. The opening at its top was too small for Martín and Luke to pass through together. Gabel covered Martín with his pistol while Luke removed the cuffs then reattached them once they climbed out. Martín considered trying to escape, but realized that even if successful Ilhui would be killed.

On the way up the mountain, Gabel Rausch's knees gave him great difficulty. As they topped the mesa, he grabbed Martín from behind. "What are you pulling? This isn't the way you described."

"I told you I wasn't sure and had to follow the path I took before," snapped Martín.

"We shall see," said Gabel. Then to Luke he added, "Watch him carefully."

Martín led the way to the rocky pinnacle that enclosed the cave. Feeling with his left hand, he found the loose stone in the wall. Dennis removed it, tossed it to one side, and then inserted the key. Not a sound came from the group as the lock clicked. It was like the hush in a courtroom just before the verdict is announced. As the five-foot door swung open, Martín could feel the tension rise like a teapot coming to a boil. His own heart raced. Fearful of telegraphing his adrenalin surge through the handcuffs to Luke, he forced himself to relax.

When the door was half open, Gabel shoved Luke and Martín to the side, bent over, and limped into the cave. "Yes!" he hissed as his flashlight illuminated the boxes and crates piled along the walls nearly forty feet away. In a frenzy of anticipation, the rest of the group swarmed inside, jamming Luke and Martín against the door.

Luke was as anxious as the rest. As the last man passed by, he stooped and brutally jerked Martín's right wrist. Martín piggybacked on the force and, using their tethered wrists as a fulcrum, propelled himself in an arc around and in front of his captor. As he came around, he stiffened the palm of his left hand and opened his thumb wide. With every ounce of force he possessed, he drove the rigid V-shape into Luke's throat. He used both speed and power and focused the blow's energy at the precise moment of impact, the way a professional golfer drives for distance. Luke gagged as the energy capable of shattering a cement block lifted him off his feet, crushed his trachea, and drove his head into the top of the low doorway. Martín clutched him in an awkward embrace, preventing his weight from pulling them both to the ground.

In spite of his concentration on the treasure, some sixth sense caused Gabel Rausch to wheel and aim the light in his left hand at the cave's entry. Seeing what was happening, he drew his pistol and fired. But just as the gunshot boomed in the confined space, Martín swung Luke's body around. Instead of hitting its

target, Gabel's bullet struck
his colleague in the back, and the impact sent him and
the already unbalanced Martín backward onto the
ground.

As Martín scrambled desperately to his feet, he saw
that Gabel's shot had panicked the others. Taking
advantage of the diversion, Martín quickly dragged
Luke's body the short distance outside the door, flung
his entire weight into it, and closed it just as another
shot rang out. Heart in his mouth, he twisted the key,
but it refused to lock. At any second he expected the
German's weight to be flung against the door. In a
panic, he threw his shoulder into it, pushed with all his
might, and again turned the key. This time he heard
the click as the iron bolt shot home. He breathed
deeply, realizing that had Rausch's knees been sound
the outcome would have been far different.

Martín heard two more muffled shots, then
pounding on the door. Seeing that it did not move, he
lowered Luke to the ground and checked for a pulse.
Finding none he turned him over and inspected the
bullet wound in the man's back. He turned him over
again but could find no exit wound. Another lucky
break; if it had passed through him, Martín would
probably have been hit.

A quick search found a small key attached to a steel
ring that fit the handcuffs. Martín released his wrist
and rubbed the circulation back into it. He also
extracted a wallet and slipped it into his own pocket.
Then he took off the gun belt and strapped it around
his own waist.

He saw no way the men could escape from the cave
any more than the Spanish soldiers described by
Abuelita had been able to and was grateful not to have

given El Vengador more accurate directions. On the other hand, the man knew generally where the treasure was
located, so Martín decided to remove any evidence that could lead to it.

He dragged Luke's body to the edge of the mesa that was farthest from the pathway down to the house. He rested a moment, then rolled the body over the edge and listened to it crash into the darkness below. On his way back, he extracted the key from the cave door. Rather than take it to its hiding place by the lower cave, he put it in the alcove by the keyhole and then found and replaced the stone that concealed it.

CORTÉS FINCA

Picking his way down the steep path, Martín worried as much as had Federico Alvarado so many years ago on that same trail, and over essentially the same things: his life and the lives of those he cared about. In spite of his vow to Abuelita, Martín didn't worry much about the treasure's ultimate fate. After witnessing the horrific death of Ilhui's friend, he knew the only things of importance were the lives of the people he cared for. What remained of the Cortés fortune was nothing but a tool to save Ilhui's life. And the people who had cold-bloodedly watched the heart ripped from a woman would not think twice about interrogating and killing Trini on the off chance he knew something that could help them. While in comparison the treasure meant nothing, for the moment it had to be kept safe. It was the only way to keep his remaining family alive.

It helped that he now had fewer adversaries. Glendaring's men, the Iranians, and four of El Vengador's rebels were locked in the cave. More importantly, the thick walls of the cave and lack of cell service prevented them from communicating with El Vengador or Glendaring. But there was still the guerrilla leader himself and God knows how many of his men, not to mention Glendaring. Some inner voice of caution, possibly concern that the police had identified the finca, had obviously caused Glendaring to send Gabel Rausch to the cave in his stead, but he and any other cutthroats he employed were still at large.

El Vengador said he would be in touch with his men. Ilhui had earlier told Martín the area had no cell service. But, accustomed to rough country, the man must have satellite phones. Martín was nearly certain that none of the men in the cave had one. In any case, the impenetrable rock walls would undoubtedly make communication impossible. Whatever instrument they had would be with the man waiting below in the van.

But even if his men were not able to notify El Vengador of a problem, the very lack of communication would soon do so. Rather than suspecting Martín, he might assume that Glendaring or the Iranians had double-crossed him. Martín's newly formed plan counted on encouraging that impression.

Had the guerrilla with the van been warned by the gunfire? Maybe. All the shots except the first one had occurred with the cave's door closed. Because the first one came from inside, that would have muffled the noise. He had no idea how well sound carried under the circumstances, but he knew that it could travel amazing distances in strange ways, depending on the topography, wind, and humidity. If alerted, the man would have tried to call his leader. Whether he got through or not, the driver would undoubtedly have found a hiding place with a clear view of the van where he could await events and take action. The most likely spot was somewhere in the grove of trees between the house and the mountain. Martín decided to act on that assumption. If the man had remained in the van, things would be that much easier.

CORTÉS FINCA

When Martín emerged from the small cave at the base of the mountain, he veered to the left, in a direction that would bring him around the far side of the house. That and the van would screen him from the trees where he guessed the guerrilla might be. He moved carefully, trying to take each step in complete silence.

After what seemed an agonizingly long time, he peered around the edge of the house. The van was still parked in the same place, about sixty feet to his left, but he could not see inside it. The moon was still swathed in dark clouds, and the breeze seemed insufficient to shift them anytime soon.

Martín decided to approach the vehicle from a point three-quarters to the rear. That meant that if the man was in the driver's seat, he would have to turn his head way to the left to see him, at least until Martín was within view of the side mirror. If he was in the trees, the van would still screen him.

He flattened himself on his stomach and began to crawl. The rocky surface was not kind to his body, nor was it easy to move noiselessly, so progress was slow. He hoped that from a distance he would seem to be just another shadow. As he came within range of the side mirror he moved with even more caution. When he was just behind the driver's side door, he withdrew the pistol and began to rise. As his face came level with the window, he leaned slowly forward until he could see inside. The driver's seat was empty.

Martín holstered the pistol, lowered himself again, and rolled under the van. That was the last place the guerrilla would look for trouble. Depending on what happened, Martín could emerge from either side. Now he could only wait. The tiny light on his watch showed ten minutes before midnight. He hoped that the guerrilla had instructions to call on the hour.

What about Glendaring? Martín guessed that when he heard nothing, he'd contact El Vengador. *No matter what he's told, Glendaring will assume a double-cross. When was the banquet in his honor mentioned in the radio report? Tonight?* Martín couldn't remember. In any case, even if Glendaring and/or El Vengador came here it would be difficult for them to find the treasure cave, certainly not without spending a great deal of time. The mostly flat top of the mountain was probably the last place they would look, and the cave's door was well camouflaged.

His watch now said midnight, and almost immediately he heard footsteps. With no attempt at silence, they came from the direction of the trees below the mountain. Seconds later, Martín saw two legs appear below the passenger door, two feet from his face. The door opened and the man climbed inside.

Martín wondered why he had gotten in on the passenger side. As he drew his pistol, he saw the man get out again and stand beside the van. Almost immediately he heard a scraping noise. The man got back in the van, closed the door, and Martín heard the electronic tones of a phone being dialed. The sound was so clear that he assumed the van's window was open. Then he heard the man ask for *El Comandante*, and Martín prepared to move.

The driver began to explain that he had heard nothing since what he thought might have been a gunshot. Martín slid from under the van on the passenger side and rose to his feet well behind the

window. A device resembling a small laptop computer sat atop the
van's roof. From it a cord led through the open window into the vehicle. The conversation continued and Martin edged forward. Craning his neck to peek in the window, he saw the guerrilla speaking into a telephone receiver.

In one swift motion Martín stepped forward, reached inside with his left hand, grabbed the man by the hair, and jerked his head back. With his right hand, he jammed the pistol into the man's cheek. "*Quiero hablar*, I want to talk," he said.

The driver froze. Martín slapped him in the face with the pistol barrel, released his hair, and snatched the phone from his hand.

"El Vengador," said Martín into the phone as the driver moaned. "This is Martín Cortés. There's something you need to know, and I'll give it to you in just a moment."

He put the receiver on top of the van and wrenched open the door. With his left hand, he grabbed the guerrilla by his jacket, jerked him out of the van, and pushed him face down onto the ground. Ordering the driver to remain still, he removed the man's pistol from its holster. Back on the phone, he said, "Are you there?"

"Yes."

"I'm sure you wonder why you're talking to me. It's simple. I did what you asked and led the men to the cave with the treasure. As soon as Gabel Rausch saw what was there, he gave a signal to the brother of the man I was handcuffed to, and they started shooting. I was still at the entrance and couldn't see who was hit. I surprised my guard, jerked him outside, and knocked him out. I was able to close and lock the door with the others inside. Now I have a proposal for you."

"I'm listening," said El Vengador, his voice revealing none of the emotion he must have felt.

"What I ask is as simple as what just happened. I want you to release Ilhui within two hours. If you don't, I'll turn your man over to the Mexican army and describe your headquarters to them. It won't take them long to find you, and there goes your precious revolution. Once you free Ilhui that will be the end of it as far as I'm concerned. If you think I'm bluffing you should know that some time ago I met Captain Raul Rodríguez. I assume you know who he is. He suspected Ilhui's involvement with you and asked for my help. If you don't do what I ask, he'll have that help." Martín waited, his heart thudding like a jackhammer.

El Vengador paused only moments before dashing Martín's hopes. "You must think I'm a fool! As soon as Ilhui is free you'll run to the authorities. You have to blame someone to clear yourselves of the murder charges. My position won't change, except I'll have less money.

"As to your threat, as convenient as this place is, too many outsiders know about it. I've already decided to leave. Go ahead and call *Capitán* Rodríguez. By the time he gets here we'll be long gone, and unless you do as I say, all they'll find is Ilhui's body in a condition that will haunt you until you die."

Martín had not really believed his ultimatum would work but hoped the shock of his news might cause the man to decide to cut his losses. That was not the case. He desperately wanted to lash out, tell the guerrilla leader what he intended to do to him, but he knew the threats would sound hollow and could result in Ilhui's death. With monumental self-control, he said, "All right, what do you want?"

"You can have Ilhui unharmed in return for two things: the Cortés treasure and five hundred thousand American dollars in cash."

Martín's hope turned to despair and then the rage he could no longer suppress. "You fucking son of a bitch! Now you're the fool. You can have the treasure. Too many people have already died for it. But I can't raise that kind of money. Once I could have, but your partner, Colin Glendaring, stole everything my family owned. Do you expect me to rob a bank? If anything happens to Ilhui, I'll hunt you down and personally kill you, which is exactly what I'm going to do to Glendaring."

"Please, Mr. Cortés," said El Vengador, sounding suddenly weary. "I know your circumstances and certainly don't expect you to rob a bank. You would only fail, and that wouldn't help either of us. It will come as no surprise when I tell you that I no longer consider Glendaring my partner. That, my friend, is the solution to your problem. You see, he keeps a large sum of money on hand to buy antiquities and to pay bribes. There is also the money he took from the Iranians. It must be in the hacienda he's renting near Mitla. You just need to find it!" Then he added, "If he has more than a half million, you can keep it."

"There may well be more," retorted Martín. "The Iranians alone had $400,000. Why don't you get it yourself?"

The pause lasted so long that Martín was afraid the connection had been broken. Finally, El Vengador said, "I imagine I'm going to be rather busy staying away from Rodriguez, and there are considerations you know nothing of. But think about this: You may find other items of interest to you in that house."

That statement struck a chord with Martín, but under the stressful circumstances, like a long-forgotten song, he couldn't quite identify it. Nevertheless, he grasped at the straw. "How can I get it?" he asked.

"Tonight, Glendaring will attend a formal dinner in his honor in the city. He won't return home until late, and I think he has no servants at the house. The German is the only one of his people staying in the hacienda. Here are the directions."

Martín carefully memorized them.

El Vengador said, "After you bring me the money and lead me to the treasure, Ilhui will be freed."

"She goes free as soon as I bring you the money. If not, you'll never see the treasure."

"We'll see," said El Vengador. "For obvious reasons this telephone will no longer work, so listen carefully. We'll meet the day after tomorrow. You'll either have the money by then or you'll never have it. Come to the village of Zaachila, south of the city. As you enter it, you'll find a large restaurant on your left. Come in the afternoon at four o'clock—alone or you'll never see Ilhui again, at least not alive. And one more thing," he added, "I know you'll need the van, but release my man just outside the city."

"What if there's a problem, a temporary delay," exclaimed Martín.

"How can I contact you?"

"You can't. Just remember the Mitla directions and Zaachila."

Martín swallowed and shook his head. Would

nothing ever be easy? He had to move quickly and knew he couldn't pull off what he needed to by himself.

OAXACA

Forced to modify his original plan, Martín hoped his Spanish was up to his needs. After assuring El Vengador's driver that if he cooperated he would be released, he ordered the man to show him how to use the satellite phone and give him its number. Martín dialed the Cortés family home in Oaxaca, praying that Trini would be there. With the manhunt, he didn't want to go to the restaurant. Although concerned the line might be tapped, Martín concluded that he had no choice.

Trini answered on the second ring. Disguising his voice and speaking in oblique generalities to confuse any listeners, Martín spoke slowly at first. Trini quickly caught on, signaling his understanding by joining in the game. Martín carefully outlined his needs.

Fifteen minutes later, Trini called back from a public phone, gave Martín a phone number, and said the person he wanted to talk to was waiting for his call. Then, speaking more openly, he told Martín that he had tried to explain to the police that Martín and Ilhui could not have had anything to do with the family's tragedy, but they ignored him. The fix was in due to Glendaring's influence. Martín asked Trini to stay near the phone.

He dialed the number and was elated when Captain Raul Rodríguez answered.

Martín explained what had happened, but did not mention the guerrilla he now held prisoner. He finished by saying, "We can help each other. We both want Ilhui unharmed, and we both want El Vengador stopped. Our goals are the same."

Rodríguez was silent for a long moment before

saying, "I have a large degree of autonomy and could mount an attack on the guerrilla headquarters, but based on what you said, we'd be too late."

Martín began to despair until Rodriguez added, "However, without consulting my superiors I can help you get the money. Not in an official capacity but on my own...I'll take the risk."

Spirits soaring, Martín said, "In the meantime, is there anything that can be done about the manhunt for me?"

"No, there's too much pressure from above. Proof will be necessary."

When it came time to decide on a meeting place, Martín was ready. Less than an hour later, he dropped off the driver.

Moments later he pulled the van beside a building across the street from the pharmacy where he and Ilhui had met the guerrillas. He had considered having Raul come to the *finca*, but if the man betrayed him its dead-end location would make escape impossible. A glance at his watch told him he was half an hour early.

Martín hid the van from anyone approaching the pharmacy and waited. At two o'clock a silver motorcycle ridden by a man wearing a black and red helmet—the vehicle and outfit Raul had described—slowed in front of the pharmacy and then cruised around to the back. Martín waited five minutes but saw nothing suspicious. So far, the captain had kept his word. Martín trotted across the street.

An hour later, the two men remained huddled near the pharmacy's back door. Martín had related the events as far back as Glendaring's destruction of his family in Santa Fe. They agreed they couldn't fool the guerrilla with a fake ransom, that to save Ilhui *and*

catch El Vengador they would have to get the money from Glendaring. That
evening sometime after 8:00 p.m., about seventeen hours away, became the obvious choice. The man would undoubtedly attend the banquet in his honor. On a large-scale map, Raul traced the location near Mitla described by El Vengador and then gave the map to Martín.

"I live in military housing," said the captain, "so you can't stay with me. Go back and rest at the *finca*, then around 4:30 p.m. follow the map to the hacienda."

"What about the people in the cave?" said Martín. "They have no food or water."

"There's nothing we can do until we get—or don't get—the ransom money. To take them I'll need several men, and my superiors will hear about it. If that happens before tomorrow, I can't help you." He slapped Martín on the shoulder. "Don't worry, it takes longer than twenty-four hours to die of thirst. Would they have worried about you?"

"One other thing," said the Captain. "In the hospital, I told you I believed we might become rivals for Ilhui. Until she's safe we need to put that aside."

Martín grinned. "Would I have called you if I hadn't already decided to do that?"

They shook hands.

MITLA, OAXACA

The sun's descent hastened as Martín neared the rendezvous location near Mitla. Shadows raced across the land, and the last of the tourist buses heading back to Oaxaca disappeared in his rearview mirror.

He'd driven the guerrillas' van through the city and to the outskirts of Mitla with no more than a glance from the two policemen he passed. As the sun disappeared behind a mountain, he pulled to the side of the highway. He'd memorized the map and thought the turnoff to Glendaring's rented hacienda lay between the entry pillars he had just passed. In the fields beyond it stood row after row of the majestic maguey plants used to make mezcal, most of them taller than a man.

It was six-thirty, and a U-turn took him to the other side of the road, facing back toward Oaxaca City. Glendaring would go that way, and Martín could watch him leave. Of course, he might have already gone. Rodríguez said the banquet would begin at eight o'clock, so Glendaring would be gone well before then—unless for some reason he decided not to attend. Martín lowered the window and caught a delicious sweet scent that he guessed came from the magueys.

Half an hour later, a black Jeep Cherokee turned out of the drive and headed toward Oaxaca.

Another half hour passed before a distant light materialized into a motorcycle, and Raul pulled up beside the van. He wore a black T-shirt, jeans, a black leather jacket, and gloves. "Ride with me," he said after being briefed.

Martín stretched and sat behind Raul as the bike carried the two men through the entry and onto a road cut between neat rows of towering magueys, their now unmistakable scent like a blind date's unfamiliar perfume. Over a low rise, the white walls of the hacienda loomed in front of them. Beside the front gate stood a small gatehouse with light coming from the window. Raul pulled to the side. "Stay here, I'll take a look." He bent low and jogged toward the gatehouse, using the magueys as cover.

Minutes later, Raul returned. "There's an old man; he's listening to a radio. To be safe, we'll have to go over the wall on the other side."

Giving the gatehouse a wide berth, they bumped slowly through the silent agaves. Behind the hacienda, Raul parked the bike beside the wall and removed his helmet. Standing on the cycle's seat, he stretched to his full length, which left his fingertips a foot shy of the top of the wall. He pulled a roll of heavy canvas from the back of the bike, unrolled it, folded it in half, and tossed it over the wall. "In case of broken glass."

Raul crouched and then sprang upward, like a basketball player at the tipoff. His hands went well above the wall, and on the way down his fingers fastened like grappling hooks. Scrabbling with his toes, he pulled himself to the top, took a quick look around, and turned to Martín. "No glass. Come on," he whispered.

From the top of the wall, Martín saw that the back of the house was about sixty feet away. They dropped to the ground as lightly as well-trained commandos. "What now?" whispered Martín.

"Check for an alarm system." Raul trotted to the back of the house.

Martín joined him, and they moved carefully along the wall, examining the visible wires with quick flashes from Raul's penlight. When they completed the circuit, Raul whispered, "I don't think there's a permanent system. This house was built before electricity and all the wiring is on the outside. But there may be battery- or plug-operated devices." He motioned to a door at the right rear of the house. "Let's go in through the kitchen."

The door was locked, and a quick examination revealed an old-fashioned bolt.

"Let's find something easier, but not in front," murmured Raul.

A quick tour found no better alternatives, so they returned to the kitchen door.

Raul extracted a hacksaw blade from a zippered pouch and fitted it between the door and jam above the bolt. "This may take a while."

"Let me do it," whispered Martín, grasping the end of the blade.

While Martín worked, Raul jogged around to the front of the sprawling building to make sure they were alone. When he returned, Martín handed him the still-warm blade, his fingers covered with bits of metal.

Raul eased the door open, peeked in, and flashed his light around the dark space. They paused to listen. Hearing nothing, Raul led the way through the kitchen into the dining room with a large table surrounded by high-backed chairs, and a credenza along one wall. A door at the far end led to a spacious living room, furnished with two leather couches, a few overstuffed chairs, and some threadbare Indian rugs on the worn tile floor. Two lamps provided weak illumination. The place smelled like mold with a dash of Lysol. To the left was the entry foyer, and across the room a door opened into what looked like a den. Raul's flashlight showed that the den was more a library than anything else, but the stacks of bookshelves were empty, as was a small closet. The only other furniture was a straight-back chair and a small antique desk on which sat a lamp that Raul turned on. Moving back across the living room to the unlit foyer, they found a wide staircase leading to the second story.

Turning to the right, Raul stepped toward the front door, froze, and then aimed his light to one side of the jam. The beam revealed a small rectangular device with a one-inch clear plastic window. He moved the light to the other side of the door, where it found a similar device, and beside it a small box.

"There must be a beam projected between them," he said. "If you break it, an alarm goes off. The devices are probably attached with Velcro or glue and use batteries, so it can't be very powerful. The alarm may not be loud, but I suppose it could somehow be transmitted to the man at the gate, or it could record the fact that the beam was broken. Look there," he exclaimed, pointing the light at the front door handle. "It isn't locked. He thinks anyone like us will come this way, open it, and set off the alarm. *Gracias a Dios* we didn't."

He moved back to the stairway, carefully flicking his light around the walls, and then again motioned for Martín to remain still. "Another one," he said. He pointed to a pair of similar devices, one on the wall and one on the bannister about a foot and a half above the second step. "If we're careful, we can go over it."

In slow motion Raul turned sideways to the stairway. Bending his knee, he raised his right foot above the devices, carefully stepped over the invisible beam, and placed his foot on the third stair. Shifting his weight, he repeated the motion with his left foot. Nothing happened, so Martín mimicked the movements and joined him on the stairway.

Carefully, they moved down the second-floor hallway, opening the doors to two bedrooms that looked uninhabited, and then on to a larger room with a television and a disordered bed, obviously recently used.

"Look for an office," said Martín.

Inside the last door, Martín saw a desk at the far end littered with papers and files. He turned on the lamp beside it. Scanning the papers, he discovered they were in English. "Nothing much here. They're correspondence about the canal project. But no projections or other details." Then he looked up at Raul. "I don't see a computer or briefcase, or much of anything else. There must be more!"

He had considered what El Vengador had said: "There may be other items of interest to you in that house," and was hoping to find something that would incriminate Glendaring in the death and looting of his family in Santa Fe.

"Let's go back and check the bedroom," said Raul.

The dresser yielded nothing but underwear and socks. Martín opened the closet door and found a rack of men's clothes. His eyes moved to the shelf above them. "What the hell's that?" Raul's light revealed an electronic device. It was plugged into a receptacle screwed into the socket of the closet's overhead light. Handing his penlight to Martín, Raul examined it carefully and then traced a wire from it to a smaller device, no bigger than a man's ring with a piece of

316

Velcro on one side.

"This is a video recorder, and this," he added, fingering the tiny device, "is a very small camera and sound recorder, the kind used to make secret films."

"Things he could use for blackmail?" said Martín.

"*Claro que sí*," nodded Raul, "or maybe for other reasons."

Raul clicked open a door on the machine and extracted a tiny cassette. "It's set at the beginning, ready to record."

Replacing the cassette, he ran his fingers over the top of the closet door. "Aha." He picked up the recorder and pushed it onto a tiny piece of Velcro on the closet's door jamb. He took his hand away and the device remained in place. He smiled. "With this, Glendaring could record almost anything in the room."

"What do you think it means?" said Martín.

"Why do *you* think anyone would make a recording in their bedroom?"

Martín held his wrist under the light. "It's only 8:30. We should still have plenty of time. Where else can we look?"

Raul thought for a moment. At first, he scowled and then nodded and snapped his fingers. "Maybe downstairs!"

Back in the living room, Raul crisscrossed the space, eyes fastened on the dark tile floor. Stopping beside an Indian patterned rug in one corner, he looked up at Martín. "Strange place for a rug. "He pulled it to one side. Stooping, he placed the forefingers of each hand in two small holes about two feet apart. The muscles in his legs and back straining, he straightened. A section of the floor tile attached to boards came away,

317

revealing a hole about three feet square. "Most haciendas had a place for the women to hide during Indian attacks, and this could be it."

Martín hunched over and peered into the hole illuminated by the flashlight. It was about seven feet deep. A vertical stone stairway led to the bottom. "Let's take a look," he said.

MITLA, OAXACA

Martín and Raul moved slowly down the stairway, coughing in the musty air. The flashlight revealed a room about ten feet square, with a ceiling just high enough to allow the two over-six-foot men to move comfortably.

Around the walls stood piles of cardboard boxes, a small table with a laptop computer, and a large hard-sided briefcase. The sight of a large steel safe caused Martín's heart to race.

Raul pulled a tiny chain on a ceiling fixture with a bare bulb. Under the now adequate light, Martín bent to the safe, slightly smaller than the trapdoor and about four feet tall. He tried in vain to move the latch and looked up at Raul. He pointed to a heavy-duty dolly in the far corner. "They must have lowered it with a block and tackle and wheeled it over here with that. We could get it on the dolly, but we'd never get it out of here. I don't suppose you know anything about opening safes? The money must be in there."

Raul said, "No, and there's no time to find a locksmith. That means we'll have to wait for Glendaring." Then he added, "With this hiding place and the safe, no wonder he doesn't have a more elaborate security system."

"In the meantime," said Martín, "let's see what else is here. It's a little before nine. I doubt he'll be back before at least eleven, but we better assume ten to be safe."

Raul opened the briefcase and scanned the file titles. "These are in English. You better look at them."

Martín saw that a third of the files were in a section labeled "Canal

Purchases." Beside them, he pulled out a thick appointment book next to a packet of small-sized binder paper secured by a rubber band. He laid it on the table, extracted the individual files, and thumbed through them.

"These look like land purchase agreements," muttered Martín. "They seem to be between various individuals and a company called TierraMex. 'LandMex,'" he translated. "They're in Spanish; come take a look."

Martín quickly discovered a separate file also labeled "TierraMex." Inside it were articles of incorporation from Colorado—Glendaring's home state—listing him as the sole stockholder. Other documents in both Spanish and English detailed the transfer of shares in TierraMex to six men with Hispanic names. Another bilingual agreement was between Glendaring and the same six men. It called for all profits on land sales to be divided equally.

As he reviewed the names, Raul gave a low whistle. "I know two of them. One is the governor of Oaxaca, and the other is my commanding officer!"

"Oh shit," said Martín. "I'm sorry. What should we do?"

Raul raised his eyebrows. "If we're lucky, no one but you and I and Glendaring will ever know what happened tonight. And he may not live long enough to say anything."

Raul's expression and the tone in his voice both startled and chilled Martín. Then he reminded himself that he was in Mexico and nothing should surprise him. Hadn't he, himself, recently vowed to kill Glendaring?

Raul seemed to read Martín's thoughts. "Don't

worry. That will probably not be necessary. I'm not in uniform, so he'll have no idea who I am."

"Let's see if this is charged." Martín opened the laptop. He pushed the power button and the screen immediately lit up. When it had booted, thankful that it was not password protected, Martín scrolled through the desktop files and stopped at one labeled CanalSum. It was a profit and loss statement, titled "Canal Pro Forma." It listed "Land Sales" at $50,000,000. There were only two categories of expenses, "Commissions and other Fees," which totaled $625,000, and "Land Cost" of $5,750,000. Martín wished he had time to total up the value of the sales agreements in the files, but guessed they would equal the latter amount. That meant the group, including the governor of Oaxaca, had convinced the State to pay nearly ten times the actual cost of the land.

"Look at this," he said to Raul. "Nearly $44 million profit. Not bad."

"We may have something to say about that." Raul's expression was again grim. Then he glanced at his watch. "According to our schedule, we have a little over thirty minutes."

Martín's eye lit on the leather-bound appointment book. It looked like the Day-Timer his brother had carried before he got an electronic model. He picked it up and saw that it held pages for each day of the past, current, and future months. He opened a page at random. The date was five days earlier. On the facing page was the notation "Cortés—decision." Each page held similar notes. The day before yesterday's simply had Martín's name in block letters with a line through it.

Martín wondered what he might find on the pages during the time his family had been ruined, but that was several months ago. He was
putting the book aside when he remembered the packet of small binder paper. Grabbing it, he stripped off the rubber band and unwrapped the piece of brown paper that protected it. Sure enough, it contained the book's entries beginning in January. He flipped immediately to the day on which his brother's body had been found, ostensibly after committing suicide following the murder of Johnny Carillo and his family. There was no entry. But the day before, the day his brother had called and confronted Glendaring threatening to expose their arrangement, the neat handwriting said, "Abel uncooperative, Gabel to handle—and also Carillo." Further on, about the time Martín's belongings disappeared from his safe deposit box, he found another notation: "Gabel re Martín SDB." *Surely safe deposit box; God knows what else is in here.*

"Raul," he said, eyes gleaming. "I think I've found evidence that could help bring down Glendaring. By itself I don't know...but with everything else the FBI has, it may be enough."

"And these boxes," replied Raul, as he waved at the pile along the walls, "are full of illegal pre-Hispanic relics, enough to send anyone to jail for a long time. We have to decide what to do."

"Yes," agreed Martín, suddenly feeling guilty at taking his mind off the real reason he was here. "We've got to get the money. Assuming it's in the safe, how are we going to get him to open it?"

Raul flipped open the blade of a high-tech fighting knife Martín had not seen before. "I will carve him into little pieces, and he can watch me feed his body to the ants, like tiny tacos. He'll open it."

Again, Martín shivered. "I don't doubt you, but I've got another idea that might give us even more. If not, we can still try your way. Do you think you could make that video recorder we found in the bedroom work in another part of the house?"

Raul nodded. "I used to make videos as a hobby before I joined the army." He listened to Martín's plan, after which they exited the underground room and replaced the trap door and rug in their original positions.

MITLA, OAXACA

It took Martín and Raul forty minutes to complete their arrangements, and they were none too soon. As they finished, headlights flashed through the living room curtains. Raul hurried into the den, and Martín seated himself on a couch just inside the living room, out of sight of the entry. Luke's pistol rested in his lap.

The front door opened, and Martín heard Glendaring say, "Just a moment," and then, "Please come in."

A woman's voice said something he couldn't hear.

This was a complication he hadn't anticipated, and his grip tightened on the pistol. Wearing a dark suit and turtleneck, Glendaring, followed by his companion, came into the living room and flipped on the light. The woman stood over six feet and had the exaggerated figure of a comic book heroine. She wore a glossy black leather top, pants, and boots and carried a large leather bag. Her mouth gaped as she caught sight of Martín.

Before either of them could speak, Martín lifted the pistol. "Good evening, Colin. I hope the banquet went well?"

"What the hell is this!" demanded the woman in heavily accented English. Her black hair was pulled severely back from the angular face into a single braid that stretched nearly to her waist.

"Shut up," exclaimed Martín. "Colin and I have some business to discuss. That's all you need to know." He turned to Glendaring. "We're going to review recent history in detail. Do you want this woman present?"

Glendaring spoke for the first time. "I would tell you

that you will regret this—more than you can ever imagine—but I fear you will pay no attention. In answer to your question, I would prefer that we meet alone."

"Fine," said Martín. "Where can we put her so she can't leave? Any rope to tie her up?"

Silence.

Martín thought for a moment, then fixed his eyes on the woman's leather bag. "Shove the bag over here with your foot, but be very careful."

She looked at Martín and Glendaring and exclaimed angrily, "You pigs, this is nothing to do with me. Let me go."

"Unfortunately, you're here," said Martín. "Now do what you're told," he added, motioning with the pistol.

She dropped the bag and shoved it with the sharp point of her leather boot to Martín. Keeping his eyes on Glendaring and the woman, he worked the zipper open and upended the container, spilling the contents onto the floor. What he saw brought a grin that morphed into a wry smile. Around his feet rested a set of handcuffs, a leather mask, a cat-o-nine tails, and a selection of adult toys, including what seemed to Martín an immense, black-plastic dildo attached to a belted harness.

He turned to Glendaring. "This I might like to watch, if there's anything left of you when I'm finished."

With his left hand, he picked up the handcuffs and saw the key attached with a piece of string. Placing the cuffs on his knee, he unlocked them and dropped the key into his shirt pocket.

He nodded to the stairway. "I think that iron bannister will work fine. Attach her to it by both

wrists, and put it above the fifth step.
That'll give her a good stretch, and keep her away
from your little alarm."

Martín tossed the handcuffs to Glendaring, who
caught them deftly. From the woman came a torrent
of curses.

Beginning to feel exhilarated at for once being in
charge, Martín said, "Lady, I know you're pissed off,
but if you would rather be dead than inconvenienced
just keep mouthing off."

Glendaring cuffed one of her wrists, passed the
chain around the bannister support above her head,
and then secured the remaining cuff to her other wrist.

"Now, into that room," Martín snapped, motioning
toward the den with his pistol. He followed
Glendaring into the room and directed him to sit in a
straight-back chair against the empty bookshelves that
faced the nearly closed closet door. Martín took the
only other chair.

"I assume you wonder why I'm here and why you
haven't heard from your thugs?" he began.

"For once you are correct."

Although infuriated at the man's confidence and
badly wanting to hurt him, Martín decided to follow
his plan. "You should be more careful with the help
you hire. As soon as we got inside the cave and your
pet German saw the treasure, he pulled a double-cross
and started shooting. One of the first things he hit was
Luke, who was still handcuffed to me. I used him as a
shield, dragged him outside, and locked the door. I'm
not sure how long people can live without water, but
whoever wasn't shot in there is about to find out."

"Do you really expect me to believe that?" snorted
Glendaring.

"Gabel would never do such a thing."

Martín knew the story he had given to El Vengador and now Glendaring was not improbable and decided to stick with it.

"Colin, you act like it's my job to convince you. The truth is, I know what happened. Maybe you and the truth have been strangers for too long. Actually, I don't give a fuck whether you believe me or not."

Martín stood up and stretched, but kept the pistol aimed at Glendaring's chest. "Here's tonight's agenda." He resumed his seat. "You and I are going to have the nice long talk I've been wanting for a long time. Then I'm going to ask you for something. If you give it to me, you might leave here alive. If you don't, you won't. I'm in no hurry. I just need to be gone before daylight."

"Cortés," said Glendaring, some of the sneer gone. "Let us move directly to the bottom line. You plan to convince me that you'll kill me. I know you'd like to, but that's not logical. I assume you need me to help save your charming little Indian from our mutual acquaintance. If not, I would already be dead."

Martín grinned. "Gee, Colin, if you keep this up you may get to skip sixth grade. But first, we have some other things to discuss. You swindled my brother, and then, after our father died from the shock of what happened, you killed Abel, making it look like a suicide—after you also killed Johnny Carillo, his wife, and five-year-old daughter. Why?"

Glendaring smiled. "You think you're in control because you have that gun, but here's the reality: I'm a close associate of the governor of this state and others equally well placed. On the other hand, you're wanted for murder and can't even return to the United States.

327

Now do you begin to understand?"

A white-hot cloud engulfed Martín as he heard the threat to his carefully considered strategy. "None of that'll help you if you're dead!" he yelled. "Now answer my question, you son-of-a-bitch. You have two fucking seconds." His gun arm stiffened but remained steady.

Glendaring saw the knuckles on Martín's trigger finger turn white.

"All right," he exclaimed. "It's obvious and doesn't really matter at this point. Your brother tried to renege on our deal, and Carillo was also in a position to destroy it. It was simply a way to solve both problems."

With some of the arrogance returning, he locked eyes with Martín. "Of course, the chance to own the Cortés hacienda and the equally interesting family heirlooms were also inducements."

"And why was it necessary to kill the Cortés family in Oaxaca?" said Martín.

Glendaring shook his head. "That was indeed a shame and counterproductive. Things did not go as planned. But we're wasting time. We both need something. Can we not reach a mutually agreeable arrangement?"

"I said we'd get to that." Martín used all his willpower to keep from pulling the trigger. "I'm a little afraid to tell you the truth—it's so foreign to you—but here goes. You hinted earlier that you could help me get Ilhui from El Vengador. You were right, but not in the way you thought. I'm sure that when your thugs didn't turn up you called him. You couldn't reach him, could you?"

Glendaring started to open his mouth then closed it.

Martín continued. "You couldn't reach him because after I left the cave I called and told him what happened. He had the sense to believe me, and for some strange reason he doesn't trust you anymore.

"Anyway, he's left the hideout and is out of touch. He offered me Ilhui in exchange for $500,000. I told him I didn't have it. He reminded me that you stole nearly that much from the Iranians before you contacted him and still have one of the emeralds, plus whatever money you brought to bribe people for your canal project. That's almost a quote, and it's why I'm here. Now, as you said, we can help each other. I need the money, and you need your life."

Glendaring raised his arms, stretched, and folded them in front of him. His confident smile again showed Martín the toughness he knew the man possessed. "Let me see," said Glendaring. "You want me to give you half a million dollars, and you expect me to believe that you will then let me go? Why should I believe that?"

Martín returned the smile. "The reason you can believe me is because you know I'm not a killer and will do almost anything to keep it that way. Notice I said 'almost anything.' No, I don't expect you to believe that I'll just let you go, but I have a different way to take care of you."

"And that is?" Glendaring reached behind his head and fiddled with the silver clasp that held his ponytail.

"Keep your hands in front of you!" snapped Martín.

Glendaring complied, but slowly enough to show his disdain.

"How will I deal with you? The answer has several parts. First, I have proof that you, in cahoots with the governor, plan to cheat the State of Oaxaca out of

nearly $44 million. I haven't decided who to give it to first, the governor or the newspapers, but I'm leaning toward the former. I figure he'll decide to cut his losses. That means you! Probably you'll be reported killed while resisting arrest after
being discovered trying to defraud the citizens of Oaxaca."

For the first time, Glendaring looked shaken. His skin turned nearly as gray as his hair, and Martín detected a tremor in his fingers.

"What proof do you have?"

"You don't really have to ask that, do you?" smiled Martín. "I think you already know. You just want me to confirm it. Okay, it's in your little basement stash just a few steps from here. And that tells you a lot of other things, doesn't it? Like that I also know where you probably have the money."

"You mean that safe? It was there when I got here; I don't even know the combination."

"Imagine that," retorted Martín. "And whoever left the safe there also left the dolly to move it around, and right next to your stolen artifacts. How thoughtful. Next, you'll tell me the money you took from the Iranians is in a bank—with all the records that would entail? Not likely. Anyway, if you can't open the safe, it'll be more your problem than mine. I'll still be alive to find a locksmith."

Glendaring's eyes creased into slits. "You know, Cortés, you just might be angry enough to kill me, but not the woman. She will prove a most reliable witness. A lot of important people saw her leave with me."

He nodded, as if to himself, and continued. "You suggested you would reveal whatever you think you found regarding my little project here in Oaxaca. How

330

could a dangerous wanted criminal get someone in authority to listen to him, or any reputable journalist for that matter? I'm sorry, but it will undoubtedly be *you* who is shot. No, young man, you simply have to think rationally, which brings us back to where we started: you want the girl and I want to be left alone."

Martín had not expected this to be easy, but it was proving tougher than he'd thought. The strength of his arguments mattered nothing if Glendaring refused to capitulate. He decided to go further. "And I'm sure you have a rational suggestion?" he said.

"Indeed I do. I have $50,000 that's not in the safe. If you allow me to destroy the evidence you so thoughtfully mentioned, I will show you where it is and we can go our separate ways."

"You know as well as I do that El Vengador won't settle for that. But maybe he'll give me credit for your dead body."

Glendaring considered for a moment. "In that case, I have no alternative but to call your bluff."

"You think this is a game?" snarled Martín. Plainly it was time for more extreme measures. "Okay, you've seen a couple of my cards, but I've got more. Let's see how you like the next one." He turned his head toward the closet door. "*Amigo*, please join us!"

As the black-clad army officer stepped out of the closet holding a semi-automatic pistol, Glendaring's eyes widened in surprise. Martín said, "This man holds a responsible position. He can corroborate my story and ensure that I get a hearing with the right people. He also lacks my squeamishness."

Raul pointed his pistol at Glendaring. "What Martín said is true. There's been enough talk. You will now open that safe!"

Glendaring said, "Exactly who are you?

Raul said nothing, so Martín answered. "I've told you all you need to know. This isn't a game or some business negotiation. Open the fucking safe!"

"Once again you're wrong. This is serious business. This man knows that my arrangements are with powerful men, that there is nothing you or he can do except destroy yourselves. I have offered you an equitable outcome, and you would be advised to accept it."

In an instant, Raul was behind Glendaring. He grabbed the man's ponytail and jerked his head back. The pistol had disappeared from his hand and was replaced with his wicked-looking knife. The razor-honed blade flicked open, and in one lightning sweep Raul sliced off the top half of Glendaring's right ear. He screamed and clutched at the wound as blood flowed through his fingers.

Pulling Glendaring's head back to an even more critical angle, Raul sliced off the tip of the man's nose as if it was the stem end of a carrot, causing another howl of pain.

Raul glared down at Glendaring. "That's only the beginning. Until you open the safe, I'll continue until there's nothing left. I'm sure you understand how the sculpture process works: You remove material until it's finished, and I've just begun." He moved the blade to Glendaring's other ear

At first, Martín was horrified, then mesmerized.

Glendaring wailed, "All right, all right—stop." He began to sob. His body shuddered, and his face went slack as he seemed to crumble before Martín's eyes. It was like the end of a horror movie when the vampire turns to dust.

In two quick strokes, Raul sawed off the pony tail above the silver and turquoise clasp, snatched Glendaring's left hand from his damaged nose, and shoved the gathered hair into it. "A bandage for you."

Glendaring continued to whimper, and his hands trembled as he clutched the hair to his wounds and blood streamed over his cheeks and neck.

Surprised that he felt no compassion, Martín snapped, "And that's not all your troubles, you arrogant piece of shit. We borrowed the video recorder from your bedroom and everything you've just said is on tape. Not exactly what I imagine you intended to capture, but it'll make a nice companion piece to the material in your spider hole. Now, the safe before my friend decides to continue carving."

Glendaring had indeed broken, and five minutes later he pulled the safe open to reveal stacks of hundred-dollar bills. Martín quickly estimated they would easily exceed what he needed to give El Vengador. The emerald gleamed on another shelf.

Back on the main floor, the woman now stood quietly with her head bowed, hands still cuffed to the bannister above her head. Glendaring's screams had apparently suppressed her arrogance. Martín retrieved her leather bag, returned to the basement, and filled it with the cash, the precious stone, the cassette of Glendaring's confession, and the files he knew would be useful.

After zippering the bag closed, Martín caught Raul's eye and gave a questioning glance at Glendaring. The gathered hair was still pressed to his face, and he slumped near the safe, obviously expecting a coup de grace.

Raul said, "You think I'm going to kill you?"

"That's what he would do," interjected Martín.

"I said I wouldn't if you cooperated, and eventually you did. I expect you'll suffer much more if I leave you alive. I'll even promise you twenty-four hours, enough time for you to leave the country. After that, this information will reach the highest levels in Mexico, and if you're still here you'll wish I had put a bullet in your head. Where you go is your business, but I'm certain that Martín will
provide the authorities in the United States with enough evidence to make that country a poor choice. Two other things you must do for me to keep my promise: make sure you are gone from here before daylight and give the man at your gate enough money for him to disappear for the next month.

Raul looked down at Glendaring, who nodded, looking even more defeated. "Just one more thing," said Raul. "You said you had $50,000 in a separate place. Where is it?"

Glendaring's eyes rolled wearily upward. "In the car's center console." He lowered his eyes.

Without another word, the two men climbed up to the living room. As they passed the woman, her eyes followed them.

"Wait here a moment." Raul left through the front door and returned in less than a minute with a small leather bag. "The fifty thousand," he said. "Put it with the rest. If there's enough, you should consider reimbursing me for expenses. Now leave the way we came and I'll join you in a few moments."

ON THE ROAD TO OAXACA

The bike pulled to a stop beside Martín's van. As Martín dismounted Raul said, "We need to talk. Help me put this thing in the back so we can ride together."

Traffic was sparse, and the outskirts of Mitla were soon behind them. Martín accelerated to just below the speed limit and turned to Raul. "Thanks for what you did. I'm sorry I wasted so much time."

"Don't worry, you're an artist. I understand what physical pain will do to a bully. You probably wonder why I let him go and gave him twenty-four hours. Two reasons: it would have taken at least that much time to get the taped admissions and evidence from the safe to the right people. And if we had killed Glendaring, the woman would talk, and I'd be accused of taking the money for myself. As it is, she's too scared to say anything."

"Won't she talk anyway?

"No, I gave her $5,000 and told her what would happen if she breathed one word."

"Martín patted his shirt pocket. "Shit, I've still got the key to her handcuffs."

"Another problem for those two," Raul laughed. "Although the situation isn't perfect, it's better that he leaves and the canal project falls by itself."

"I understand. You think he'll really go?"

"He knows it's his only choice. And we left him the artifacts, which are obviously important to him. He can disappear with them, transfer money from the United States, and go to someplace like Venezuela."

"Okay," grunted Martín, "but we better make a plan. Now that I've got the money, I'm afraid to give it to

El Vengador. He may kill Ilhui anyway. And what about the people in the cave?"

"Because some of them are associated with Glendaring, and because he can be connected with my general, I'll probably be ordered to make them disappear."

"Wouldn't it be better if they weren't killed? The Iranians can testify that Illhui and I had nothing to do with killing our family. And once they know they've been abandoned, Glendaring's men might be convinced to verify what happened to my family in the U.S."

Raul considered. "That makes sense. There will be no killing if I inform the Federal Police before reporting to my superior. I know the head man, Inspector Alvaro Vasquez. He'll cooperate if we take care of him. I'll have some problems, and it will be expensive, but if I'm very careful, I can use the information in that leather bag to make things okay." He chuckled. "Maybe more than okay!"

"I'm beginning to understand how Mexico works. Now, I have an idea how to handle El Vengador."

After hearing the plan, Raul smiled. "You'd make a good Mexican."

As they neared the city, Raul motioned toward a convenience store.

"Pull over there. I still have some equipment and will edit any mention of El Vengador out of the video, and then find Vasquez. Go back to the *finca* and hide the rest of the evidence and money. Call my cell in three hours."

Moments later as he mounted the bike, Raul added, "Just remember that when this is over and Ilhui is free, you and I may not be quite so friendly."

336

CORTÉS COUNTRY HOUSE

When Martín parked at the old country house, he noted that he had a little over two hours before calling Raul. Although shivering—as much in reaction to the night's events as to the temperature—he decided not to make a fire. Even though he believed the authorities knew nothing of the *finca*, the smoke would signal his presence in case anyone did check. He left the lamps unlit for the same reason.

Upstairs, a beam from the waning moon came through the window in the room Ilhui had used. With its light, he sat on the edge of her bed and counted the money; it came to just under $600,000.

After temporarily stashing the bag on the top shelf of the iron baking oven, he wrapped himself in a blanket and sat on the couch near the dark fireplace, as if it might provide warmth by association. The wind had risen sharply, and the sighing trees sounded like the voices of everyone who had ever lived in the house speaking at once. He wondered how many of them had faced life and death situations in this same building.

He should be pleased. The confrontation at Glendaring's house had gone well. He had the money and enough evidence to clear both himself and Ilhui, and probably enough to convince the U.S. authorities to indict Glendaring and restore much of his family's stolen property. The problem was that Ilhui was still in danger. Besides that, nothing else mattered.

El Vengador's unpredictability added to his concern that Glendaring might not willingly fade away. A double-cross by Raul or the *federale*, Alvaro Vasquez, or both together also required consideration. That sort of thing seemed to be *de rigeur* in Mexico. Nevertheless, he had to admit things seemed on track, and just the thought of ending Ilhui's captivity sent a restorative shot of adrenalin through him. By the time for the telephone call, he had made certain arrangements that raised his spirits even more.

Raul answered on the first ring. "Everything went well with Inspector Vasquez. We'll arrive in the morning about eight with both soldiers and policemen—to keep each other honest," he chuckled.

Then he became serious. "Vasquez has agreed not to arrest you, but he'll question you thoroughly and could change his mind. You need to blame the whole thing on Glendaring. Don't even mention El Vengador, certainly nothing about any previous relationship between him and Ilhui. Of course, when the cave is opened and El Vengador's men are found, there could be a problem. By then, I trust that your generosity will persuade Vasquez to overlook almost anything. Do you understand what I'm saying?"

"Perfectly."

"You should say that after killing your family in Oaxaca Glendaring came to the *finca*, captured you and Ilhui, and took you to his hacienda in Mitla. He then forced you to come back and lead his men to the treasure while Ilhui stayed with him. When you and I later went to Mitla to rescue Ilhui, Glendaring claimed that she had escaped from the hacienda and stolen one of his men's cars. After that, when you returned to the *finca* from Mitla, you found she had been there before you and left a note saying she was going to stay with a friend in Mexico City.

"Don't say anything about Glendaring's money, only

the evidence—and don't give it to him right away. Tell him that copies are being made and he can have it later today. I showed him the video after cutting out any reference to El Vengador. That and the fact that your story will match mine should satisfy him until then. I assume you understand the reason for these precautions?"

"Yes, indeed," said Martín, pleased he had already taken measures to prevent undue extortion by the *federale*.

CORTÉS COUNTRY HOME

Martín slept fitfully in Ilhui's room until sunrise. The location made him feel closer to her and also allowed him to see anyone approaching from the gate. Although way behind on sleep, a hot shower followed by the chilly morning air invigorated him.

Raul and Inspector Vasquez arrived just after eight, followed by a small convoy of police and army vehicles. After introductions in the living room, the two Mexicans shared a thermos of coffee and some shortbread-style pastries with Martín. He thought Vasquez's buzz-cut gray hair, granite jaw, and rugged build made him look more like an American Marine than a member of Mexico's Federal Police. Even his black plastic glasses resembled military issue. After coffee, Raul excused himself.

"A few questions, *Señor* Cortés," said the *federale* in a voice made gravelly by the cigarettes he chain-smoked.

"Of course, Inspector," replied Martín, grateful that his Spanish was now nearly fluent. "I appreciate your help, and you have my complete cooperation."

"*Muy bien,*" said the man with a nod. "Please describe the events of the last few days, especially the murder of the Cortés family and what happened last night."

Martín first related what Glendaring had done to his family in New Mexico and then his Oaxaca family's meeting with the Iranians. "My family thought they seemed quite genuine, but they must have somehow joined forces with Glendaring."

"What were the Iranians buying from your family?"

"I wasn't there, so I don't know precisely. Probably coins with historical value, or maybe a codex.

340

Glendaring was once an archeologist and went to a lot of trouble to steal the ones I had."

Martín explained that he and Ilhui were sitting in this room while the crime was committed in Oaxaca, and learned of it only when Glendaring's men arrived and took them to Mitla. He ended by describing how he had locked the men in the cave after they turned on each other, never mentioning El Vengador or his men.

"How did you find out that the girl escaped from Glendaring?"

"After I locked the men in the cave, I called Raul, told him what had happened, and asked for his help in freeing Ilhui. We went to Glendaring's house. No one was there, so we began searching it. A half hour later, Glendaring returned, and he told us she must have escaped from the locked room where he'd left her. On the way in, he'd noticed one of his cars was missing.

"When I got back here, I discovered a note from her saying she was going to stay with a friend in Mexico City."

"Do you have that note?" inquired the inspector.

"Yes," replied Martín, pulling from his shirt pocket the message he had carefully forged the night before.

The inspector squinted several times, but seemed satisfied. Then he got to the two other items Martín had anticipated. "This treasure, is it true that it came from Hernan Cortés?"

"That's my understanding, although I only know what I was told by the family."

"What is its value?"

"I don't know. I saw it only briefly on a dark night at the end of the cave. I think there are some valuable codices, and if the boxes I saw
are full of gold and silver they could also be worth a

fortune. At first, I was surprised at how little I saw. However, after more than 450 years that would be natural. I don't know Mexican law, but I assume that the government will have a claim to any items of archeological significance."

Inspector Vasquez ignored that. "We'll soon know for sure. Now, about the evidence that Raul described." He paused and fixed his penetrating gaze on Martín. "I want to see it. Some extremely powerful people are involved in this canal affair."

"Certainly, Inspector. It's being copied, and I can have it delivered to you this afternoon. In the meantime, arresting the men and cataloging the treasure should occupy us."

As he said the last words, Martín looked the man directly in the eye. "I should tell you that I believe the Iranians will be able to completely clear Ilhui and myself. And Glendaring's men may provide evidence proving he killed my brother and a client of the bank, and stole my family's property in the United States. Should those things happen, I will be extremely grateful."

"Mr. Cortés, I have no problem obtaining information from criminals. If they have it, so will you. After you bring me the evidence."

Martín smiled. "I understand; you shall have it early this afternoon."

"*Muy bien*," said the inspector, offering his hand to Martín. "Please remember that you are still wanted for murder. Until I actually speak to these men in the cave and see the evidence...you understand?"

"Certainly." Martín again shook the inspector's hand.

Raul stepped into the room. "The police and army

squads are ready." Sensing the mood, he smiled at Martín.

On the way up the mountain, Martín avoided the lower cave that allowed bypassing the brush-covered cliff. Instead, he led them in a traverse up its least steep portion and over a barbed-wire fence.

At the top, the sun had risen well above the distant peaks and the wind was still gusty. Raul and Vasquez stood together making final plans. Since the men in the cave were criminals, they decided that the *federales*, rather than the army, would take the lead.

On the windswept mesa, Martín turned the key in the stone door's lock as quickly and silently as he could. The inspector, who now wore a gas mask, jerked it open. Powerful lights blazed into the cave's interior and were followed by a canister of teargas. Standing out of the line of fire, Vasquez yelled through a bullhorn for those inside to drop their weapons and come out or be killed. Although he spoke in Spanish, Martín assumed the meaning was obvious to the non-Spanish speakers. Either that or the many hours without food or water had taken their toll. Blinking and coughing into the blazing lights, the men filed out, hands over their heads.

Martín watched Glendaring's men, Gabel and Dennis, file by, followed by the Iranians, one of whom limped. Dennis's shoulder was stained with blood as were the pants of the limping Iranian. None of El Vengador's men appeared. Inspector Vasquez waited a moment for the air to clear. Then ordering his men to stay put and holding a stubby automatic weapon at the ready, he charged into the cave.

Vasquez stopped briefly to check four bodies at one side about halfway down. He gestured toward two pistols on the floor and then made his real priority clear by rushing to the back of the brightly lit space. Martín decided there must have been a falling out, and Gabel had killed the guerrillas, or maybe he had done so in frustration. Eyes watering from the residual gas, he remained still. Raul hissed into his ear. "Inside, quickly, but be careful."

He shoved Martín forward, and the two of them moved swiftly to the back, keeping their hands in plain sight. Besides the remnants of the gas that brought tears to Martín's eyes, the air was fetid with the aromas of body odor and human waste. Strewn about the floor were coins and ingots of gold and silver. Around them were haphazard piles of bark paper covered with drawings, obviously discarded in frustration.

The inspector faced them and quickly masked the excitement on his face. He motioned with his weapon to the bodies behind them. "Those four are long dead. Who are they?"

Without hesitation, Martín said, "They were with Glendaring."

Vasquez gave him a hard look, obviously not convinced. Nevertheless, he nodded. "Whatever you say. I'll list this property and ask you to sign it."

Raul cleared his throat. "For the sake of efficiency, I suggest that Martín and I assist your men."

Noting that two well-armed soldiers had appeared behind Raul, Vasquez gave another curt nod.

Martín said, "Inspector, I'm anxious that whatever needs to be done to clear Ilhui and me be done as quickly as possible. Your help will be greatly appreciated."

Vasquez glanced at his watch. "It's now a little after nine-thirty. If you bring the evidence we discussed to

344

my office at one-thirty we should have preliminary results from the interrogations by then, including a comparison of bullets between the ones used to kill those four and those used on your family. If all goes well, I should be able to withdraw the charges before the *comida*. Perhaps you will join me?"

"Thank you. That would be a pleasure, but please allow me a brief postponement. I am anxious to find Ilhui's brother and see if he knows where she is. They're the only family I have left."

Vasquez winked at Raul. "Of course! We Mexicans can be both efficient *and* understanding."

Martín nearly laughed out loud as he suddenly realized how obtainable justice was in Mexico—for those who could afford it. But he worried about the approaching meeting with El Vengador, all too aware that Ilhui's life, and possibly his own, still hinged on the outcome.

Raul's men had brought small cloth bags and an electronic scale, and Martín watched carefully while soldiers and *federales* separated the gold and silver coins and ingots and then weighed and scooped them into the bags. It took nearly forty-five minutes. Martín counted fifteen bags of gold and twenty-five of silver. After recording the weight of each bag, Vasquez estimated the total. Not considering the historical value of the coins, which Martín thought might be considerable, it came to $1.5 million.

Inspector Vasquez made notes on a clipboard as the drawstring on each bag was closed. When the counting was complete, he handed the board to Martín and asked him to sign a statement attesting that the count was accurate. Seeing the total, twelve bags of gold and twenty of silver, Martín looked up. The inspector's eyes bored into him. Gone was any sign of their recent collegiality. Vasquez and Raul stood rigid and silent while Martín paused to confirm his calculation that the missing bags were worth about $300,000. The atmosphere thickened to thunderstorm consistency. Then, without regret, he scrawled his signature and shook hands with Vasquez.

The tension broke, and the inspector smiled. "I will see that these are delivered to the bank of your choice."

On the way down the mountain, Raul touched Martín on the arm, pulling him to one side. "It's good luck that the guerrillas are dead, and I told the Iranians not to mention El Vengador. Copy the evidence and get it to Vasquez as soon as possible so you can make the meeting with El Vengador."

"If I can get hold of Trini, I'll have him do that. If I show up, Vasquez might try to hold me up for a few more bags."

"Good thinking,"

When they reached the bottom, it was Martín's turn to steer Raul aside, allowing the group to pass by. "Follow me," he said.

Moments later, he opened the door to the small cave at the base of the mountain. From the bag of money and evidence he had placed there last night, he extracted the $50,000 they had taken from Glendaring's car and handed it to Raul.

"Thank you," said Martín. "And whatever you get as a share from the good inspector is fine with me."

"I...," Raul began, and then smiled. "*Gracias*!" If you ever decide to emigrate, you just passed the Mexican culture portion of your citizenship exam." He extended his hand, and then, changing his mind, he gave Martín a hearty *abrazo*. He gripped Martín's arm. "I wish I could go with you, but my presence would ensure Ilhui's death." He shook his head and added, "See you later today as we agreed. *Vaya con Dios*."

ZAACHILA

When Trini picked up on the first ring, Martín assured him that things had gone well and asked him to come to the *finca*. He hung up, feeling like a gambler on a winning streak. His luck had held, and he was nearly certain El Vengador needed money so badly that if the exchange was properly handled, he would free Ilhui. But he still worried that the guerrilla leader would try to take the ransom and then kill Ilhui and himself. He couldn't banish the image of the angel-faced blond girl painting her naked body with the heart of Ilhui's dead friend.

Trini arrived forty-five minutes later in the family's Jeep Cherokee, his Ralph Lauren khakis and polo shirt giving no hint of his female persona. The reunion was emotional, and Martín was surprised by the young man's obvious concern for him amidst the tragedy in his own life. After hearing what had happened, Trini agreed to make two copies of the evidence and take one of them to Inspector Vasquez's office. He also said he would make arrangements with a bank for a place to store the gold and silver. Martín then traded him El Vengador's van for the Jeep.

After Trini left, like an athlete before an event, Martín paced the old house trying to visualize success, but was quickly frustrated by the unknowns. Making a decision that he realized could mean life or death, he divided the $500,000 portion of Glendaring's money demanded by El Vengador into two bundles. One he placed in a paper bag and locked in the small cave at the bottom of the mountain; the other he stuffed into a white canvas tote bag. He drove through the gate just before 2:00 p.m.

The satellite phone no longer worked, so he stopped at the public phone in the village. Trini reported that his meeting with Vasquez had gone well. "Apparently the Iranians are cooperating, but the Americans are not. Inspector Vasquez said he needs a little more time before rescinding the charges against you and Ilhui, but he promises that will happen later today. He agreed to transfer the gold and silver to the bank I found, so I don't think he's trying to grab more."

Elated that one more tangle was unraveling, Martín left, hoping to undo the most crucial knot of all. Instead of bearing southeast from the city as he had done on his way to Mitla, he drove nearly due south, first on a highway and then a rural road that drew him into the hills. Knowing that he was still the subject of a manhunt, he drove with caution. Interference from the police at this point would be tragic.

He cruised through sleepy villages, past small farmsteads, and across clear streams flanked by irrigated fields. He kept his window open to the brisk country air, perfumed with the scent of new-mown grass. The road constantly twisted and turned so that different pastoral vistas opened before him like a slide show. He hoped that someday he could make the same drive under more pleasant circumstances. Finally, around a turn on the left he saw the restaurant where he would be contacted. He made out one long, low-slung building and several outbuildings of stone and brick with pitched corrugated tin roofs. As he slowed to a crawl, a tall, open-sided shed with a metal roof set well away from the other buildings caught his attention. About ten people milled around the perimeter. The nearby parking lot held only a sprinkling of cars.

His watch said two-thirty, half an hour early. He drove through the village and parked on the far side, behind a stand of trees at the back of a dry-goods store, where it was unlikely to be noticed. He hefted the bag full of money and began walking toward the restaurant.

Twenty minutes later, he entered the grounds with five minutes to spare. The parking lot was nearly full, and a much larger crowd had gathered around the small building he had noticed before. Since he had no further instructions on how to make contact, he joined the group.

Under the steel-framed canopy sat a stone structure about the size and height of a twin bed. On top of it a mound of dirt held a flower-covered cross, obviously imitating a grave. As he tried to reconcile that image with the general attitude of merriment among the bystanders, two young men in white shirts, pants, and caps moved through the crowd. One of them grabbed the cross and pulled it slowly from the mound, revealing a rope tied to its bottom that disappeared into the dirt. The other man grasped the rope and gave a mighty tug. A cheer went up as a liter bottle of golden liquid, followed by wisps of smoke, swung free from the loosely packed soil.

Martín felt a pull at his sleeve and turned to find an Indian girl in an embroidered *huipil* and voluminous skirts offering him a small clay cup. He took it, and a moment later one of the men poured some of the liquid from the bottle into it. A glimpse at the label confirmed his guess that it held mezcal, now quite warm.

By this time, the men were removing shovelfuls of dirt to one side of the "grave." As they did so, more tendrils of smoke appeared and the aroma of smoked meat filled the air. As they reached the stone base, one of the shovels clanged on metal. Donning gloves, the two men removed a thin, bed-size piece of corrugated tin to reveal a still-smoking pit filled with items wrapped in what looked like banana leaves. The cooking smells were intoxicating, and Martín realized that Mexico's famous black humor had attached itself to a ceremony celebrating the unearthing of a traditional *barbacoa* pit.

The area continued to take on the aroma of meat roasted with exotic herbs and spices, and Martín remembered he had eaten nothing since the pastries he'd shared with Raul and Vasquez early that morning. He took a tiny sip of mezcal, afraid to drink more on an empty stomach. For a moment he pictured himself there with Ilhui for a celebratory meal, but reality quickly returned. He clutched the sack of money to his side and walked slowly through the outdoor seating area toward the open-air kitchen behind it.

He sat on a bench under a canvas awning, slightly away from the other customers but where he could easily be spotted. Behind him was a cook-stall where a stout Indian woman in a spotless white dress embroidered with pink flowers flipped huge tortillas on a convex griddle. Other cooks stirred the contents of steaming *cazuelas*.

Martín watched a group of *mariachis* circulating through the tables. Several times they sang a song, received payment, and moved on. Partially for something to do and partly because it calmed him, he took several more sips of the smoky mezcal. After ten minutes, he was beginning to fear that nothing would happen, when the four-man musical group again caught his eye. In full *charro* regalia of sombreros, waist-length embroidered jackets, and belled pants over cowboy boots, the men had bypassed several tables and came directly toward him. They formed a semicircle, screening him from the other tables, and began to sing.

The tune seemed both distinctive and familiar. At the first refrain, Martín recognized the ballad he had heard in the bar in Zacatecas, the one his companions told him recounted the exploits of the guerrilla leader, El Vengador. Carefully, he looked into the faces of the musicians. Three of them were middle-aged and nondescript. But the slender bass player's deeply creased, hawk-like face looked at least seventy, and his eyes glittered with intelligence.

As the song concluded, Martín pulled two ten-peso coins from his pocket. In the sudden quiet, he handed them to the old man who stepped forward, removed his sombrero, and bowed, revealing a shock of pure white hair. As he finished the bow, the man said in good English, "Go behind the kitchen and across the field. Follow the path past the tractor into the hills." With a flourish, he returned his sombrero to his head and followed the rest of the group to the next table.

Martín waited a few moments and then stood and made his way to the restroom at the far end of the open-air kitchen. He emerged with the bag of money in his left hand and strolled behind the building, where he found a newly plowed field. At the far end was a tractor, and behind it stretched brush and tree-covered hills that rose steeply into the distance, where the lowering sun backlit the rough landscape with a dusty haze. Martín felt the first chill of evening in the air.

Picking up his pace, he strode through the field to

the rusted old tractor that had obviously not moved in many years. He remembered reading that years ago the government had bought such equipment for peasant farmers. They used the machinery until the first time something broke, then having no parts or mechanical expertise they
abandoned it, reverting to their age-old stoop labor tradition.

Behind the tractor, a trail wound along the bottom of a narrow valley westward into the range of mountains. Easy to follow, he thought the primitive pathway might precede the introduction of the wheel to Mexico by the Spaniards. The air was crisp, and as Martín climbed he saw that the hills on either side grew taller and steeper. He felt unseen eyes, but after glancing up the hillsides despaired of spotting watchers.

The trail zigzagged higher, leveled out, and then bore sharply to the right into another narrow valley, at whose far end rose yet higher peaks. As happens in mountain country, the sun was dropping quickly. At the end of the valley, he made out a stand of tall trees at the base of the next mountain. He had walked quickly and in spite of the cool mountain air, perspiration seeped into his shirt. The sudden cessation of birdsong and a general feeling of unease caused him to sense that he neared his destination. He slowed his pace to conserve energy and became more cautious. He had not shaken the feeling he was watched, and when he reached the trees it was confirmed.

The grove was thicker than he'd thought, and he approached it carefully, the tote bag firmly at his side. The light dimmed, and the temperature dropped further. Ten feet in front of him, a man stepped from behind a tree and pointed a pistol at him.

Martín actually felt relieved to recognize one of El Vengador's guerrillas and quickly complied when he was ordered to drop the bag and raise his hands. From the other side, another man approached, frisked him, and checked the contents of the bag. Surprisingly, he handed it back. "Follow," he ordered.

With the first man behind Martín, they went through the trees and then a short distance up the mountain to a level clearing under a rocky overhang. "Wait here," ordered the man in front, motioning for him to sit on a nearby boulder.

For ten minutes, Martín watched the shadows lengthen as the sun continued its descent in earnest. Then, with not even the sound of a snapping twig, a small party of men and one woman headed by El Vengador materialized from the left. Martín's heart leaped at the sight of Ilhui. Her head was bowed, and one of the guerrillas had a hand on her left arm. As she looked up and saw Martín, she jerked herself free, ran to him, and threw her arms around his neck.

"We'll make it okay," he whispered into her ear, for the first time really believing that.

Ilhui held him tightly, her face pressed into his shoulder, then she slowly disengaged and stepped back, eyes lowered.

Surprised at her attitude, Martín said, "Are you all right?"

She nodded but still did not meet his eyes. He saw an angry bruise on her cheekbone, probably where El Vengador had hit her at his previous headquarters.

Before he could say anything, the guerrilla leader stepped forward and looked pointedly at the tote bag, now dangling from Martín's left hand. "I presume you succeeded?"

"To a point."

"What does that mean?" The man's handsome face, framed by his nearly shoulder-length hair, lacked expression and, surprisingly, his tone held neither pique nor threat.

Martín met the guerrilla's eyes. "What I mean," he said slowly, "is that I got the money you demanded, but the man who destroyed my family—both families—is alive and well. That is, if you ignore some damage to his ear and nose. He has either left or soon will."

El Vengador shook his head. "His jet's at the airport, so he's still here. I understand your wanting revenge. Be patient and that could happen sooner than you think." Then almost as an afterthought, he said, "The money please."

The bag changed hands. As the guerrilla looked inside Martín said, "I'll save you the trouble. There's $250,000 in there. You'll get the rest *and* the treasure after Ilhui is free."

Martín braced for a storm, but El Vengador merely nodded. "That was not our arrangement, but as you wish. One of my men will take her back to the restaurant. You'll come with us, another way."

"No," said Martín. "I'm keeping our bargain. Now I need assurance that she will really be free. We go with her to my car at the far side of the village so I can watch her drive away."

Again, El Vengador nodded. *Too easy—what the hell's going on?* wondered Martín.

"Come with us to our van."

El Vengador placed Martín and Ilhui in the center of

his group of six men and set off on a path that approached the village at a different angle from the one Martín had followed.

The sun dropped lower and shadows crept furtively about them, like a band of natives stalking a column of explorers. Ilhui walked beside Martín, neither looking at him nor speaking. "You really okay?" he asked.

She gave a bleak smile. "Yes, physically. It's just that...we can discuss it later."

Martín stayed by her side as they descended toward the village. *What's happened? The fire seems to have gone out of both Ilhui and El Vengador.* He decided he had more important things to worry about—at least he hoped so.

The next half hour passed with no further conversation, and without warning the sun disappeared behind a mountain. The trail became less steep and widened into a well-packed road. Around the next bend they turned sharply to the right into a small draw at the end of which stood a van, similar to the others used by the group, guarded by the same driver Martín had surprised at the *finca.*

When they neared the village, Martín gave directions to his car. About a quarter mile before they reached it, the guerrilla leader ordered the van pulled to the side and two of his men to get out and look for a trap.

Martín shook his head. "I told you I'd give you the money and take you to the treasure if you release Ilhui. I'll keep my word. And don't forget the people locked in the cave. You'll have to deal with Glendaring's men and take care of yours and the Iranians."

"I haven't forgotten."

Fifteen minutes later, the two men returned and reported no sign of a trap or surveillance of any sort.

356

Although Ilhui sat next to Martín in the van, they didn't speak. When the van pulled in beside the Cherokee, Martín pressed the keys into her hand. "Go to the city—Trini's waiting for you. I'll make sure they call no one."

She nodded and squeezed his hand. "Thank you," she muttered, with a smile that seemed impersonal, as if directed at a stranger that had provided a small kindness in the midst of an all- consuming grief.

Even more puzzled and concerned, Martín watched carefully as she got into the car, switched on the lights, and drove slowly away.

CORTÉS COUNTRY HOME

After watching Ilhui drive away, Martín tried to focus on what was to come. But now that she was free, nothing else seemed to matter. He'd hand over the rest of the money and take the guerrillas to the cave, where Raul's men would arrest them. All Martín had to do was stay out of the line of fire. Then maybe he could find out why Ilhui acted so strangely and get on with his life.

When the van pulled in front of the Cortés *finca*, darkness had fallen. El Vengador's manner went from lethargic to hyper-alert, but his former viciousness still waned. "No more delays," he snapped, shining a flashlight in Martín's face. "Tell me exactly where we're going and what will happen."

Martín explained that the money was in the small cave at the base of the mountain.

El Vengador, carrying the tote bag with the first quarter-million dollars, eyed Martín suspiciously, but handed him a flashlight and nodded for him to lead the way.

Inside the small cave, the handover went smoothly. El Vengador barely looked at the money before stuffing it into the bag. But as they climbed the narrow switchback trail to the mountaintop, he seemed increasingly edgy. When they crested the mesa, he called a halt. A bank of clouds had blown in and obscured the moon and starlight. The boulders on the mesa were mere shadows, and the rocky pinnacle above the cave vanished into darkness.

El Vengador sent two of his men ahead, and Martín watched their flashlight beams skitter around the mesa like tiny UFOs. They soon returned and gave the all-clear.

The men assembled near the cave's entrance, and Martín aimed his light at the rocky wall, revealing the door and its lock. He handed the key to El Vengador. The guerrilla carefully inserted it into the lock with his right hand, while his left hand kept its grip on the tote bag that now held half a million dollars. Then he stepped away and spoke to his men, reminding them to be careful of their comrades inside.

El Vengador again reached out and grasped the key between his thumb and forefinger. But instead of turning it, he swiveled his head and focused his light on Martín, who had inched along the wall away from the door. For a moment, El Vengador gazed at him, and Martín held his breath. "You open it," said El Vengador, moving to the side.

As Martín stepped to the door, the guerrilla leader spoke softly to his men. "Turn off your lights until the door is open, and then immediately shine them inside." He moved to join those farthest away from Martín.

In the sudden darkness, Martín heard the lock grate as he turned the key and swung the massive door open. For a moment there was nothing, and then everything happened at once. The guerrilla's flashlight beams were immediately obliterated by far more powerful lights from inside the cave, as well as from behind them. A bullhorn reverberated across the mesa. "Drop your weapons or die. Now!"

Expecting the air to be filled with the deadly buzz of bullets, Martín hit the ground and covered his head with his hands. But he only heard a large number of men converging. Less than a minute later, Martín was pulled to his feet by Raul Rodríguez. "You certainly know how to duck."

"A very useful thing whenever you're near the Mexican army."

"That will cost you," shot back Raul. "Ilhui?"

"All went well," said Martín. "She should be home with Trini."

"Thank God! But we still have work. You need to identify El Vengador."

Martín examined the line of guerrillas blinking in the glare of powerful spotlights, and his stomach clenched. "He's not there. Before the lights went out, he was right here." He pointed to a spot on the other side of the open door. "I thought he was going to open the door, but at the last minute he ordered me to do it. Something must have warned him. How the hell could he have gotten away?"

Raul shook his head in disgust. "During the short few seconds when we took off our night-vision glasses as the lights went on. If so, he was lucky. I assumed that between the men in the cave and the ones who came from the edge of the mesa no one could escape. I do have two men guarding the van below. I'll warn them even though he probably won't go there. Did he have the money with him?"

Martín nodded.

"If he's as smart as I think he is, he's probably gone."

"Shit," grunted Martín. Then glancing toward the six handcuffed guerrillas, "What will happen to these men?"

Raul glared. "You work for Amnesty International or something?"

"No, but I want to know."

"I told you before that the official government

policy is that there's no organized guerrilla activity in Oaxaca. It's my job to ensure that. What you've done in the last few days took a lot of courage. Now it's time for us to go our separate ways, especially regarding Ilhui."

Martín looked him in the eye and smiled. "At least for a while."

"*Claro que sí*, of course!" Raul laughed. The two men embraced.

After the *abrazo*, Martín grabbed a flashlight, turned, and made his way down the mountain. As he neared the bottom, he heard distant gunfire from above. Sick to his stomach, he continued. Then he realized that with the van in possession of the army, he no longer had transportation.

When he reached the house, he found the family's Jeep parked beside the guerrilla's van and the house lights on. Ilhui and Trini waited for him in the living room. "Is it over?" cried Ilhui, her face showing the strain and bruises of the last few days.

"Yes," said Martín. "At least I think so, but El Vengador escaped."

Her face remained a mask.

Trini came to Martín and gave him an *abrazo*. "Thanks for everything."

Yeah, thought Martín, suddenly depressed. *Thanks for bringing Glendaring to Oaxaca.*

Trini said, "Let's go to the city; we can talk on the way."

Martín looked at Ilhui. Her shoulders slumped, and her once golden skin seemed palid, making her look ten years older. Her eyes fixed on his, and she came and put her arms around him. They held each other tightly and then separated without a word.

OAXACA

It seemed like months rather than days since Martín had seen the Cortés townhome. Trini had cleaned it thoroughly, so there was no evidence of the recent tragedy. Even Dragón had recovered and lay yipping in a dream on the floor by the door. But each room held reminders of Hector, Martha, and Abuelita, who had spent their lives in the place and whose souls Martín suspected remained nearby. He wondered if their presence was what troubled the dog's sleep.

Neither Martín nor Ilhui had eaten since breakfast and thanked Trini when he placed bowls of his eighth *mole* and a basket of hot tortillas on the table. With it, he served mugs of frothy, chile-laced hot chocolate. After dinner he produced a pot of *café de olla*, the traditional coffee made with *piloncillo* and a dash of chocolate.

During the meal, Martín's concern deepened. Ilhui said nothing, and when he caught her glancing at him, she turned away. For the first time, her arms were bare of bracelets.

When they were done, Martín pushed his empty plate aside and looked at her. "Let me tell you what happened." He described the trip to the country house, locking the men in the cave, and the events at Glendaring's hacienda. When he finished, he said, "Financially, here is where you stand. Unless Vasquez finds some way to extract more than the $300,000 I allowed him to steal, there should be about $1,300,000 left, plus the emerald at say another $200,000. There is also about $75,000 of Glendaring's money that I didn't have to give El Vengador. All in all, enough for you to live well, but maybe not a great deal for future generations. Of course, there are the codices, which could be worth a fortune by themselves. Do either of you know if the government will take them?"

"You know as well as I do they'll take whatever they can get." Trini fixed his gaze on Martín. "You keep saying 'you.' *You* are part of this family, not just by blood but because you've earned it. At the very least the $75,000 from Glendaring belongs to you."

In the ensuing silence, Trini glanced at Ilhui. She gave a slow nod, but her expression and body language remained lethargic. Martín had hoped for a hero's welcome from her and had expected at least a hint of gratitude. But he realized that what had happened, including the deaths of her family and especially watching Greta's brutal murder, had been about as traumatic as anything a human being could experience.

As Martín sought a way to break the awkward silence, a thought hit him. "Wait a minute. Vasquez left the codices in the cave, and I doubt Rodriguez or his men took them!"

At that moment the phone rang. Trini answered and handed it to Martín, mouthing "*El Capitán.*"

It was indeed Raul. He told Martín that he had just spoken with Inspector Vasquez, and that all charges against Martín and Ilhui had been dropped. He also said that the canal project signing ceremony was still scheduled for the grounds of Monte Albán tomorrow at noon, and that he and his men were providing the security. "I doubt that Glendaring has the nerve to be there, but I suggest that you, Ilhui, and Trini attend. The press will come, and that will give you an opportunity to remove any doubts about your innocence."

"Great," said Martín. "According to El Vengador,

Glendaring's jet remains at the airport. Now tell me about the status of the codices?"

"The Cortés family has suffered enough. Do what you want. I left the key where you kept it in the small cave. Now, I want to talk to Ilhui."

During their conversation, Martín watched Ilhui carefully but could detect no change in her attitude, even when she learned about the dismissed charges. At least Raul convinced her to attend the ceremony. Despite his better judgment, Martín said, "Ilhui, tell us about it, what happened."

Ilhui sighed and said, "I wasn't harmed. I was blindfolded most of the time, and he kept the bitch that killed Greta away from me. But something happened. He seemed to change completely after we moved from the cavern below the ruins to a small house not far from where we met you. He dismissed most of his men, told them to return to their homes. Once I saw him cry, and he argued continuously with the girl."

"Any idea what happened?"

She shook her head and looked away. Reluctantly, Martín concluded that tomorrow, after a good night's sleep, would be a better time to dig deeper.

They were about to go to bed when the doorbell rang. Trini answered it and returned holding a business-size envelope. On its face, in bold slanted cursive, was written "*Señor* Martín Cortés." Martín carefully tore it open and unfolded two pages covered in the same hand. He read aloud:

Señor Cortés,

You must think me a brutal, unprincipled man. I

have certainly given you enough reasons for that, so you may not believe what I am about to say. But I assure you it is the truth. Under the ancient city, when you asked me what I was doing and why I was doing it, I dismissed you, convinced that my actions were appropriate. I have spent the last years fighting to create a better Mexico, and I remain convinced that the current system has no chance of improving life for the majority of people. Those in control are simply too selfish to do what must be done. Later, when I thought about it and about what you said regarding the pattern of revolutionaries becoming dictators, I concluded you were right, and that I have indeed become something I am ashamed of.

On the way to our new headquarters, I realized that what you said was correct, that a less violent course is possible. When I thought of the things I have recently been part of, especially killing Greta, it made me ill. Even the name I adopted, as you pointed out, is an indictment of my motives. My father who died for nonviolence would be horrified and ashamed of me, and I am ashamed of myself.

What the future holds for me I do not know, but I can assure you that it will not involve violence, so you have nothing to fear from me. In fact, despite your attempt to capture me, I am in your debt. I suspected a trap, and your manner outside the cave convinced me I was correct.

Although it comes far too late, I wish to apologize to you, Ilhui, and your entire family, and I wish you every happiness in the years to come.

Sincerely,

Luís Marcel Gorgón

At the bottom was a postscript:

"Please believe that when I said your concerns about Colin Glendaring may soon be resolved, I was not speaking idly. Also, I fully realize that what I have set in motion and the fact that I do not intend to return the money you brought me makes what I said above seem like a lie. Nevertheless, I am comfortable with what I plan to do next and how I will use the money."

When Martín finished, the silence held until, with more energy, Ilhui said, "Luís Gorgón, so that's who he is. He was in the news about five years ago, a professor at UNAM in Mexico City, outspoken in his criticism of the government and suspected of being involved in revolutionary activities. One day they found his wrecked car just outside of Acapulco, reportedly the result of a dispute with other revolutionaries. I heard no more of him." Saying nothing further, she rose and walked toward the stairs.

Knowing he should give her time but unable to contain himself, Martín said, "Ilhui!"

She stopped but didn't turn around. He stood and went to face her. "I know this is a bad time, but we need to talk."

She said nothing as Trini disappeared through the doors into the patio.

"Please?" said Martín.

She moved her head affirmatively, and he gently took her arm and steered her to the couch. After they sat, he said, "I know I should give you some time, but I'm impatient; I can't help it. This is too important! Here's what worries me: before all this happened, even after it began, I believed we were getting along well, more than well. I know we felt an attraction, and while we realized we had a lot to learn about each other, we were both excited at the prospects. Something's happened. Not knowing what is driving me crazy. I beg you to tell me!"

Ilhui kneaded her hands in her lap. "It's quite simple," she said, looking up at him and speaking forcefully for the first time.

"Whenever I really care about someone or something, I seem to make the wrong decisions. In the past, only I suffered. Now, because I misjudged El Vengador, most of my family is dead. And even though I know you aren't to blame and that if you had not come Glendaring would probably have come anyway…. The truth is, I'm disgusted with myself and everything around me."

Martín took her hand in both of his and looked into her eyes. "I've thought about that carefully. El Vengador admitted he sought the family out because he had *already* heard about the treasure. Even if you hadn't encouraged him, he would still have helped Glendaring. As for me, Glendaring had no idea I was here before he started his search for the source of the emerald and codices that he stole from me in New Mexico. He was coming to Oaxaca anyway and would have pursued it even without my presence. Believe me, Ilhui, it's natural for us to blame ourselves and maybe even each other. But it's unfair. Was working with those children also a mistake?"

She shook her head, seemingly in agony. "I just don't know. So many times I've been sure I was right and then turn out to have been wrong! I know I sound like a stupid parrot that always says the same thing, but please give me that time you mentioned." She stood and went upstairs.

Martín remembered one last call he had to make. The last time he
had spoken with Herb Gonzalez, his best friend and lawyer, was from the American Embassy after being kidnapped. Moments later, the familiar voice boomed through the line. "Martín, where the fuck are you? The last thing I heard you were wanted for killing part of your family in Oaxaca. Since then, nothing...*nada*!"

Martín apologized and summarized the recent events, beginning with the reappearance of Colin Glendaring and ending with the uncertainty regarding what the man would now do. Herb remained quiet until Martín finished, and then he said, "That evidence in Glendaring's Day-Timer and his recorded admissions about the killings of Abel and Johnny Carillo... I'm not certain if the recording can be used in court, but the FBI and FDIC will sure want to hear it and to see the rest of that stuff. That may be all we need to make you whole. Can you get it to me right away? And when are you coming home?"

To the first question Martín responded quickly, "I have everything but a copy of the recording and will overnight as much as I can tomorrow." The second question caused him to pause. "I'm not sure where home is, but I'll be in Santa Fe within a few days. I'll let you know as soon as I can."

As he hung up, he turned to see Trini staring at him.

MONTE ALBÁN

The next morning, Martín returned to the house after an early walk to find Trini waiting for him. "I'm ready to go with you to get the codices."

When they entered the cave, the codices still littered the floor, like windblown trash. As they gathered them up, Martín marveled at the collection. The bark-paper drawings depicted scenes from the very beginning of the conquest, rendered in the folkloric style of the Aztecs. The principal subjects included Spanish ships, men on horses appearing to be one animal, and drawings of Spanish soldiers. A few resembled the ones stolen from Martín in New Mexico, and some of the subjects were easily recognizable as Hernan Cortés.

"Montezuma's spies illustrated what they saw," explained Martín. "They're worth a fortune! But with the ownership cloudy it may not be safe to keep them in a bank where the government could grab them, although an official institution may be where they ultimately belong." They placed the documents in large plastic containers they had picked up at the market and then returned to Oaxaca.

Later that afternoon on the way to the canal ceremony at Monte Albán, Martín, Trini, and Ilhui rehearsed what they would tell the reporters. Ilhui said she planned to say as little as possible, and all agreed that Martín should speak for them. Unspoken but on all their minds was the fate of Glendaring, the man responsible for the death of so many Cortés family members. Would he attend the ceremony? If not, what had happened to him?

As on his last visit, when they reached the ancient city, Martín felt he was on top of the world, and a sudden energy flooded his body. At the entry they discovered their names on the list of authorized attendees, undoubtedly put there by Raul. As they entered the grounds, they saw that a dais had been set up overlooking the majestic ruins to one side of the sunken court where the Zapotec Indians had played their life and death ballgame. Sloping stone walls descended to the narrow, grass playing field. At its far end, a giant stairway rose again to ground level. Beyond it stood flat-topped pyramids. It seemed to Martín to be on a grander scale than even the largest modern sports stadiums. In front of the dais in a semicircle were rows of folding chairs.

The press quickly spotted the Cortés family and spent the next fifteen minutes asking questions. After Trini and Ilhui deferred to him, Martín related that the family was murdered when robbers discovered that the valuables they sought did not exist, that he and Ilhui were mistakenly blamed when one of those arrested lied to the police.

The arrival of the dignitaries caused the reporters to scurry on to greener pastures, and Martín, Ilhui, and Trini took seats toward the back. As an official tested the PA system, Raul Rodriguez, in full dress uniform, approached and pointed out the mayor, the governor, and his commanding officer. Everyone of importance seemed to be there except Glendaring. The captain bent to Martín and whispered, "His jet is still at the airport," and then he passed a small package to Martín. "Your copy of Glendaring's taped confession." In return, Martín handed Raul a copy of El Vengador's letter, which he folded and slid into his pocket.

The time for the event to begin came and went.

Even though punctuality was not a priority in Mexico, after half an hour the dignitaries began glancing toward the entrance to the grounds, and the crowd started to murmur. After an hour, the portable speakers crackled into life and a man in a dark suit explained that although one of the principals had been detained, the proceedings would begin.

The mayor of Oaxaca stood and, in glowing, self-important terms, introduced the governor of the state. His Excellency rose and gave appropriate thanks in the same flowery manner. Then he began to describe the benefits the canal project would bring.

As the governor spoke, the hum of a powerful engine intruded. As it increased in intensity, all eyes were drawn to its source. A sleek jet approached from the direction of the airport, moving at frightening speed. "It must be Glendaring," whispered Martín.

Like a vengeful demon, the plane streaked toward the mountaintop. Martín's pulse raced as he remembered movie scenes where helpless people were chewed up by strafing aircraft. The shriek of the engine became deafening, and Martín could clearly make out the pilot's chalk-white face as the plane crested the mountain and headed straight toward the crowd. Panicked, Martín shoved Trini and Ilhui to the ground and then joined them. Nearly everyone else also hit the turf.

At the last minute, the plane danced on its tail, and with a thunderous roar streaked upward, like a rocket blasting into outer space. Most of the crowd, including Martín and Ilhui, came to their feet, craned their necks, and squinted to watch the elegant machine continue its climb toward the sun. Seconds later it disappeared in a blinding flash, as if vaporized by a space-age laser. That image was followed by a deafening explosion, and debris rained onto the crowd. Martín pushed Ilhui to the ground and threw himself on top of her to protect her with his body. Then he clasped his hands over his head. A piece of torn metal fell nearby, and he heard shrieks of pain.

When the deadly cascade subsided, Martín looked up to see the charred, still-smoking remains of the plane littering the field and the injured writhing in pain. The dais lay on its side and the dignitaries were sprinting up the hill toward the exit. Raul and his men rushed about attending to the most serious cases. Trini was already standing and Martín helped Ilhui to her feet. They rushed after the panicked VIPs through the exit gate.

On the ride back to town, Trini said to Martín, "You think that's what El Veng…rather Luis Gorgón meant when he said, 'Your concerns about Colin Glendaring may soon be resolved'?"

"I imagine so. It was probably a bomb set to go off when the plane reached a certain altitude."

OAXACA

Later that afternoon, Martín, Ilhui, and Trini sat in their living room. "Is it really over?" asked Trini.

"Yes, at least the bad part." Martín sighed.

"Good," said Trini. "I'll open the restaurant tonight. It's time."

"That's great! We should do everything we can to get things back to normal." Martín noted that Trini was not in drag as before when he went to the restaurant, and Ilhui seemed naked without her bracelets.

Martín asked Trini for the extra copy of the evidence to send to Herb. As he left for the DHL shipping office, Trini stopped him. "I postponed the funerals for Hector, Martha, and Abuelita, hoping you could attend. I heard you say you were going back to Santa Fe, and I...?"

"I should have discussed that with you. Schedule the funeral when it's best for you; I'll be there. About everything else, we probably feel the same. Too much has happened too quickly for us to have done anything but react. In my case, I came to Mexico to get away from my problems and gain perspective. On one level I found the opposite. On another I found a new family and a new world. But then I lost part of that family."

After composing himself, Martín continued. "I have some business that can't wait, and it may be good for Ilhui to have some time alone. The worst thing I can do is to try to push her into something before she's ready. If I stay here, that's exactly what I'll do."

Trini shook his head. "I don't understand what she's thinking any

better than you. While you're gone, I'll talk with her.

Stay in touch. You and she...there's too much there to lose."

"Thanks, I agree," said Martín and gave Trini an *abrazo*.

SANTA FE

On the flight to Albuquerque, Martín experienced both sadness and anticipation. Sadness at the previous day's funeral and anticipation of what was to come, especially his reunion with Pancho. When he caught sight of Herb Gonzalez outside security, he felt a flush of triumph, the opposite of the despair that had engulfed him at their last meeting.

Inside Herb's Range Rover on the way to Santa Fe, Martín pushed his seat all the way back, stretched out, and brought Herb up to date. "Raul Rodriguez, the army officer I told you about, drove me to the airport. He said the investigation of Glendaring's crash indicated that a bomb destroyed the jet, probably one set to explode at a certain altitude."

Herb shook his head. "How do you think that happened, and why the hell did Glendaring buzz the event?"

"I'm pretty sure El Vengador placed the bomb. He inferred as much more than once. Why did Glendaring do the flyover? I told Raul my best guess is that Glendaring knew he was finished and decided to leave with an act of contempt, his way of giving the finger to the world. Raul agreed on both points. He said that placing the bomb was one of the last things El Vengador did.

He then explained that the previous day his men caught one of the guerrillas. "After some 'encouragement' he led them to a cabin where El Vengador had hidden in the mountains behind Zaachila, near where I found Ilhui. Raul couldn't tell if it was occupied, so his men surrounded it. They were about to go in when they heard the angry shriek of a woman followed by two gunshots. A moment later, a young blond woman ran from the house screaming and holding a pistol. When they ordered her to stop she shot at them. They killed her. Inside the cabin, they found El Vengador, shot to death."

"Was that the same woman who murdered Ilhui's friend?"

Martín paused, remembering the sickening site in the cave below the ancient city. "That's what I asked, and Raul said he thought so but needed to be certain without upsetting Ilhui. We stopped at the morgue and I identified her." Martín shook his head. "What a waste! She was so beautiful and seemed so innocent that her face looked like the death mask of an angel. Then, just before we got to the airport, Raul told me that the Iranians had been taken from jail and escorted to a private jet by some grim-looking men representing the government of Iran. I wouldn't like to be in their shoes."

After digesting the news, Herb said, "I found a bunch more incriminating entries in Glendaring's diary and gave them to the FBI with the rest of the evidence. They didn't seem too excited, and I want your situation given a high priority. I've scheduled a press conference tomorrow morning to turn up the heat."

After catching up on less significant news and learning that Herb had a car for him, Martín lapsed into silence. For the rest of the drive to Santa Fe, he watched the familiar mesas drift by under soaring thunderheads, feeling like a ghost passing through a former life.

The next day, the first thing Martín did was pick up Pancho. The huge dog leaped joyfully on him, nearly knocking him down. The reunion turned out to be a highpoint of his return, and from then on, they were inseparable.

Later that day, the press conference had the desired effect. The news that the hometown family might soon be exonerated saturated the media. A week later, Martín was given the keys to his family's home and assured that the bank would also be restored to Cortés family ownership, as soon as the various hearings and formalities were concluded. Martín found it difficult to describe how he felt. Elated, yes, but in a bittersweet way.

He had decided not to visit the family hacienda until the ownership question was resolved. At daybreak the next morning, he turned into the driveway and scanned the fenced, wooded thirty acres before his gaze settled on the house. It was exactly as he remembered, but seemingly from a nearly forgotten dream.

The huge oak front door creaked open and Martín walked slowly into the spacious living room. Everything looked the same, but the place felt cold and empty. He moved hesitantly across the room to the double mahogany doors to his father's study. He paused, for a moment, feeling he should knock, and then slowly pushed them open. In front of him stood the old desk, its surface bare. Beside it sat his father's empty wheelchair. He released a breath he was unaware he'd held. The fact that Glendaring had changed nothing, possibly had not even been in the place, caused him to smile. The ensuing torrent of memories brought tears.

The next week was a blur of activity. Aunts, uncles, and cousins paid their respects, awkwardly trying to paper over the way they had treated Martín. He ignored them. The rest of the family had always resented his father's success and they had never been close. Reporters asked for interviews, and he declined.

His artist friends welcomed him with open arms and urged him to resume painting. He was pleased but somehow unmoved, and told them nothing about his work in Oaxaca. Mainly it triggered a yearning to see what he'd done again, to make certain it was as good as he remembered.

He visited the graves of his mother, father, and brother, and shed tears as he wished he could have brought bouquets of the spectacular orange-gold marigolds called *cempasuchil* used in Mexico to celebrate the Day of the Dead.

One afternoon, a gleaming new Porsche nosed into the parking area, and Laura, his former fiancée, came to the door. She hugged him, and through tears told him how worried she'd been. She seemed to have forgotten that long before he left, she'd stopped returning his calls. Martín was polite but distant as he told her his life had changed. "The last thing I want to do is hurt you; that's just how I feel."

Stone-faced, she turned on her heel and left, confirming Martín's earlier judgment that this one instance had worked out for the best.

Every few days he called to speak to Ilhui, but she was never available. He did talk regularly with Trini, who told him she still seemed despondent and confused. Then one day he received two letters. One came from Raul, who told Martín that any rivalry they had regarding Ilhui was over. "Although she seems uncertain about most things, she was definite about having no interest beyond friendship with me. Even though she wouldn't admit it, I'm convinced she's in love with you. You should return as soon as possible."

The second letter came from Trini and said essentially the same thing. He concluded with, "Martín, please come back! The enclosed is my most valuable possession. I give it to you as a token of my love." Inside the envelope, on expensive bond paper, was the recipe for the treasured eighth *mole*!

Martín suddenly realized how lonely he felt in Santa Fe. Although he had the comfort of early associations, what had happened during the last year diminished them to unimportance. After Oaxaca, Santa Fe seemed artificial and contrived. As he looked at the tourists and locals affecting Indian dress, and the shops filled with howling coyotes, images of Kokopelli, and fake men's ponytails, he was put in mind of an adult theme park. The endless preoccupation with things like "natural" foods, "self-realization," and every kind of foreign spirituality irritated him. Only the Indians selling jewelry in the plaza struck an authentic chord. In the midst of all the artificiality, they somehow remained apart, maintaining their dignity.

His mind kept wandering to Oaxaca: the markets and the daily life they represented, the wild mountains and disorderly *milpas*, the enchanting courtyard in his family's house. Most of all he envisioned Ilhui, and each memory triggered a different emotion. He saw her telling him about herself in the country house and then kissing him passionately after she saw his first painting. He saw her sitting happily in the old house full of children, and he saw her being slapped by El Vengador. But most of all he saw her confused and distraught before he left.

Intuition told him he could not just go back. He

believed what had happened caused so much emotional damage that any positive change would come at a pace so slow that it would drive him crazy, cause him to say the wrong things, make the wrong moves. It took him the rest of the day to devise a plan, and the sun had set when he made the call to Mexico City. After listening to Martín, the man he spoke to said, "Leave it to me, I know exactly what to do." A week later, the man called back. Martín grinned and made his own arrangements, promising Pancho that, one way or another, this would be the last time he would leave him at the kennel.

OAXACA

After he disembarked at the airport in Oaxaca, Martín passed a newsstand. One of the newspaper's headlines caused him to stop. *State Governor and Garrison Commander Resign for Unspecified Reasons*. He raised his eyebrows and gave a half smile. Raul must have been busy with his copies of the Glendaring evidence.

As on his initial visit to the city, Martín had given his family no notice of his arrival. Even though he had a key, when he reached the Cortés home, in midafternoon, he knocked. This time no one answered. No Marta or Hector with welcoming smiles. No Abuelita waiting for him in the courtyard.

He decided to follow his intuition and walked past the art supply store and up the several blocks to the base of the hillside. From there he climbed up to the house where Ilhui worked with the children.

Sister Beatriz answered the door. He had equated her with the iron-fisted dragon who had run the girl's dorm at the University of New Mexico and was taken aback when she immediately smiled and said, "Yes, Ilhui is here. I'm glad you've come."

Basking in the warm welcome, he was pleased to discover that his Spanish was now instinctive. The time in Santa Fe had apparently allowed his mind to sort things out, like a computer reorganizing its hard drive.

Ilhui sat on the floor surrounded by children with whom she played a card game. Her hair shone like black silk, a perfect complement to her golden skin. With her full sculpted lips and extraordinary eyes, he thought she looked like a big exotic cat curled up on

the rug, and he
realized she was even more beautiful than he
remembered. He also noticed that her arms still held
no bracelets. As she looked up, Martín watched
carefully for her first reaction. When she recognized
him, her eyes widened in surprise, then lit with
pleasure. But instantly a cloud formed over them. She
dropped the cards she was holding, and her hands
clutched each other in her lap.

"Please don't stop," said Martín. "Forgive me for
not calling, but I wanted to surprise you—with good
news for a change."

She smiled as he came and sat beside her, and this
time the pleasure lingered in her eyes. Looking up he
saw that Sister Beatriz was watching Ilhui as intently as
he was. "Go on, keep playing," urged Martín.

As Ilhui retrieved her cards, Ana, the little girl who
had taken to him on his first visit, came and sat close
to him. She remained silent but could not take her eyes
from him. Martín patted her on the head. "See, little
cousin, I told you I'd return."

She continued to gaze at him, as if he had just
performed an astounding feat of magic.

Later, as they walked down the hill, Martín said.
"Everything in Santa Fe is working out well, but I
wanted to come back."

Ilhui looked up at him. "I'm glad...I..."

"Don't say anything right now," Martín held up a
finger for silence. "I want to tell you what's happened,
and I have a surprise for you—something that has
nothing to do with us or anything that's happened.
Will you come with me to the *finca*? Tonight. It's
important."

She seemed uncertain, and then Martín watched the

doubt in her eyes gradually replaced by a long-absent sparkle. She squeezed his arm. "We can leave right away. I'm glad you came back."

CORTES COUNTRY HOME

Before they left the city, Martín took a long look at the courtyard where he'd first met Abuelita. He could see her there by the fountain, reading or just gazing at the tropical foliage, perhaps receiving visions of the future. He went upstairs to his painting of that scene and the other one. Like his impression of Ilhui, they had improved during his absence.

As they got in the car, Martín said, "A quick detour if you don't mind."

At the cemetery, they stood inside the marble-walled enclosure that marked the burial plots of generations of the Cortés family. In front of them stood the newly chiseled inscription that simply said, "Abuelita, who loved her family."

"How do you think she knew what she did?" asked Martín.

Ilhui shook her head. "I don't know, but she was never wrong." She squeezed his hand and added, "She was right about you."

Martín felt a sudden lightness, as if an enormous burden had vanished. He looked again at the inscription and could almost feel his father patting his shoulder.

Ilhui drove and Martín told her everything that had happened in Santa Fe. Interrupted only by a pause to open the Finca's gate, he finished his description of events as they pulled into the parking area near the entry.

Everything seemed just as before, including Ilhui. After leaving a note for Trini, she had once again stacked her forearms with bracelets, and her old smile came quickly and often. *Maybe because nothing awful happened here,* guessed Martín.

He had anguished over what to say to her. Should he tell her he'd discovered that Santa Fe was nothing but the husk of a former life, that for him leaving it would be like a snake shedding a useless skin, that most of what made Oaxaca so special was her? Or should he begin by asking how their separation affected her, find out if she still blamed them both for the tragedy and deal with that?

He needn't have worried. In the living room, he turned to face her and discovered her closer behind than he had realized. Only slightly shorter than Martín, she barely needed to look up to meet his eyes. Without a word she put her arms around his neck and nestled her cheek against his. After they'd held each other for a few moments, Martín kissed her on the forehead. "Does this mean that you've forgiven me—and yourself—for what happened?"

Again, she looked into his eyes. "Sometimes forgiveness comes with understanding. Both of us did the best we could at the time, and the only good that can come out of what happened will be what we now do differently. I've worked with the children nearly every day, and I can't tell you how good that makes me feel. And when I saw you!" She shook her head in wonderment. "After my earlier stupidity, I was depressed and managed to act even worse. I didn't think you would come back. When you did, I realized you understood, and I felt so *increíble.* So incredible!"

Ilhui closed her eyes and tipped her head, offering her slightly parted lips.

Two hours later in Ilhui's room, moonlight washed over them as they called a temporary halt to their lovemaking. She put her head on Martín's chest and looked up at him. "What about the surprise you promised me?" she asked.

"Do you feel shortchanged?" he inquired with mock sarcasm.

"No. Just the opposite, I can assure you. I just wondered."

"In the morning, I promise."

Ilhui remained silent for a moment. Then her voice now serious, she said, "There's something I've wanted to ask you." She paused again until she saw he was paying attention and continued. "Does anything seem odd to you about the treasure?"

Puzzled, Martín asked, "What do you mean?"

"There's plenty for us, but not much more. It doesn't seem reasonable that Abuelita would have continued with—what do you say—business as usual if that were true. She was always concerned with future generations."

"I only knew her for a short time," said Martín, "but that makes sense. She put the family's future above everything, including her life. I remember when I first discussed becoming a *guardián* with her. She said something to the effect that although the treasure had decreased over the years it was still 'sufficient.'"

As Martin stroked Ilhui's cheek, he had another thought. "I also remember when I first saw the treasure in the cave. My expression must have indicated I was surprised at how little there seemed. She said, 'Do not be deceived, the treasure is greater than it appears.' But we listed everything there. No chance anyone took anything without me knowing it."

"Unless there's more of it in a different place?" said Ilhui. "And one other thing: Abuelita and Hector almost always sold emeralds, perhaps one or two every other year. They only used gold or silver coins for small, unexpected things. Maybe those two emeralds they tried to sell to the Iranians were the last ones, but I'm not convinced."

"That makes sense," agreed Martín. "Besides that, it's a helluva climb to the cave, and I could barely move the iron door in the ceiling in the first cave. I assumed that Hector probably went with her."

"You wouldn't know this, but when she brought back emeralds, she always came here alone."

"If there's more, where could it be?

"*Quien sabe?*" said Ilhui. "Who knows, except that from everything I remember it would be close."

"Wait a minute!" exclaimed Martín, snapping his fingers. "I told you Glendaring hid his stuff in a small basement below the hacienda. Raul said that all old homes in the countryside had them. Places where women hid during Indian attacks. Is there one here?"

Ilhui came suddenly to her knees and faced him. "Now that you mention it, I remember something from when I was very small. It's vague, but I think the kitchen has a place like that. I had wandered in there and Abuelita grabbed me. I remember her pointing at a hole in the floor and telling me it was full of spiders that would kill me. I've been afraid of them ever since."

"Maybe under that baking oven you told me Abuelita had installed?"

"Let's go see."

Martín looked at her kneeling beside him, her breasts not far from his face. "If it's there, it's been there a long time and can wait another half hour."

It was actually closer to an hour before they found themselves in the flickering glow of the kitchen lamp.

Martín had previously paid little attention to the iron oven. He now saw that it was about four and a half feet wide, five feet high, and two feet deep. He also saw that its feet were bolted to a rectangular piece of wood made of oak planks. He thought someone had gone to a lot of trouble and expense when a cheap piece of plywood would have served just as well to protect the tile. He also wondered why the stove had been bolted to it and why it was over two feet longer than the base of the oven.

Grasping the oven firmly, he tried to move it. It wouldn't budge. He put his shoulder and full weight into it with the same result and turned to Ilhui. "Do you suppose those bolts go all the way through the wood and into the tile and concrete?"

She got on her knees and began to inspect the base inch by inch. She had gone nearly completely around it when she exclaimed, "There's a small hole on this side of the wood. I have an idea: bring me an icepick from the drawer by the cooler."

Martín returned with two of them. "Take your pick," he said, "no pun intended."

Ilhui giggled. "I understand! My English has improved as much as your Spanish."

Taking the pick, she inserted it into the hole, and there was a metallic click. She looked up. "Try it now."

Martín pushed, but to no avail. He said, "There are two picks, which seems odd. Maybe there are two holes?"

Ilhui had nearly completed her survey when she exclaimed, "Here it is!"

She inserted the other pick and produced another click. Martín pushed on the oven, but still nothing happened. He stepped back and looked at it carefully, then slapped himself on the forehead. "Of course. It must revolve, and I've been trying to push it from the middle."

Moving to one side of the oven, he shoved on it. It moved with very little pressure but just a millimeter or two, where it seemed to hang up on the icepicks. Seeing what had happened, Ilhui removed them. This time the oven moved easily on its base in a circular motion. "It's like a giant offset Lazy Susan," he said. "Probably on ball bearings."

With almost no effort, the heavy appliance continued to revolve until it had gone ninety degrees and revealed what was below it.

"There it is!" Martín pointed at a hole in the tile floor, nearly two feet square.

Ilhui handed him a flashlight. The beam illuminated a ladder built into the basement wall that descended over six feet to its floor. Getting on his knees he looked inside. "It's about two meters square and about half full of wooden boxes."

Still afraid of the place, Ilhui stayed above while Martín went down. Moments later, he handed up some wooden boxes and then climbed back out.

As the lid to the first box opened, they saw the dark green glow in the dim light, and sucked in their breaths. "My God," whispered Ilhui.

Forty minutes later, the inventory was complete. There were two large boxes nearly full of uncut emeralds, a few of them as large as the ones Martín had seen before. Most of them were much smaller, but still big by current standards. The rest of the boxes contained ingots of gold and silver.

Sipping brandy on the couch, Martín said, "It looks like enough for another 450 years!"

Ilhui narrowed her eyes. "Too bad there will be no Cortéses to enjoy it."

Martín burst out laughing. "What are you talking about? There may be at least one on the way as we speak!"

She giggled and stood. "Perhaps we should go and make certain."

CORTES COUNTRY HOUSE

Althought exhausted from the previous day's activities, the next morning Martín arose early and went to unlock the gate.

At midmorning, Ilhui joined him in the dining room. Over eggs scrambled with *chorizo*, she said, "With all the excitement you probably think I forgot about the surprise you promised. But something in your voice told me it's important."

"It is," he replied, beginning to worry about what he'd set in motion. After glancing at his watch, he added, "You'll see in about half an hour."

Forty-five minutes later they heard the crunch of tires on the driveway and the beep of a horn. "Is that it?" asked Ilhui, suddenly uneasy for no reason she could think of, except that she could tell that Martín was nervous.

"Yes," he said.

He pulled her to her feet, put his arms around her, and held her tight. "I love you," he said. As he led her to the window, he prayed he had done the right thing. Through it they saw a man standing by a dark Mercedes sedan. He was tall and thin and wore tiny, round glasses. "That's Felipe Gallardo, the genealogist who found you for me."

From the passenger side, a woman got slowly out. She was very tall and although her hair was streaked with gray, she was still beautiful. The way she kneaded her hands together in front of her testified to her agitation. She stood next to the genealogist, staring uncertainly at the house as if expecting it to disappear. Martín felt butterflies in his stomach as he realized that the resemblance was indeed striking.

Ilhui turned to Martín, eyes wide and her face drained of color.

"Yes," said Martín, trying to keep his voice from shaking. "It's your mother. Before you go out there you should know that the man who found her told me that Abuelita gave her the choice of taking you and raising you by herself, with no money and no job, or leaving you with them to be raised as a member of the Cortés family. She had to promise never to contact you. She wanted desperately to keep you, but decided to do what she thought would be best for you. She agreed to Abuelita's terms and received a large sum of money. Unfortunately, she soon lost it to swindlers and has been working as a housekeeper for a wealthy family in Mexico City ever since."

Martín held Ilhui by the shoulders and looked into her eyes. "Forgive me if I've handled this badly. I..."

Ilhui tossed her head and, choking back sobs, said, "Forgive you for what, making my dreams come true—every single one of them?" Then, tears streaming down her cheeks, she turned to open the door.

EPILOGUE

When Martín agreed to me publishing his story, I asked him if Trini would consent to allow the recipe for his eighth mole to be included. Martín said probably not but that he would ask. The answer was no, and I thought that was the end of it. To my surprise, one day after approving the final manuscript, Martín faxed me the recipe with the following note from Trini: "Until the events that you have chronicled, I felt that it was appropriate for me to keep my recipe a secret. Now that I am fully involved in all family affairs, I realize my original decision was fueled by jealously, and it is my wish to make my greatest creation known to the world outside of Oaxaca." With typical honesty, he noted that the first part of the preparation is loosely based on a recipe in Asian Grills by Alexandra Greeley. Being somewhat knowledgeable about Mexican food, I tested and adapted the recipe for the North American kitchen. ¡Buen provecho!

James Peyton

THE EIGHTH *MOLE*

Meat and rub:
1¼ pounds boneless leg of lamb
2 tablespoons fresh ginger ground to a paste
1/2 tablespoon ancho chili powder 4 cloves garlic
ground to a paste 1/2 tablespoon salt

One at a time, massage the rub items into all surfaces
of the meat, and refrigerate overnight.

Seasoning Mixture:
3 tablespoons malt vinegar
1 tablespoon fig-balsamic vinegar
3 whole cloves
6 green cardamoms slightly crushed
Vegetable oil for basting the meat
2 bay leaves
2-inch stick canela (Ceylon cinnamon)

Preheat your oven to 350 degrees.

Place the lamb in a large baking dish, combine and add
the seasoning ingredients, then add enough water to
cover the lamb. Bring to a bare simmer over medium
high heat.

Cover the baking dish, leaving about 1 inch open for
steam to escape, and place it in the preheated oven for
1 hour. Lower the temperature to 275 degrees and
continue cooking for 1¼ hours or until the lamb is
very tender but not falling apart. Turn off the heat and
allow the lamb to cool in the broth, uncovered.

Strain and reserve the cooking liquid, baste the lamb with vegetable oil, and place it in a smoker heated to 250 degrees for 30 minutes. Remove the lamb and when it is cool, cut it into 3/4 inch pieces, and reserve.

The mole:
1 mulato chile
1 ancho chile
1 pasilla chile
1 chilhuacle negro chile
2 small to medium size tomatoes
1/2 cup pine nuts
Vegetable oil
1/2 cup chopped white onion
1 clove garlic, finely chopped
4 small mission figs, stems removed
8 mint leaves
1/4 cup dark rum
1 teaspoon cider vinegar
2 ½ tablespoons light brown sugar
3/4 teaspoon dried, whole oregano
2 cups reserved lamb broth
1 1/4 teaspoons salt
1/3 cup raisins
1 ½ tablespoons grated Mexican chocolate
1 tablespoon toasted sesame seeds
Chocolate mint leaves for garnish

The garnish:
1 ripe plantain, fried and sliced
1/4 cup toasted sesame seeds
Whole chocolate mint leaves

Toast all the chiles in a dry skillet over medium heat

for about 30 seconds on each side, or until they are fragrant and soften, but do not allow them to scorch. Remove the seeds and stems and place the chiles in a blender. Cover the chiles with very hot water and allow them to re-hydrate for 20 minutes. Drain the chiles and replace them in the blender, discarding the soaking liquid.

Broil the tomatoes by placing them on a baking sheet or oven-proof skillet, as close to the broiler as possible, and broil until they are soft and the skins charred, about 15 minutes. Add the tomatoes to the blender with the chiles. Heat a small skillet over medium heat and cook the pine nuts, stirring frequently until they are just golden. Add 3 tablespoons of the nuts to the blender and reserve the rest. Add ½ tablespoon vegetable oil to the skillet, and cook the onions until they are soft but not browned. Add the garlic, cook one more minute, and then scrape the onions and garlic into the blender. Add a little more oil and cook the figs just until they begin to swell, about 1 minute, and put them into the blender, and add the mint leaves. Spoon off the grease on top of the reserved lamb broth and add 2 cups of it to the blender. Blend the mole ingredients for 2 minutes, then strain through the fine blade of a food mill. Reserve.

Sauté 4 cups of the cut-up lamb in 2 ½ tablespoons vegetable oil or lard, then add the blended chile mixture, rum, vinegar, sugar, oregano, salt, and raisins.Bring the mixture to a boil, and simmer, uncovered, until the sauce thickens, about 15 minutes. Add the chocolate and cook two more minutes.

Refrigerate overnight, reheat, and serve topped with fried ripe plantain, sesame seeds, reserved pine nuts and chocolate mint leaves.

Serves 4

AFTERWORD

My thrillers are based on personal experience and history woven into contemporary times. Martín Cortés, the present-day protagonist of The Royal Fifth (referring to the amount of stolen treasure that the conquistadors were supposed to give to the Spanish Crown), is descended from the first-born son of Hernán Cortés, also named Martín. The remarkable circumstances surrounding the birth of the first Martín Cortés, coupled with the legend of the stolen treasure, inspired this novel. Following his landing in Mexico in 1519, Cortés found a Spanish priest named Geronimo de Aguilar who was shipwrecked in the Yucatan in 1511. He had been enslaved by the Maya and learned their language, enabling the Spanish explorer to converse with the natives. After he won a fierce battle in Tabasco, the vanquished Indians gave him twenty women. He took one of them for himself after converting her to Christianity. There are several versions of her original name, including Malinali and Malitzen. The Spanish pronounced it Malinche but christened her Doña Marina. Her father had died when she was young, her mother remarried, and had a son with the stepfather. It is said that the couple sold Marina into slavery to remove a potential cloud on their son's inheritance.

Cortés communicated with Marina through Aguilar until she learned Spanish. She also spoke Nahautl, the language of the Aztecs, and became Cortes's translator. More importantly, she accompanied him to his meetings with Moctezuma and provided advice that enabled just five-hundred Spaniards to conquer tens of thousands of Indian warriors.

Following the Aztec defeat, she bore Cortés's first son. That first Martín may have also been the first mestizo. Although illegitimate, Martín was declared to be legitimate by Pope Clement VII who issued a document declaring so after Cortés sent Indian performers to entertain the Catholic pontiff. His conquest of the new land put Cortés in control of Mexico and Marina's family was terrified that she would seek revenge on them. They had nothing to fear as she is said to have been thankful for the events that allowed her to come to Christ and be with the Spaniards. After Cortés's Spanish wife arrived in Mexico, he gave Marina a dowry and saw that she was married to another conquistador.

To this day, some look upon her as the mother of modern Mexico. Others believe her to be a traitor responsible for the destruction of an entire civilization., The word Malinche is often used in curses, including a song called La Maldición de Malinche, (The Malinche Curse). My summer stay in Oaxaca several years ago was also important in my formulation of this thriller.

There is something of an otherworldliness in this ancient city that is an integral part of everyday life. Its fascinating and diverse population, unique architecture and incredible cuisine were the perfect backdrop for a compelling thriller. My hope is that you will enjoy reading The Royal Fifth as much as I did writing it.

James Peyton

ACKNOWLEDGEMENT

There is no way to thank everyone who helped with a novel, but you can certainly express your gratitude to those whose efforts were most significant. That includes the Daedalus writer's group which made so many excellent suggestions, Deanna Roy whose extensive knowledge regarding the publishing process was invaluable, David Aretha who did the formal edit, and Gary Demers of Notable Press who helped implement the publication every step of the way.

ABOUT THE AUTHOR

Award-winning author James Peyton infuses his novels with stranger-than-fiction encounters and true-to-life characters from his extensive travel and research. Realism in his plots and action comes from that background and his experience in martial arts and tactical firearms.

The Royal Fifth is based loosely on historical events surrounding the Conqueror, Hernán Cortés, and their consequences brought into the present time. It will be followed by a mystery-thriller series featuring federal policeman, Artemas Salcido. Artemas is the illegitimate son of a Mexican governor and his Yaqui servant. Following his mother's suspicious death, he was sent to be raised by the village priest. He attended Harvard on a scholarship and returned to Mexico vowing to fight corruption—only to receive his real education, where the grade is often life or death.

BOOKS BY THIS AUTHOR

Books on Mexican Food and Culture
El Norte: The Cuisine of Northern Mexico
La cocina de la frontera: Mexican-American Cooking from the Southwest
Jim Peyton's New Cooking from Old Mexico
The Very Best of Tex-Mex Cooking: with Texas Barbecue and Texas Chile Naturally Healthy Mexican Cooking

Novels
Vampires of Bustamante

Available on Amazon

Subscribe to James's list to receive free blogs and new release notices at: www.jameswpeyton.com

Made in United States
North Haven, CT
24 March 2023

34501177R00245